1

'ENTWINED'
by
JOY BURNETT
ISBN: 978-1-9999129-6-3

i2i
PUBLISHING
i2i Publishing, Manchester.
www.i2ipublishing.co.uk

3

ACKNOWLEGEMENTS

I am most grateful to all who helped me with this book, particularly, those who have encouraged me by reading it, commenting on it and making sure I put the commas in the right places! – John Fletcher, Morgen Bailey, Michael Richards, Laura Kirkwood, Michael Leonard and Pat Downham.

To my friend Andrew Cameron Young who travelled with me when I explored the routes I used in part one in Southern France and part two in Spain.

To Teresa Lister for her friendship and encouragement especially when the book was in its raw form.

Thank you to all my family and friends for their support even though the subject matter was sometimes outside their grasp.

Thank you most of all to William L Shaffer co-author of 'Illuminating Physical Experience' who intrigued me with my past life reading in 2003 and set my imagination aflame with the idea of reincarnation and the Karmic issues that could be the result of many past lives.

Thank you to everyone who reads this book. I would love to hear from you.

joyburnettwriter@yahoo.co.uk

4

Memories or imaginings
Lurk just out of reach
Touches of light in darkly deep
Who knows the truth behind the strife?
Perhaps to guide, perhaps to teach
To face a challenge yet unknown
Some tortured souls forever 'Entwined'
Their journey moves into life anew
Brings sin and fear to live again
And stays unresolved without atone
Through mists of time and endless pain
Is it true? Do we reap what we sow?
Or do we face it all again?
Another chance to right a wrong
Or do we learn and let it go?

PART 1
GUILT

Languedoc 1209 CE

At the end of the twelfth century, a group of Christians known as Bons-Chrétiens arose in Languedoc (or "Oc"), the southwest region of France. They and their 'credentes' – lay and noble followers – were considered to be 'dualist heretics'. Their belief system later became known as Catharism. The Bons-Chrétiens were pacifists who believed themselves to be the only true disciples of the Apostles and followed their disciplines of hard work, honesty, equality and simplicity and taught through example.

Catharism held to a doctrine of Reincarnation; the individual soul being born into this world of suffering again and again until it had reached the state of inner purification, which meant it could then merge with Christ.

Because they denied the power of the Catholic Church, Pope Innocent III declared a Crusade against them, bringing nobles from France and Germany with their armies, mercenaries and clergy.

So began the battles, culminating in one of the bloodiest and most ruthless Crusades that the world had ever seen. Many of the main participants were involved for gain, as the estates in those areas were valuable. Those who brought their own armies from northern and eastern regions had been promised such reward.

The vast majority of the ordinary fighting soldiers were consigned for a forty or sixty-day term of participation or 'quarantine'.

These short-term participants have received scant attention from historians. Most research provides little more than simple lists of Crusaders, no indication of their lives or where they came from, how and why they were recruited, their training or their motives.

Evidence suggests that they believed they were going on a pilgrimage against a people called the Albigensians, a broadly used term to indicate the heretics of the city of Albi but also the vast area of Languedoc where the Bons-Chrétiens had flourished.

Thousands were killed and injured, and even though they were supposed to receive a 'wage', it seems many relied on what they could loot or purloin.

This is where our story begins with **Léon Dumont,** a bright, thoughtful boy who worked happily farming the hillsides of Gréolières in the district of Grasse, persuaded by his faith and love of his father to join the Pope's army of Crusaders as they move toward Languedoc against the heretics.

Eva Rocault is the daughter of one of the elite, a *Perfecti,* of the new faith of Bons-Chrétiens who lives peacefully in the small village of Laroque-de-Fa in the Corbières Mountains.

CHAPTER 1
Early Summer 1209 CE

LÉON DUMONT
I must keep my faith and not give in was my only thought. But still I vomited. I couldn't stop. The smell of death, fear and blood was in my nostrils. The day had been filled with more screams and pleading than I could ever have imagined.

Such evil deeds that are expected of us. I had never seen so much blood before, but I had been told to believe God needs these heretics to be slain.

Our Pope and Sovereign demand we kill them all.

I was an ordinary boy not yet sixteen and until that fateful day, had lived a plain life, happily working with small flocks of hillside sheep in our remote village in the southeast near Gréolières.

Then the soldiers came.

They appeared without warning, on an ordinary spring day, when the folds of the mountains shone with wild flowers, the streams overflowed with morning rain and the early lambs were starting to fatten.

The day's work was just beginning when they arrived. Recruiting for the Pope's army, they told us. So, all the men and boys were gathered together in our neighbour's big barn. The officer in charge, a great beefy Southerner, picked out the tallest and the strongest. Being short and stocky I hoped I might be passed by. But, no! He looked me up and down, and said to my father, "Your son looks a strong lad. Perhaps he will make a good soldier. What do you say, boy? Make a man of you fighting for the glory of God?"

My heart skipped a beat. What did I know about being a soldier, good or otherwise? What did I know about war? Nothing at all, but I knew I could not refuse. Those who did so were said to deny their faith, and my father was determined that I should join the Crusade and fulfil my duty.

He would have joined himself but for the stump that was the remains of his right arm, lost in an accident ten years past, when the roof of the old barn fell on him.

He was a pious, God-fearing man, who talked endlessly about wanting to go on a Crusade. More in mind, I knew, of going to the Holy Land against the Saracens.

This was not the same but, nevertheless, it was still a Holy Crusade and we understood that we would be fighting heretics, so a noble cause it must be.

If my mother were still alive, she would have persuaded my father I was needed at home. She understood me well enough to know I had no stomach for violence. My chief joy as a child was to accompany her to Church, not because I was uncommonly good, but because I loved to listen to the prayers and Psalms, and the lilting language of the sacraments, of which I memorised long paragraphs.

I was a bright lad and had learned to read a little, but I was much more interested in animals and especially the horses bred for trading at the fairs.

"He's a thinker, not a fighter," my mother told my father when I showed no interest in the fist fighting at the local fair, that encouraged the boys to tackle a wiry, muscle-bound regular fighter for a few livres.

It was more than a year since the winter had taken my mother in a fit of coughing. Today, I missed her more than ever before.

Nevertheless, I stood tall, hoping and praying I would be rejected. But with a nod from my father, the officer selected me and the documentation was quickly completed.

In return for our services the promise was: remission of all our sins, a monthly wage, training and the chance of returning a hero.

Fifteen others from our small community joined up, most

of them willingly. Although I was sure there were some who were pushed into it by their families and who, like me, felt as unsure and deeply apprehensive about leaving home for the first time.

My father proudly clapped me on the back, thinking no doubt of the rewards rather than the possibility that I might be injured or even killed. How could I say that to him? How could I disappoint him?

Hero... I'm no hero!

I didn't want to go, but we stood in a raggedy line, swore an oath of fealty to do our duty to God and the Holy Mother Church. Then, amid cheering and good wishes, set off in the clothes we were wearing.

We walked for many days, the army increasing daily as new recruits and other armies joined us.

Once in Montpellier, I was told that we would get some serious training before moving on toward Oc, where the fighting would begin in earnest.

Most of the boys treated it like an adventure, play fighting and backslapping with jokes about sinners and salvation.

I could only think that I would not see my beloved animals and father again. My old dog Tipo would miss me. And Father always forgot to feed him.

None had ever seen such a great army. According to the experienced Crusaders, this one was far bigger than any to the Holy Land. It stretched a full league long as the great procession tramped the dusty roads. The thunder of hooves and wagon wheels filled the air, startling the birds from the trees and sending herds of goats and sheep skittering off up the surrounding hills and mountains.

There were many different types of people, with different languages and trades, divided into groups each with a commanding officer. Most of the farm boys were employed as muleteers, with the knights' horses or with the animals brought along for food.

There were armour-clad knights, a shimmering mix of brightly coloured attire, with their own archers and infantrymen. Pilgrims by the thousand, clergy with great retinues of followers, teams of cooks, craftsmen, surgeons, farriers and grooms, many carrying their tools of the trade. Great wagons with tents and supplies: mead and wine, machinery, the blacksmith's wagon with anvil, tongs and bellows, new arrowheads and a portable furnace.

Fighting equipment was in another, and all accompanied by pack mules and herds of stock.

When we joined the main army camp in Montpellier we were issued with a leather jerkin, a belt, and a knife each, and told that we would get a club or an axe or perhaps a sword, once we had done some training. I had no idea what that would mean as I had never done any kind of fighting. Now was the time to learn if I was going to survive the next few weeks.

The majority of the commanding force came from France, others from the northern provinces of Germany and Italy. Some were noble sons with large armies but with no estates of their own, because they had older siblings who by law inherited the family lands.

We were promised great rewards, but the knights and barons would gain the most, as punishment for heresy allowed the confiscation of the heretic's properties and the disinheritance of descendants.

As an extra incentive to join the Crusade, the Church promised to pay all outstanding debts and the Pope would absolve us of our sins. All the mercenaries, vandals, adventure-seekers, gangs from the streets, and the unwashed mass of riffraff from the prisons along the way had been given the chance of salvation.

Such men thought nothing of killing or inflicting pain if it gained them a good meal, a pair of boots, or a woman for the night.

This was not where I wanted to be at all.

Allocated to a group, I was travelling under the banner of a knight from Chartres, Guy de Pressau, whom I hardly understood when he addressed us, as he spoke in a soft French dialect.

I'd been assigned to work with the oxen and the great horses that pulled the catapults; the trebuchet and mangonels used to bombard resistant castles and fortresses where the heretics sought refuge. Being with the horses was my only pleasure, and they were beauties. Old Tantho, Ferro, Hans and Grenod were trained warhorses and scarred from many battles. I drew strength from their huge, overworked bodies and tried to give them as much nourishment as I could.

CHAPTER 2
Training

LÉON

We marched again for many days. With us was Arnaud Amaury, the Abbot of Citeaux, sent by the Pope to lead the Crusade against the heretics. He was a fat Cistercian abbot, hard-faced and richly dressed, with a great retinue of protectors and supporters.

Many holy men accompanied us – medical monks and priests who attended the physical and spiritual needs of our army. Most were in the Crusade to fight rather than preach but that didn't stop the most pious ensuring that our belief in our mission was justified and honourable in the eyes of the Church. At every opportunity we were ensured of our place in heaven if we fought and gave our lives to God's words. We all had to attend daily mass.

Simon de Montfort, Earl of Leicester, joined us with his own army and soon became our new military commander. I was told he was a brilliant soldier, having proved himself in many former Crusades, but I knew little of him.

Once we were camped on the hot, grassy plain to the south of Béziers, the coastal town in the north of Oc, we waited. Our time was spent building the great ornate pavilions our leaders occupied, pitching tents, cleaning armour, constructing the massive catapults and machinery, and tending the beasts, while knights practised with their lances, swords and axes.

Several days passed, the activity intense. As we prepared for a long stay, scouts and messengers hurried in and out of camp daily, reporting on evidence of heretics' positions and support.

I had no time to ponder what I was doing there. I was kept working from dawn until I collapsed on my straw pallet late at night.

None of the new recruits understood what to expect until Arnau de Suis, our immediate officer and a grisly war-hardened mercenary, shouted, "Still negotiating! We'll not go to battle today. Nor tomorrow I reckon. We must wait now, but we'll use our time for training. We'll learn you how to use a good blade, eh, boys? You'll thank me when you need to, so let's start."

De Suis led our group to the blacksmith's tent where our weapons were honed to their sharpest edges. The forge was hotter than Hell itself. The great muscled arms and sinewy throat of the huge blacksmith at the anvil glistened in a sea of sweat. His apprentices sat alongside, working on hauberk links with strips of wire.

We trained in open ground alongside a field where the bowmen practised, shouting triumphantly at every good hit.

De Suis loved to show off and demonstrate. He was wiry and strong and fast on his feet, so could disarm almost anyone, even those much bigger than himself. He liked nothing better than to humiliate the younger lads, so he picked on the smallest of our group, Victor, a black-haired gypsy from Montpellier, to torment. Twisting him savagely, de Suis held his knife to the lad's throat, and demonstrated the quick slice that would cut and kill instantly.

When de Suis let him go, the boy was gasping and spitting, and his throat bled from the nick the officer had inflicted. The lad's dark eyes were venomous. I saw the thought flash that he would turn his weapon on de Suis. But I caught his eye and gestured for him to take a care. He was no match for our cruel superior. He nodded an understanding to me, but I could see the determination written clearly on his face. I had no doubt that he would not allow himself to be bullied again.

I was paired with a tall, lanky lad called Guillem. He had been trained to use a sword by his father, but was incompetent with a knife. I, on the other hand, had worked with knives and could slaughter a beast, but the thought of cutting a person's throat sickened me. I easily outshone Guillem with my skills, although I really had no natural talent for anything bigger than a knife. Although quite short in stature I was strong and agile and managed to hold my own. I was pleased with myself until Arnau de Suis said, "This could be your forte, lad. Slitting the throats of heretics will earn you a place in heaven."

Arnau de Suis watched me leap on Guillem and hold the knife as he had demonstrated. "Prove yourself in the field, my boy. That is of course if you can," he added sarcastically as I released my hold on my opponent's head.

De Suis's crooked face challenged us to defy him.

"You lot *will* obey me," he thundered at every opportunity. "I am going to tell you to do things you have never done before. If you disobey or complain, you will be punished. If you fail, you will be punished or you will die. So, listen carefully to what I teach you or you will suffer. You are here to do God's work. Remember that."

Never in my life had I known anyone like him. He was a brutish-looking man who had spent most of his life as a mercenary. Originally a pike man with the Swiss army, he told us with pride that he had seen many battles. His nose was bent and notched, and one eye had a scar through it that made it look lower than the other. His fat mouth hung open and he had a furrowed forehead that gave him a look of near animal stupidity.

He pushed us hard, demanding that we take even our practices to a scary level. We were all tired and hungry but laughingly de Suis told us that this was nothing compared to real battle and that we all needed to toughen up!

Ha!

I could hardly stand up, let alone walk. All I wanted was a hot meal and a warm bed.

Not much chance of that!

CHAPTER 3
Laroque-de-Fa in the Corbières Mountains

EVA ROCAULT

It was approaching midsummer, the sky full of light wispy clouds, the hillsides alive with butterflies and bees. Spending a day like this was a treat for us. We were so happy to be out in our beautiful mountains.

Everything had been fun even though our hands were sore and discoloured from collecting the herbs, nuts and figs that grew on the steep mountainsides around Laroque-de-Fa.

It was the time of year when we could harvest the wild fruits, lovely aromatic herbs and nuts that grew so abundantly here in the Corbières.

Our neighbour Vivenny and her children, Matilde, who was eight, and the six-year-old twins, Jacob and Jusef, had joined my brother Roul and me on our foraging expedition.

My greedy little brother had eaten most of his collection of fruit when we stopped for lunch by the waterfall, and now waddled along the track, his panniers nearly empty. Well, he was only four!

Vivenny's children raced ahead, their feet bare and their tatty shifts exposing their little pink bottoms, all the while carefully carrying their large baskets of figs and nuts.

Vivenny and her family never had enough clothing, or anything else for that matter. She'd been widowed two years earlier and had few means to support herself and her children.

Her husband's parents, Leilah and Samuel Hasdai, and my father had helped her ever since her beloved husband, Mucky Tom, had been killed in a fire. He wasn't really mucky. He had been very handsome and dark-skinned, his parents having come to Languedoc from Portugal before he was born.

"Leilah and Samuel are coming to see us next week. You must come and meet them," Vivenny said as we turned for home.

"I will. Of course I will."

"Eva, you know they are Jews? They had to leave their home when their king declared that he and his kingdoms were to become vassals of the Pope. That didn't bode well for them, the Jews who lived there," Vivenny said. "They don't talk about their past at all, but they are good people who keep themselves to themselves and practise their faith quietly and discreetly."

Popping a large ripe fig into her mouth she continued. "They are genuinely kind *and* they don't have a problem with me not being Jewish. We're going to spend the winter with them – somewhere near Aleth-les-Bains. They've offered to help me with the children so that I can work."

"I'll miss you," I said sincerely.

"I know, but you'll be busy with your studying, and soon you'll be going off preaching with your father."

"Not until Roul is a little older. I can't leave him yet."

"We can't wait to go to Aleth. While we're there I'll steer clear of Tom's sister Ruth, though. I don't like her at all." Vivenny laughed. "Nor do the children."

"Why don't you like her?"

"Oh, she's just nasty and brittle, has no sense of fun, and is openly hostile to me and everyone else. She runs the Hasdais' business now, but complains all the time. She's just plain mean, even to the children."

"Oh, no."

"Luckily she's not around too much when we're there. I will just have to try to ignore her." She shrugged as she said, "I know the children will be better off there with their grandparents, though. They are very good to us."

"Oh, Vivenny. I can't imagine life without you around."

"We'll come back and visit in the spring," she assured me.

We continued to talk of Vivenny's plans to leave, and while the children enjoyed running and climbing the rough hillsides, we harvested the yellow figs, almonds and the aromatic herbs. Vivenny's children watched over my little brother and, apart from a scary moment when he'd found a wasps' nest, all had gone well.

Almost all the fruit and herbs we'd gathered that day would be dried for the winter or traded in the weekly market in Laroque. We were sun-drenched and tired as we headed home.

As the sun dropped behind the mountain, we watched a storm approaching. It was getting late and a mass of dark clouds bustled through the valley. We hastened our efforts to return to our croft before the skies opened. By the time we reached the village, we were wetter than the ferns beneath the waterfall where we had stopped at lunchtime to eat. It was still so warm that we didn't care.

We ran laughing up the hillside to the nearest building, the old barn on the edge of our little croft, offloaded our packs and shook the water out of our clothes and hair. We stood watching the torrents of rain turning the parched earth to mud, knowing it would be dry again within hours. It was still midsummer, and the hottest time of the year.

A sheet of lightning lit up the sky.

"Wowee!" yelled Roul clutching at my skirt, his blue eyes wide with alarm. I put a reassuring hand on his little blond head. We stood in awe of the great waves of lightning that illuminated the evening sky with the crashes of thunder that sent the children squealing behind the straw bales at the back of the barn.

Reaching for my hand Vivenny asked seriously, "Do you think we'll be safe?"

"What do you mean?"

"You know... the Crusade... I know they're seeking out

Bons-Chrétiens, but the Jews are also hated by the Catholic Church, and there is no tolerance in some places, as there is here."

Her concern showed on her work-worn face. "Oh, Eva, what will happen if they come here? Your family should leave and go to one of the fortresses where you'll be protected. Have you made any plans?"

"No, we haven't decided on anything," I said. "Father and I have talked of it, about where we would go to be safe. Only *if* it becomes necessary, but I think we have time. The armies are still far away and will probably be defeated before they get here."

But we all had our reservations. Only yesterday, when we had taken our cheeses to the market in Laroque-de-Fa, the news was bad. We heard from the travelling merchants and jongleurs that the Crusaders were moving from the east, determined to eliminate everyone who stood in their way, and were now camped outside Béziers ready to attack.

News circulated quickly along our valley, and everyone was praying that the army would be defeated before they got as far south as our village in the Corbières. Nevertheless, everyone was fearful.

CHAPTER 4
Otherspace

EVA

I, too, was afraid, but I said to Vivenny, "We must live in hope, and pray that we are spared. Our Lord Trencavel in Carcassonne will keep us from harm."

"You must not delay, Eva," Vivenny said.

"No, we'll decide soon," I replied as I wrapped my arms around her.

Struggling alone with three children had taken its toll on her. Vivenny was barely twenty-three to my fifteen years but she could easily be taken for my mother. It would be good for them all to go to Tomas's family where they would be taken care of.

The fun and laughter of our day dissipated as our conversation turned to the events that were threatening to overtake us.

Taking her hand to reassure her, I added, "Come, let's race back."

It was just a few short paces to our little croft so we lifted our baskets and dashed, the children ran laughing through the rain and mud to our respective homes. Across the valley there were other small crofts and villages that were part of the same estate. We were a peaceful and well-cared-for population. Our love of the countryside kept us from the noise and bustle of the cities and towns, and until recently we had lived calm, peaceful lives.

My father was knelt in prayer, deep in spiritual contemplation, when we returned to our sturdy stone croft that stood with five others on the hillside overlooking the valley. Roul and I slipped quietly into the back of the room and carefully sorted our fruits and hung our herbs. We both knew this was a special time for him. As he sang his prayers it was easy to see his shining aura, a light so clear it vibrated through our tiny house warming it with pure, loving energy. I was so proud of my good father, his faith in the power of love and his calm optimism.

Bernard Rocault had been a credente of the new faith all his life, and through his devotion had become a *Perfecti*.

As part of his road to perfection he was expected to love no one but Christ, but he loved Roul and me. He had also adored our mother, Christiana, who'd died giving birth to Roul.

I was only ten years old when she died. Roul was a small, sickly baby, so Papa decided, instead of travelling and preaching as he had done previously, he would stay in Laroque and take care of us.

"Because I've refused to give you up, I will have to go through the ceremony again, back to the sacred caves of the Sabarthéz to receive the *consolamentum* – renew my baptism. It is unusual but the cleansing is needed before I can move fully into the spirit again," he told me. "But I love you, and Uncle Stevan has taken my place now."

It was his only dissension with the new faith, but he argued that if we should love everyone, why not our own flesh and blood.

Uncle Stevan, who had lived with us, was already travelling, preaching, and working towards his own perfection.

Finding it hard at first, Papa taught and ministered in the local area only.

By adhering to the strict rules of chastity, simplicity and poverty, he was working towards spiritual light. He tended the sick and gave peace to the dying by transmitting loving energy to them so they could move towards the spirit in joy and safety, to evolve into their own perfection. He was proud of the fact that we had no Churches, or clergy to maintain, putting our resources into learning and cooperation. Nor did we have the need to force people to take oaths of fealty to their beliefs. We offered example in our words and deeds.

The Crusade against us was beyond our understanding, as we were Christians too, but didn't believe the dogma of the Church and the Holy Trinity. Nor did we believe in violence and killing, neither man nor beast. None of the *Perfecti* we knew would kill even in self-defence. Jesus taught us *not* to kill. Our doctrines and beliefs follow Him, for He *was* our earthly lesson, and only by purification of the flesh could we obtain our spiritual peace to meet God.

"We need no superstitious rituals," Papa assured our followers, "nor relics of dead saints, consecrated buildings, images of torture and mindless obeisance. We don't need to rule our people with tyranny, as does the Church. They have betrayed Christ's message. We yearn for a newer and purer faith."

It was true. Over the years the followers had increased and included many of the noble families who ruled our lands bringing peace and harmony to our lives.

One day I would be ordained, I had already taken a vow of chastity and knew that I would never marry or have a family of my own, so I would be received into the world of spirit as a virgin, undefiled and pure. I was too young to receive the *consolamentum,* the spiritual baptism. My father had explained how I would be expected to leave my family, and he didn't want that. He himself had defied his own belief by marrying our mother and having children.

I was sure I wanted to follow in his footsteps, and always listened carefully when he explained his beliefs.

"Compassion," Papa explained to me one sunny day when we were sitting on a hillside, "by its very nature is a mix of love, empathy and goodwill, and the feeling of pain – physical or emotional – must not remove that compassion, for only in this way can we move on and be purified."

"But, Papa," I said, "how is it possible to love someone who causes us pain?"

"We must love everyone, saints and sinners alike. It's hard, I know, but the experience is only transitory."

"I could never be so brave. I know what hurts and it is *so* real, I couldn't just wish it away," I replied laughing, recalling a fall a couple of years ago from a peach tree, and a painful broken arm.

"If you take yourself away from the physical body, you will feel no pain," he explained, "I know you can do it if you practise. You have the mark of the priestess and the eyes of the knowing."

True signs, my father told me. I had violet blue eyes and a dark tiny cross on the side of my neck. These, he assured me, are recognised as proof that I had the ability to transcend to the spirit world with ease.

So I'd practised hard, whenever and wherever I could, and over time I learned that I could lift out of the physical into my *otherspace* without too much effort, and it *was* a safe, pain-free place. It taught me that I *could* escape from the physical. It gave me confidence too because I learned to understand another dimension of myself.

CHAPTER 5
The Fall of Béziers and Carcassonne

LÉON DUMONT

Quite unexpectedly, one day, we were called to join the first siege of the town. A handful of bored mercenaries, itching for a fight, had incited a reaction from the townspeople, so the battle began. The leaders had forced their way into the city and were urging us to arms.

Panic clawed with icy fingers at my belly, but I grabbed my weapons, headed for the city and followed the foot soldiers across the river into the suburbs of Béziers.

I ran and screamed with the horde of hooligans and soldiers, the scent of battle driving us forward, but my sword remained dry, whereas most had the blood of many dripping from them. I could not slash and kill as others were doing that day. To my shame, I pushed my sword into a dead woman to make it look as if I had done my duty.

We rampaged through the city streets, the houses and even the churches. I ran, hid, ducked and swerved while others were killing and maiming. Nothing in my life could have prepared me for what was happening. No one was spared. Few prisoners were taken.

I watched as my comrades raised their swords or axes and struck men, women and children, raining blows again and again so that their blood spurted and their guts fell out.

I'd never known what was inside us; those holes in the bodies exposed what should have remained hidden.

Mothers screaming for their families and the crying of babies haunted and sickened me. Yes, I had run with them, but I was *so* ashamed of what I was doing. I was frightened and horrified of being so. I was there to do my duty but I felt as if I had passed through the gates of Hell.

Buildings were ablaze, bodies were everywhere, and as I

ran I trod on a baby whose tiny rosebud mouth streamed with blood. Beside her lay her mother, arms outstretched across the alleyway, reaching for her, but with her head severed, their blood running together in a slowly coagulating stream. My stomach lurched and, as I sped on through the streets, I was overcome with disgust and nausea. I hid for a while in an abandoned house by the city wall where I vomited until I could hardly stand.

The massacre of Béziers was cruel and murderous, and we were killing everyone regardless of their faith or who they were. Weren't we here to kill the heretics? Everyone in the city was being massacred. It made no sense to me. I thought we were doing God's will, but this could not be so.

Ignoring the carnage, the rabble of mercenaries and soldiers were taking whatever spoils they could as they plundered the houses and shops, even though we had been told that no one could steal for his own gain. All plunder belonged to the knights and would be divided once Béziers was taken.

Troops of armed knights attacked anyone caught stealing. Nevertheless, the streets were covered with objects discarded from the looting. Books with pages torn out, quilts slashed so that feathers swirled in the streets like snow, drifting in the wind. A great roll of scarlet silk, muddied with footprints, rippled and unrolled in a gusty alleyway. Broken pots and glass mixed with the blood and mess.

Fires were blazing everywhere. I ran along the city wall looking for a way back to the camp, wanting only to escape the noise, the stench and the blood. I could barely see where I was going for the smoke and fumes.

Behind me the great Cathedral of Saint Nazaire collapsed in the fire. Turning a corner and pushing past men with arms full of plunder, over the bodies that lay everywhere, I found myself running down the surrounding hill toward the river. I could see no sign of the bridge we had crossed to enter the city.

People were running in all directions. Across several fields and in the distance, I could see a small clump of trees. I ran and ran, my breath heaving in my chest, my heart beating so hard I thought to die there and then. I pushed through a hedgerow, until I was alongside the fencing and the small copse. As I reached the shadows, I pushed my body under a spiny oak and again puked with such force that I could hardly breathe. As I could not let my officers see me like this, I stayed in my hiding place for an hour or more.

As the sun went down, I knew my comrades would be returning, so, guessing the direction of our camp, I ran as fast as I could, keeping away from the main paths, so as not to be seen. As the light disappeared from the sky, I spotted our army and quickly joined a few stragglers. Some, with arms full of stolen goods that they were sneaking into the camp, out of sight of the officers' tents and pavilions.

With nothing left in my gut and little appetite, I returned to the noise, to the all-pervading odour of stale bodies, abandoned armour, the cooks, serving girls, and the mangy dogs that lurked in corners in the hope of a few scraps. But the smoke and the smell of the rabbits, birds and boars cooking on the spits added to my queasiness.

As I entered the huge tent, my assigned billet, Guy de Pressau, my commander, was shouting my name. I rushed over to where he was seated with a great bowl of vegetable soup and a hunk of bread in his hands. Once again I was overcome by faintness and sickness.

Fighting to maintain a look of obedience and enthusiasm, I knelt.

"Dumont! At last! Where have you been? Come have your supper, you're too... what you say? Skinny... yes? Have you tended my horse?"

Lifting an eye toward me, he enquired, "Are you ill, boy?" I had to listen carefully as he spoke with a strong accent that I found difficult to understand.

"Sire, I am tired and not used to so much excitement. It has but a temporary effect, I am sure, but I cannot face any food. I will make up for it tomorrow," I replied, trying to keep from retching again. "I'll attend your horse now and retire. With your leave, Sire."

He nodded. I'm not sure he understood me well either, but his attention was taken by another knight who had a suit of armour and was showing it off. His fortune came no doubt from what he had taken from one of the rich houses in the city.

I moved away quickly to the corner of the tent where a few old, smelly, fly-infested blankets had been thrown. A small brown dog growled and skulked away. I squeezed my eyes shut, wanting to blot out the images from my mind, but I couldn't. Before I could sleep, I knew I had to attend to the knight's fine dapple grey stallion tethered behind the tent.

Still with the dirt and blood of battle on him, the horse looked tired and depressed, his grey head hung low. As I approached, he shivered violently, kicked out his back foot and stamped it down, his tail thrashing back and forth.

Although shaking and weak myself, I spoke to him softly, pushing my breath into his flared nostrils and stroking his muddy muzzle with my fingers. As he relaxed, I carefully relieved him of the heavy armoured saddle and hardened leather caparisons. I brushed him well before walking him to the pasture, where I let him free to graze with the hundreds of others.

It was a long walk back to the tent, and the smoke and fragments of ash that blotted out the burning city made my head hurt, my nose and eyes sore.

I lay in a dark corner, hot, exhausted and ashamed, but I couldn't sleep and was tormented by the visions of the massacre that we had inflicted on the poor souls of Béziers.

What was I doing there? I felt completely lost in a world I

had no understanding of.

"Be on your way with God as your guide," my father had said as I left home, but even so, I was unable to recognise what was expected of me.

I had been told that heretics were sinful and denied the Catholic Church, but it was so hard for me to believe. The few Bons-Chrétiens who had lived near our home in Gréolières had fled many months before, when the Pope had sent his emissaries to search them out, arrest, or convert them. They mainly came from a country called Bulgaria and always seemed to me to be good, peaceful people, and I had little cause to want to kill them.

Once the prospect of fighting for my faith would have thrilled me. Certainly, when I was very young, I dreamed of being a hero, listened to stories of the Crusades and imagined myself with a white cross sewn to my tunic and a large sword in my hand, a great steed and a fortune in reward to bring home to my family.

Such childish fancies. I know that now. I'd seen those returning from the Crusades broken and weary, sometimes wounded beyond repair. It led me to appreciate my quiet life and know that I was not brave, nor could I have enough dedication to the sport of killing for my faith. But to make my father proud would be better than any amount of money or wealth.

Until the soldiers came, we'd been blessed with a calm and peaceful life. Our small community had kind nobility who allowed us more freedom than most, so life *was* tolerable.

We never starved as others did. In fact, we considered ourselves very lucky, as the taxes we paid were small compared to those of our neighbours, who were bondsmen to Viscount Jacques Dentrellier. He was a cruel, greedy landlord who made many demands on his people, using bullying and harsh methods. His tenants worked harder and stayed subservient, often leaving their families with barely enough to survive. My family and our friends had often tended the children of our nearest neighbours who had been ill or half-starved.

Of course, Viscount Dentrellier was here, having volunteered his own small army of troops in the hope of gaining more land as a payment for his services.

I tossed and turned trying to make some sense of it all until Pieté Chamise wandered over to where I lay. We came from the same area, but he was much older than me with a large, hard labourer's body. His family were the brickmakers in the village.

He was really enjoying what he called 'this adventure' and seemed immune to the bloodthirsty task we were involved in. Back home, he was a big clumsy adolescent who mocked Jews and cripples, and got into fist fights outside the alehouse. Pieté and some of the others I knew from our village seemed to be possessed by a lust for blood, and having been pushed into the killing, they were now in determined pursuit of what they had been told were the enemies of the Church, and nothing but more blood, more screaming and more death would satisfy them. They were like foxes in a henhouse.

It was hard to understand but I think they killed because they were scared. I was shaken by the knowing, and guessed I too would soon be the same as they were, killing without question.

Pieté settled himself on the rank bale of straw I'd slept against. It had helped keep out the chill of the night but stank of mould and urine. Pieté seemed immune to it, was filthy dirty and his matted hair had the remains of dried blood in it. He was gnawing on a huge hunk of bread with dirt-encrusted hands.

"Where you bin? I di'n't see you when we came back." And, noticing my shivering, said, "You ill?"

"No, I'm okay now," I replied, sitting up.

I wondered if I could summon the courage to say what I was feeling. I felt my heart pound. I had tried to keep my doubts to myself, and I was afraid of how he would react to my question, but felt compelled to ask him why we needed to do this.

I took a deep breath and said, "I don't like what we are doing, Pieté, and I can't see the sense in it. What's it all about? We're killing Catholics too, just because they live here in harmony with the Jews and the Bons-Chrétiens. This surely can't be right. It's not like going to war, having an enemy, having someone to hate or to defend our homes or loved ones against. Many of these people are not even resisting and we don't know who we are killing most of the time. Are they not our own countrymen?"

"Yeah, they are, but God'll know his own, according to our officers. That's... when the time comes. How would I know? I don't. Anyway, the Jews have left and gone to Carcassonne," Pieté replied as if that justified our actions.

For a moment a small look of regret crossed his ugly features, but it passed and was replaced by a greedy, heartless grin.

"What about the rewards though? Already I've got loads of stuff to take home – new boots, knives, even some jewellery. Stuff I can sell. I have them hidden, of course." He gestured towards the fancy tents of the knights and nobility. "Bastards won't let us keep anything if they want it themselves."

"So, this is a war about greed rather than God?" I sighed.

"Well... it has been worthwhile." Then he added, "No, this is our duty, too. We're fighting for our faith and the Pope. *And...* our love of God. If the Pope's ruled that the heretics be killed then it must be so."

"So, if the Pope says the moon is square, it is so?"

"'e has the last word, 'e is the authority. 'e is the emissary of our loving God." Pieté obviously considered that was good enough reason to be involved in this, but I could not agree.

"What is there about God to love? All my life I've been good out of fear that I might offend Him, the Church, or my father. That is not a good faith. Look where it has got me. Here I am, killing my fellow countrymen and I know not why. My whole life is governed by fear. I've never felt the love of God, never been able to have fun or have anything to show for my miserable existence. My only enjoyment in life has come from working the land, caring for the animals, the birds and wild creatures I watch quietly when I'm on my own."

Pieté raised his eyebrows and smiled. I knew he didn't understand. I bent my head and pulled at my matted hair, then rubbed my hand across my forehead and swollen eyes, for I had cried many silent tears. My sorrow must have shown on my face. I couldn't hide it.

Softening a little, Pieté asked, "Why 'r' you questioning the belief of your family, Léon Dumont? Don' you wan' to conquer the heretics who threaten our faith?"

"What makes them heretics?"

"They defy the laws o' God and the Church."

"Does that make them evil? Where are they?"

"What?"

"The laws of the Church! I only know them from what I'm told to believe."

"God's will's written in the 'oly books and in our reverence to the sacraments. You denyin' your faith, are you?"

"No, I am not, Pieté. I want to know wherein lies the happiness of life that is taught by the Church. We're not allowed to own or read the Holy books. It is only our priests and clergy who do. That is, if they *can* read. Some of them don't, have never learned and don't even recite them correctly. They learn the sacraments off by heart."

"'ow do you know they don't recite 'em right?" scoffed Pieté, stuffing the remains of his bread into his mouth.

"I've heard the prayers and sacraments hundreds of times. I know them by heart and how they should sound, so I know when they do it wrong. Even though they are spoken in the Latin. They miss whole sections, mispronounce parts, and often have no idea what they've said."

Pieté laughed at me then. "Oh, you are so clever, Léon, too clever for y'own good, I fear. You'd better watch it or you'll be called a 'eretic yerself. You'll go to Hell when you die, you know… C'mon, get yourself some grub."

Off he lumbered to where the cooks had brought some fresh bread and trays of smelly sardines.

I won't know the difference because I'm in Hell already, I thought. I'd better keep my thoughts to myself and get on with what's deemed necessary or I shall never get through this. There must be others who question these things, but the mass of people here seem to me to have no doubt that we are delivering God's will. So who am I to question that?

For several days we camped, while the wounded were attended. Some were sent back to their homes with injuries so awful that they would never work again. Others, who were in pain or distressed, remained in camp with our medics.

We moved on towards the rich trading post of Narbonne, led by Arnaud Amaury and all the Papal Legates with their brilliant crucifixes and in their fine, richly embroidered clothes. The counts and knights came with their own colours and armies, and rode alongside. For miles behind, the thousands of men, horses, mules, machinery and stores streamed across the harsh terrain with the hot winds of the summer exhausting both man and beast. The great horses and oxen puffed, pawed and strained to pull the loads of equipment that it took to wage war against the fortified towns and cities.

Without warning, we were urged to change direction. We heard from the generals that Narbonne had surrendered to us, the Crusaders, with promises that all heretics, whether Bons-Chrétiens, Jews or Saracens, would be delivered to us, and their properties confiscated.

As fear dictated the surrender, terms were negotiated very quickly, with only a few small skirmishes along the way, so we camped again without battle. Other places, hearing of the downfall of Béziers, gave up their arms and cities without a fight.

Thank God, was my only thought!

The army restocked from the grain and fruit stores and moved on. Prisoners were taken away to be tried as heretics. In Azille and La Redorte, some were burned at the stake. I did not witness these horrors but I was told that the prisoners sang all the way to the pyres and died bravely, preferring martyrdom to conversion.

By now it was midsummer. We marched across the hot plains towards Carcassonne where the heretics were known to have their greatest influence.

We were told there would be many bloody battles and it would take many months as the heretics had spread north past Montauban and Albi, and south through the Corbières mountains to Spain.

As we travelled, we found many hamlets and crofts deserted, and we stripped them of anything worthwhile. Swift reprisals were doled out to any resistance we encountered along the route.

I found several ways of avoiding being involved, usually with the stock or horses. I became an expert in immersing myself in a job too arduous to walk away from. I managed to keep away from the beatings and abuse. I knew the time would come when I would have to account for my absences from the daily round-up of prisoners.

CHAPTER 6
The Battle for Carcassonne

LÉON

After a violent and brief storm, the heat diminished and three days later we made camp a good distance outside the Carcassonne city walls. The turrets and spires of the city sat high on a slope in the valley of the river Aude. We knew this would be a hard battle as the defences had been doubled since the atrocity of Béziers.

It was hard work erecting the tents and stalls for the stock, unloading the huge wagons and digging latrines. Halfway through the night, we collapsed with exhaustion. I stopped trying to think for myself or understand what was going on. Like everyone else, I just obeyed every order without question.

"Gather up, lads," Arnau de Suis shouted as we rose early the next day from our dusty beds.

"After Mass we are to attack immediately. It is imperative that Carcassonne is captured if we are to succeed in our mission."

As we lined up to collect our vittles, we watched a party of knights ride down from Carcassonne and assumed they had come to negotiate the surrender of the heretics. They obviously had not reached terms that satisfied our leaders as they left very soon afterward.

Later, Abbot Amaury, dressed in an embroidered white and purple robe, and holding a spiked mace, took Mass surrounded by his retinue.

Holding aloft the mace, he pointed it in the direction of the city. He was sweating profusely, but lifting both arms high he spoke to his followers. "Here rules the heretic Lord Raymond-Roger Trencavel, Viscount of Albi, Nimes, Razès, Béziers and Carcassonne. He is guilty of harbouring the sinners. Even members of his own family are committed to the monstrous superstitions of these heretics. Prove the reality of your faith and rid the world of these evil-doers, this filth, that deny our sacraments," urged the Abbot as one of his congregation swabbed his glistening forehead. "They pollute our faith. Let's get to our mission and slay them all." His voice rose. "Your salvation depends upon your actions today. Rome has decreed it. As good and holy men, soldiers of Christ, go forth and strike the sharp sword of death to all advocates of the devil and those who are contaminated by them."

He spoke with such conviction that it was hard to believe we were not justified in killing them all. Around me men were nodding and cheering, spurred by his words and restless to get it over and done with. So it began.

That day I heaved and strained with the huge boulders used in the great slings of the trebuchet that we piled up to bombard the fortifications. To protect me from the arrows, I wore a brigandine shirt and a mail coif that chafed my throat and forehead. The heat was so intense that it was difficult to breathe.

It was August, and the hot air shook with the noise of the relentless attack from the catapults of rocks and logs, while great storms of arrows and missiles flew back at us. To get close enough to bombard the walls of the city, we had to move uphill through the suburbs, so, as the people fled, we harnessed the oxen and horses and heaved the great weapons closer and closer.

Bodies lay all around, heaps of men and horses, dead or dying. Infantry streamed past us, and the mounted knights, with lances and swords, pushed toward the great fortifications.

The noise was terrible. The cries of the wounded and maimed rose in a chilling twist of steel meeting steel, or the thwack as the swords reached their targets. Day and night blurred into one as we continued the attack, great clouds of dust flying from the disintegrating stones and bricks, smoke drifting through the rubble. The tangle of bodies was all around me, running and falling, calling and dying. The ground beneath me turned slippery with blood.

My whole body was covered with dirt, blood and dust. My eyes burned and were watering, forming rivulets of mud on my cheeks. My mouth was so dry I couldn't speak. My hands were raw and blistered from turning the windlass of the trebuchet. The thud of the counterweight and the creaking of the capstan will live in my dreams; so constant was the noise, that I could hear nothing else.

We were given no release, and as the boulders diminished, anything, including the dead, was hauled into the catapults and sent flying over the ramparts. There was blood and guts everywhere but I could see little, my body aching, bruise on top of bruise, and my mind numb with the horror of it all. I felt I must be in Hell itself.

It took many days for us to take Carcassonne and I experienced emotions I never knew I had. I ceased to feel my body and had no rational thought other than taking my next breath and surviving the nightmare. It was the middle of the summer and there was no respite from the heat, the flies and the stench.

It was only when we had cut off the water supply to the fortress that the surrender finally came. Even then, there was no rest as we rescued the few fortunates who had reached safety, moved bodies, buried the dead and took apart the catapults, ready to move on. Kites circled overhead, dipping occasionally to join the scurrying rats that brazenly picked at the slaughtered pieces of human and animal flesh.

My horses were in a bad way and my favourite, old Tantho, coughed till his throat bled. There was no help but to rest the horses. Some were so badly injured they had to be replaced. I had led as many as I could across the river to pastures where they could rest and recuperate. I wished I too could stay and lie down in the summer fields, and forget what was happening.

Every part of my body hurt, and although I couldn't eat, my thirst was enormous. I stopped at every stream and river to try to sate my dry mouth and throat. The sun was dissolving into liquid gold over the hills behind Carcassonne, and a slight breeze began to stir, drying the muck and perspiration across my forehead. For a moment, I felt the balmy heat of the sun streaming over me. I had a flash of vibrant memory: leaning on a fence in a field of prickly stubble, the scent of the newly cut hay on the terraces around my home in my nostrils – and I remembered for a moment how good life had felt then.

My hands curved around the hilt of my blade as I looked over to the devastation that was the remains of the city and wondered again. When will it all end?

As the days wore on, hundreds of Bons-Chrétiens were herded away from the city, without clothes or possessions.

Where will they go? I wondered. Wherever it is, they will be hunted down by the merciless troops of this, the Pope's Holy army. Others, including Raymond-Roger Trencavel, who had tried to negotiate a cessation of the bombardment, were taken prisoner.

It didn't seem right to me that he should have been captured while on a mission to seek a compromise for the people of Carcassonne, but instead was held, then imprisoned, in his own dungeons at the Château Comtal, inside the ramparts of the city.

Many prisoners were wounded. Some, who were unable to walk, were sent to the castle dungeons where they would die of their wounds or await their trials. Others were marched away to be tried, tortured, hanged or burned at the stake.

In the tents, men and boys recounted their battles,

showed off their scars or bragged about the great piles of plundered goods, which they were wrapping and packing, ready to take back to their families. One small group from Lyon who had finished their quarantine even had a cart piled high with every imaginable household item, from weighing scales to carpets. They set off home happy. Many spoke of returning after the harvests were gathered for another term of duty. To me, only a fool would want to repeat the experience of battle and all it entailed.

From Carcassonne, our troops divided again as the terrain got higher. We moved on to areas where it was impossible to take the catapults. The machinery and the great siege ladders were to be transported to other large cities: Albi, Fanjeaux, Castelnaudary and Castres, places I had never heard of, but were apparently overrun with heretics.

With the fall of Carcassonne, we were told that Simon de Montfort would become viscount of the confiscated territories of Raymond-Roger Trencavel. The troops were reorganised yet again. New routiers and other mercenaries from the north came, and several more nobles from France, with their own armies, joined our host.

In the following weeks, the weather cooled as we moved south to reduce more towns and villages to dust. Garrisons were set up, prisons constructed and new orders issued. Where there was news of groups of heretics, or where they were supported, troops were sent out to arrest or destroy them with the unanswerable argument of force.

We reached the high mountain range of the Corbières as autumn tightened its hold, the bitter winds and freezing rain making the mountains a treacherous place to be.

The high crofts and villages that spread in the valleys and on the slopes harboured many of the heretical faith and their sympathisers, so we systematically attacked and raided them. Moving mainly at night, prisoners were dragged from their homes to be questioned and tried. Many were killed running or trying to escape.

It was a tough expedition that took us high up, through wooded mountains and along deep, dark valleys. We had with us some hardy mules carrying stores and weapons, but we were expected to carry our own armoury and clothing.

Two priests accompanied us to convert the sinners. Those who refused would be arrested and tried. At every opportunity, the priests bombarded us with stories of the heretics' sins, and how they contaminated the world with their practices and beliefs. They told us strange tales of baby sacrifice, sodomy and other dark sins.

One afternoon, Arnau de Suis ordered a group of us to prepare for a journey south to a town called Laroque-de-Fa, where there were rumoured to be many of the new faith who had not converted. As usual, we were ordered to search the crofts and villages all around the town and round up the sinners.

"A good opportunity, lads!" shouted de Suis as we collected our arms. "No knights with us so we can collect whatever we want. Earn your rewards, my boys, and let God see your worth. Let's get rid of these heretics once and for all." He pranced along, inspecting our weapons. "Prisoners will be taken and runaways killed. Now, Dumont, try to get yourself a bit of booty, eh?"

I had collected nothing. As my comrades filled their sacks and boxes, I felt I needed something to take back for my father. I had nearly completed my quarantine, and would be returning home very soon.

After what I had seen and experienced, life could never return to normal, but I was beginning to believe that I was weak and stupid, as de Suis had suggested on more than one occasion. I should put my feelings away and take whatever I could, as others were doing.

Did it matter what I felt? Perhaps at some time I would be able to understand and know it was justified after all. But in my heart I feared I had become like the others; I was now resigned to the job we were doing.

The dark of night was descending as we crossed the bridge of the river Sou that surrounded the town, but we could still see that Laroque-de-Fa was a beautiful place. Small stone houses nestled in the shadow of the rocky hills where swallows swooped and dived. The town had an air of peace and prosperity but was soon filled with the fearful cries of the inhabitants as they were roughly pushed into groups so that the priests and commanders could question them. There were small flurries of violent fighting, quickly dealt with. Knives, axes and swords flashed as the townspeople were gradually dealt with.

I no longer wanted to puke at the sight of beatings inflicted upon the villagers. I repeated in my head the words of our leaders and imagined myself glorious in the eyes of our Lord.

Although many refused to divulge the names of the heretics, speaking of them with high regard, there were a few who did talk if enough pressure was applied.

"Cooperate or your town will be destroyed!" shouted our black-robed man of God. "You know what happens to those who collaborate with sinners."

De Suis held an old woman who was being questioned. He snapped her head backwards while her screaming baby granddaughter was held aloft by her feet. The old woman was so distressed that she told de Suis about a meeting place for those of the new faith – close by – where they would find an *elite* of the sect.

"Bernard Rocault is his name," she sobbed, her voice shaking as she reached and clutched toward her granddaughter. "He lives there with his children. He has a small son, and a daughter already versed in the scriptures and going to be a *Perfecti* herself. Please," she wailed. "Please give me the child."

I, along with twenty others, followed de Suis to the edge of town and up a hillside to the croft the old peasant woman had described. This was where Bernard Rocault and his family lived, and where the *Perfecti* met.

CHAPTER 7
Attacked

EVA ROCAULT
I woke with a start, fear flooding through my body, my heart beating frantically to the sound of soldiers running, banging, shouting, baying for blood. Their voices were raised and excited in the glory of their mission. Panic gripped me, my knees trembling beneath my nightgown.

Even though we knew Carcassonne had fallen, we were unprepared, not thinking they would come so soon.

Living with the fear of this day, I remembered nothing of our decisions or plans. I heard my father being dragged from his bed. Poor Papa, he was old and tired. I knew that he would not resist.

I strained to hear.

"What do you want with us?" he called out.

"*Perfecti*... heretics, sinners!" screamed one of the men. "Let us burn them now... They defile us all. Heretics all o' you and those who support you."

My dearest Papa, so highly regarded and admired everywhere for his pure and loving attitude to all living creatures, was being dragged from his home as a heretic against the Holy Catholic Church. It was unthinkable that anyone would see my father as a sinner. So many noble families had entrusted him with the spiritual education of their children and he was good to his very bones.

I grabbed my blanket, wrapped it tightly around my head, and slid away from my bed. Standing pressed to the wall, every instinct told me to flee, but my body was stiff with fear. Cold chills were pressing into the back of my neck and I could feel my stomach cramp. Then the warmth of my pee running down my legs.

Holding my hands across my chest, I thought I had even

stopped breathing. Trying to think clearly, I remembered there was a space between the house and what remained of the old barn. I could hide there. But I couldn't move.

Over the screaming and shouting, I heard Roul's terrified voice, somewhere in the distance.

"Eva, Eva." Although I knew I had to hurry, my limbs were heavy and leaden. I could only move in slow motion.

"Eva!"

With sudden clarity, I realised he was outside my room in the alley between the house and the pigpen.

As if my body had been released, I threw myself under the heavy canvas sheet that covered the opening, over the wooden ledge, and fell on top of poor Roul.

Gasping for air and choking back sobs, he fell backward. I hoisted him quickly onto my hip and ran as fast as I was able, until we reached the end of the house. The ground was slippery, my bare toes squelched noisily in the mud. Edging along the wall, I found the small gap between the building and the barn.

I could hear the men stamping and shouting, people screaming and begging. In a moment they had found my room and were jumping through the window after us. We crept into the tiny space and I held Roul against me.

"We must hide under the barn, Roul." I whispered, "I'll be right beside you."

He wrapped his arms tightly around me, his snotty nose pressed into my neck. I pushed him hard and he let go with a whimper, sliding quickly toward the narrow space. Moving him into position, I pressed him down with my bare foot. I knew that with a wriggle, he could disappear into this place with ease, as he had done so many times in games of hide and seek.

Being small for my age, I too squeezed in, and was almost instantly alongside him. From there, I could see nothing but the dirt floor beneath my nose and smell the soil mixed with the decaying herbs that had been swept out of the house. Roul choked back his sobs and clung onto my arm.

I could still hear my father and others being dragged away. Their screams set me shivering so hard that my teeth were chattering.

Roul was still whimpering, but I held his hand and stroked his forehead, until he lay still.

I was so sure that at any minute rough hands would drag us from our hiding place. We would be marched away, or be imprisoned accused of heresy. So much for our plans!

But now the time had come. And they had come. Some of our people had fled to the fortified castles or mountain caves. But as most of us could not imagine leaving our homes, we stayed in the hope that we would be missed.

As I lay shivering I tried to pray, but the image of my beloved father being badly treated brought hot tears to my eyes. My poor Papa would not judge them, nor would he fear them. He would welcome death because he would escape from the imprisonment of the physical world. Not to fear death was a crowning achievement, but my sweet, gentle father would suffer on the way to his final glory, for he would remember us, his children, and know that we were not yet ready.

We had been taught to be tolerant and compassionate, and believed that these were the most basic attributes for us to strive for.

Could I feel compassion for these men who were enjoying the pain, destruction and havoc they caused? I thought not, as I held my frightened little brother and the cold crept into my bones.

It was difficult not to be afraid. Learning not to fear, not to hate, were the most difficult lessons of my faith – too difficult at that moment for me. In my head I understood, but my body betrayed me and, as I shivered, I wondered whether I could ever become completely 'perfect'.

I closed my eyes and told myself I should not judge, should not allow myself to be held by worldly emotions. I tried to relax and think of His teachings, and the words of the wise ones. All should be respected and honoured.

I ran my finger across my birthmark, tracing the outline of the tiny cross on my neck. I deliberately slowed my breathing, feeling myself relax. I brought down around me my spiritual shawl, my comfort and protection. In a moment, I heard nothing, my body relaxing into a state of weightlessness. As the awareness of my cold body diminished, I was floating with great white clouds above me. Soft blue and gold wrapped around me like a drifting mist, comforting and caressing me.

I was in my *otherspace* where I felt protected and safe. Here, my thoughts became clear. All troubles diminished into insignificance. Time passed in a different way whilst I was there. Everything became soft and muted. The silence was so beautiful. I felt only pure joy. There the world was no longer a place to fear.

CHAPTER 8
Flight

EVA

It was still dark when, with a small tingling sensation, my essence and flesh became one again and I became aware of Roul's body next to me. Slowly and painfully, I eased myself around so I was facing him. He was deeply asleep but I could feel his breathing. He was so cold. I tried to reach out for him to bring him close but found that we were too cramped. Not wanting to frighten him, I gently touched his forehead. He stirred and whimpered.

"Roul, wake up. We must find somewhere else to go," I said.

He lifted his face. I could just see the whites of his eyes as they widened, as he too remembered our plight. My poor, frightened little brother looked so small and vulnerable. My heart was filled with love for him. "Don't be afraid, Roul, we will find somewhere warm and you can go back to sleep."

Getting out from beneath the barn was difficult. My feet were stiff with mud and numb with cold. I shivered violently again. Rain was falling in grey sheets. I could see little movement except the large old tree bending in the wind. Pushing my hair from my face and listening carefully, I knew we were alone. Even the village in the valley was deserted.

Struggling from our hiding place, I wrapped my arms around Roul. As I lifted him, he clung to me and laid his head on my shoulder. I inched forward along the wall towards our front door.

"Where will we go, Eva?" he whispered.

Before I could answer, a movement caught my eye. I tensed and stopped, held to the spot. Just to our right, next to the pantry window, there was something moving, and I could hear a crunching, slurping wet sound. Holding Roul close and moving slowly forward, I saw a dark form scraping at something on the muddy ground. It was a large dog, or perhaps a wolf. It was eating, pulling and tearing at the flesh of another larger animal.

The wind rose and bent the old cypress tree so that moonlight momentarily lit the pathway. The animal looked up, growled, and hurried off. But in that moment, horror at what I saw overtook me.

I dropped Roul and pushed him back behind the wall. Stepping forward, I stared at the remains of a body lying face down in the dirt. There was a huge dark ring around it, sticky and wet. The one remaining leg oozed blood. Halfway down, the leg bone was sticking out. It had been chewed into a bloody pulp. The side of the body was exposed where the clothing had been ripped off. A huge hole had been torn into the flesh.

In the puddles of bloody mud on the ground lay entrails like long, slimy black slugs.

Holding both hands across my mouth to prevent myself from screaming, I saw that it was Vivenny's daughter, Matilde. Pretty, sweet Matilde who loved to sing and skip, and always smiled at everyone. Lying at an odd angle, her dark shiny hair was spread out over the top of her head and her face was partly hidden. Her head was almost severed.

A huge black, bloody wound ran across the back of her neck. Her bare, pink little bottom was the only part of her that remained intact. I wanted to cover it, but I couldn't move.

I looked away from Matilde's mutilated body and saw a few feet away there were others. It was so dark, I couldn't tell who they were.

I was still standing with my hands over my mouth when I heard Roul whimpering. He had been particularly fond of Matilde. She had cared for him when Papa and I went to prayer meetings.

He could not see this.

All was deserted, no living soul to be seen. While we had hidden, everyone had been taken or driven away.

Laroque-de-Fa was burning and the acrid smell of smoke drifted through the wet darkness to our little croft.

As Roul's sobbing became louder, I quickly turned, lifted him and held him close.

"Hush, Roul," I whispered.

Poor child! He was so frightened; his body was shaking, and I knew I had to get him away from there as quickly as possible. What if the soldiers returned? We started to move across the hill toward the forest. Then, realising how wet and cold we both were, I decided to get us some warm clothing. Lifting Roul, I moved carefully and slowly back towards our house, avoiding the open spaces where the bodies lay.

The door was broken and although it was dark, I could see the muddy footprints of the soldiers who had dragged my father away. The coarse blue robe he had been wearing lay on the floor. He would be cold but I knew he would not complain.

The whole place was eerily quiet. Even the animals had gone. The only sounds were of the rain and rustling trees. Quickly, I helped Roul put on as many clean, warm clothes as possible, with his heavy-hooded cloak over the top. I helped him pull on his squirrel-lined boots. We took a few extra clothes in a small bundle.

Somehow I managed to pull on my own clothes, wiped my muddy feet, and put on warm stockings and boots.

Moving quickly to the pantry, I packed all the food I could find into a small sack.

I had no plan, but knew that we should leave this place before the soldiers returned or the dawn revealed the carnage. We would hide till daylight and find someone to help us. Throwing on my own heavy-hooded cloak and taking Roul's hand, we ran across the slope away from the croft and the village, down the valley towards the forest. Poor Roul was gasping, so I heaved him up onto my hip and moved as fast as I could with my bundle of clothes while Roul clutched the sack of food. His other hand grabbed the back of my neck. His little fingers transmitted his fear.

Running away from everything I knew and loved left a feeling of deep emptiness in my heart.

My life as I had known it for the past fifteen years was disappearing forever.

Would our days ever again be filled with fun and laughter?

The great lands and estates around us had been peaceful for my lifetime, and now all I could feel was worry for Roul. How would I keep him safe?

The wind was rising as we reached the edge of the forest. My teeth were chattering again.

A bigger storm was brewing, the breeze was stirring up the dead leaves and sending them spiralling around my ankles.

Stopping at the edge of the forest pathway, I remembered the little dell where we used to play hide and seek, and a thicket with a small opening into a flat patch of ground. We could hide there, out of the cold – a good place to rest until morning.

I ran as fast as I could, my legs screaming in protest and my breath burning my throat. All I could think was that we needed to get as far away as possible. It was so dark and several times I thought that we were lost, so we had to keep stopping.

At night everything was different. But, finally, sobbing with relief, I found a path that I knew. Deep clinging darkness lay ahead, muttering and sighing in the wind. Dark shadows formed and reformed. The forest changed shape, giving it an unworldly and menacing spirit. Great teardrops of rain fell from the trees. My flesh crept, the overwhelming vastness of the sky making me feel small and vulnerable. The forest sounds were menacing too – so close – sounds I usually heard from a distance and in the safety of my bed.

Staring around the forest, I knew I couldn't carry Roul any further. "We will be safe in a moment. We will sleep in the dell," I whispered, as much to reassure myself as him. "Let us walk now. We will stay there and soon be warm."

His eyes were wide. His thin, little face, dirty and tear-streaked.

"Where shall we go?"

"Tomorrow we will go to the Château d'Arques and ask for help from the Seigneurs of Termes," I replied, hoping he wouldn't ask again as I had no idea whether the Seigneurs would be there. Certainly, their own small army would be fighting the Crusaders, but they were usually based in Termes, a long way to the east. I was sure if they were there we would find protection, as many of their family were of the new faith themselves.

The brambles had covered the opening to the dell. I had to get a heavy branch to push aside the prickly, grasping lengths of stems so we could crawl through. A pungent odour of animals and dead leaves made me pause for a moment, but fear pushed me ahead.

Dropping to my knees, I crawled in. Although the darkness was intense, I could feel the warmth of earth that had not yet succumbed to the chill of autumn. The leaves inside were dry.

"Roul, come on," I urged. "Hold my skirt and come inside." But he did not move.

I turned, caught hold of him and dragged him forward. I pulled him close, wrapping my cloak around his shaking body. "There, there. We'll soon be warm."

Placing the bundle of clothes under his head, I sang a soft lullaby, holding him like a baby, stroking his soft blond hair.

As his body warmed and relaxed, his breathing slowed.

Through the long night, while Roul slept, I was busy trying to decide where we should go. Papa had planned we would move east to a safer place, a fortress in the Aude. But we heard that the main army was moving from that direction. I would have headed towards Carcassonne and sought refuge if the Trencavels had still been there. I couldn't move north because there were huge army camps outside Capendu and Rieunette.

Where would we be safe? I knew not. Nor did I know where the prisoners would be taken and held. Where was my beloved father now? Where would we be safe?

I needed to sleep, but could only worry. I was uncomfortable with my brother laid across my lap. On the verge of drifting into slumber, I sensed his breathing change to hollow rasping. I stroked his brow, it was hot and sweaty.

'Oh Roul, please don't fall ill,' I thought, 'I have nothing here to help you.'

Finally, I slept.

CHAPTER 9
Regret

LÉON DUMONT
I squeezed my eyes shut, trying to blot out the images of that night. The little girl's face as she fell, her eyes pleading and terrified, her hands reaching out toward me, the sound of the thwack sending her blood spurting from her throat ran and re-ran in my tortured mind. Dark-haired and brown-eyed, she looked just like my little cousin who laughed and sang and talked of having her own babies when she was grown, her life full of dreams and plans.

I had stared at the body of this young girl who could dream no more, who would never again see the sun or the stars, never become a mother or feel the love of her family, and my heart split in two. As the darkness hid the hot tears springing to my eyes, I vowed, from that moment on, that I would cry no more, just get the job done, do what was expected of me.

We had captured the old *Perfecti* and many of his followers, but some, including the little girl, had run away, been mercilessly cut down and left to rot. Everyone else from the croft was herded away to the garrisons for questioning. Only those who accepted the sacraments and recanted would be released. The rest would go to the pyres.

We collected the few goats and hens to take back to camp. With our many prisoners taken to the garrison outside Limoux, our group headed back to the great camp near the river.

We would regroup for another battle and move on to attack other fortresses in Lastours and Cabaret.

I curled into a ball in the corner of the tent and tried to wipe out the jumbled pictures and thoughts racing through my head. I didn't want to think. I could make no sense of any of it.

I'd always enjoyed the solitude and independence of the countryside and had no desire to be anywhere else. Certainly not here! Now, even the thought of going home gave me little joy.

Victor, my little gypsy friend, appeared. "Come, Dumont, de Suis is dishing out the ale. We need a good drink after today's work."

"Good idea."

I got up, vowing to make the best of this ghastly life. I would drink myself into oblivion as all the others did. Perhaps that was a good way to cope with it all.

Several hours later, with a belly full of mead and ale, I collapsed in a heap and fell into a deep sleep, waking a few hours later to vomit most of it into the pot by my pallet. Then, till daybreak I tossed and turned, hating my life and myself.

CHAPTER 10
Escape

EVA ROCAULT

As the light of dawn peeped into the tiny entrance of our refuge, Roul opened his eyes. He was pale and wanted a drink. I told him to stay still and hidden. I crawled outside with the small bowl I had packed with our food and crept to the stream that ran close by.

In the morning light, the place looked more familiar. The early sunlight sparkled on the tumbling waters of the stream as it ran down to the Le Sou River.

I felt my spirits lift. In better times I had spent many hours in that rocky valley and those woods, collecting nuts, herbs, berries and roots, hoisting kindling and logs.

The forest glistened in the shimmering light and, as I hurried over the open ground, my feet lifted the dew, splashing the hem of my skirt. As the pathway was muddy, I worked my way quickly across the driest parts and concentrated on getting Roul some fresh water. I washed my face and, having quenched my own thirst, filled the bowl and returned to the dell.

I had almost reached the opening when I heard the sound of horses galloping through the valley. I ducked down. A moment earlier I would have been in their path. I shuffled backward into the opening, pulling a loose branch behind me and, with a finger to my lips, gave Roul his drink.

Peeping through the branches, I saw the banner of the leading horseman. It showed a fork-tailed lion, which I knew to be the insignia of Simon de Montfort, the Pope's man, the military commander of the crusading army sent to eliminate us.

We'd been told of its design at the market the previous week by Marcus, an old market trader who, many years before, had fought with de Montfort on a Crusade against the Saracens. "Puts fear in the heart of everyone. His reputation is fierce. He was young then and looking for glory. Now he wants estates and wealth for his growing family," he told us sagely.

The horses were sweating and lines of white foam on their withers and around their mouths showed they had been ridden hard.

Quickly gone, they left the path churned heavy with the mixed odour of men and horses, the disturbed earth and rotting leaves. They were heading north, perhaps to their camps by the great river Aude, or around Carcassonne.

My fear returned, cramping my empty stomach. I lay still, watching Roul sipping from the bowl. His eyes were closed and his brow beaded with sweat. He coughed and lay down without a word.

How can we move on with all these men trying to kill us? Who will protect us? Would they know we are of the new faith? We are children and there are many orphans on the streets of the towns and cities. If we get far enough away, nobody will know us. That's what we have to do. Get to a place where we can find good people who will help us.

Father has been teaching me to read. I can cook too, so I could perhaps find some work in a castle or chateau.

Staying for a while, we shared an apple, some bread and a few nuts, and finished the water. Roul ate quietly, very slowly.

"Can you walk awhile, Roul?" I said, as I wrapped his hooded cape tightly against the chill wind.

He nodded. "Where are we going?"

"I'm not sure yet but we will soon find somewhere safe," I assured him, and taking his hand we set off.

CHAPTER 11
Camp Life

LÉON DUMONT

Next morning, as the rain was so heavy, we did not decamp as expected. Rivulets of water flowed through the huge tents. Those who slept outside covered themselves the best they could. The stench was awful.

Once again, I was overcome with nausea. Nevertheless, that was infinitely preferable to the slaughter and bloodshed that had been my life since I had left my home.

The days passed with endless rain and mud everywhere, great streams filled with waste from the overflowing latrines. Everything and everybody began to smell and look the same colour, except the noble knights and the clergy. They had hordes of servants keeping them dry and clean.

The horses and stock stood wet and bedraggled in the pens. Tantho's cough had improved, though, so he would be back on duty in the next siege.

Fights broke out amongst the men, bored with the card games, knucklebones and inactivity. In the meantime, of course, business flourished in the whores' tents.

Other than my usual duties with the animals, I and the rest of our group were assigned to dig more latrines further away from the camp as those closest had flooded, and many of the great tents and carts of food and drink had to be moved.

As the day progressed the rain eased a little.

Side by side, Victor the gypsy and I slithered together in the mud as we hauled and secured the last of the great ropes holding the tarpaulin over the blacksmith's workshop. Victor laughed as I fell, and I took a playful swipe at him as I struggled to my feet.

"Come on, Dumont, let's eat!" he shouted as he ran off

towards a large group gathered around a fire, a huge blaze set in a rectangular pit under a long spit. It was an enormous construction on which dozens of geese, hens and rabbits were being turned. The cooked meat was being sliced onto big wooden platters. The young kitchen boys in leather gloves and aprons dodged between the hungry men, passing it around with speed and skill. Having been served, the men wandered off to be replaced by others as they braved the rain and mud to get their suppers.

Victor and I stood in line and took as much as we could, having been driven hard all day by de Suis.

Crouching inside the nearest tent, we sat on our haunches, wolfing down our meats. We were wet and muddy, and hardly recognizable, as our clothes were stuck to our bodies and our faces caked. Bits of mud had dried as we'd stood in front of the burning pit waiting for our food and it hung like shards of brown ice from our chins.

"Jesus... God," said Victor suddenly, his eyes misting. "I can't wait to go home. I'm so sick of all these bloody heretics. Bastards. Let someone else kill 'em. I've had enough."

"Do you have no pity for them?" I asked, thinking of the little girl who reminded me of my cousin.

Victor shrugged. "There is no point in being soft-hearted. You have to be strong and do what's needed. God's will is that we rid the place of 'em. We have to be ruthless."

"Blessed are the meek for they will inherit the earth?" I quoted.

"Pah... I think not, the world is too full of violence." Victor's eyes became vacant for a moment, as though searching deep within for an explanation. "You have to be strong to preserve the true religion."

He picked some of the dried mud from his chin. "I want to go home now. I've done my duty. Just a few more days and my quarantine will be over, then I'll never have to set eyes on de Suis again. The prick never leaves me alone. If I stay any longer, by God, I'll kill him."

I understood his anger. De Suis always picked on Victor and took enormous pleasure in stirring him up, as if daring him, goading him to react so that he had an excuse to beat him up. De Suis was an evil person who always made me feel that something unclean had crawled across me. But he left me alone most of the time. He often called me names by telling me I was lily-livered or stupid, but I could cope with that and did not let him anger me. I, too, would be returning home soon, so I decided to stop trying to rationalise what we were doing, and get on with it.

CHAPTER 12
Lost

EVA ROCAULT

Oh, the endless rain! A soft persistent stream of water that dripped from the trees in great, fat drops so that our clothes were soaked through in minutes. Within a very short time, with the weight of our soggy cloaks, walking became harder. However much I tried, I couldn't keep us dry.

We kept away from the main pathways through the forest and headed west, hoping to find help at the Château d'Arques.

I had travelled this area before but the terrain was rocky and the ravines deeper than I remembered, so we stayed close to the river as I knew it would eventually join the great waterway of the Aude.

Roul did not complain as we walked and climbed that day, but had hung onto my hand so tightly, so trustingly, that I knew I would do anything to keep him safe. He'd not asked about Father. It was as if he already knew our fate was moving in a different direction.

Approaching a small croft, we could see it had been raided and torched. I tucked Roul into a corner of a small lean-to at the side of a burned-out house and set off to see if I could find whether anyone was still there. Perhaps even find something to eat.

Everything was deserted. There were several recently dug graves in the next field. I stood for a moment and prayed that wherever Papa was, he was at peace. I tried hard to remember all he had taught me. It was not easy. How could our lovely valley have been reduced to this in a few short months? I tried not to think of the devastation we had run from, but I could not forget the sight of Vivenny's daughter, poor, sweet Matilde, and the good life that we'd had.

Returning to Roul, I chased away two dirty, skinny boys, probably in much the same state as we were. They had stolen what little food we had left. Poor Roul was distressed and crying.

"I couldn't stop them, Eva. They were bigger than me," he sobbed.

"I shouldn't have left you on your own," I said, and resolved not to do so again. "Come on, we'll find some help soon, my lovely boy. Let us sing a song and skip along awhile."

After that we met nobody at all. It was as if a great hush had descended. The valleys and mountains were main highways, usually with traders and travellers moving from place to place. Herds of goats and flocks of sheep often grazed near the river or on its lush banks. But today, everywhere was silent and deserted. Even the animals and birds had disappeared.

Some time later, we saw a small herd of feral goats grazing on the steep slopes where the sparse grass tufted towards the sky, but taking our scent, they scampered up the rocky hillside and disappeared.

I tried to stay light-hearted and sang as we walked, but we were both so tired. Stumbling along a mossy bank, we found a bird's nest full of large eggs and my spirits lifted. I wrapped them carefully in my sack. We were both hungry and I still didn't know how far we would have to travel. But luck was on our side. As the light dropped and darkness threatened, we came across a small dwelling tucked into the side of the mountain. I breathed a sigh of relief as I recognised it. I knew who it belonged to; a hermit monk called Boris who came occasionally to Laroque-de-Fa and sold what he called 'Holy Wishes'.

Villagers believed he could change their fortunes and, once, Vivenny bought one. The following day, as she was harvesting beans, she found three dinars pushed into the soil. She was convinced it was Boris's 'Holy Wishes' that had brought them to her. Boris was a quiet, bony old man and no one knew where he came from or what he was doing living in the mountains. He had been there for many years.

I now had my bearings, as I knew his home was close to the Château d'Arques on the road to Aleth-les-Bains. If we got there we would find comfort.

There was no sign of Boris and the place had obviously been deserted for a long time. I pulled aside the rush matting that covered the opening to a small cave set in the hillside. I could see nothing. I stepped in. It was warm, dry and deeply dark inside. As my eyes adjusted, I could see he had constructed a chimney in the corner under which lay a small hearth with a pile of twigs and dried moss.

We could shelter here from the rain and get dry. There was a flat ledge in the rock with a small cross, a shiny piece of stone, and a bunch of dried flowers and herbs. On another shelf sat cooking pots, cups, knives and a ladle. Under a dusty old blanket I found a flint and steel, and managed to light the twigs and moss. Piles of kindling and logs sat stacked in a corner so I soon had a good fire. In a wooden box, I found some nuts and seeds, and some wheat flour. In another corner a cask of ale. With the eggs I had collected I made us a good meal. As I ate my own food, I watched Roul struggle with his. After he had drunk some warmed ale, he curled up by the fire and slept.

It was good to be cosy and dry. Soon, I too fell into a deep, exhausted sleep.

The following morning, I studied the seething mass of grey clouds moving in our direction.

"Can we stay here?" Roul asked. He had found a bag of coloured pebbles and was happily sorting them into piles.

"Yes, until you feel better, lamb," I said. I had already decided that we would stay in the shelter at least another day.

The weather did not abate. But we had a little food and we needed the respite. While Roul played and rested, I used my *otherspace* to relax and gather strength to help me believe that all would be well.

CHAPTER 13
New Orders

LÉON DUMONT

October blustered in full of gloom. The day was brittle and cold as I listened carefully to what Guy de Pressau was explaining. He stood on a makeshift stage made from an old cart and pallets that were usually tied to the horses to pull our gear.

We were gathered on the wet hillside to hear new orders about the war against the heretics, and to witness the punishment of two deserters who had been hunted down during the night and were now going to be flogged. They were no older than me, and had been tethered together and stood upright all night, so they were exhausted and broken. One was crying uncontrollably. I knew neither of them. My hollow insides and weakened state had deadened all feeling and I hardly registered what was going on around me or what de Pressau was saying. He was shouting about our duty to God. I willed myself to listen, hoping that something would inspire me to believe his words.

Arnau de Suis stood behind me. As I pulled my cape tightly around my shivering body, he leant forward and whispered in my ear, "Take heed, Léon Dumont. I have been watching you. I know your heart is not in it." He indicated the deserters. "This will be you if you disappear again."

So, he had noticed!

I turned to face him. His scraggy face was contorted and mean, so I moved away, knowing that very soon I would be able to return home. I had already finished my quarantine, but had been told that I had to stay until the weather improved and continue to work as ordered.

Our commanding officer was issuing new instructions. His accent was so strong I couldn't understand all he was saying. Even though some around me were repeating his words and translating for those of us who didn't know his odd way of speaking, I still did not understand.

"We have new orders," de Suis told us. "We are to capture rather than kill so that justice will be seen to have been carried out. All heretics will be tried, as the law requires, and we are to be allowed to take only from those found guilty. There is to be no more looting, and any caught stealing will be severely dealt with."

Those around me were laughing and jeering. Looting had never been allowed, but nobody obeyed the rules and they took whatever they could, whenever they could.

"Tha's what we're 'ere for!" shouted Pieté. "My time's up so I'll take what I can."

Disgruntled and angry, the crowd dispersed muttering about the new edict.

Arnau de Suis followed and then gathered us around him. "Listen, you lads. Do not be seen with your plunder. Be smart. Keep what you get well hidden, and capture rather than kill. You'll earn your salvation if you bring in prisoners. Here is the list of the heretics and their preachers. They've been openly condemning our faith and our God. We must capture them!" He waved the list. "We will not move forward until the rain has stopped. But we will have new supplies and fresh bedding sent from the town today. So get some rest. We still have serious work to do."

When the beatings began, I ran back to the muddy camp, knowing that Arnau de Suis was right. It could have been me on the receiving end of that whip. I couldn't wait for my quarantine to end. I was empty and distraught. I knew that I must put aside my fears; carry out my orders so that I could go back to my father and my village with pride. The only way I could survive that shitty world was to remember a better one at home with my animals. I was determined that I would do anything to get back soon.

The great mounds of fetid dung, waste and rubbish slid along the trenches down to the river. At least the rain would clear some of it away. I found a large tent and stood inside away from the endless downpour, and watched the squires polishing the suits of armour, each trying to outshine the other.

Wet saddles were laid out to dry, and two of the smaller boys were cleaning the ornamental bosses. The horses snorted and kicked in the pens outside. They didn't like to be tied in the rain.

With nothing better to do, I wandered over to the horses and stood for a moment, breathing in the damp pungent smell of them, infinitely preferable to the terrible stink and filth around the camp. I walked over to Tantho. Looking up, he snorted a greeting. As I caressed his soft muzzle, I wondered what it must be like for the horses, travelling all those miles, involved in the noise and pain of the battles, constantly pulling the great weights and rarely getting any affection. Did they wonder, as I did, whether life would ever be peaceful and free again?

CHAPTER 14
Aleth-les-Bains

EVA ROCAULT

The next day was cold and misty. The rain still fell sharply across the mountain slopes, but we could stay there no longer. Keeping warm and dry was impossible. Roul was shivering as we left the forest, passing through fields of soggy grass, over shale and rocky hills.

We walked all day but made slow progress because often I had to carry Roul and we couldn't find the Château d'Arques.

As I knew there were great caves in the high mountains of the Corbières, which many people and some followers used as permanent homes, I decided to look for them instead.

All day we searched. We headed upward across the towering rocks, but we found none of them. In the misty, miserable weather, we veered off track. We found no one. When the rain stopped, everywhere was eerily silent. No sound of birds or insects, no breath of wind.

Nothing, but the rustle of our movements and the dripping rain!

Roul became feverish again, so we slowed down frequently. He hardly responded although I sang and talked to him.

The next night, we slept in a goat-herder's shed built in a ditch on the side of a rocky hill. All that remained of our food was a few seeds and two dried figs. Roul had lain down on the smelly floor and closed his eyes. He slept for a long time and then I couldn't rouse him.

The following morning, I lifted him across my shoulder and ran from the scruffy hillocks to a flat, fertile plain spotted with vineyards, deserted farmhouses and workers' huts. At last, I heard the sound of the river and saw, in the far distance, Aleth-les-Bains surrounded by its protective moat. Oh, what relief. Here we would be safe!

As we drew closer, I saw the spires of the Abbaye Sainte-Marie. I had been there once with my father, preaching and spreading the Light.

The fortified city of Aleth-les-Bains was a prosperous place where the hot, thermal waters were said to be healing. In normal times many people visited, and I knew there were hospitals and rehabilitation centres on the surrounding mountains where the springs rose and bubbled to the surface. It was the perfect place to get help for Roul.

I set off with renewed determination. My boots were caked with mud, and just lifting my feet was exhausting. Roul had mumbled and cried all morning but was now quiet and as pale as a dove's belly, trying hard to walk.

We had to cross the river; it was flowing fast from the heavy rain. Great swathes of trees and rubbish were being swept along so the banks were covered with driftwood and debris.

Head down against the weather and intent on reaching the bridge, I heard a loud rumble from across the hill, the road from Limoux and Carcassonne.

Suddenly the hillside was filled with people, whole families, foot-sore and soaking wet, heading for the city. Bedraggled children with tear-stained faces, and older relatives sat resignedly on top of the carts with watchful, sad expressions. With them were their horses, donkeys, sheep and goats. Chickens and ducks clacked noisily in cages tied to the sides of wagons.

Like us, they were fleeing the Crusade, looking for refuge. My spirits lifted and, ignoring my blistered feet and Roul's weight, I hurried toward them. We joined them as we reached the bridge that spanned the frothing water. Everyone was hurrying, taking little notice of us, until a gruff old man pulling a handcart strode along beside me. He took one look at Roul and said, "I'll put him in the wagon, Mistress. He don't look too good." He gently lifted Roul from my aching shoulders, placed him in his cart on top of a tarpaulin and covered him with a soggy blanket.

"Where will they all go?" I enquired of the man as we walked toward the city.

He shrugged. "My guess is to relatives and friends, but some will camp and others find refuge in the hostelries. I don't know. Many of us will travel further west or south."

We crossed the sturdy wooden bridge, the water roaring beneath us. It had risen so high it was almost at the roadway, but it was quickly negotiated and the wagons and carts were carefully pulled over without incident.

The drawbridge across the moat surrounding the city was down. My heart lifted again as we were joined by others heading in the same direction. The city stood on a hill and soon the whole roadway, across the hillside, was filled with people and wagons moving toward one of the main gates.

As I walked alongside the cart where Roul lay, we passed makeshift tents and stalls everywhere. It looked as if many families had been camped there overnight. Some were loading up again to get inside the city walls. A gaggle of geese was being herded upward.

There was no sign of the Pope's soldiers but it was obvious they were expected soon. Everywhere, people were preparing for the inevitable siege. The walls of the city were being extended, and a huge wooden walkway constructed for the archers. Stone, wood and boulders were being piled high, ready for the ballistas and slings.

Some of the many workmen were digging small trenches to release the accumulated water so that it ran down the hill alongside the road, grey and bubbling toward the moat. Others were constructing extra walls along the slopes outside the main ones. We paused as we reached the gates, and Roul was lifted from the cart and placed back across my shoulder.

"Go up that road to the top and you will find a physician," said my gruff companion, indicating a road up the hill. "I'm only staying here a short while and then moving south again."

"Thank you, sir. I am grateful for your help. Good luck on your journey," I said.

Inside the city walls, more stalls, tents and improvised shelters had been constructed. Many seeking refuge clearly had nowhere particular to go. Once again, I wondered how Roul and I would survive.

Further on, the market was alive with people buying and selling, moving about, intent on getting what they wanted and hurrying away out of the rain. All sorts of goods were on sale. Small pens of scrawny goats and sheep, chickens hung by their feet, squawking and flapping, tiny wire cages filled with birds, rabbits and ducks.

Although tired and hungry, the crush and noise and the smells of the market place were comforting.

I had to find help soon, but everyone was rushing about intent on their own problems of getting out of the rain and finding somewhere to stay.

There were calls and cries from every direction and no one took much notice of us.

A fat, slack-faced woman was heaving a great bundle of wet firewood. She glanced our way but hurried on before I had a chance to speak to her. We moved slowly through the city, searching for a kindly face, a helping hand. We paused outside a large open courtyard where material was being felted – not a job for the weak or faint-hearted. The men and women working there had strong bodies and muscular arms.

Big bags of fuller's earth and bales of cloth stood under the extended roof at the back of the premises. Two men, with large poles with a bat-shaped end, were pounding and grunting, their backs turned and determinedly ignoring anything but their work.

Although it was still raining, the sun suddenly lifted in the sky. I was hot from the effort and the heat coming from Roul's feverish body.

A broad-shouldered woman carrying a large bucket in her raw red hands glanced our way, so I took the opportunity to speak to her.

"Madam, can you help me please? My brother is ill. Where can I get help?"

"If you have money," she grunted, "go to the physician's house, which is two lanes away. If not, call on old Therese. Go across the square, up by the castle wall. Next turn left." She poured her bucket of water into the huge trough where the men were pounding the cloth and turned away.

Coopers rolled barrels up the slope toward the abbey and the chateau, clattering over the cobbles. Carts rumbled past, laden with goods. A small girl cajoling a scrawny goat, its udder swollen with milk, passed by, making me wonder what had happened to Marielle, our goat.

Roul's limp body had exhausted me. Carefully wiping his forehead, I leaned against a wall.

Muttering feebly, he asked for a drink.

I shifted him on my aching shoulders.

"Soon," I said with more confidence than I felt.

I had to find Therese.

CHAPTER 15
Facing Death

LÉON DUMONT

Walking through the endless mass of grubby tents, I headed toward the river. A few of the men were setting up smaller shelters under some trees. Like me, they were soaked and filthy.

Victor was with other lads from our group. I lifted my hand in greeting.

"Come, Léon, we are to play la Soule." He was carrying a large pig's bladder, stuffed with straw and covered with leather.

"It's too wet, Vic," I replied. "It will be as heavy as a cannonball in a few minutes' play."

I knew everyone was bored but playing la Soule when the ground was treacherous and slippery would probably end up with a few broken bones. It was a rough game with little skill and a lot of brute force.

"Lily-livered, scared of everything, snotty little Léon Dumont! Get out there and play. Show a bit of spirit, why don't you?" sneered de Suis as he swaggered towards Victor and took the soule from his grasp. "Give it to me, gypsy boy."

Raising it above his head, and holding it with both hands, he hurled it fast through the air towards me. It hit me in the chest. I bent, winded, gasping, and dropped to the soggy ground, trying to catch my breath. I heard his coarse laughter as he strode toward me and kicked me so hard in the head that blood spurted onto the ground in front of me. The pain was terrible and my head was buzzing. From the corner of my eye, I saw Victor swing toward de Suis and heard him shout, "You filthy, sadistic pig."

Turning, de Suis punched Victor hard. I heard his nose

crack and, as I straightened and took a breath, I could see blood pouring down Victor's mouth and chin.

Hurling himself toward de Suis, he gave vent to his pain and anger, and brought his fists one after another hard into de Suis. He managed a couple of swift punches but he was not fast enough for our leader, who dodged and dived, then rushed toward Victor with a thump. His feet slid from under him and together they fell, de Suis onto his back and Victor on top of him.

Getting to my feet, my heart leapt into my throat. I took a step backward, my muscles tensing as I realised what de Suis had done.

Victor lay across him, and with a swift movement he pushed the slack body to one side and snarled, "Anybody want to take a chance, eh?"

His long thin dagger had killed Victor instantly. Nobody moved.

I felt like a child that had been tumbled into a mad world. Flashing before my eyes and leaping in my belly, I could see and feel all the horrors of this insane quest we were enmeshed in. In a moment my anger rose, exploding and expanding at the bloody senseless war, the endless rain and de Suis. It erupted into an unbearable explosion of boiling rage.

De Suis turned to retrieve his weapon.

With a great howl from deep within, I leapt toward him, landing heavily on his back. With my arms clamped around his head and neck, the impact of my weight brought us down. Using all my strength, I twisted his neck while holding him on the ground. But he was too strong for me and, with a thrust backward, elbowed me in the ribs. I fell. Punching and growling at each other we rolled through the wet mud and thorns. He managed to pull himself free and, getting to his feet, turned, his ugly face contorted into a grin. "Ah, so Léon Dumont thinks he can hurt me."

He laughed as I too leapt to my feet.

I was raging with a blood fury I had never felt before. The dagger flashed as he dashed toward me. Unexpectedly, it was in his left hand, but I caught his wrist in mid-motion, my forearm and biceps straining with the effort to hold him. He struck at me with his other fist, I felt my eyelid split open and was blinded with pain and blood. Loosening my grip, his dagger swung downward and through my clothing into my upper arm. I kicked out as hard as I could and caught him in the bollocks. He bent double, twisted out of my reach, but straightened so fast that I could not get to him. He swung with all his might, and his right fist struck me hard. I felt his knife slice through my tunic and sweep downward into my leg as I fell. A spasm of agony ran down my body as I felt the gushing warmth of my blood across my knee.

I was so full of fury. I no longer cared whether I lived or died. I jumped up and kicked out, missing his body but hitting his left hand. Eyes flaring, he pivoted, his dagger flying through the air. Undeterred, he lunged forward, punching me hard in the stomach. I fell again, which gave him a chance to lift me up and heave me forward toward the river.

I was hoisted rapidly over the bank as if catapulted like a stone from the trebuchet. I fell and hit the water, hard. The filthy black murk filled my eyes and mouth, clogging and suffocating me. The fast-flowing force and tangled mess of riverweeds and debris pulled me down. The morass stretched in all directions. I didn't have the strength to free myself.

I sank and rose, sank deeper, and was forced around so I couldn't tell which was up and which was down. Water invaded me. There was pain in my ears and behind my eyes. My throat and lungs were hurting.

Oh God, I was going to die!

There was nothing but panic and pain. I flailed, uselessly,

trying to find the surface. I had to breathe... but the river sucked me down further and further away into a dark, black void.

CHAPTER 16
Friends

EVA ROCAULT

Roul still lay slumped across my shoulder as I hurried on. I turned the corner in between the tall, dark buildings the woman at the felting yard had indicated. Faced with a maze of dark alleyways and a gloomy succession of buildings, I didn't know which way to turn. The sun had gone down and the evening chill set in. Dark clouds scurried across the sky. I was dispirited and afraid.

A cobbled yard on my left afforded a little light and I saw a small, open doorway where an old woman was sweeping. Just as I was about to approach her, I heard a familiar voice calling my name. I turned and saw Vivenny running toward me. My heart nearly exploded with joy. Behind her were the twins with an elderly couple carrying large bundles.

Before I had a chance to speak, Vivenny, breathless, her face full of sorrow, pulled me tight against her chest and wrapped her arms around Roul and myself.

"Vivenny," I gulped as tears of relief poured down my cheeks. "You are free. I can't believe it is you. Where is Papa? Is he here too?"

I turned into her soft, familiar chest and released all my pent-up emotions in great shuddering sobs. She too was crying, but finally explained, "No, Eva, he is not here. He is still under arrest at the garrison near Limoux." Wiping away my tears, then her own, she asked quietly, "What has happened to you? What is wrong with Roul?"

"Roul is ill, we have no food left. Vivenny, it is a miracle that you have found us."

I told her of what had occurred at the croft, about finding Matilde. But she said, "I know. I went back as soon as I could. Of all those who were taken, only seven of us were released." Her face crumpled again and she sobbed. "We went back together and buried Matilde and the others. Doucelina Maçon, Audric Faceux, Sebastien Royer and little Geffroi Baudin were all slaughtered that day. We could not stay there, so we left straight away and travelled to Tomas's parents."

She beckoned to the elderly couple standing a short distance from us, holding the twins. "They were planning to leave as the Crusaders were getting closer. Your Uncle Stevan is coming soon. He is helping the Bons-Chrétiens to leave Limoux. Come, let us help you with Roul."

I was still holding my brother across my shoulder as Vivenny introduced me to Leilah and Samuel Hasdai. They immediately showed their concern, and Samuel took Roul from me. Seeing how still he was, he beckoned for us to follow him. "Come, this way," he said, walking swiftly down the now dark alleyway.

We left the noise and bustle of the market and headed toward the far side of the city. My arms and neck, relieved of Roul's weight, relaxed a little, but I could not stop the tears. As little Jusef took my hand, Vivenny wrapped her arms around me and silently we all followed Samuel. Leilah was explaining to Jacob where we were going. Her face was lined and weary, but her features were soft and gentle. Leilah's grey cloud of hair was swept up into an untidy bun. She walked with a swift, easy grace and had no trouble keeping up with us. Her body was lean and upright, as was Samuel's, who was taking great strides across the squares and through the dark alleyways.

"We will find help here," Samuel assured me as we hurried under the overhanging balconies in the narrow streets. We passed the abbey entrance and moved along the wall until we came to the back of another building. There was an arched doorway with a small hatch, above which was the Star of David. Over that, a sign which I did not understand, but I knew it was the Jewish quarter.

CHAPTER 17
Alive

LÉON DUMONT

I lurched awake on a desperate, gasping breath. I opened my one good eye and groaned, aware only of the sound of the rushing water and rustling trees. I was still halfway in the river, with the top half of my body tangled in a great bough of willow tree that had washed up onto the sandy shore. Coughing up the dirty liquid and mud, I choked, tried to take a breath but could only gasp. Pulling backwards, I managed to throw off the branches. Flopping over onto my hands and knees, and groaning with pain, I threw up the remaining water.

My whole body hurt. The rotten smell of the river was in my mouth, my nose and my head. My fingers and feet were numb and I was shivering so hard I couldn't stop my teeth from chattering.

But I was alive!

A cold wind blew across the heaving, brown river. It was still raining. A soft, heavy rain that collected and dripped from the sparse trees on the riverbank. A few paces away stood a deeper forest, perhaps a bit of shelter where I could rest for a while. Dragging my sodden body off the shore, I leaned against a tree, trying to steady myself. Taking a deep breath, I lifted my tunic. My side was covered with bruises and was tender and painful. When I finally gained sufficient control of my shaking hands, I explored my hip and shoulder bones, my spine and chest. Blood was oozing from a small hole just under my ribs. I had a large gash on my right leg and another on my upper right arm. Nothing appeared to be broken.

I was relieved to see my knife still in its sheath and strapped to my belt. Why hadn't I used it on de Suis?

I headed slowly towards the trees, every footfall torture. My feet sliding and slipping on the wet pine needles and earth, my breath rasping, blood pumping in my head. I didn't know which way to turn. I stood and thought. I didn't really care where I went. I just wanted to be dry and warm.

My fear and pain turned into a bitter hatred of the Crusade, de Suis, and my life. Hatred was growing like a weed on a rock face, forcing its way into the cracks where it flourishes against all odds. I could no longer feel any compassion or understanding for the sinners who had brought me here.

Panting, I fell, my nose still full of the stink of the river.

My head was spinning – whether from the pain or from loss of blood I did not know. I slid down beside a slippery fungus that, pale as parchment, clung to the side of the great beech tree. I landed on my face in the slimy, wet leaves. I had no idea how long I lay there by the river.

Arnau de Suis will think I am dead, I thought grimly, before I lost consciousness.

CHAPTER 18
Awake

LÉON

Bodies fall all around me. Arms and legs float, heads turned upside down. Horses run through me. Animals scream in pain. My old dog moves toward me, sniffing and excited. But he bares his teeth and turns away. He doesn't know me. I call to him but he runs away. My father, his missing arm restored, waves a flag with a white cross. He looks happy but he too doesn't answer when I call to him.

Hundreds of wandering, naked people pass by, holding bags bursting with food although they are hungry, skinny and haggard. Swords covered with blood fly through the air, slicing at my head and face. Blood everywhere... I am screaming but no one hears me. Why? I see a face above me in the clouds... Is it God? A great clap of thunder and a flash of lightning.

"Prove yourself, lily-livered Léon. God is your witness."

Suddenly I was awake. Fear and pain crawled through my body like a flame on the move.

Where was I?

I knew I had been asleep a long time. It was dark and I was alone. My bandaged right arm was folded over my head. Although my left eye was covered, I could just discern a beam of light with the other, but had no idea where it came from. I couldn't turn and look. I was warm and lying on something soft but I couldn't move my left arm at all. I was contained, confined.

Perhaps I was a prisoner! Although I was in pain, I was alive. Someone must have tended me.

Twisting my head, I could just see that the shaft of light came from a far corner of the room. A half-open door lit a small area on the stone floor but I could see nothing else. The sharp smell of something medicinal hung in the air.

As I tried to move to see more of the room, the rhythm of my heart changed and another sharp pain hit my chest. My stomach lurching, I drifted away again on a grey cloud of fog.

Waking again, all my limbs were wooden and stiff, and when I opened my one good eye, I still couldn't move. My eyes and throat were gritted and sore. Panicking, I found I could move my feet and toes so I wriggled them until I could feel my lower legs.

My heart was beating with a kind of fury that matched my pain. Taking a deep breath, I attempted to sit up but I could only shuffle slightly sideways. Nothing about my body was doing what it ought. I heard sounds of doors opening and closing and lay still. Someone was coming. Perhaps it would be easier to know where I was and who had taken care of me if I remained 'asleep'.

Then I heard indistinct and muffled voices, as if through cloth, softly at first, moving toward the room. My hearing was not good as my ears felt as if they were still full of the cold river. I only caught an odd word or two.

"Must be a soldier... cannot leave... will return... refused... No."

As I heard the door slowly opening, the voices grew louder. I held my breath. The accent was difficult to understand.

"I'll leave you to watch him then, Mikhail. Eva or Leilah will relieve you later, or perhaps Ruth when she arrives. Let me know if he stirs."

I carefully opened my good eye. As the old man pulled up a chair, an arm's length from the bed on which I lay, I couldn't see the other man, but he too sounded old.

"Remember, he is a prisoner, so if he wakes, take care," said the retreating voice. The door closed.

So, I was a prisoner!

My keeper settled into his chair. He held a sheaf of papers that he studied intently, and didn't look at me at all. He obviously assumed I was still asleep. I continued to wriggle my toes and feet until the door opened again and another voice asked, "Can I see the soldier, Mikhail?"

A child's voice!

"Is he tied up?"

"Come, Roul. You are obviously feeling better. Yes, you can look but don't go too near. He is still asleep, but he could wake at any minute."

"Will he try to kill us all when he wakes up?"

"No, I don't think so. He is badly injured."

I could feel rather than see the child's closeness. He was obviously very young as the top of his head only came in line with my arm. I could feel his breath as he said, "He doesn't look very dangerous."

"That's because he's asleep," said Mikhail.

"What will happen to him?"

"I don't know. You go back to bed now. Abraham says you need at least three days' bed rest. Your sister and Leilah will be up to see you soon."

I heard the child leave and the door shut. Keeping my eyes closed I tried to remember what had happened. I saw de Suis's ugly face, felt the blade of his knife and the icy water of the river. I knew I had finished my quarantine and should be on my way home. But, instead, I was a prisoner with no idea where I was, how I got here, or who these people were.

CHAPTER 19
Safe

EVA ROCAULT

So began our stay in Aleth. Roul was recuperating and happily making friends with the other children.

Vivenny, the twins, Leilah, Samuel and I were in an adjoining building, which was usually hostel accommodation. It was so conveniently close we could visit Roul at any time.

Abraham told us about the hostel. "It was a hive of activity until this year and this damnable war. Many patients came for restorative treatments, although of course only those of our faith stayed here. Now it is being used to house everyone fleeing the Crusaders. More are coming today."

"Is this the only hospital in Aleth?" I asked.

"No. There is a large spa hospital on the northern side of the city. It is outside the walls, but has wonderful pools of hot, sulphurous water."

"Where does it come from?"

"Deep within the mountains," answered Abraham. "There are many passageways under the city. They lead to an underground lake which has bubbling jets of crystal clear water. Very therapeutic! It is good to drink and to bathe in. We use it for all sorts of ills. We are extremely lucky to have a few of those pools in the Jewish quarter, although there are others both in the city and the surrounding district. There are many inns and houses that cater for the wealthier clients but now they too are being filled with refugees."

Abraham sighed.

"For many centuries we have had peace and tranquillity here in Aleth. Sadly, now we are faced with a crusading army intent only on killing and destroying."

He turned to leave.

"Perhaps when you are settled you could come and help in the wards. We've had quite a few admissions and are short of staff. The soldier is here too. Been in the river and is badly wounded. He has not yet regained consciousness but his wounds do need attention. There are a few patients with infections from wounds and one poor soul who has been tortured."

Leilah and I volunteered our services.

"Ruth will help too when she arrives," Leilah said. "She might need a little persuading but she is strong and capable. I'm sure she will."

I had never been in such a large house before. The hostel was a great solid stone building with three floors and many rooms, large kitchens and gardens, which made it a perfect place to stay. We found two rooms on the ground floor, a small one for Leilah and Samuel and a larger one for Vivenny, the children and me.

Abraham told us that we could remain for as long as we needed, but others escaping the Crusaders would soon join us.

The rain was pounding on the rooftops as they arrived, wet and tired. The noise grew as more and more people with their crying and mewling children came looking for shelter.

As most needed something dry to wear and somewhere to sleep, Vivenny and I helped with bedding, straw pallets and some clothing from the stacks on the shelves in the cupboards in the corridors.

Many had brought their precious belongings, so the rooms and passageways were soon piled with boxes, rugs, trunks and baskets. Others had escaped with only what they stood up in.

The huge kitchens already had a large stock of food, casks of wine and mead. Great bunches of drying herbs hung from the ceilings. The resident cooks set up a spit over the fire, where at least twenty chickens were cooking. Bread was baking in a large black oven. Several tables were set up for people to eat when needed.

A few contributed whatever they had brought with them to the food store. Others had come with nothing, but all were fed equally.

For me, it was good to be with Vivenny and the twins and to know that Uncle Stevan would be coming soon. But we all mourned for sweet Mathilde, and when Roul asked where she was, poor Vivenny broke down again.

"She is safe in the spirit," I said, trying to reassure her.

"Eva," she said, wiping her wet cheeks, "that is your belief, not mine. But I would like to believe she is happy, wherever she is."

"She will be, I promise you. Death is not the end. Her soul will rejoice in its freedom to join the Light. You will see her again when the time is right. Uncle Stevan will explain it better."

"I believe that too," Leilah said unexpectedly. "In death we do not cease to exist. We are on a journey. We always were and always will be." She wrapped her arms around Vivenny and allowed her to sob her loss onto her broad shoulder. It was a very sad time for us all. We lived in fear of what could happen if we were attacked and, although I had no fear of death, dying was harder to imagine.

Mostly, I missed the warmth, love and wisdom of my father and hoped that he was not suffering. But the news from the surrounding district made us all fearful. Troops were combing the area for dissenters of any kind. Much of the army had moved northwest to the cities of Castelnaudary and Saissac.

No one knew whether the Crusaders would attack Aleth, but preparations were in full swing. Scouts were out and the moat was closed, the sentries on guard only opening up for the newcomers as they arrived.

Leilah and Samuel's daughter Ruth, from whom they had

been separated when they had left their village, had finally arrived. She was accompanied by others, including Ezekhiel and Gelda Navarro and their five sons. Ezekhiel had been a respected moneylender in his home village, Montréal, west of Carcassonne, where he had worked for one of the local squires there. Anyone who employed Jews and did not surrender them would themselves be punished, so they had been turned out of their home with nothing but the clothes they wore. The journey had taken its toll, and the boys were distraught, hungry, wet and weary.

Gelda Navarro, in at least the sixth month of pregnancy, had fallen and badly cut her knee so was struggling to walk without assistance.

Samuel and Leilah smiled with relief when Ruth arrived safely. She was carrying a huge basket of food.

Leilah looked appalled. "Why haven't you shared it, Ruth? These children haven't eaten for days," she said.

Ruth screwed up her nose and shrugged, "Why should I? They are nothing to do with me."

She walked away looking for blankets and a pallet to use as a mattress for herself. She paid little attention to anyone, even though I noticed that she kept glancing at me. She must have been wondering why I was with her family.

While Vivenny and Leilah bathed the boys, found them warm, clean clothing and collected a bowl of soup for each of them, I dressed Gelda's knee.

They were a pleasant family. While Samuel and Ezekhiel helped others bring in their belongings, we found a vacant room where they could stay and Gelda could settle the children.

"Thank the Lord for a bit of peace," Ruth moaned as she dropped her long, bony body onto the pallet she had dragged into our room. "Those babes have done nothing but whine for hours. We had to take a different route as we saw some of the Crusaders' scouts and a troop of knights riding along the river road. We took the mountain track in the end. Hard going, though. Need some sleep."

Turning to Vivenny and her parents, she said, "You could have waited, especially you, Viv. Nobody's interested in you. It's us, the Jews, they are moving on. You shouldn't even be here. Couldn't you go back to Laroque? You'd be better off there."

There was something in the way Ruth said it, a glimmer of repressed glee in her voice, that made me shudder. Her eyes rested on me for a moment and a look of understanding crossed her face.

"Isn't Vivenny a part of your family too?" I said as I watched Vivenny move away, her face flushed, her shoulders heaving with apology.

"Is this your heretic neighbour?" Ruth asked Vivenny, ignoring my question as she removed her boots and massaged her feet. "This hostel is for Jews only. She can't stay here."

"At the moment I have no choice," I replied.

"She is safer here with us," Vivenny intervened. "You know her father is awaiting trial and her brother is sick in the hospital. She will stay with us till he is better and her uncle arrives."

"Is he a heretic too?"

Although I wanted to walk away, I said angrily, "None of us are heretics. We are of the new faith."

"Who needs a new faith when you could become a Jew?" Ruth said angrily. "The oldest faith in the world. Don't you know that? Why has Viv brought you here?"

I saw the distress on Vivenny's face. I was somewhat concerned by the hurt that had been inflicted on my friend. I cleared my throat. "Be kind to Vivenny. She has just lost her daughter, as well as her home, so don't you think it would be better if she stays with her family."

"Ah, family yes, but we are not really family now are we?

She is not really one of us. And nor are you."

"Ruth," Leilah interrupted. "Stop that! Your father and I brought Eva and her brother here. We are all in danger, and it matters not of what faith we are. These are good people. Vivenny *is* family. We all have to work together to get through this terrible time."

"But they have brought this terrible time, have they not?" Ruth sniffed. "It's because of them that the Crusaders are here."

On the far side of the room, Jusef and Jacob were playing, balancing sticks, and noisily play fighting.

"Shush, you boys!" Ruth glared at the twins, showing her dislike of her nephews. "I need another room, a place away from these children. You can't expect me to stay here with all this noise."

She rose and marched purposefully out of the room. I hoped that she would find another room as soon as possible.

Ruth was several years older than me and I found her hard to like. She was haughty and selfish. Although attractive, with dark glossy hair, her turned-down mouth and sulky attitude gave her a hostile look. She was tall and angular, built like her parents, but her face had neither the gentleness of her mother's nor the strength of her father's.

Daily, Ruth's dislike and distrust of me grew, and she went out of her way to make both Vivenny and me uncomfortable, so we tried to keep out of her way. She didn't manage to find a vacant room so her pallet was pushed up alongside mine, as far from the twins as possible. Nevertheless, she was constantly complaining about them.

Some nights she didn't return to our room and Leilah worried that she might have found a man to sleep with. Once she was missing for two days and two nights but she shrugged off questions with her usual hostile glare and never gave any indication of where she'd been.

I was hoping Uncle Stevan would arrive soon. Then we

could leave the Jewish quarter and although I would miss
Vivenny, the boys and Leilah and Samuel Hasdai, I would
not miss Ruth.

CHAPTER 20
A Prisoner

LÉON DUMONT

When I next awoke, the dressing on my right eye had been removed. The soft, wet stroking across my face gave me a remembrance of my mother, of the day when the tup had kicked out when I was pushing it toward the ewes. The cut on my cheek, although minor, had bled profusely. My mother had refused to let me work until she had bathed it with yarrow water.

Was she with me? No. She had died... When was that? I couldn't remember, nor could I bring to mind where I was. I kept my eyes closed, lay still. I could hear a gentle humming, the sound of children laughing and a distant hammering. Somewhere in the far background was a sorrowful moaning.

A soft hand swept across my forehead. Then a sheet was pulled up to my chin. I suddenly recalled where I was and knew that my situation hadn't changed. I was still a prisoner! My left arm was firmly restrained so I couldn't turn. But the pain in my head had diminished and my ears had cleared. I was safe and warm and dry. Someone was taking care of me. It felt good, not something that I felt in all the months I had been away from home. My mission as one of God's fighters seemed to have paled into the distance so guilt swept through me. Wherever I was, I should not be here.

I opened my eyes. The girl stepped backward but not before I saw her violet eyes.

In wonderment, I gulped. Have I died and gone to heaven? She was beautiful, her eyes blazed with light and life. Surely she was an angel! She stood still, holding the bowl and a soft cloth. She was somehow familiar. Have I seen her before? This was someone I thought I knew. I was sure that she knew me too.

"Hurr," I croaked, my voice dried to a whisper.

"Hello," said the angel. "I am Eva. I will get Abraham."

As she leaned over, I noticed a small birthmark, a dark cross, on her neck. It brought to mind something I could not describe, a faint memory, a drifting picture of long ago. Suddenly, I was thinking of my grandmother and I could feel tears rising.

Eva turned to leave. In my limited view, I saw her blonde hair tied in a long braid down her back. She disappeared and I heard the door close.

'Come back,' I cried through my tears. 'I want to know who you are!'

CHAPTER 21
Destiny Begins

EVA ROCAULT

Around him, a soft gentle aura tinged with gold and, as he moved, sharp jagged spikes of maroon and black came and went but eventually disappeared. He was young and strikingly handsome. Bandages covered one arm and one leg. A huge, oily dressing lay across his stomach. Although he had been washed and covered with clean bandages, his hair was matted and dried dribbles of blood were around his wounds. I had removed the padding from his eye and had bathed it gently. The split on his eyelid was healing well.

I knew that he had refused to speak to anyone, even though he had regained consciousness briefly and was obviously able to understand what was said to him.

When he opened his eyes, I was startled! A feeling of warm understanding and compassion rippled through my body. I wanted to touch him again. No one had ever attracted me with this type of intense feeling. I had never viewed a boy in any way other than as a friend. I was alarmed to know I could feel the heat of physical attraction.

I stared at his mouth as he tried to speak and I felt myself flush from top to toe, a pleasant feeling that I had not encountered before.

When I told him my name, he'd gazed at me with such gentleness and pleasure, my insides melted like butter. After I had brought Abraham, I left as quickly as possible, confused and unnerved, but I wanted to know more about him.

CHAPTER 22
Meeting Ruth

LÉON DUMONT

I must have drifted off into sleep again. When I opened my eyes next, there was another young woman standing gazing at me. Her eyes were the colour of wet mud. She was tall and dark unlike the petite, violet-eyed girl I had seen in my dream. Or was it a dream? I could not be sure.

"Hey, Mister Crusader, the physician has been and gone. You went back to sleep again. Little Eva said you tried to speak to her. Better not, eh!" The girl wrinkled her nose and pursed her lips. "You can speak to me, though, if you like. Do you know you are a prisoner? *I* would have let you die but perhaps they think they could do some deal for you. Unlikely though, eh, little soldier boy?"

Contempt flitted across her dark features. She dropped her gaze. "Think you are doing fine? Comfy, are you?"

"Who are you?" I managed to whisper.

"Ruth," she said. "And who are *you*? Nobody seems to know where you came from. The Crusader army is miles upriver, but you have a Crusader's cross on your sleeve. Are you one of them?"

I decided not to reply. I feigned a lack of understanding with a slight shrug.

"Have you got a name?" she continued.

Give no one your name if you are captured. Tell nothing of what you know. Do not repeat any plans that you have been told. Do not divulge any information whatsoever about the Pope's men.

I shrugged again. If I stayed silent, no one would know what to do with me, and as soon as I was well enough, I would try to escape. But I needed to know where I was, so I cleared my throat, and croaked my question. "Where am I? What is this place?"

"Ha," she laughed, "the last place you would expect to be. You are in the Jewry of Aleth. Aleth-les-Bains, of the healing waters! Lucky you, eh? So, little soldier boy, who *are* you? Are you going to tell me your name? You don't look much like a Crusader."

I did not answer.

She waited.

But I stayed still and watched her.

I had no idea where Aleth was, though I had a vague notion, from the maps we had studied, that it was a fortified city. In my head, I pictured the lie of the river, flowing south. But since I had no idea how far down the river I had been swept, nor had any recollection of being brought here, I did not know.

"So, you are not going to tell me?" she said, taking hold of my bandaged arm. "I have to change this dressing. Lie still."

Without any more conversation, she quickly changed the dressing. "Although, I don't know why they are bothering with you," she said. "If we get attacked they will never get in. We have enough stores to last a year and, anyway, I hear the army is moving north so you will probably die here."

She paused. "Haven't you anything to say?"

I turned my head away and closed my eyes, contemplating her words. I was in a Jewish hospital in a place I could not recall. Even if I could escape, how would I get back to the army if they had moved north? I could only hope that a few troops had stayed in the area to round up the heretics from the surrounding villages as we had done when the main army had moved on. I did know that a garrison had been set up to hold prisoners before their trials in the town of Limoux.

"So, you're not going to talk to me? I could help you, you know." I stayed silent so she turned to leave. "Your choice then, soldier boy." The door slammed.

Opening my eyes when I was sure she had gone, I found I

could move my head and see a little from my still swollen eye. I turned as far as I could and pulled at my left arm. It was firmly secured with two clamps with long metal pins, one on my upper arm and one on my wrist. I pulled again but could not move. The pain in my right arm had receded so I stretched it out to investigate the other dressings. The large one across my right side felt damp and I raised myself up enough to see it was soaked with some sort of oil. I could not reach the one on my leg. The small effort of trying to move exhausted me and I realised it would take a while before I had enough strength to attempt an escape.

Later, a tall elderly man, who did not speak, brought a foul-smelling medication. I took it without complaint, as I knew that my recovery would need all the help I could get.

I prayed. 'Blessed Father in Heaven, why am I still alive? Everything had been against my life being saved. I even wanted to die, did I not? That you have spared me must have some significance. I pray you reveal the divine plan that I must fulfil. Blessed Father, I beg you show what I must do to gain your favour?'

CHAPTER 23
Preparing for Hanukkah

EVA ROCAULT
We were preparing for Hanukkah, eight days of feasting and prayer. During this time no one would be allowed to enter or leave the Jewry and the gates would be locked on the inside. We still had two weeks before the festivities began. Thereafter, the gates would be locked on the outside for the rest of the year.

"After Hanukkah," Abraham told me, "we are locked in during the Christian Holy Celebrations, as Jews are forbidden to be evident at that time. That is the reason for the external locks on the main doors to the Jewry."

"What will happen to the Jews who come here?" I asked. "Will they too be locked out?"

Shaking his head, Abraham assured me, "They will not come during Hanukkah, nor in the Christian festival. If by chance any arrive, our scouts will guide them in. We have many passageways under the city. There is one from our hospital gardens here in the Jewish quarter which leads to a cave where the waters bubble up from the depth of the mountains. It is possible to walk along the internal channel and reach the northwest side of the mountain. We can escape through there if it becomes necessary. We can also bring people in that way. But it is unlikely that the Crusaders will attack during the religious festival. Many will go home, I guess. The leaders will be planning their next move."

Roul was almost back to his normal self, although still not sure how we came to be here. He was attending the morning school that had been set up by Rabbi Gerton ben Levi in the hostel. The rabbi, who had arrived after us, was trying to bring normality back into the children's lives.

Everybody was busy helping to prepare for the feasting

days. We took turns to help in the hospital, kitchens or wherever we were needed. The hospital was now almost full and we still had the prisoner to care for.

One morning while Ruth was on duty, Leilah and I sat in the kitchen rubbing herbs. Powerful aromas of sage, rosemary and thyme filled the air. Leilah was in a pensive mood.

"Do you ever think of returning to your homeland?" I asked her as we worked.

"I used to," Leilah said, "but it was a long time ago and it had become impossible to live as Jews. The new king made it intolerable for us. When we arrived in Languedoc, we settled in Limoux. We were pastry makers. It was hard work, but we did well, and then the babies arrived. We often talked of returning to Portugal but, when Tomas told us he was going to marry Vivenny, we gave up all ideas of leaving. They told me that they had fallen in love on the very first day they'd met. She was seven and he was eight."

Leilah smiled as she remembered. "Tomas was one of the children sent every summer to the big estate for the fruit harvesting. There was another boy called Tomas in their group, and so to identify the different Toms, our boy was named 'Mucky Tom' because he was so much darker than the rest of them. From that year onward, that was always his name."

Leilah turned her lined face toward the fire, and the undercurrent of old, sad memories lay in the silence that followed. "He was a lovely son. So handsome too! At eighteen, he married Vivenny and... then the grandchildren came. Matilde and the twins arrived. But, of course, you knew my Tom as they all lived in the croft next to yours," she sighed. "We never expected to lose our Tomas, and now Matilde."

I remembered when Tomas died. He was working in a sawmill just a few miles from Laroque-de-Fa. One hot July day, a fire had started in the surrounding forest, the wind rose and, as the flames spread, the men at the mill became trapped. They decided to make a run for it but died in the fire. When it finally burned itself out, the mill was found intact and undamaged. But that was no consolation for Vivenny, an orphan herself with no family other than the Hasdais. It seemed right to me that she should be with them now, even if Ruth disagreed.

Finishing the herbs, we moved to the far side of the kitchen where a few of the women were preparing the candles for the nine-branched menorahs. I knew little of the Jewish festivals but Hanukkah was special, particularly now that so many were in danger. It was a time for music and dancing, games and a celebration of their faith. One candle was to be lit for each day that passed and placed in the menorah.

Uncle Stevan arrived just before Hanukkah. He had taken those of our faith who had arrived with him to safe houses in the city. When he heard where Roul and I were, he came straight away to get us. My happiness at seeing him was mixed with dread of the news he brought. I hadn't seen him for many months and immediately noticed how he had aged. His face was lined and his body thin and wiry. He looked ill with exhaustion. He hugged me tightly when I told him of our flight from Laroque.

"All will be well, Eva. Common sense must prevail and, if it does not, we will join the Light with joy. Perhaps for us this life's lesson is over. We cannot change our destiny."

"Even for Roul?"

"No, not even for Roul." He smiled as he spoke and I knew in my heart it was true.

He told me a little of his journeys and the trials he had faced. While he had done his best for as many Bons-Chrétiens as he could, he had failed to get my father released and, as a credente and preacher, he had put himself in danger.

"As the daughter of Bernard Rocault, you are also on the list of heretics. You must stay here in safety, Eva."

I nodded as he told me how he had taken up arms to save the people he had brought here. I could see it saddened him to the very depth of his being. He was devastated that he had killed a soldier.

"Even though it was self-defence," he said angrily, "it makes no difference. I have failed my faith."

The kindly physician, Abraham, asked us to stay until after all the religious festivals were over as he could see that Uncle Stevan was exhausted and needed to rest.

The pain of uncertainty about our future gnawed at my heart as I pulled myself from my bed. I missed the beautiful quiet and solitude of our mountain home, but no amount of persuasion could convince me that my father and the wise men and women of our creed were bad or wrong in their beliefs.

It was a cold November morning when Uncle Stevan and I left the Jewry and headed for the great drawbridge where more Bons-Chrétiens had arrived looking for refuge. Some had travelled long distances and were cold and exhausted. Some carried a few belongings, books and tools of their trade, but there were others carrying only their children and babies. The courtyards were jammed with people, shouting and crying, shattering the peace that had been here an hour before.

The next week was the beginning of Hanukkah so Roul and I would stay there for the following eight days and then I would leave and join others of our faith for the December celebration of the birth of our Christ.

As I was hungry, we headed straight for the great warm kitchen for some soup and bread.

"Where have they all come from, Uncle?" I said once we were seated at the table.

"Mainly from the north of Carcassonne," he said. "It seems that the main army is heading for Albi, where there is a huge community of credentes and *Perfecti*. Many of them have great estates and control the schools and businesses in that region. They will defend their lands and there will be more bloodshed."

"Eat some soup, Uncle," I said, but he refused any food.

"No, I cannot." He was obviously distressed, his face grey with worry.

"Tell me what is happening, then?" I asked gently.

"Raymond-Roger Trencavel has been found dead in his own prison," he said. "Simon de Montfort has been made Viscount *and* awarded Trencavel's lands and estates for his service to the Crusade. We need all our courage now. We have to look after ourselves. I will move out tonight to support our people through the coming days but you must remain with the Hasdais until the end of Hanukkah."

"Is it over for us then?" I asked as Uncle Stevan held his head in his hands.

CHAPTER 24
Making Plans

LÉON DUMONT

"Take Eva, when you escape," Ruth suggested as she renewed my dressings. "She is a priestess of the new faith and should be tried along with the rest of them. It is their fault that we are in this awful situation."

So, Eva was of the new faith, therefore a heretic. I thought she was a Jew, like everyone else there. I had watched her quiet administrations with pleasure, been fascinated by her beautiful violet eyes and her gentle demeanour. I'd never spoken to her or anyone else, except Ruth, who, in her own harsh way, took pleasure in telling me what was happening with the war against the heretics. She had an intense dislike of them, and constantly complained that the Jews would probably have been left in peace, if not for the Bons-Chrétiens.

Her views interested me not one bit.

Fulfilling my duty and getting home as soon as possible was all I cared about.

This war was not of my making but of God's, and I'd had enough.

"You will be a hero if you capture someone like her. She is well known as a priestess of the new faith."

"How can I arrest her? Even if I could, I can't get her back to the army to hand her over. I am still a prisoner."

Looking straight at me, Ruth grinned. "I know a way out."

"Do you now?"

"Yes, I do," she said, "and I can help you. There is an underground passageway that leads directly from our hospital gardens to the north of the city, close to the river and to your army encampment."

"How can I take her?"

"You'll have to figure that one out, soldier boy," she sneered. "But you're strong now. Our gates will be open for one day after Hanukkah ends and before the Christian festival begins. Then they are locked on the outside after that. She'll probably not be missed."

"Why's that?"

"She plans to move out of the Jewry that day to go preaching at the Christian festival with her Uncle Stevan. He's already left. My family will think she has gone to the Bons-Chrétiens in the city. Her uncle will think she has stayed with Roul who will not go out until after the holidays. He's staying here awhile. Apparently, it's important for him to attend school!"

She grinned impishly and said, "On the last evening of Hanukkah, I will create a diversion so that I can get you out of here. I'll show you the entrance to the cave. All you have to do then is follow the pathway alongside the underground stream. It will be dark and slippery, so take your time or you will find yourself in the river again."

She snorted her haughty laugh. "We will wait until the Christian festivals begin. As I said all our gates will be locked on the outside. Everyone will assume that you are still within the Jewry when you escape. No one will know I have helped you. It will be a blessed relief for me not to have to put up with Eva's sanctimonious ramblings about the spirit world."

"Is it difficult to get out?"

"It's not very long," she said, "and if you're careful, it's easy to negotiate. I've used it several times at night. I met a man on my journey here. He was not a Jew and it was fun for a couple of weeks. That is how I know where your army is positioned."

With Ruth's help, I would escape, arrest the heretic priestess, and take her as my prisoner. If the tunnels under the city were close to the army camp, I could hand her over to be tried. That would gain me as much prestige as I needed to leave my quarantine with pride.

My strength was growing daily, my wounds healing well. Only my leg still pained me. For three weeks, Ruth had been coming daily to talk to me and, although others were caring for me, it was to her that I confided my longing to go home.

Although the physician had tried to find out about me, I had told them virtually nothing. Soon I was given more freedom, allowed to go to the latrine on my own, to wash and feed myself. Although I was still restrained, I could sit rather than lie in bed all day.

My filthy clothes had been washed and my boots dried and cleaned. I had no idea where my belt and knife were. But Ruth promised she would find them before I made my escape.

I had made up my mind to go ahead with the plan.

At last, God looked kindly on me, saved me for some purpose. It all had to be for a reason. I would return home glorious, even though I knew the life I was going back to wasn't the life I had left behind.

I was not the same person who had left home in the early summer. Everything was changed. Nothing of what had been done could be undone. But I felt a thrill, pleasant and unpleasant at the same time, at the thought of the glory I would achieve by bringing in an important heretic.

She would be punished. I would be a hero and get my life back in the sure knowledge that I had served God and the Mother Church. My father would be proud of me.

So, I realized, the sour bitterness of my life became my salvation. I had been spared for this very task. God had saved me. He had work for me after all!

Ruth found my belt and knife. She brought me some rope and some cloth to tie around the heretic's mouth. She also found out how to unlock my manacles. She was not a very likeable girl, but she was wily and determined. I couldn't help but admire her and was grateful to have her as an ally in this strange place.

CHAPTER 25
Out of the Jewry

EVA ROCAULT
The days passed with little news from outside the city. We were busy, though. We collected and stored wood, salted and bottled fruits and vegetables.

Ruth continued to take pleasure in insulting and being uncooperative with Vivenny and me, but spending time with Leilah and Samuel more than compensated for her barbed comments.

The Hasdais were always so kind to us, and admonished Ruth regularly for her harsh remarks. It didn't stop her though but, as the days passed, she spent more and more time helping Abraham in the hospital, avoiding the kitchens and us, if she could.

One evening, just before retiring, Ruth told us haughtily that the Crusader talked to her daily. "His name is Léon and he comes from a village far away near the Italian border, where he lives with his father and his dog. He wants to go home. His duties here are finished. He wants to know what is to happen to him and no one has given him any indication of what is intended. I told Abraham that he should have let him die, but he just told me 'that's not what we do.' Would've saved us the trouble of looking after him. And now no one knows what to do with him." She shrugged. "It's kept me amused, though. He's a good-looking boy."

"Perhaps it would be best to release him," suggested Leilah, ignoring Ruth's surly remarks.

"I think not," Samuel snapped. "What are you thinking of? He will probably return to his army and go on killing more innocent souls."

"Ruth says his quarantine is over. He wants to go home," retorted Leilah. "We should let him go."

"He should be tried for all those he has slaughtered, not allowed to wander off home as if he is not responsible. He is one of them, therefore he should be punished."

"Ah," said Leilah. "'Should' is a great word, but hardly applies when there is a war on."

So the discussion continued. No one was sure what would happen to him. I hoped they would let him go home. I was still disturbed by my reaction to him, and my heart beat a little faster each time he came to mind.

I was preparing to leave, as Hanukkah was coming to an end and I was needed among the credentes here in Aleth, so I would probably never see him again.

I planned to go out through the gates that evening and join Uncle Stevan in a chateau on the east side of the city. It belonged to Viscount Chep de Cantrec, a *Perfecti* of high standing. I would be sad to leave Roul behind, but he was well and happy, and I knew the Hasdais would take good care of him.

Ruth suggested we harvest the remaining vegetables in the frosty garden and, as the weather was dry, Leilah, Gelda, whose leg was now healed, and two other ladies set off with spades and baskets. I joined them to help collect carrots, turnips and hardy greens. They were needed as the stores were depleting rapidly and, although there was plenty of dried food, fresh vegetables were in short supply.

The garden where they grew was on the side of a small hill where areas had been cleared between the bushes and trees. There was a high slope to one side and a small old wall. But where we were digging was flat and even.

It was hard work, but we were in good spirits having enjoyed the Hanukkah celebrations, and I was happy at the thought of joining Uncle Stevan that evening.

As the day was drawing to an end, I began to feel uneasy. I started to move back up the hill toward the others who had been collecting with me. Surely I was safe here? But I had the feeling of being watched. I tried to ignore it, and carried on picking the last of the turnips that we had dug up. The uneasiness suddenly intensified, and the conviction that someone was close was so strong that I picked up my basket and started to run up the hill. I shouted to the others, but the wind had risen. They had their backs to me, moving away, so they didn't hear me.

The next moment I was sure, I could hear the panting breath of my pursuer.

I turned. It was Léon, the Crusader from the hospital.

"What are you doing here?"

With a quick glance up the hill to check that no one was in sight, he edged toward me.

"What are you doing here?" I repeated.

A breath – a change in the wind – touched my spine... tingling apprehension. A moment of panic! The look in his eyes told me.

Why should I fear him? No one but the family knew about me. Unless... Someone must have helped him. Ruth. Of course! She knew, and it was she who had suggested harvesting in the garden that day.

Without a moment's hesitation Léon moved toward me. He wrapped a long rope around my body. I struggled but I knew I was no match for him. He threw my basket into the bushes.

What could he be thinking of? Before I had an opportunity to ask, a strip of cloth covered my mouth, another he wrapped around my eyes.

All he said was, "Hush, and walk where I push you."

I had no choice but to obey. I lurched forward, and stumbled across the rutted earth.

Within a minute I heard a creak, and a cool bitter phosphorous smell invaded my nostrils. I tried to pull back but Léon kept me tightly held. He was grunting and heaving. But I had no idea where we were or what he was doing.

The following hour or so was only a confusion of sounds, unfamiliar feelings of being pushed, rushing water, and Léon's voice telling me where to put my feet as he held me tight to his chest.

I moved blindly forward as he instructed, my heart pounding and my breathing sharp and laboured.

I was terrified!

CHAPTER 26
Going Home

LÉON DUMONT

Getting out of the city had been easier than I could possibly have imagined. I'd not been concerned about getting captured. After all, I was already a prisoner.

Ruth had guided me to the garden, having started a small fire at the back of the hostel next to the hospital wall. It had caused enough confusion to allow us to sneak out and across the ornamental gardens to the gate of the vegetable garden.

Capturing Eva was easy. The only difficulty had been opening the door that led into the cave. Set in a slope, the heavy, rusty door needed a good pull. Eva struggled but she was so slight that I had no trouble holding her and, once the door was open, I pushed her through.

I thought it would be pitch dark, but there was an eerie light that played off the flowing water, onto the walls and the steps. The well-worn pathway led down to the fast-flowing stream, which hissed and bubbled with a phosphorous glow.

The walk through the tunnel had been relatively simple. I held Eva close to me, and guided her along the most treacherous parts, so we had moved fairly quickly. The pathway opened into a huge cave where bats and other animals wheeled and prowled. At the far end, the water cascaded in an impressive waterfall down to the level of the lake. We were high up, and I had not felt any indication of climbing upward. I believed it must just be the lie of the land.

But I was free, and standing at the top of a waterfall with a prize heretic as my prisoner! I sighed with relief as I removed Eva's blindfold. I felt her shudder as she saw where we were.

"Go on," I said, "down."

She turned to me with fear in her eyes. As she had to walk ahead of me, down the wet and rocky pathway, I released the rope slightly.

"Don't worry. I'll hold you," I said. "You are as light as a clock of dandelion seeds. I won't let you fall."

Nevertheless, parts of the descent were difficult. Because it was dark by then, it took us a long time to work our way down, but she was nimble and light-footed.

When she struggled to breathe, I took off her gag. She whispered thank you and carried on.

I could see she was shivering, whether from fear or cold I no longer cared. She was my prize, my reward, my redeeming glorious act in the eyes of my God.

And against all the odds!

Ruth had assured me that if we followed the lake north we would reach a farm where there were good Christians, people who had no sympathy for the Bons-Chrétiens. We could spend the rest of the night there.

All we had to do was find the farm. We walked for several miles. Eva did not speak. Neither did I, nor did I want to as I was intent upon my quest.

At last, we reached some farm buildings and crofts. I wrapped the cloth around the girl's face and mouth again. As we approached the farm, several dogs set up an alarm. Rough men emerged from the farmhouse carrying axes and knives. It did not take them long to recognize me as a soldier of the Crusade and the girl as a heretic prisoner. They told us soldiers and prisoners had already passed that way recently, so they knew we were heading for the garrison near Limoux. They were happy to let us sleep in the stables.

A stable boy snored in the corner and an ox and a large brown carthorse stood in the smelly pen. But we were warm and comfortable at last.

I'd pulled it off after all!

CHAPTER 27
Facing my Fate

EVA ROCAULT

When my blindfold was removed, I turned to look at Léon. I had not spoken to him since leaving the lake. My shivering had ceased and my breathing steadied.

"Léon," I said, "let me go back, please."

He shook his head. His eyes were hard, the pupils wide and black, intent on me. His expression, one of resolve, told me nothing would change his mind. His aura was changed too. No longer soft, but harsh and dark with prickly spikes of crimson and black.

"No."

He stepped toward me, grabbed my hair, jerking my head back so the skin on my neck was pulled tight. He held his blade close to my throat. Although his hands shook, he held firm.

I stopped wriggling.

"Don't speak, heretic," he snarled, "or I will cut your throat. Just move your head to answer me. You are, are you not, the daughter of Bernard Rocault, the *Perfecti* heretic?" His voice was as cold as the flagstones in the church.

"Yes," I whispered, my voice straining. He released his hold long enough for me to say, "I am, and proud of it. But he is no heretic. He is a Christian but of the new order."

"Ha! I am sure of it," Léon said sarcastically. "That's all I want to know. I don't really want to talk to you. You are now my prisoner. I found you by chance and you are my piece of luck."

His mouth was close to my ear, but his voice quavered.

"None of us can be certain of what lies ahead, but I will do my duty as God has instructed. I don't want to be here, never wanted to come, but I have yet to prove myself. You will be that proof."

I stood still as he pulled my arms behind me and secured them to a wooden post.

As he moved away to pull a bale to sit on, I asked quietly, "Will my death help you?"

At first he didn't answer. Then he said, "I will take you to be tried. You don't have to die. If you admit to your sins, you will be spared. Go to Mass. Go back to the Church. Make amends."

"And bow down to Holy relics," I said, my voice rising, "swearing oaths and allowing lesser men to have control over me. No, no. Never! How can I believe the Pope is the sole earthly guardian of absolute truth? Why would I? It is all based on lies. I don't, and never will believe in the Church as you know it."

He stood then so he could look me in the face. With his jaw clenched in anger, he said, "No, I know that, but you don't have to believe it. Just do it to save your life."

"Never. You could release me now."

He hesitated, but then the look of resolve returned. "It is through our prayers and duty to the Church that we will find our place in Heaven. I must do what I believe to be right."

"Your beliefs don't make you a better person," I said. "Your behaviour does. In our faith we do not swear, lie or commit brutality and evil against each other. How does that make us heretics?"

He sat back down on the bale of straw and let out a deep sigh. "To disagree is treason. Why not repent? Save yourself."

"I am already saved. Death is not the end. Look around you, Léon. All over our kingdom, people have turned away from the Church because it is cruel and joyless, and only vindicates those who can support it."

"I hold my faith," he said. "But I know we live in a world

where terrible things happen without explanation or justification. I am not a fool. What use is reason and free will if we cannot use them in the world in which we live?"

"'Tis blind faith in what you have been told. Nothing to do with reason or free will. Divinity lies in the uniqueness of the individual. Choice is a universal gift. Tolerance and personal liberty are that we believe and adhere to."

CHAPTER 28
Confusion

LÉON DUMONT

I had never come across such simple certainty. This young girl made it sound so obvious. I didn't want to talk or listen to her, but I couldn't stop myself. Yet the consequences of not doing my duty reminded me again of my father and my God.

Once you have a task to do, it's better to do it than live with the guilt of not doing it! Or perhaps the guilt will be greater if I do it! I was confused. All I saw now was darkness. At least my life on the farm was ordered, and I believed what I was told about God's laws. Then it was easy not to question. After all, who was I?

"You have no choice now, do you?" I said, pulling the rope tighter and tying it more securely to the hook on the post. "I will take you to the holding place for the Bons-Chrétiens, where you will be tried with all the other heretics."

The stable lad stirred in the corner and the horse snorted. I walked over to him and breathed in his comforting odour. The chestnut lifted his lips searching for food, but I had none. I rested my forehead on his scrawny neck.

My bravado made me feel sick, but I knew I had to follow through with my mission. In saving my life, the Lord, my God, had shown His love for me. Now I must do what would earn me praise from my superiors.

I watched the girl from where I stood. This was my test, but I had to carry on. That was the task I had been given. That is why I am saved, I assured myself again.

"As you wish," she sighed, turning her big violet-blue eyes towards me. "But I will be condemned. You do know that, don't you?"

"No. No... I have to take you in, in the name of God. I cannot let you go. You are a dualist; you believe in two Gods, do you not? That makes you a heretic. There is only one God whose son was Jesus Christ."

"That is *your* belief. Everything we are or think we are derives from matter and energy of the universe, and there is good and evil, and the flesh is the making of evil. I don't know how I know this, but it is so. Where is your vengeful God? Can good and evil exist in one God?"

"Of course," I answered, not entirely sure what she was asking.

"Is your God not wholly good? How can you make sense of your beliefs? What of the evil that men do in His name? Is this Crusade an act of your loving God? Your belief rests entirely on faith in the translations of the old book made by greedy, self-interested, pious people who want to control you. It is the Church who gets richer and more powerful, not the people. It makes no sense. It is all about control, Léon."

"Don't speak my name," I spat. "No! No, the Holy Book tells us what we must do and what we must believe!"

"Interpreted by whom?"

"The elders and wise men of the Church. Our Pope –"

"Those men are ambitious and greedy. Just see how they live in comparison to the poor, the serfs and the slaves of society. Do you never question your faith of another's interpretation?"

"Yes, I have, but I have learned not to question."

"We do, and we have found that there is a better way." Her violet eyes were wide with a sincerity that made me hesitate.

She flinched as I banged my fist hard against the wooden post to which she was tied.

"No, no. It is your denial of the sacraments and ceremonies of the faith, is it not? I would that I could spare you, but I cannot. I must do my duty. It has to be. I will return to my home, put all this behind me and get on with my life."

"But it is your actions that shape you," she said. "You cannot deny them. That is what makes you who you are. You will carry it with you, even if you would rather not."

Her words pushed my thoughts from side to side in my head, their message clearly had to be denied, so I projected myself into the role of competent soldier and Crusader for the Faith. I had to stand firm and not question my beliefs, so I said, "I will not listen. It is you who has to change. You'll not be punished because of your father. You can live if you want to. Do you not believe in Heaven and Hell? In the final judgment? You will burn in Hell for your sins if you don't recant."

"I don't believe in the last judgment. Evil is not of God's making but of Man's. You see it every day in the world in which we live."

"How can you not believe in Hell? What happens to the wicked then?" I asked, not sure I wanted to hear her answer. Nearly all my fears were about going to Hell if I did not follow God's laws.

She spoke calmly and easily. "Another life, another body. So that each may work out their sins and come to an understanding of pure goodness. Each person chooses the path he takes."

"Hah," I sneered. *That* could not be so. But my thoughts were galloping away from me. Everything she said felt so true. Yet I could not allow myself to believe any of it. She was so sure. It was as if I was seeing her for the first time. Such perfect faith!

A tingling sensation ran through my whole body, rousing and quickening my heart and my sleeping senses. Without thinking, I reached forward and took her hand. Our fingers meshed together as if forging a link to some unknown future.

I looked into her eyes. "Shall we meet again?"

"We will," she said, looking into mine. "Each of us is born with a light within us, but to be lit, it needs the breath of love, which is the nourishment of our inner selves. Without love, it will not burn brightly or warm the world with its glow."

CHAPTER 29
Destiny

EVA ROCAULT
A whole dimension of my being fell away, leaving a raw space in which a tender grief welled up in me. But I felt no fear.

"Aren't you worried about dying?" he asked.

"Death? No, no," I said. "Death comes to us all. There are many things worse than death. My body does not matter; my soul will rejoice in its freedom to join the Light. I am afraid of dying, yes, but it will be fast and I will take myself to my *otherspace*."

"What is your *otherspace*?"

"I don't really know... a great bright funnel of light takes me there. It reaches out and takes me out of the physical into the pure spirit. I will stay in there until it is decided when I shall take to the flesh again. I am, after all, only a credente."

"A credente?"

"A follower, not a *Perfecti*. I have not yet learned all I need to. I will come back again, eventually overcome my fears and learn to purify my words, my deeds and myself. Sometimes it takes many lifetimes to reach perfection."

"Will I too come again to face the torments of life?"

I stood very still and gazed into his eyes. "You will, Léon, until your soul is pure, but in the meantime you will remain with the torture of a guilty soul. Wounds can be healed. Poison drawn off with a leech or a knife, but the guilt of your actions will live within you. It cannot be plucked out like a splinter or be salved with herbs."

"Enough," he said. "You confuse me with your arguments."

CHAPTER 30
Duty Fulfilled

LÉON DUMONT

The following morning, the ink blue of the sky was starting to pale into a soft violet, almost the shade of Eva's eyes. It was cold and we walked fast through the haze of misty grey shadows towards the garrison. Eva would be detained and I would be free. We'd had little sleep but Eva was quiet and determined, walking tall and singing softly. She had assured me that I was to do what was needed of me. She was unafraid.

But I *was* afraid. A deep sadness had overtaken me, but I forced myself to carry on with my mission. I could not turn back, however much I wanted to. God had given me this chance. I was not going to fail because of this young woman with her violet eyes and heretical beliefs.

But the sadness of my actions crept deeply into my aching heart. Some deep, intense yearning to see my actions through to the end moved me onward.

A necessary completion!

Four days later was set as 'the day' of the burning. I wanted, needed, to see it. It was a cold day with a raw harsh wind, the sky the colour of slate. Pushing through the crowd, I watched the mounted soldiers herding the prisoners, some roped, others chained together and, in consequence, jostling and stumbling as the older ones lost their balance and fell, dragging others down.

Mostly their faces were calm and, although a few looked fearful, others were speaking to them quietly, reassurance and acceptance on their faces. Many wore the simple blue robes of the *Perfecti*.

And they were singing.

Did they not realise they were about to suffer the pain

and agony of Hell fire?

Some soldiers were striking those nearest to them, shouting obscenities, spitting and jeering, prodding them as they made their way down the street to the square where the pyres were being built.

A procession of priests and black-clad friars with their silk banners, and carrying on high a huge cross bearing the suffering Christ, moved across the square towards the outskirts of the town where dozens of wagons were arriving, loaded with wood for the burning.

Great piles of logs, boughs, brushwood and tubs of tar surrounded the posts set in the ground and secured with weights. Each post had a pathway left free of wood so the guards could lead the heretics to the poles to which they would be tied. More brushwood was placed around them so the crowd could see them from the waist up.

As Eva was led to her post, I caught a glimpse of her long plait of blonde hair. Bile rose in my throat. Waves of sorrow and guilt overwhelmed me as I watched her turn to be tied. I was responsible for this!

Eva held her head high and she was calmly singing with the others.

At that moment, everything I had believed in crumbled to dust.

CHAPTER 31
Toward the Light

EVA ROCAULT

Finally, the day has arrived. It is now.

I will be with my beloved father again. I had not known he and many others had been imprisoned for months waiting for this day. Together, we will travel onward.

There are so many people, watching and waiting, some jeering, others waving their fists. The soldiers push us along like cattle, their faces cruel and distorted with hatred. Icy panic fills my stomach until I hear my father's voice. He is singing to the glory of the Holy Spirit. The haunting hymn reminding me of the perfection that awaits us.

Catching sight of my father, and seeing how unchanged he is in his resolve, gives me more strength than I had dared to hope for. He turns and smiles at me.

Taking a deep breath, I too start to sing, and others around me join in. Our voices move us forward and I hold my head high, pushing the sound from my chest into the cold air.

A long, deep, humming sigh echoes from the voices around me, and slowly the crowds hush.

It is time.

One by one we are led to the poles, tied, and surrounded by more wood. The cords are biting into my ankles and my wrists as they are twisted and bound together.

Although I feel deep sadness for the loss of the pleasures and loves of this life, I know the life force that flows within me will continue into another.

I am trying hard to hold my father in view. His eyes are closed and I am concentrating on the prayers and moving on into a new dimension.

The pyres are lit.

CHAPTER 32
Guilt

LÉON DUMONT

The flames start slowly. But in a brief moment, the cold wind lifts them into a furious blaze.

All I can hear are the moans and screams from those whose lives are being cut short by the flames. Some in the crowd are weeping, some cheering. As I push forward, I catch words here and there.

"Surely no one deserves this –"

"Can't believe it –"

"– and those children –"

"See them heretics burn!" screams a fat priest dribbling down his cassock, his eyes bulging with excitement.

Some move hurriedly away. Small children with dirty, frightened faces run from the smoke and smell. The stench of burning flesh is foul, and those closest to the fire hold cloths over their faces.

But for me, an overwhelming feeling of tender pity for this beautiful young woman, who has touched me to the depth of my being with her faith, simplicity, goodness and love, pushes me forward.

I am standing against the barrier surrounding the burnings, as the heat increases. Great billowing clouds of smoke sweep up and around, surrounding the pyres. I can't see Eva. The singing is lost in the cries and screaming of the prisoners as it echoes up into the grey swollen clouds.

Then, suddenly, the wind lifts away the smoke and I am looking directly into her tortured eyes.

Her suffering makes my heart explode with grief. I am tormented with waves of guilt that I could allow myself to let my beliefs overcome my compassion for such a beautiful spirited girl. I should have let her go but my desire for glory was too strong.

My guilt overwhelms me. My tears cascade down my tortured face.

"Eva," I scream. "I am so sorry."

CHAPTER 33
Into the Spirit

EVA ROCAULT

I have closed my eyes and am trying to ignore the noise and the intense heat. I am taking slow, deep breaths, hoping that death will come quickly. My throat feels raw from the hot pitch and smoke, and I stop singing. I am willing myself to relax, but the pain is terrible. My skin is burning, and as my body heaves and strains, my wrists and ankles are tearing against the restraining cords, cutting them deeply. I am writhing in agony and the flames have only reached my legs.

I can hear the crowd howling and cheering, but the noise, the fear, the bodies of those around me, their mouths contorted with agony as the flames rise, deny me my freedom.

I am beginning to choke and my body is shaking with the pain as if I am having a fit. I am trying to slow my breath again but it is too intense. I am gasping.

Suddenly I hear my father's voice lifting in joy and singing the Pater Noster. As others join in, a smooth rhythm of noise overcomes the sound of the flames, the crowd and the fear. I close my eyes so that I can concentrate on the prayer.

"Our Father who art in heaven, hallowed be thy name... thy kingdom come..."

The terrible heat grows and flames are moving upward. I breathe in as deeply as I can, inhaling the dense pine pitch smoke, and whisper my 'Amen'.

I know I must concentrate on moving to my *otherspace*. Agony and fear rise in my chest so that I feel it will burst. I must move out of my tormented body.

I open my eyes. Through the smoke I can see Léon's face in the crowd, contorted with grief and sorrow. His mouth is open, screaming my name, tears flowing down his face.

The agony of betrayal.

Poor Léon... But it is his will, his pride and his beliefs that have brought me here. He needs to know what he has done.

Watch my pain, Léon. Watch it so that you will never forget the cruelty and injustice of this day. Watch it so that every thought from now on is etched into your daily life. Never forget, Léon. The time will come when you will have to face your actions, as all is repeated through the realms of time and nothing is forgotten. Your God will not reward you for this terrible sin. You will be made to repent.

A deep bitterness toward him and his faith winds its way into my thoughts and I am ravaged again by scorching agony. How can he be so cruel?

With my anger, my suffering intensifies.

I am dying for my beliefs and it is neither right nor fair. Just for a moment, regret for the life I had assails me. I pray that Léon and all those who have perpetrated such cruelty will suffer too.

I know these are not the thoughts or desires of my faith, and I hear again my father's words.

"Pain is only transitory and we must love everyone, saints and sinners and those not fortunate enough to have our love, empathy and goodwill. They will not be purified and honoured as we are in our spirit form, but will return life after life to suffer until they too can be Perfect."

A great gust of wind intensifies the fire and with it my whole body burns. My heart suddenly goes out to Léon and I acknowledge the gentle spirit that lies within him. My own fear swiftly subsides and I can see the Light moving over me. I am quickly at peace, very sure it is happening.

I am sliding towards it, a shimmering connection, away from the fires and the evil, away from the present into a timeless, endless space. I am suspended between the past and the future, between the then and the now, the pain and the smooth iridescent pathway ahead.

I am surrounded; soft and loving arms caress me. I am travelling from one dimension into another; a safe place, away from the hatred and ignorance of the present.

It is left behind as I move away from the confines of my body into the spirit.

Everything is silent. I am cleansed in that beautiful, white, weightless world.

I will see you again Léon. That I know! But you will suffer the agonies of this day yourself. You will not be allowed to forget your guilt.

I am now free to move on... and on...

PART 2
REVENGE

Catalonia, Spain

During the reign of Ferdinand of Aragon and Isabella of Castile, the Spanish Inquisition was in full flow.

In 1483, Pope Sixtus IV agreed that the Inquisitor General Torquemada, already active in Castile, could extend his powers to Aragon with the authority to appoint Inquisitors all around Spain. He set up extensive courts.

To create a united faith, it was deemed necessary to rid Spain of all those who did not follow the faith, take Mass, attend confession and adhere to the laws of the Church. Originally the Inquisitors focused on the heretics, the Conversos; converted Jews and the Moriscos; converted Muslims and those who had given lip service to their conversion but still practised their own laws, in some places quite openly.

However, overly zealous Inquisitors found themselves searching out many other sins – sins of the flesh, sorcery, coveting, blasphemy, bigamy, harbouring and thievery came within the jurisdiction of the courts and were all harshly dealt with. The 'Santa Hermandad' were the religious police of the time, whose general duties included arresting those suspected of heresy or misdeeds, protecting pilgrims on their journeys, rural patrols and enforcing taxes.

A Court of the Inquisition set up in Cuenca, La Mancha in
Spain changed the lives of all who lived there, especially
Evangelina, a novice in the convent of Santa Hilda, and
Leopoldo Sanchez, the new Inquisitor.
A residue of Karmic memory surfaces when they meet.

CHAPTER 1
Spring 1493 – Convento de Santa Hilda, Spain

EVANGELINA

The sky was an extraordinary shade of deep dark blue. Rolling black clouds, heavy with rain, menaced over the valley and raced towards our convent. I would have to work quickly as a storm could devastate our crops and plants which we had worked so hard to cultivate that year.

I knew Sister Donna-Marie would not be happy if her precious seedlings got washed away, so I set about protecting our garden. I tied up the beans and covered some of the fruit. I quickly dug a channel alongside the patch of ground where our herbs grew, and directed it toward the hillside stream that sloped down to join the Jucar River.

The weather had been unusual. The snowstorms and exceptional high winds in the winter caused drifts so deep that they took weeks to melt. The wet, never-ending spring meant that it would be extra difficult to get a good crop.

Feeling happy and contented, I sang a few bars of the song Isabelle had taught me on our journey here. Singing or humming outside the chapel wasn't really allowed, except during carnivals or saints' days. But no one could hear me. The garden was far from the main building of the convent, and all of the other nuns and novices were attending Prime, the early morning Mass.

I didn't really care anyway. I only worried about what Donna-Marie thought of me. She, who had helped me so much and whom I loved more than any other being I had ever known.

For the first time in my life I was well fed and cared for. Nobody here knew about my past but Donna-Marie.

When I arrived at the convent over two years before, I was a filthy little street orphan. A travelling friar who had found me by chance brought me here. Good fortune shone on me that day, for I had wanted so badly to escape the awful life I had in Burriana, I was prepared to travel anywhere and with anyone. The good friar offered me the chance of a new life and I jumped at it.

Coming to the convent was the best thing that could have happened to me. Far better than starving in the gutters or dying in agony as my mother Riba had done. She's gone now and it served her right, lifting her skirt for a few worthless maravedis. She got the sickness and it ate her away slowly and painfully until, in the end, it was a relief for both of us when she died.

My mother had been a sad, bad-tempered, unfeeling woman, who raged at me for everything I did or didn't do. She struck me too, many times. But then, as she'd become weaker and weaker, her blows had become cursory and feeble. Nevertheless, she would flail and shriek at me if I failed to bring her money or food.

The day before she died, I had nothing. She screamed at me that I was a useless, clumsy, hoof-handed, grape-eyed, stinking slut that would never be good enough to please anyone.

I ran away and, two days later, luck was on my side. I met the good friar, Father Matias, who offered me another way of life. It involved a long journey, he told me.

So much the better, I thought. The further I am from Burriana, the happier I will be.

I had no regrets about leaving. It seemed the only thing to do at the time.

Another child, sweet Isabelle, accompanied us on our long journey to the Convento de Santa Hilda. My time travelling with her and Father Matias were some of the happiest days of my life.

On our arrival at the convent, the sun was dropping from the sky, casting glorious shadows through the valley. All I could think was that this must be Heaven. The beautiful, peaceful convent in Palomera, near Cuenca, was built on a flat plain overlooking the river. Alongside stood a chapel, an orchard, and a huge garden with shaded paths and archways of flowering shrubs and trees. Surrounded by mountains, this was where my new life would begin.

Although I knew nothing about my future then, I had a feeling of tranquillity and overwhelming joy to be so far away from the foulness of my previous life.

It had been a long, hot day. Isabelle and I were led to a tiny room and given a bowl of soup. We were so tired. We slept, curled together on the big soft bed like a couple of exhausted puppies.

"Get up, you are wanted in the kitchen," a surly voice had whispered on the first morning after my arrival. A young, plump girl with a tight wimple that made her face look pink and round had shaken me. My heart missed a beat. I jumped up instantly, thinking I was back in Burriana.

"I am novice Junã. Come follow me. No smelly little girls are allowed to have their breakfast here. And leave the boots," she ordered as I tried to pull them on.

It had been a long time since I'd had a pair of boots, so I tucked them under my arm, refusing to put them down. Junã tut-tutted and indicated that I should follow her. My little friend Isabelle slept on, undisturbed, rolled into a ball against the wall.

I wondered what was in store for me as I followed Junã along the cold corridors. I was so full of questions, so many things I wanted to ask. Questions that swept through my mind like a flock of birds. I was tongue-tied with anticipation. My new life was about to start.

It was still dark as she took me into a large kitchen, told me to wait, and then disappeared without another word.

In the middle of the room was a huge tub of hot water that smelled of lavender. I thought it was far too big for a cooking pot.

Looking around, I saw that there was more hot water in a smaller pot over the fire. I waited, enjoying the warmth and wondering what was going to happen next. My life had changed so much in the past weeks.

I was suddenly very afraid as I watched the flames dancing under the pot, the scarlet and golden heat from the logs reddening my cheeks. My fear was a long-standing one. I could not go anywhere near a flame or even eat hot food. A strange fear! It wormed its way into my dreams, so that I would wake sweating, with my feet and hands burning.

I kept my back pressed against the wall as I recalled the dream I'd had that night. I'd expected to sleep more soundly once we reached our destination. After all, it had taken many weeks of rough and disturbed nights to get here. I had curled into the warm blankets and fallen instantly into a deep sleep. But the dream disturbed me and left me afraid and shaking. It was always the same. A thousand candles burned around me, moving slowly forward like an advancing army. In the flames, faces full of fury, with flickering tongues of fire, leaping and lashing.

Once, a priest came to Burriana and preached about the flames of Hell that awaited all sinners. I couldn't sleep for weeks.

As I stood watching the dancing fire, I was overcome with trepidation, not only of the flames but also of knowing nothing about this new life that I had willingly walked across the mountains for.

I didn't hear Sister Donna-Marie enter.

"Are you ready for your bath?" she asked in a soft voice, making me jump out of my fearful daydreaming.

A bath? No. Not me. I'm not having a bath. I'll get ill, I thought, as I spun around and faced her.

She was smiling, rolling up her sleeves purposefully.

"I'm Sister Donna-Marie and you are Lina. Are you not?

Come, take off your shift."

"Don't touch me," I hissed at her, and backed into a corner with my fists raised when she tried to get me to take off my filthy dress.

She moved toward me and carefully took hold of my raised fists, so I spat at her as hard as I could. My aim was good and my spittle hit her on the chin and dribbled down onto her habit. I pushed her and spun away, moving to the other side of the room.

"I am not getting in there. It will burn me," I shrieked at her as she wiped away the spittle.

"It will not hurt you, Lina. It's not so hot as to burn. The Abbess says you must be cleaned up before you can be allowed to eat."

She smiled. "Now come. You will want to eat, won't you? You must be hungry."

I was shaking at the thought of going anywhere near the bathtub, but her gentle voice reassured me that I would come to no harm. In all my fourteen years I'd never been washed in anything but cold water. As I calmed, she encouraged me softly. She helped me remove my raggy dress and coaxed me toward the warm water. She was almost as small as me, with a round face, lovely blue eyes, and she smelled sweet, like a garden full of flowers. Her gentleness emanated from her like a cloud of silk.

"I have a lovely new outfit for you, and breakfast is good with lots of honey and milk," she said as she swished her hands into the water. "Come, feel. It is warm, not hot. It will make you feel good."

My hunger overcame my trepidation so I put my finger into the water. It did not burn as I had expected.

Donna-Marie waited. I lifted one leg and dipped a toe into the sweet-smelling water. My fear subsided so I stepped into the tub.

"How long have you been alone, Lina?" she asked as I

tentatively sunk into the warm, soapy suds. It was heavenly
and I relaxed enough to say, "All my life, I think."

Even though I'd had a mother, I had always been
neglected and hungry, not used to any sort of care. Sister
Donna-Marie was gentle and kind as she poured warm
water over my raggy mop of hair and carefully massaged
sweet-smelling soap into it. She did this several times until it
squeaked with cleanliness.

"Tell me," she said.

"Why would you care?" I sniffed.

"Why would I not?"

I looked into her face. I had never seen such loving regard
from anyone. It made me want to cry. I never normally cried,
but as she gently stroked my hair, I rested my head back
onto her hands and let the tears of years slide down my face.
She slipped a cloth into the water and softly stroked it across
my cheeks.

"You might send me back," I spluttered.

"Back to what? You have no family, do you? Why would
we send you back?"

"I would rather be dead than ever go back."

"Tell me, Lina," she said again.

I told her the whole story.

Oh, the relief of it!

CHAPTER 2
Telling My Story

EVANGELINA

I needed to leave my past behind forever, but I wanted to tell her. Once I began, the words tumbled out in a torrent.

I told her how when I was a ten-year-old virgin my mother Riba had sold me to the highest bidder. The memory of that day I'd blotted out completely, but it was then that I started to hate my life and to shut off my feelings to the foulness of it all.

"When my mother was taken ill, selling my body was the only way to keep us fed," I said. "I hated everything and everybody but I had no choice. She was really ill, dying. I stayed with her, tried to help, but she was screaming at me when her husband Selvin Lendos arrived."

Donna-Marie was watching me silently.

"He wasn't her husband of course, he was a dirty Greek bully," I explained. "He'd been a sailor, jumped ship in Spain, and found a way to earn a living without working himself. He said he was our protector, but he didn't protect us. He had no regard for my mother or anyone else. He came and just stood looking down at her. She always stopped shouting when he was around."

I shivered as I repeated Selvin Lendos's words to my mother as she lay suffering. "He said, ''Tis you that has the cankered sheath and 'tis you whose earning days are over, you stinking drudge. Do not revile your daughter. She's worked hard for you whilst you have lain here rotting.' He brought her a bottle of cheap brandy to help deaden the pain and, although she drank every drop, she died that night, screaming in agony. He didn't care for her at all. He had her body removed and taken to the pauper's grave."

Donna-Marie stroked me gently, "Did you stay there?"

"I had no choice. He stayed with us. We'd shared the

room with his two other girls, Mar and Julianna. His only interest was that we went back to earning for him as soon as possible. He said to me the very next day, 'Get ye'self out to work now, Lina, but clean ye'self up and put on something bright and pretty so that you can find a decent punter. Ge'down to the docks; there are new ships coming in all this week. Flash those pretty purple eyes and find a rich dick. Don't go the way of your sluttish mother,' he ordered me. Something pretty? What a joke. I didn't have anything pretty!"

I shrugged and Donna-Marie smiled.

"The only thing I owned was what I stole from a washing line. My other dress was ripped off by an overenthusiastic butcher. What was I supposed to do? I couldn't use one of Mar's or Julianna's. Nothing they owned would fit me. They are both tall and skinny with big saggy breasts."

I cupped and bounced my hands at my waistline, and Donna-Marie laughed.

"The port where we were expected to work was a long walk. I told Juliana I was too hungry to go out. I just lay on my flea-infested cot staring at the rotting ceiling, feeling nothing. I wondered why I couldn't cry for the woman who had brought me into the world."

I sighed and tears flooded into my eyes again.

"I thought I was worthless. My life was only worth what my body could earn and I hated everything about it. I hoped to die."

Donna-Marie patted away my tears and then helped me out of the tub. She wrapped me in a towel and gently ran her fingers through my wet hair.

"Now you are here. You are safe. We are lucky to have you, Lina," she said. "Did you always live in Burriana?"

"No," I sniffed. "When Selvin Lendos found us, I was only little, and we were living on the streets of Valencia. I don't really remember being there. We moved many times.

Sometimes we slept in the woods, on the beach, or in a dirty gutter. I learned when I was very young to run and hide, who to avoid, and to live on scraps thrown over the city walls. Lendos took us to Burriana. It's where foreign ships come, mainly to load the oranges that are grown on the Plana Baixa. He promised my mother work and a good life. He is tall and good-looking, and my mother believed that he would take care of us. But right from the beginning he drove her out to sell her body and encouraged me to beg or steal whenever I could. Mostly, he ignored me, until I was old enough to earn him money with my body."

I told her of the stinking room, the rough, sweaty men, the hunger, and the people around me who cared little for me. That day Julianna had made enough for us all to eat. She bought some local sardines and a hunk of bread. She wasn't usually so generous, but she'd had a friendly relationship with Riba and was the only one who would miss her.

"Lendos left the next day and told us all to get to work. He would be back soon to collect our earnings. Two days passed, and I hadn't been out of our stinking room. Julianna and Mar refused to share any more food with me and I was hungry and weak. They were furious," I explained as Donna-Marie listened carefully, holding my hand as if to help me with the pain of remembering.

"What happened?" she said.

"They were afraid of Lendos. 'You will be in trouble, Miss Misery,' Mar spat at me when she came in from work with a dirty face and a new bruise on her cheek. 'When Lendos gets back he'll whip you, you know.' 'I know, and I don't care what he does!' I shouted back at her. But yes, I knew what he would do. So early the next morning, I set off into town, onto the streets to find a pocket to pick or a pie to steal. Instead I had found a scrawny, smelly sailor who paid me for my services, pulled me into an alleyway, and as he dropped his trousers pushed my head towards his filthy equipment. I took one look at his flabby old dangle and bit his bollocks so hard that he squealed like a pig."

Donna-Marie's face was a picture when I said this, but I saw a small smile curve the corners of her mouth.

She picked up a brush and started to tug at the knots in my hair, so I continued. "Then, of course, I ran as far and as fast as I could, over walls and through gardens, ending up in the church of El Salvadore in the Calle de El Barranquet. I stayed there a long time, under a pew which smelled of rotten leaves and mouldy feet, listening to my heart beating and my stomach rumbling, wondering what to do."

"So? Did Lendos find you?" she asked.

"No, I fell asleep I think, because it was really late when Brother Matias found me cold and hungry, clutching the few coins that the sailor had given me. I told him I was a homeless orphan. That *was* true. And, that my mother had worked in the kitchens of a count's castle, before it was taken by the State because he was a Jew. Which *wasn't* true."

Donna-Marie laughed. "What an imagination you have!"

"Oh, there's more," I told her. "I gabbled a silly story of a jealous cook who threw me out on the streets. I told him that I had come to the church to pray and give the only money I had left to God in the hope that he would help me. I showed him the coins and used my eyes to plead with him. I must admit this was the first time I had used my 'womanly ways' on a man. A man of the cloth too! It seemed to be effective as Brother Matias smiled at me and said, 'Well, my dear child, God has seen you and He will always reward those who have such faith.' I dropped my head and managed to squeeze out a few submissive tears so that they dripped onto the stone floor. Suddenly I heard him gasp. 'What?' I thought. 'Has he changed his mind already?' I was about to implore his help, but I could feel his fingers hovering over the side of my neck where I have my little birthmark. Then, much to my surprise, he suddenly exclaimed, 'you have the sign of the cross upon you, my child. I believe you were sent. Come with me, and we will find you something to eat and something to warm you. Your devotion has served you well.' That was good enough for me... He thought I had been sent! From where? I know I have a birthmark on my neck but I can only feel its outline. Never seen it, but I guess it's a similar shape to the cross that towered over the altar."

I turned and pointed it out to Donna-Marie.

"I had already noticed it," she said simply, so I continued.

"He treated me very well. That night he fed me things I'd never seen before, as well as ham and bread and a big jug of watery wine. I gobbled it all so fast it made my stomach ache. I was so afraid that Lendos would find me. Then Brother Matias asked me if I had a vocation. 'What's that?' I asked. 'A desire to serve our Lord,' he said. 'Oh yes,' I answered. Then he asked me whether I would be prepared to travel to a new life? I would have to give up worldly desires and devote my life to God?' 'Yes!' I said. 'Yes, of course I would!' The further the better was my only thought."

Donna-Marie was still struggling with my matted hair as she asked, "Did he know about Lendos?"

"No. If he'd known of my background he probably wouldn't have suggested that I came here with him. I told Brother Matias that I had no one who would miss me and that my only known relative, my mother, was now dead. He told me that he was a travelling friar, on a Holy mission to the convents and monasteries in the north and west. His bishop had sent him up from Murcia to make his yearly tour of the convents, to take confession, and ensure that Mass was being properly performed."

Donna-Marie nodded. "Yes. His journey takes many weeks, always ending here."

"He told me that he was always on the lookout for truly pious young people to bring to the convent and monasteries as they always needed new recruits. He said, 'I'm going to take you to a lovely convent in Cuenca where you will be very happy and you can devote yourself to our Lord.' Great! I thought, but I had no idea what would be the consequences of my decision. I just decided to make the best of it."

"It is a lovely place," Donna-Marie said as she carefully untangled another knot of hair, "and you will be well cared for here."

I felt how gently she worked on my tangled locks and knew that she spoke the truth.

"Brother Matias told me about Isabelle," I said quietly. "She is to stay here too. All her family died of the plague in Murcia except an old uncle who paid Brother Matias to bring her back to Cuenca. Isabelle's family originally came from Castile. Even though many had died including the priests and nobles, Brother Matias told me he believed that he had been spared because the pestilence would only punish the wicked."

"Indeed," laughed Donna-Marie. "But don't you think he is a good man to care for you both?"

"I do. But I am sure he only brought me because it was a good idea for Isabelle to have a companion. She is only eight and needs a bit of watching. 'Fine,' I said, 'I can do that,' at the same time thinking what a bore it would be. I'm no nursemaid."

"I understand that you have looked after her well," said Donna-Marie.

"She is a perfect friend and she makes every day fun. I have never been happier in my life."

"Good. Now go on with your story. It is nearly time for breakfast but I would like to hear about your journey."

I told her how we had set off before dawn and saw no one as we headed through the darkened streets toward the orange groves that surrounded the town. We had a mule and two donkeys to carry us and our baggage. I had none of course, but Brother Matias had stores of salt, spices, pots, wax for candles, ink and paper, plus bales of hide and cloth for the places we were visiting.

"Isabelle is a devout, golden little girl who behaves very well and says her prayers daily. She seems to me to be very happy, despite the sad fact of her parents' death. She'd got boxes of clothes and boots and even gloves... none of which fit me so I travelled in the rags I had been found in, and the cloak and boots that Brother Matias had given me from the poor box," I explained, and then found myself relating the whole journey to Palomera.

CHAPTER 3
The Journey

EVANGELINA

We were an odd pair; we couldn't have been more different. Isabelle was so pale-eyed, pink and fleshy, and obviously well fed and well cared for, whilst I, being only slightly taller, with my violet eyes, was dark and skinny, my long hair as black as a raven's tail.

We travelled west through the endless groves of orange trees, through Betxi and Onda, each step taking us further away. Then north through the forests and over the rocky hills past Olba to a deep valley, a place called Arenoso where there was a great lake of turquoise water. Brother Matias caught some big scaly fishes that we cooked over a fire in the evening.

Each day after that, the mountains got higher, the gorges deeper, and we had to lead the animals and walk ourselves. Brother Matias huffed and puffed, and Isabelle often ran ahead to find the easiest way. At first my legs hurt all the time but gradually, as the muscles got accustomed to the walking and climbing, they became stronger. I had never seen places like those, nor been so far away from the seashore before. I was entranced with the wild flowers and the great forest trees. We travelled through gorges with towers of rock so high I had to lean back to see the top of them. I hid carefully from the assorted travellers going towards the ports of Castellón and Valencia, so that word would not get back to Lendos.

Everywhere we went we were offered food and shelter, and Brother Matias preached fervently about the dangers of sin wherever and whenever he could. We climbed again across steep pathways where we could hear the flap of a bird's wing or the spring rain dripping from the trees.

My whole world had changed, from the hustle and noise of Burriana to the soft hush of the mountain pathways. We stayed for two days in a monastery in Virgen de la Vega and offloaded some of the goods that Brother Matias had brought for them. Sleeping in a real bed for the first time ever and with a full stomach, I indulged myself in daydreams of my new life.

What would I do? Would I be expected to work, or pray? I had never prayed in my life but occasionally watched others do so, heads down, appealing to some unknown force for an easier life.

Isabelle and I were left to our own devices and explored the fields and surrounding woodlands, often catching sight of deer and wild boar, while Brother Matias took confessions, Mass, or christenings, and even performed a wedding as there was no ordained priest in the village where we had stayed.

'We've got to get going now, girls,' Brother Matias told us as we set off across the mountains again. 'We have a long journey ahead. It will take many weeks to reach Cuenca.' The further the better was my only thought. I was now beginning to feel that Lendos would never find me, and I was enjoying being with Isabelle who accepted every day with a smile and never seemed to be tired or worried.

One day it rained so hard that we had to stop. We found a smallholding where an old couple let Isabelle and I share a tiny bed in the loft whilst Brother Matias had theirs. I had no idea where they slept, probably with the goats and chickens in the tiny lean-to against the house.

In the morning Isabelle and I attempted to milk the goats and, as we laughed and giggled, the old man watched us with a sad smile.

"How much I miss having young folk around," he said to Brother Matias who was busy pushing another slice of goat cheese into his greedy mouth. The couple's two boys had long since moved to Valencia for work.

All too soon we had to move on. We travelled across a flat plain to Teruel, a largish town with a big market square where we were given bread, fruit and lots of provisions. All the stallholders were happy to give the friar sustenance, and we loaded everything onto our donkeys.

"Brother Matias made me laugh when I exclaimed at the amount of food we had for our journey," I told Donna-Marie. "'What, young lady?' he said. 'I took a vow of poverty, not starvation.'"

"He's an upright and God-fearing man, and other than straying a little from the pathway with his greedy appetite, he takes his priestly vows seriously," Donna-Marie said.

"Oh, I know that," I laughed. "He's a saint in my eyes. That day we nearly lost Isabelle who had a habit of wandering off. Brother Matias was so distressed. We found her happily chatting to a stonemason who was carving a huge angel into the rock on the hillside that overlooked the square. Brother Matias warned her that she would not be allowed to leave his side in future and, seeing his concern, Isabelle replied, 'I won't, Father, I promise.' Phooee... what a nice little girl she is!"

I went on to relate how the journey took us across more wooded mountains and rocky hills. How fine the weather was and how all I could do was think that I was escaping. I loved being free and in the fresh air. Even though the riding was difficult, as I had never even sat on a donkey before, I thought it was wonderful. The sun was warm and we stopped by streams and rivers. Isabelle and I soaked our sweaty bodies, enjoying the icy water that flowed down the mountain toward the sea. But not Brother Matias, even though sometimes it was so hot that his little round shaven head and face dripped with perspiration. I never saw him remove any of his clothes. He was a bit stinky, but he was always kind, and tried to make our journey as pleasant as possible. He told us stories about his travels and his life. The time passed quickly as he described the buildings and parks of the south where there were long, long miles of shimmering sand, the beautiful gardens of Madrid and Seville, and his many pilgrimages to saints all over the country.

We sang as we travelled too. Isabelle knew many songs and rhymes, and she taught me to count. She was a sweet child and never complained, although I did, often, when the heat was too much and the ride too long.

We made a funny little family, trundling along, laughing and singing our songs. Isabelle was full of fun and waggled her bottom, pointing to Brother Matias's large one swaying from side to side on his mount. He looked over his shoulder and smiled as we giggled. Laughter was something that had never been part of my life before, and I enjoyed my days enormously. Our journey took us across a flat plain covered with vines and then into the mountains again with twisting pathways, where we only met a few goats and wild rabbits. Once we slept in an old church, another time in a large barn. Not always the most comfortable places, but we had a store of fruits, cheeses and biscuits to eat and, best of all, I didn't feel that I was on my own anymore. Within days, I felt my spirits lifting. All I had to do was smile at the old Brother and he patted my cheeks and told me of the wonderful life I would have at the convent.

At night, Isabelle and I huddled together under the blankets that Brother Matias had brought for us. I was the closest I had ever been to being happy. So much better than the smelly streets of Burriana with the sailors, merchants, slaves and whores.

By the time I had finished telling Donna-Marie about our journey, she had cut and pinned my hair away from my face.

"Time for breakfast," she said. "You can finish your story later."

"There is no more. I am here," I said simply.

Although I had no regrets about leaving that life, I hadn't wanted to come to a convent. It seemed the only thing to do at the time, and I was glad now.

Donna-Marie never judged me or treated me other than kindly, even though in the beginning I'd spat and screamed at her like a wildcat.

She had cleaned and medicated my scabby, flea-bitten back and shoulders, smoothed a soft oily lotion into the scars on my bottom, and cut my tangled hair from my face. She had gently washed me till I was pink and smooth, and rinsed my hair with rosemary water so that it shone as it dried.

She placed me in a soft warm shift with a pale blue cord around my waist. It felt strange to be clean and sweet-smelling, my hair cut short and the relief of the tears shed as I had recounted how I came to be here.

No one had ever shown the slightest interest in me or my feelings before, and I was exhausted from the remembering. This loving soul had taken it upon herself to look after me and help me gain some self-worth, of which I had none when I had arrived.

I felt like a different person. I *was* a different person! I was clean and dressed and I smelled of lavender and rosemary.

CHAPTER 4
Convent Life

EVANGELINA

At breakfast that first morning, Isabelle and I sat together and watched as the novices and a group of small children, all girls, went quietly about the business of clearing away the remains of their meal. We were then sent to meet the other nuns. The novice-mistress Sister Magdalena was put in charge of us. She was the oldest nun in the convent and had breath like a pig's behind. Brother Matias had explained that she was known for her wisdom and kindness to the novices and orphans. We were to obey her every word.

Chubby Sister Beatrix, in charge of the kitchens, permanently red-faced and greasy-handed from her cooking pots.

Little Sister Enetta, a widow who was recently sent to the convent, scrawny and pale as a sun-drenched pebble, endlessly twitching and nervously fiddling.

Sister Belen-Sualita, who lived in happy ignorance of where she was and existed in a state of placid bewilderment doing whatever she was asked with no idea why. A sweet novice called Olivia was especially assigned to ensure that Sister Belen-Sualita stayed within the confines of the convent and didn't stray.

All welcomed us cheerfully, but I was unsure of what I was doing there as they all showed devout and obedient natures, of which I had none. But it was Donna-Marie's affection and support that convinced me. She offered Isabelle and I a colourful picture of life as she knew it in Santa Hilda.

"We live long, contented lives here. No family, other than that created by the sisters. No randy, drunken husbands demanding a poke, leading to endless children, exhaustion and collapsed wombs." She laughed with a small wink directed at me, and added, "We are healthy, eat well, and the citizens of Cuenca are good to us. Some of the girls here are incarcerated into the convent by fathers unable to secure them a husband, or unwilling to maintain them. Others come willingly with vocations or due to circumstance, or in some cases forced by family tradition. Not all are impelled by holy vocation, though. There are a few widows, too old to remarry and perhaps unable to do so, entered of their own accord, often bringing with them the riches of their departed spouses. We have our orphans too, twelve at the moment. They will stay only as long as they want to."

Two years passed.

At first my moods were storm-tossed with defiance; I was expected to restrict not only my movements but also my speech. I'd never known any form of real discipline, only endless bullying and violence. Adapting to the eight sessions of daily prayers, the chattering rosary beads, the convent rules of silence during working hours, made me realise how different my life was to become.

But, as time passed, I worked hard, learned the prayers and the psalms, and managed to stay on my knees instead of fidgeting during the endless services. Only for Donna-Marie would I do this, as the words meant nothing to me, and I didn't really believe any of the sermons. I envied the simplicity of her certainty of Christ's majesty.

"Why so much praying?" I asked Donna-Marie one sunny day whilst we were working.

"Prayer lifts the heart, gives you a look toward Heaven. It is a way of showing your gratitude and love for your life and your love of God. It enlarges the soul and unites it with our Lord."

"Oh, does it?" I moaned. "Well, I don't like it that much."

Isabelle, on the other hand, now a pretty ten-year-old, loved the prayers and order of the convent and was obedient and happy. She worked and studied with our Sacrist, old Sister Agnes, and was able to read and write well enough to keep the convent's documents in order. She was already taking responsibility for our bookkeeping and expenditure. She was such a clever girl, and there was no doubt that she would eventually take over as Sacrist.

We were considered to be slave-novices as we came with no dowries. In Isabelle's case she had a tiny income from her uncle, but it was by circumstances playing a part in our respective fates that we both came to be here. We were expected to work and serve others in order to earn our place.

The convent of Santa Hilda supplied olive oil, wine, medicines, liquors, embroidered cloth and hand-copied religious works to the local bishops, gentry and citizens of Cuenca. This added to the income from the dowries of the nuns who often came with properties bequeathed in perpetuity.

Those who came to be treated, helped, or requiring prayers from the Holy sisters and who had no money to pay would often donate gifts: candles from the candlemakers, cloth from the weavers, and food, milk and manure for our garden from the farmers.

I was happily assigned to work with Sister Donna-Marie. She was the convent dispensary, a healer and a lover of all nature with a curious gift of insight. She knew instinctively what was going on, how people and animals felt, understood what their needs were, and she seemed to be tuned into something… something that *I* never saw or perceived.

She taught me about plants; how flowers, seeds, roots, berries and trees had healing properties. They held amazing secrets that could kill or cure.

"There is a very fine line between doing good or ill," Donna-Marie explained to me one day when we were set to work in the pharmacy. "Many plants can do either depending upon their administration. These plants, for instance," she continued, indicating the leaves she was crushing in a mortar. "The Mandragora. They can help or harm, as both the leaves and the roots have wonderful properties, but the dose wrongly applied can kill. Like henbane and belladonna, they have been included in many a witch's brew, but I am told pharmacists in the east use it as a sedative when performing surgery. In the right dosage it will put the patient into a deep sleep and alleviate pain and anxiety, but if I give too much the person will die, so I have to be really careful. My father's teacher called these plants 'reremt'. The fruits are like small apples, and if sniffed or dried and crushed into a drink can act as a stimulant. Some say for erotic purposes."

She smiled and then giggled uncharacteristically.

"Not that I have ever tried, of course," she added seriously. "These plants were originally brought by a traveller from the warmer region of the southern coast and we keep them covered with straw in the winter and close to the wall to protect them. They don't like cold weather, but if we carefully nurture them we can use them in our stocks of medicines and cures."

Donna-Marie pounded with the pestle until the dried leaves she was crushing became a fine powder, which she carefully poured into a tiny mixing bowl. "Today I will mix these with oil of hypericum and lavender for Sister Belen-Sualita who has an ulcer on her shin. It will soon help the sore, I'm sure. Can you find the oils for me, Lina?"

I had learned to recognize the labels on the hundreds of bottles in the pharmacy, so easily found the hypericum and the lavender. We worked all day as she was also preparing a poultice for Sister Francesca who had a sore and swollen abdomen.

I watched carefully as Donna-Marie mixed some torn leaves of geranium with cornflour and resin and rose oil. She explained that too many of the leaves could also irritate the skin, so once again I was learning about dosage. We were also assigned to making lozenges for the bishop across the valley.

"He suffers from constant throat soreness, so I make him these." She indicated the small pile of round, sugar-coated sweetmeats. "They are made mainly of honey mixed with ginger and lemon, hyssop and pennyroyal. They seem to help him with his long... long... sermons." She laughed gaily. "Although sometimes prolonging them tires everyone, including me."

Donna-Marie knew so many of the secrets of nature, and as each season came and went I learned how to identify the different species of wild flowers and trees, the various properties of the berries, seeds, leaves, blossoms and bark. Also I learned when to pick and harvest them, prune the fruits and vines, sow seeds for our foods and herbs, how to prepare, macerate, and make tisanes, press olives, mix food spices and make perfumes. I was learning so much every day and wondered whether I would ever know enough to make the mixtures without her guidance.

It was so exciting and each season offered different wonders. I began to understand what nature could do. She explained how too much rainfall could change the way they worked. How the soil in the valleys and the mountains produced different properties. She showed me a place where the honeycomb was toxic because the bees feasted on the juniper trees that grew only on that hillside.

"Sniff it, Lina. Can you tell how different it is? We must not eat honey from here, but we *can* use it to help the healing of wounds and sores."

How wonderful were the things I learned from her!

We also extracted fragrant oils from the herbs and blossoms by folding them in layers of goose fat pressed between old clay serving dishes that had been discarded from the kitchen. These were held together in boxes made with old planks of pine. Every few days, we refreshed the plant material onto the fat and pressed them together again. It was hard work to lift the planks and the clay dishes, but we would gather the blossoms and herbs early while they were still fresh with morning dew, and press them into place before breakfast. In time, when the fat had absorbed all the aromatics from the plant, we scraped it all into a large pot and heated and strained it. In this way we made pomades and unguents.

Depending on the plants, some were used for infections and wounds, others for breathing problems or stomach pain, and still others for painful limbs and joints. Some of the impregnated fat we mixed with grain 'alcool' so that it separated the aromatic oils from the fat.

Donna-Marie made beautiful lotions and poultices, and scented the altar candles with relaxing fragrances that made our prayers and meditation calm and beatific.

We also dried and ground herbs, seeds, berries, flowers and the bark of the willow, and carefully potted and labelled them. She prepared herbal infusions and knew exactly which to give if sleeping was a problem, for a gastric ailment, or an infected wound.

"You know so much. Did you learn it all here?" I asked one day when she had been explaining the properties of the geranium leaf.

"No. My father worked with Abdul, a *Moriscos* in an apothecary in Teruel, and, between them, they taught me most of what they had learned over the years. My father often took me with him when he went to see patients, but the rest I have learned from books, and sometimes with careful trial. I have found out for myself what works and what doesn't."

"Did your mother and father put you here?" I asked.

"No, I never knew my mother, and my father died when I was fourteen."

She smiled happily as she told me. "I joined the convent,

not just to survive, but because I also had a 'calling' to become the bride of Christ. I wanted to come. It was here that I could carry on with my learning and healing. I was already an accomplished nurse and midwife but I have always wanted to do more, and this place gives me that opportunity. Here I can script my knowledge and gather more information that will help others to learn too."

In time I could easily identify local flowers, trees and mushrooms, all of which we collected and used on the various ailments that were presented, both in the convent and on our rounds of the local people.

We secretly collected child-bane for women of the area who had no wish to bear more children, and Donna-Marie explained that dried and ground, taken daily it would prevent conception. It had to be kept a secret, as this was not within the church edicts.

Donna-Marie was the gentlest human being that I, Evangelina, had ever met. The curing arts she practised brought relief to many, especially some of the older nuns who suffered from pain in their aching joints. She made a cream from olive oil, beeswax, extracts of willow bark, cypress and floral water that she massaged into their painful knees and stiff fingers.

The people of Cuenca knew her well and appreciated the help she gave so lovingly and willingly. Donna-Marie, as well as the local physician, an old barber surgeon who was better qualified at pulling teeth than midwifery, had attended almost every newborn baby in the town. Everyone loved Donna-Marie. She was so devout and I followed her example whenever I could, and pretended that I too had the same feelings as she. But I did not. For me there was no logical reason to believe in God. I could not have faith that nothing is something, simply because I had been told so.

God didn't seem to have been very evident in my early life.

CHAPTER 5
1493 The New Inquisitor – Cleansing Begins

LEOPOLDO SANCHEZ

My uppermost thought, as I unpacked my trunks and arranged my desk, was that here was another new place full of sinners.

I had been assigned 'Casa Inspiradora', a large, well-furnished villa on the outskirts of Cuenca. It afforded me the luxury and the security that I deserved. Standing on a hillside, it was surrounded by high walls and locked wooden gates. The gate to the west was big enough to accommodate a carriage, but my personal one opened into a long, covered archway that led to my equally sturdy front door, giving me the security and privacy I knew I needed.

Inside the walls were ornamental gardens of great beauty, small lodges and pathways that led through a thick wall to the back of the house where a conglomeration of outbuildings housed my servants and my personal soldiers, my own police force, the Santa Hermandad.

Buildings added over the years and scattered around and against the back wall included a small forge, a butchers, a glasshouse for propagating plants, storerooms and a huge bake house. There were stables and coach houses, kennels for my hunting dogs, and a small chapel. The house had belonged to a disgraced noble who had joined with a group of the nobility of Valencia who had not looked kindly on the Inquisition. He had been expelled with many others and had left with his family the previous year.

I had brought with me a trusty servant, Oskar, who would attend to my personal needs and become taster of all my food and drink. A necessary precaution in this new place, I had been told!

Oskar was a dull and wily man who obeyed orders well

and would investigate all who worked for me. The house was neglected and needed a good housekeeper, a cook, kitchen and housemaids, and a laundress. Oskar could take care of all the domestic issues so I'd leave everything to him. Also accompanying me was my personal confessor Pedro-Anton, and Dunkan, my bodyguard, a member of the Holy Brotherhood. Both were part of the team who had been with me in Segovia.

I thought of the Holy men, Gaspar Juglar and Canon Pedro Arbues, who had come here eight years before and were murdered by *Conversos,* one poisoned and one stabbed in the throat. Surely I had nothing to fear now. I *should* be welcomed. Nevertheless, all my food would be prepared and tasted in this house. My own chickens, grouse, goats and sheep were in the large meadow at the back of the stables, well guarded, and also surrounded by a wall. I had my own abattoir and roasting ovens too. Every precaution had been taken.

My love of God and dedication to my work had earned me a great reputation in the eyes of the Church. I had done well and was pleased with my new posting. Few with such a humble background had risen to the rank of Inquisitor of the Realm.

I had been with the Holy Office under the guidance of Tomas de Torquemada, our Grand Inquisitor, since its beginning ten years before, when we took over the jurisdiction, power and authority that had previously belonged to the bishops. I had proved myself in the courts of Medina del Campo and Segovia, so I was sent to Cuenca to set up a new court for the Inquisition. Here, Jews and Muslims who were disregarding the new expulsion orders, and *Conversos* who had not executed their conversion to the full, would be tried, burned, or hanged.

I loved my work and had been blessed with the task of searching out thieves, bigamists, adulterers, heretics, sinners and sorcerers who do the work of the devil. The hand of the Lord will lie heavy upon those who stray from His Law. They will suffer for their sins. This was work I was good at, for I knew that I was the instrument of the Lord.

With the taste of anticipation in my mouth, I considered my forthcoming duties, and what they would entail.

I had worked hard and now I was the sole Inquisitor in this area, and the powers invested in me were manifold.

I was confident in my team. My police force and my preaching monks would search out the sinful so that I could do my work.

Local taxes had been increased so we could afford to pluck out the enemies of faith and country and set up the courts to deal with them.

It is a big responsibility but I vowed to bring the Lord to these people.

My work here is just beginning!

CHAPTER 6
Summoned to the City

EVANGELINA

The black-clad monks arrived late in the day as we were preparing supper and the sun was going down.

Abbess Alissa was informed that they were here, with orders from the new Inquisitor. He had arrived the previous month to search out heretics.

Everyone from the convents, monasteries and outlying farms was to be in Cuenca city the following day. The new Inquisitor had demanded that we all be gathered together in the city to be questioned.

"Why would they want to question us? About what?" asked Sister Francesca.

A question we all wanted to ask.

"We have nothing to fear," said our Abbess. "They are looking for sinners, sorcerers, and heretics, Jews and Moors. There are new laws to deal with those not practising the Faith, and I suppose they have come to deal with that."

The next morning we set off. Abbess Alissa took the lead, her skirts lifting the dry dust along the pathway down to the river that led from Palomera to Cuenca city. She had asked us to pray and sing along the way, as the journey would take most of the morning. Sister Francesca, our chorister, led us and we sang and hummed all the hymns we knew. We'd set off early and were soon joined by others summoned to the city, including farmers and the monks from La Melgosa. All but the very infirm walked across the hills and valleys to the deep gorge that surrounded Cuenca. We passed the caves cut into the rock where the poor lived.

Donkeys, horses and people vied for space on the long uphill path to the city. The limestone walkways narrowed as we climbed, so it was slow going. By the time we reached the city centre, the sun was high in the sky.

Donna-Marie held my hand and told me not to worry.

"These things happen occasionally, according to the whim of the bishops, the nobles or the sovereigns," she explained as we huffed and puffed up the last alleyway. "We have nothing to fear. I expect the new Inquisitor wants to make his presence known. I am sure he will not bother us."

We were all hot and thirsty so we went first to the convent house 'Giraldo' in the Calle San Pedro where six of our sisterhood lived and worked. They stayed in the town to work on the tapestries for the new apse aisle planned for the 'Our Lady of Grace and Santa Julian' cathedral. The sisters were famous for their needlework, and Sister Monica-Alma had been there for many years. She welcomed us with drinks and fruit, and told us all she knew about the new Inquisitor and his searches for sinners. It wasn't much, and didn't make us feel any easier about being there. She told us of other Inquisitors who had been before and not been accepted, even to the point of being murdered, but that was many years ago, she assured us.

As we left the convent house, the black-clad preaching monks and the Santa Hermandad, distinctive in their green and yellow, were gathering everyone together from the villages and towns, directing them toward the churches, halls and city squares where all were expected to listen to the sermons.

Everyone was 'persuaded' to attend.

The Holy Brotherhood sent us up the steep Calle San Pedro to the new courthouse at the top of the hill. We ended up standing with groups of weavers and spinners outside their workplace opposite the courthouse steps.

A tall, hooded monk, all in black, stood in the centre of the steps with his arms in the air, waiting for silence. Several others stood around, watching the noisy crowd as if to search out anyone who was not attending or looked guilty.

Eventually the great masses of people settled and were quiet.

On the steps of the courthouse, tables were set up. Scribes sat waiting for instructions, and attendance was being recorded. At the centre stood a darkly handsome, velvet-clad man with small beady eyes that swept through the crowd, occasionally stopping to point out someone to his scribes, who then summoned a member of the Santa Hermandad to bring that person forward.

So, this was the new Inquisitor.

I held tightly onto Donna-Marie's hand, and little Isabelle had her hands together as if in prayer waiting for the next sermon. She wasn't afraid. Why was I? Had I not led an exemplary life since being at the convent? Possibly now, but not in the first few months, when I screamed and shouted when told what to do, stole extra food or hid during prayers.

That was over two years ago. But, I was not a believer. If there were a God, He would know for sure that I was a sinner.

"Good people of Cuenca, God is everywhere and He sees your sins." The booming voice of the monk on the steps was confirming my fear. "We travel here to help you, charged with the duty of ending the devil's work in this place. Let us pray to Him that observeth every misdeed and passeth judgment. Guide us today so that we may restore piety to the city of Cuenca. Root out evil and those who support it. Drive out the demons of sorcery, treachery, those lacking in faith, and all mortal sin. Who will be the first?"

He stopped for a moment and looked into the crowd, his eyebrows raised in question.

"Who will be saved? If you confess and repent *you will be saved* from the burning fires, from the pain, the torment of hell."

He paused for effect, dropped his eyes as if in thought, and then continued with a raised voice.

"We have had too much plague and pestilence, too much sickness, and it is because of YOUR SINS!"

He shouted this pointing to the crowd, picking out an occasional face or a posturing youth who appeared not to be listening. I saw an old woman, the cook from the Castillo de Belmonte, crying as she was being questioned, and marched away out of sight minutes later.

The friars were skilfully inflaming the crowds.

Two others stood outside the 'Our Lady of Grace' cathedral, and others in the new courtyard of the 'San Miguel Church', their voices echoing around the city.

"It is in your own hands. Cast out your demons. Know that we have around us those who divide our faith. God demands that everyone is to break relationship with anyone who does not keep the Holy Laws or who are false Christians. They pervert our society. Especially the Jews, they and they alone are responsible for killing the Son," he said, exploiting the fear of everyone with his words.

"Your sins bring down the wrath of God, your sins bring all the unfortunates, the bad crops, the death of your herds. This is the work of the devil... the devil in YOU. Cast him away and confess," they urged. "The faithful must repent their sins and change their ways."

I dared not move for my body was shaking so uncontrollably that I felt I should fall if I did so. This was no ordinary fear, but a crippling, stomach-churning, sour terror.

How could any divine Creator test his subjects so? Killing them and tormenting them, leaving them hungry or in pain? Who would create a world where all pleasure was a sin? I was terrified that at that moment someone would read my mind, someone would discover what a heathen I really was.

CHAPTER 7
Eternal Fires of Hell

EVANGELINA
In Burriana, I had paused once or twice to listen to the preaching monks, but little they said affected me, as I was far more afraid of Lendos's belt and my mother's fist than the devil.

But that day, such was my fear that I would answer anything they wanted. I would lie, pretend, and accept that I could change nothing.

The green-coated men walked amongst the crowd, taking names and sending others to be questioned. Without warning, one walked to where we stood. I held my breath as I thought that he had come to take me, but he pushed me aside and motioned for Donna-Marie to go forward. I reached out and held her hand tightly but she turned, releasing me, and said quietly, "Stay with Abbess Alissa."

Before I knew it, she was taken into the main hall where the questioning was being conducted.

"Let us pray," said the friar.

I stared wildly around the throng of people, seeing all heads bowed. Isabelle had dropped to her knees. Most were quietly hushed with the impact of the words that echoed around us.

"Who shall provide the first testimony? Who will redeem himself?"

I stayed watching the doorway through which Donna-Marie had been taken. Others pushed around me but I could not turn my eyes away. Many advanced, some whispering and fearful, others willingly stepping forward to denounce or confess their sins to be absolved or punished.

The sermons had stirred the crowd to believe that it was their sins or those of neighbours, in-laws, friends or untrustworthy spouses that were the cause of their misfortunes, and I could hear shouts and denials and a few fights.

Like a statue, I waited whilst the sun dropped and the heat of the day disappeared.

Time stood still, my fingers were pressed together and my lips trembled. The crowd slowly dispersed and diminished until just a few were left. Isabelle took my hand and tried to pull me down the hill and back toward the path to the city gates.

As I reluctantly turned to walk with the others, a hand took me by the elbow. I was so startled that I almost fell, so weak in that moment. I thought with relief that it was Donna-Marie, but the grip increased and I found myself being led toward the courthouse door. The tall, green-coated soldier pushed me up the steps past the scribes and monks, through the great hall and into a panelled room.

There he stood, our velvet-clad Inquisitor. At the desk a scribe, quill poised. I dared not raise my head.

"I am Leopoldo Sanchez and I will be asking the questions. Do you understand?" I could feel his breath as he leaned over me, his lips were close to my ear and I managed to nod.

"What is your name, Sister?"

"I am Evangelina, a novice. I have not yet taken my vows," I whispered.

"Señorita, do you know the woman Donna-Marie, who is accused?" I nodded again. Accused? Of what could Donna-Marie be accused? It is I that should be accused. I am the unbeliever.

"How well do you know her?"

I was shaking so hard that my throat was closing, but I replied, "Er... I work with her, Excellency."

"Is that all? And do you help her with her potions? Do you know of her spells and charms? Her sorcery? Her pact with the devil? If you unduly defend a sorceress, you become part of that heresy. Who would place themselves in that position? Would you? Anyone who sees sin and does not denounce it will burn in the eternal fires of Hell."

His voice lifted and bounced through my head like a physical pain.

"Do you understand what I am saying? It is even worse to tolerate sin around you than to commit it. God will forgive those who commit the sins but not those who tolerate it. No forgiveness for them... None!"

I stiffened, took a deep breath, and replied, "I know of no sin, Excellency."

Eternal fires of Hell? I imagined the pain, the agony of heat. I cannot go there. I will not. I will say anything he wants, but no hell, no fires, no heat. My legs shook and I was shrinking into a quivering ball of fear.

I would be found guilty too if I did not denounce her, my friend, my beloved sister. I could say nothing that would help her. He believed that she was guilty already. The Donna-Marie of whom he spoke did not exist; she did not in any way resemble the picture of her that he was painting to me.

Terror coursed through my body. I could not look into his face or listen to his words so I studied the stone floor. It was shiny from the footfalls of many, and in the tiny cracks dried leaves and dirt were deeply encrusted. I kept my eyes resolutely lowered and tried to think, to concentrate on the many who had walked this way through the years, the suns and moons that had passed. I did not want to hear his words. I could not.

"... honour to be God's servant... an earthly hand to do his divine... tell the truth... Donna-Marie cannot be... others... those who repent will be saved..."

He stopped talking and stood in front of me, waiting. As I lifted my eyes I was looking directly into his face. Although I had never seen this man before, a dart of recognition flashed through my thoughts. I knew him. How could I? It shook me because I knew that I had never set eyes on him prior to this day. I could feel a sense of familiarity in the marrow of my bones. I blinked hard and, still gazing at him, my terror disappeared and I was no longer shaking.

He was a handsome man, but his nose and mouth were large. He was not tall, but had a rigid, powerfully built body that he held upright with his chin tilted down so that he looked down his nose. His long black hair was tied back and mostly covered with a round, stiff cap. His black velvet robes trailed the ground. But it was his eyes that haunted me, full of light and shadow and yet so dark and deep that something in my heart responded to the mystery within them. My mind felt hazy and my memory obscured.

He stared at me for a moment and then recoiled as if he too recognised me. He turned quickly away, and then returned to stare at me. This time I kept my eyes fixed on him and he moved quickly past me to another novice that had been brought in behind me.

I was allowed to leave, but I was told to be aware that there would be further questioning. I was sure of that too.

CHAPTER 8
The Pleasures of the Task

LEOPOLDO
The candles flickered while I waited, the walls of the cellar lit and faded as the flames danced. The drip, drip of water somewhere in the recesses of the deep dungeon added to the irritation. In the far dark corners of the room hung two bodies, tied with their arms behind them and weights on their feet so that their shoulders had dislocated, one unconscious and one moaning hoarsely.

On the far side of the room, with a desk and a tiny candle, sat José Fernandez, the scribe. I watched him as he waited quietly. He never spoke or gave any indications of any personal feelings and recorded exactly what he was told. He had white, spongy skin from a lifetime spent in the gloom of the castle dungeons and cells. His job was solely to write the confessions to ensure record of guilt for the courts.

I was excited and my heart was thumping in anticipation, but my head hurt and interfered with my thoughts. A continual long pain with stabbing highlights that reached a pitch of such great torment that, at times, I wanted to tear out my hair or beat my head against the wall. Of late, this affliction had increased so that there were days when it was hard to focus my eyes or even walk in a straight line.

I took a deep breath, which calmed my excitement and the increasing nausea. I hated to lose control. I liked to take my time, everything to build slowly, to see them hold out as long as possible, so that I could extract every single drop of pleasure from their pain. Especially the women!

The climax was their confession, a split second of exquisite elation. I always had a plan. I worked to achieve that final perfection. Experience had shown me that every stage releases its own particular flavour, its own particular pleasure. From the first moment of arrest, to that spirit-lifting moment of final capitulation, the spectrum of sensuality supplied by the execution of my perfect planning.

"Bring her in, Dunkan," I said.

Dunkan, the most experienced and toughest member of the Holy Brotherhood, pushed Sister Donna-Marie into the dimly lit room. The walls were thick and curved so that screams would bounce back into the room, rather than be heard from outside.

I looked at the girl brought before me, I guessed her to be about twenty-five years, perhaps more. My men had taken her that morning and charged her with sins against the Holy Church. Sister Donna-Marie was pretty, not so very young as I had first thought when I looked at her closely. Perhaps nearer thirty-five? Nuns do keep their youthful looks. Were not their lives easy? I noticed that her hands were rough and work-worn, and glanced at the written information that I had about her. Ah, she was in charge of the convent gardens and orchards. She grew vegetables and herbs, as well as the strange plants that she used to make her spells and potions.

It had been during an interrogation of a fat peasant woman that we had learned of Sister Donna-Marie's ministering to the locals with her special touch and healing herbs, her ungodly chants and suggestions of nature as a way of healing, rather than prayer and dedication.

My friar Pedro-Anton had been questioning all the villagers, and it seemed that Sister Donna-Marie had been practising her black arts for some considerable time.

An old man had confessed to using her potions for his wheezing chest, and his wife, when questioned, had told them that they made her husband 'frisky'. Another woman allowed Sister Donna-Marie to give her a potion for her nightmares and melancholy, and told her that she could see a better life ahead for her and her children.

It is not possible for her to foresee. We believers know

that goes against the Church. Only those vested with Holy ordination have the power. She has the devil working within her.

Today I will enjoy her pain, and by tomorrow she will admit her sins and eventually be tried for sorcery.

I will get the other one too, the little novice girl who helped her at the convent. She'd stayed in my head, her violet eyes and dark good looks touched a knowing chord somewhere deep within me. The great wave of apprehension that had swept through me as she lifted her head, and looked at me so accusingly, had for a moment confused me. But I would deal with her. I had no doubt that she too has been involved. Evil had been at work in that place.

The woman, Donna-Marie, showed no fear. She was smiling.

How could she smile at a time like this?

"Ah, so you are not afraid, Donna-Marie? You will be here until you confess, you know. No one is coming to help you. Not today, nor tomorrow, not at all, any time."

"No, I am not afraid," she replied quietly. "I have done no wrong. My Lord will protect me for He knows the truth."

I was so disgusted. Her Lord! Her Lord was indeed the devil.

Hurt her! whispered the demon in my brain. *Enjoy it, and make her pay.* I felt my nerves tingle and trickle along my spine.

"What is it you do, Donna-Marie? Potions and silly spells for the weak-minded? Do you interfere with what God intends?"

It was hard to read her expression. She lifted her shoulders as I sneered at her and then dropped her head so that I could not see her face.

"You dare to think that your Lord will protect you from your sins? That in itself is a sin!" I shouted in her face. "Only if you confess your sins you may be favoured once more in

His eyes. I will make you suffer, for the Devil is your Lord and no other. He has allowed you to believe you can heal. Is that not so?"

"It is nature that heals. I use only those things nature provides," she replied as she lifted her eyes. Her insolence was plain to see, but it excited me.

"God is in everything I use, for He created in nature some form of alleviation for every ill," she added defiantly.

"Indeed, and who showed you these evils?"

"There is no evil in what I do." Her voice quavered slightly. "I learned all I know from my father and his partner, both were respected apothecaries and physicians from Teruel."

"Their names?"

"Alberto Santiago and Abdul bin al Kindi. Both are now gone to their graves. My father was old and Abdul died in an accident. Now, may I return to the convent as I have work to do?"

"God is the only physician because *He* is divine. You are here to confess."

She didn't move or flinch at my threat.

After a long pause, I shouted at her. "I know you have sinned! You will be burned as a sorceress if you refuse to admit and repent your sins."

Hurt her... hurt her. I wanted to watch her contorted in pain, begging and confessing.

"Only devotion and prayer and the miracle of the saints can heal." As I said this, I thought of my own pain and the headaches that tormented me. I prayed a great deal and showed my devotion to God by self-flagellation for my sins and I wore the spikes. I had addressed many prayers to Santa Adela, Encratia and Jorge. I had to do more, perhaps go to the El Pillar Basilica in Zaragoza and show my devotion. I knew that my afflictions were a result of the demons that haunted and tormented me. My own sins were great, and I knew that only repentance would reward me. Through my love of our Lord I would be healed. I knew I was a sinner but the Lord would forgive me.

Not so this woman. I had to work harder to seek out the heresy that surrounded us.

"Confess," I urged. "You are a sorceress, are you not?"

The woman lifted her hands toward me, palms upward, showing the smooth hard skin.

"I'm just an ordinary person through whom God works. These hands tend only what our Lord allows. Everything I use, every herb, root or flower is a remedy that comes from nature and the earth, which along with the stars and the heavens were created by Him for us to worship and use."

"You lay your hands upon people and let them believe you can heal them?" I said.

She ignored my question and said confidently, "Compassion, contact, touch can indeed help people to heal. I believe God has chosen to use me in a very special way. If my touch can relieve pain or anxiety, I know it is the Lord who is healing."

"Your Lord is tainted with sin. Your Lord is the Devil. Is it not so?" I let my voice rise.

She hesitated and I could see that she was chastened. "No. It is not so." She sniffed as the tears ran slowly, silently down her pink cheeks.

I was progressing. I leaned toward her and said, "The Inquisition is a delicate and finely tuned procedure. You will be questioned so that you understand that you will be condemned on the evidence that exists. You will be encouraged to tell the truth. Will any defend you?"

"Of course they will! I have helped many people and everyone at the convent will speak for me." Her lip trembled and her face crumpled.

I was pleased. Yes. I was going to break her slowly!

"Ask her again," I said to Dunkan as I picked up the hook

of the strappado that was attached to the ceiling.

I knew that the pleasure I felt was part of my gift from God. I thanked the Lord daily in my prayers that these pleasures were allowed to me because of my given role as the Teacher of Righteousness.

"Do you see these?" Her eyes showed the beginnings of fear as I lifted the hooks towards her. "These I will attach to your wrists. You will be hoisted slowly upward so that your shoulders dislocate."

My excitement increased. I was filled with Holy light at moments like this. It was a great honour to be a servant of our Lord.

If she did not confess, I would start on her devil-working fingers or her seer's eyes. I would get a confession from her and she would be tried and burned, as all sorcerers should be. I knew how to bring each sinner a degree of pain that would make them talk yet keep them conscious and alive. It was not my remit to kill, only to help them confess and repent. The judges in the court would sentence them.

It did not take long: the woman was slight and, although strong-bodied, she could not endure the pain as her arms dislocated from her shoulder joints.

She screamed and cried and was then silent.

To do this work for my Lord was so blessed, and the cries of pain and fear could not affect me, as I knew deep in my heart that it was necessary and honourable. The outcome proved the morality of my actions as nearly all cried out their sins to God and admitted their guilt.

"Mark down every word, José Fernandez. I shall return in an hour," I instructed my scribe. "We must take our time."

The pain in my head was increasing so I left, worrying only about my own pain and the workings of our Lord that I should suffer so.

I went to the church to pray for relief, for lately it had become almost unbearable.

CHAPTER 9
The Trial of Donna-Maria

EVANGELINA
Over the next few days I hardly slept, and eventually we got a message to tell us that Donna-Marie had been charged with sorcery. The Abbess and myself were to give evidence in the court in Cuenca the next day. We had all been praying for our dear friend ever since our return from the city, but to no avail, as the news was the worst we could imagine.

I looked at the tired, lined face of our Mother Abbess who'd cried with us. I prayed and cried until my body was weak and limp. My stomach churned for lack of food as I had not eaten since we had returned to Palomera.

Around us, the convent was in darkness, no candles glowed, other than those in the chapel where we stood. Everyone else had gone to their cells, exhausted, confused and tired from that sad day's offering.

"Come let us rest now and sleep," said Abbess Alissa. "There is nothing we can do."

"Sleep? How can I ever sleep again? How can there be nothing? Where is the Lord, our merciful, loving God, to whom we are all praying? How could he abandon her, let her suffer?" I cried angrily. "I want to kill him, that so-called man of God, the Inquisitor."

"Our order does not allow us to foster anger or a desire for revenge and we must never, never despair of God's mercy," the Abbess replied.

"I can't feel that way. How can you?" I said, full of anger and despair.

"We must keep faith. Come, Angelina." She held my arm as I tried to rise from my knees where I had collapsed in the chapel.

At the courthouse the next day when Abbess Alissa was

questioned, she stood bravely, her hands quietly together, her face lifted to the black-robed friar-judge.

I only had eyes for Donna-Marie, who stood bent and dirty with her face to the floor. Her legs were quivering uncontrollably. Her head was uncovered and her brown hair hung in raggy strands over her face. Her right hand was wrapped in a bloody bandage, and I wept and shuddered as I watched the red liquid pool on the floor at her feet.

Two burly Hermandes were holding her arms to keep her standing. She was almost unrecognisable from the beautiful, loving person that I knew her to be.

Abbess Alissa spoke calmly. "Donna-Marie is no more a sorceress than I am. She has only ever helped people with her medicines, poultices and tisanes. She takes care of those who are ill or grieving. She brought us all relief when the influenza came to us last year and so many were ill with it. She gave everyone the tisanes she had made. Made of God's medicines, pennyroyal and ragwort, it reduced their fevers. Without the intervention of our dispensary mistress, we would have lost not only our Sister Magdalena but the novices Junã and Therese."

"Why did this happen? Was there sin within the walls or within the −?"

"I am not sure I understand your meaning, sir," interrupted the Abbess coolly.

The friar-judge glared at her. "I believe that He is telling us that there is not enough devotion in Santa Hilda, that there should be more prayer, humility, discipline and obedience."

"We celebrate God with all our hearts and souls. There is nowhere more so invested in the glory of our Lord than our convent." Abbess Alissa's eyes blazed. "The art of healing is one of our Lord's greatest gifts, and Donna-Marie's expertise and devotion to her craft enriches all our lives. She is a good person who possesses a great knowledge, which she freely serves. She is a natural healer and blessed with this gift, this gift from God." Her voice lifted. "Do not condemn an innocent for she is doing our Lord's work."

The friar-judge sniffed and, ignoring Abbess Alissa, stared at Donna-Marie. "Who do you think you are? To heal? That is God's work."

Swivelling on his seat, he turned back to our beloved Abbess. "Do you defend this woman, Abbess Alissa?"

"Yes, I do," our Abbess replied as she turned to the crowd who had gathered in the courtroom. "I ask you, citizens of Cuenca. Is this not true? Step forward to be counted those of you whom Donna-Marie has helped, those whom she has released from pain so that we in turn may have her released."

I felt my heart leap in sudden joy that the Abbess had spoken thus of Donna-Marie, even though I saw fear creep into her eyes as no one moved to answer.

"How can you punish such a good woman? Her whole time here has been spent in the service of our Lord. Please, do not do this."

I pressed my hands into fists and prepared to speak, but realised that I was the only one doing so. Everyone else was standing still, their eyes fixed on the black-robed judge.

I wanted to scream out loud that she is my only friend. She is good and kind and loves everyone, especially God. But I was shaking uncontrollably. My stomach cramped so that my legs felt to give way. Is the Lord not merciful? He knows that she has never bewitched anybody as they are suggesting. He must set her free.

"Sit down now, Abbess Alissa," said the judge, waving his hands toward the onlookers. "You see, no one will speak as advocate for her? And we have much evidence of her so-called healing. We have witnesses who have testified against her, and she has confessed during questioning that the devil is behind her work."

Wiping his greasy forehead, he continued, "You must all know that we live and die according to God's mandate. It is His will if we never rise from our sickbed, if we leave this world sooner than we want. It is God's will, and you are blasphemous to think that any other has such power."

He turned again to Donna-Marie. "Do you freely admit to being in concert with the devil and do you understand that you have been found guilty this day of sorcery? Your sins are great; you let innocent people believe that you can heal them. Are there others in consort with your heresy? Do you have accomplices? Are there those in the convent who aspire to your evil or help with it?"

"Sir," whispered Donna-Marie, her voice as thin as a reed, her mouth barely moving. She swallowed hard. "I am guilty of all... all that you speak of. No others. Nobody else... only myself... no others have helped me... I resolve all sin."

I could see the mottled pink of her neck and the blood seeping through the soggy cloth on her hand, which she now held to her breast.

"In that case, there will be no more questions. You are condemned to the flames as all witchery must be eradicated from our midst."

No, no, how could that be?

All around me people gasped and shrank into their own guilt for not defending this woman who had been a comfort to most of them at some time in their lives.

I couldn't breathe. My world had fallen apart in a matter of minutes.

The following day, Donna-Marie and seven other 'sinners' were burned at the stake in the square courtyard outside the courthouse.

CHAPTER 10
A Good Day's Work

LEOPOLDO
I knelt in my chapel and gazed at the great crucifix. It was so beautifully carved that I could see the curves of tender flesh, and feel the pain of our Lord. Perhaps my work would negate my own sin and relieve me of my irksome pain.

I prayed that I would continue to be blessed. I felt satisfied with myself and with the outcome of the trials.

"My good Lord. I pray that you are pleased with me. My days here are reaping rewards and my work gaining a reputation. In your name I will drive out all sin from this place. I will redeem myself in your eyes. I am ready and willing to –"

A cold gust of air interrupted my prayer.

Without warning, a swirling grey mist surrounded my body. My head began to throb, my body trembled, and my self-satisfaction seeped away. Lifting my shaking hands to rub my neck, I felt a weight on my shoulder as if a bony hand had come to rest. And with it a putrid breath and a whispered warning, "Sinner, bad boy, wicked boy. Repent your sins."

Would I never be free of my guilt?

"No. No," I cried. "I have done well. I have been good. Be pleased with me, Mother!"

178

CHAPTER 11
Imprisoned

EVANGELINA

I was so disgusted and ashamed that I had not spoken up for Donna-Marie. My heart was beating fast with the knowledge of what I had failed to do. I hadn't been able to defend my dearest friend. I had let her go to her death and not shouted my love and praise for her. Why hadn't I told them how she had helped people in pain and used only the power of the herbs and her gentle energy? Not spells or witchcraft. My own fear had made me deny her.

A deep loathing of myself surged into my throat and, at that moment, I resolved to somehow revenge her death.

It was very quiet. I sat heavily on one of the pews and stared at the altar. Outside, the weather had grown clement for the time of year, but the chapel was cold. I shivered and lifted my eyes to the great crucifix above the altar. The pain of Jesus Christ was hard to behold, but at that moment I believed it matched my own. We were told that through His sacrifice we were absolved of all sin, given the chance to live again. How could that be true? The words of the messages rattled through my thoughts. How could it be that He had not seen the perfection of Donna-Marie? That He had allowed her to be taken? The agony of Jesus Christ was for nothing... nothing at all if He could allow such wickedness.

In my angry thoughts, I could only repeat my feelings. 'I will avenge my beloved Donna-Marie. I will kill him. How? I do not know but I will find a way.'

Donna-Marie's words came to me then. 'This is a place of harmony and honest worship. We must love our Lord and all his wonders, not love pride or envy, jealousy or anger. Love one's neighbour as oneself and forgive those who sin.'

No. I will kill him. He deserves no love, no forgiveness.

The truth is that forgiveness can only come to those who repent their sins, but he enjoys what he does, he enjoys his power. I will make him pay for his wickedness.

'But, what could I do?' I asked myself over and over.

I knew I would be questioned again. I could deny all knowledge and go to my grave bearing the sin of betrayal, for I would be burdened with it on my conscience forever. Nothing would ever be the same again. *Or*, I could avenge her death and, if I died in the process, so be it. I would join her in her spirit life wherever that might be. Donna-Marie had absolute faith that there were other spheres, other places where we exist in a different form. She told me quietly one evening that other beings helped and guided her. She called them her angels.

My resolve grew and a tight knot of hatred began to form in my soul. I *would* find a way. My gut was so twisted into knots of anger that it was hard to stand and walk upright.

Later, I heard that in six days' time I would be questioned again. I was to be back at the courthouse, where five others and myself would be held until we could be interrogated.

That night, sitting on my hard cot and holding my tear-stained blanket to my face, I was cold and shivering. I had bitten my bottom lip so savagely that I had drawn blood, which now dripped onto my soggy blanket.

Tucking my legs under myself, I desperately tried to imagine what I could do. How I could kill the dark-eyed Inquisitor who had taken my friend.

I leaned back against the pillows, and stretched and smoothed my softly rounded curves. My breasts were large and firm, my skin once drab, now smooth and clear. Two years of Donna-Marie's loving care, good food, dry clothes and honest work had expanded the flesh on my bones. Perhaps these were my weapons?

Was this an ordinary man? Did this fiend have a heart or any feelings at all? I would find out!

I had not been into the garden since the day in court. I was amazed at how quickly it lifted my spirits to be outside amongst the plants, away from the chapel and my Sisters with their endless, useless prayers. It would make no difference now.

I felt the soft wind upon my face and strengthened my resolve.

I thought about the early days at the nunnery when everyone else there had given up trying to make me behave, attend the services, and get on with life without screaming abuse when I was told what to do. My dirty habits and foul language were a constant torment to everyone at the convent. I had really let loose after Brother Matias had left, until I realised that to eat I had to work. My early life had been full of running, fighting, arguments and cursing, and sex of course. When food was available it was gobbled before anyone else could take it.

To be a novice had certain duties, and the endless prayer and silence was something I found hard to bear. It was only Donna-Marie who had tamed me with her loving counsel. She often just led me to the garden with its beautiful aromas and colours and talked softly about the wonders that nature held. She always managed to calm me and convince me of my right to be there.

I wondered now whether I could remember all that she had taught me.

I automatically pulled a few weeds and tied a few branches whilst considering what I knew. Did I know enough to use the magic of the plants to wreak my revenge? If so, how could I gain access to the man?

The convent garden looked deserted and abandoned. It would never again be a tranquil place for me. There were so many memories of Donna-Marie there, as she skilfully twisted the twine around a handful of herbs and flowers, wrapped the fruit and vegetables for the kitchens or urged the weeds away from her precious plants.

I had never ceased to wonder at her knowledge, so I pledged that I would take time to restore it and try to continue the learning that I had gained so willingly. I would study the drawings and the description of each plant's curative powers and contra-indications so that I could use God's own miracles to kill or cure as I saw fit.

I walked around the beds of flowers and the hundreds of herbs and medicinal shrubs, letting my fingers drift through the rosemary, basil, calendula and hellebore.

Hellebore...? What had I learned of that? It could purge and cleanse, but too much root would poison. Others, like the tall lemon balm, were gentle and calming, but as I moved toward the surrounding wall, I noticed the Mandragora sitting against the walls like a fat, round rosette, the tiny fruit nestling in its centre. What was it that she had told me about its fruit? They could excite, they were known to be sexually intoxicating.

That is what she inferred, was it not? I would collect and dry the little fruit and store them carefully.

In the corner, a large bush of henbane with its creamy flowers and black centres, another of the healing or harmful plants I knew, but its uses evaded me.

I collected the hessian bag with the garden tools from the rear of the dispensary and made my way back. Soon I was immersed in the staking, pruning, deadheading and harvesting of our precious garden. It was early, so I cut the calendula heads that would be soaked in olive oil to make a healing balm for rashes, wounds and pustules. The basil and pennyroyal had gone to seed so I collected the tiny seeds and carefully labelled each. I took a few cuttings to propagate under some glass in our storeroom. We had used most of our stock when the wheezing and coughing of the winter had started.

A small yellow butterfly paused for a moment on the

purple spikes of lavender where the bees were busy collecting their nectar. It calmed my throbbing impatience as I watched these tiny creatures going about their business.

I moved to the Mandragora and picked the little apple-like fruits, carefully wrapping them. I dug some of the root too, and then moved on to the hellebore. I packaged them separately and carefully labelled them, so that I could identify them with ease.

As my hands worked, I searched my memory for all that I could remember of the plants that could be deadly.

Donna-Marie had taught me my letters so that I could read the labels of our jars and potions. I was a fast learner, but still could not read as well as Isabelle, who had long since surpassed me. I would persevere with my labelling and study all the notes that Donna-Marie had made in her little book of scripts and recipes. She had illustrated many of the things we used, so I could easily identify most of our stores.

I would study everything carefully, so that when the opportunity arose, I would be ready.

As I expected, I was summoned to give evidence of my involvement with Donna-Marie, and returned to the same room and the same questions.

The Inquisitor stood before me but, now that my beloved friend was gone, I was less afraid and my resolve for revenge had strengthened. I would lie, cheat, steal and kill if I had to. I kept my eyes down and my hands together so that he would imagine my respect.

"As a novice were you assigned to the dispensary Sister known as Donna-Marie?" Leopoldo Sanchez asked me.

"I was, your Excellency."

"Did your duties involve mixing the spells?"

"No, I only brought from the garden what she asked for. Much of my time was spent outside tending the plants. I know little of what she used."

"But did you not accompany her on her visits to patients and families?"

"Oh yes," I said as I lifted my eyes to him purposefully. I would begin my deception. "We have a tedious life, you know, and I like to get out to visit people, especially if they have children. You see, I was never really meant for convent life. I would like to care for little ones and introduce them to the love of God. I come from a large devout family; my father served the Church with tireless love and devotion. We believed in the power of prayer and, as a family, kept the strict laws of our Holy Church. Sadly, all my family were taken in the plague many years ago, so that is how I came to Palomera."

I lied so easily. I let my voice quiver and imagined it so well that I managed to bring tears to my eyes. Pausing for a moment, I watched him from the side of my eye. He had a look of surprised amazement and wariness... somehow as if he had not understood.

He turned his back on me.

I continued, sniffing loudly. "I have no wish to take the veil. I was thinking that I would leave the convent soon and work with the children of our parish. I have learned to read and write, and I can cook well and, of course, I know much about God's plants." I hesitated for a moment as he turned toward me again. "I can make tisanes and poultices and know which plants can reduce a fever or help pain."

Had he smiled or had I only imagined it? He walked around and stood behind me so that I could not see his expression. When he finally spoke, his voice was softer, but no less lethal.

"So, you deny all knowledge of the evil being perpetrated within your convent? No idea that the Sister with whom you worked was casting spells?"

"No, none at all," I lied, "I would not be party to anything that goes against the laws of our Lord."

"Even though you know of these medicinal skills?"

"I know only what has been used to help, not cure... only our Lord can cure."

I felt the Inquisitor's grip tighten on my shoulder and my heart missed a beat.

Now, I thought, show him your intent. I was sure I could seduce him into believing me.

I lifted my hand and placed it on top of his. He released me and pulled away in surprise. I turned slowly towards him, reaching again for his hand and lowering my head, raising it to my mouth I kissed his fingertips. He pulled his hand away sharply and wiped his fingers across the front of his cloak. His eyes were confused, so I dropped to my knees.

"Excellency, I apologise to you most sincerely if I have offended you, but you are so... so..." I forced my lips to tremble and tears to spring to my eyes. "I cannot help myself. I admire you so, you are good and noble, and you are ridding this place of evil beyond words. Our faith must be protected and you are proving it can be done." I kept my eyes down as I said this, but I could feel his tension.

"You..." He stopped and yanked the door open. "Cranto!" He yelled. "Get her out of here now. But keep her until I can question her again."

Oh, excellent, I thought. He was nervous already. I will bide my time.

Cranto lifted me to my feet and pulled me roughly toward the door but I was sure now. I had felt the heat rise in the Inquisitor as I kissed his fingers. He could not disguise it. He was a man after all!

I must get him to trust me so that I could get close to him.

CHAPTER 12
Weakening

LEOPOLDO

How dare she? She thinks she can play with me.

My thoughts ran on. How insolent she is!

I will teach her humility.

What was I thinking? Ah, yes. I want to see her again. Just to look into her eyes made something deep inside me spring to life. She roused in me a feeling that I had never before experienced. She thought me offended but in reality I was entranced. As her lips had touched my fingertips, I was transported. I know I should not desire her, but I will confess and repent for the sins of the flesh. I must cast out these sinful thoughts.

The words of my masters echoed through my mind. 'Women are the ultimate sin... It is through them that we have lost our way.'

My father agreed and encouraged me to study and read, and become more knowledgeable about the Teachings, the philosophy and theology of the Dominican order.

"It will be good for you, Leopoldo, and keep you busy and away from women."

"Why, Father?"

"Because women are naturally wicked and reduce a man to do things against his better nature. Wickedness is one of the natural illnesses that mankind is born with, as a result of the original sin," he told me in a whisper. "Avarice, ignorance and an inability to do good are the others, but worst of all is a woman."

I will go to confession. I will put on my cilice to remind myself that I must bring my body into subjection.

My body must be chastised.

CHAPTER 13
Biding My Time

EVANGELINA

As I was dragged away, I was afraid and thought perhaps I would not see him again – that I might not get any chance to convince him of my innocence and prevail on his goodwill.

Perhaps he hadn't given me another thought... but I remembered his look and knew that there was something about me that intrigued him. I had felt the strength of his reaction, his heat, and his confusion.

I felt it too, emanating from myself.

I was bemused by my feelings of knowing him, but that gave me confidence in a strange way, as if we were playing out a long-forgotten scene. In my heart I knew he would release me, but I knew not when or what would happen then.

I was taken to a disgusting cell that stank worse than the gutters of Valencia. The floor was bare concrete with a variety of filthy and worn straw-filled pallets pushed against the back wall. The two female occupants, my cellmates, smelled as I imagined a dead body would, but they held out their hands to lift me from the floor where Cranto had thrown me.

The slop bucket had overflowed, so the floor was wet and streaked with excretion. My habit trailed in the mess and, as I stood, I was reminded of my childhood and the filth and neglect I had known then. I was not going to be deterred in my resolve by stink and filth. I had known worse.

There was a tiny slit of light high up on the wall, which threw a streak of light across the area just in front of the heavy, studded door. I could hardly breathe at first but pulled myself upright and introduced myself.

"I am Lina. I will not be here long," I said, with a boldness

I did not feel.

"Oh really, my little lovely. I wish I could say the same," answered the twisted, toothless woman holding my arm. I wiped my hands down my habit and surveyed my temporary dwelling place.

"No. I am to be questioned again and I will be released."

I had lain in that cold smelly cell for two days with nothing but hard bread and water, allowing my intent to expand and harden so that I would do anything to wreak my revenge. I would act the innocent, I would beg or suffer, but I would not give up.

The two other inhabitants, Irma and Eleanor, were pushed together against the far damp walls. Both were haggard and of undefinable ages. Neither knew what their crime was, or why they had been forgotten and left in these filthy dungeons.

I listened to the women as they told me their stories. Irma had had both her legs broken and she could only shuffle painfully around the cell. Neither had been set properly, so they both bent the same way. She thought that she had been a whore, but would not have been imprisoned for that, as both the Sovereignty and the Church allowed fallen women to ply their trade. It was considered an asset to society to prevent adultery and unnatural practices. Irma laughed as she explained that she had been told that earthly laws could not punish them and that they would suffer for their sins when they met their Maker.

"I guess I must have done something that I can be punished for," Irma said. "But I can't remember what."

They had both been there for many years, and the younger of the two, Eleanor, had given birth to a child, which had been immediately taken from her, but she couldn't remember how long ago that had happened. They were both sad and miserable, seeing no future for themselves at all. I, on the other hand, had big plans for the future.

Somehow.... I would get my revenge on that bullyboy sadist, but I would take my time. Watch and wait and, if I die, I will do my best to take him with me. I determined he would pay for what he had done.

I sat on one of the smelly pallets and made myself another promise. When I get out of here, I thought, I will find a way of getting these poor women out too.

Time passed and, for the first time, I wondered whether I was being overconfident and I too would be forgotten. I could not let it be so. I concentrated on the reaction he'd had to my touch, and prayed.

'No... No, I did not pray. I did not know to whom I should do so. My goddess was now revenge; that, and that alone, would serve me.'

CHAPTER 14
Desire

LEOPOLDO

I followed the dark, damp corridors where the lanterns on the slimy stonewalls cast an eerie glow, flowing, moving shadows into every corner.

The dirty monotony was broken only by an occasional heavy door, locked and bolted and studded with pitted iron. I heard an odd muffled groan and crying from inside and wondered what crimes the inhabitants were guilty of.

This place was used for all manner of prisoners: thieves, adulterers and murderers, as well as heretics.

To find her cell, I bypassed the guards and descended into the gloom, just to take another look at her. I needed to see her again. Why I did not know. She doesn't look like anyone I know or care about and yet... The question ran rings around my mind. Why do I want to do this? Why do I want to see her?

Hurt her, hurt her, cried the beating rhythm of the demon in my head. That will stop this... softness, this desire to protect her. Hurt her. No. I knew I couldn't. There was something so intensely familiar about her. Those eyes haunted me. Every time I looked into them I was overcome with a searing emotion, as if my stomach was being pulled from me. The intense nausea and headache increased with the feelings. It confused and irritated me. What I really wanted was to protect her.

Protect her? From what? From me?

She wasn't even the greatest beauty. She was small and dark and only vaguely pretty. She held me with her eyes, deep violet-blue pools and almond-shaped, innocent yet with a hint of knowing too. Each time she looked at me, her gaze transported me to another place and unfamiliar emotions sprang toward me as if from some deep memory that I couldn't quite reconstruct.

I knew that she was held at the furthest end of the dark corridor as all the cells were being used. An unusually busy time of course, since King Ferdinand and Queen Isabella of Castile had announced the cleansing.

I placed my eye to the slit in her cell door. I could see little of her, but as my eyes adjusted to the dark, I gasped. She was stretched out across a straw pallet, her legs apart, and her smooth bare arms above her head. Her habit lay across her body, only barely covering her breasts, which were large and white, and firm. Her lower region was exposed to me as I panted behind the door. She sighed and turned, pulling her legs upwards and curving her bottom towards me. I desperately wanted to turn away but I couldn't. Disgust and desire were running in equal measure through my veins.

A searing pain shot through the left side of my head. The agony was unspeakable. I was shaking with the effort of staying upright.

Only as the pain receded could I move cautiously away from the door.

CHAPTER 15
Release

EVANGELINA
I had known he was outside watching me. I had curved my body as provocatively as I could and pushed my bottom forward in full view. I'd positioned my pallet close to the door even though the slop pot placed at the side of the grill was still stinking and foul. I could hear his breathing and he gasped quietly. My hope quickened, but he did not enter or speak.

I turned to a seated position and lifted my eyes to the slit in the door. I could see nothing at all as it was dark, but I could hear him as he shuffled quickly away.

Later that same day, I was hauled out of the cell, along the gloomy passageways to wait for the dark-eyed Inquisitor, Leopoldo Sanchez. I was given a wet cloth to wipe my grimy hands and face. It seemed pointless as I stank like a sewage ditch, but I wiped my face and ran my slightly cleaner fingers through my hair. I raised my head and stood tall.

When he arrived, he looked paler than I remembered, and his eyes were glazed and watery. He did not look at me, but walked to the window and looked out across the valley behind the courthouse.

"I will not detain you any longer. All the inquiries that have been made about you have convinced me that you were indeed only an assistant to the witch, and know little of her spells and potions. I expect to hear no further reports, so you may leave."

"Ah," I made a small sound.

"We will provide accompaniment back to the convent if you require."

"No, your Excellency. I require only a clean dress," I

answered with as much dignity as I could, "but I do have another request."

"Do you?"

"Yes, Sire. Those two women, Eleanor and Irma, who are down in that cell have no idea why they are there, and seem to have been forgotten. I wonder, Sire, whether it would be possible for you to enquire into their sentences. I would like to help them reach our Lord and perhaps lead useful lives again."

I was amazed at my own audacity, but I was unafraid, and, now that I was free, my resolve had strengthened yet again.

He turned then, a look of sheer astonishment on his face. But once again he recoiled when he looked into my eyes. It was as if I had not only shocked him but also frightened him.

CHAPTER 16
Tempted

LEOPOLDO

My Lord God, Father, I cannot fathom Thy truth. What is it you desire of me? Why am I tempted by the Devil?

"In nomine Patris et Filii et Spiritus Sancti," I prayed.

My knees hurt as I bent before the altar, and the metal cilice on my thighs and arms cut deeply so that the pain reminded me yet again to bring my body into subjection.

"See how I suffer for my sins, oh Lord. I must pay penance for my desires."

Over the years, Christ's naked, torn body had become more familiar to me than my own. The great crucifix in the chapel, so beautifully carved that I could see the tender flesh and feel the sting of the thorns as they penetrated the softness of our Lord's forehead. There was His body with His blood seeping from His tormented flesh. Iron nails through skin and bones, the screaming sinews taking His weight.

I twisted the cilice and pressed on the sores from my recent flagellation. How sweet was the pain, sweeter than a lover's caress? Why would I question? I must suffer as Christ suffered, I must link with my Saviour, feel His pain and know His glory.

My heart cramped with savage joy as I concentrated on my agony, so intense that a dazzling brightness surrounded me.

For what purpose? Was I becoming soft? I needed to keep my edge to do this job and seek out the sinners. I had no room for sentiment.

My thoughts suddenly changed direction. I was gazing into her eyes. Those eyes, with a softness that brought all things about life into focus. Now my heart was bursting with something I could not recognise. All that I knew from somewhere in the depth of my consciousness was surfacing. Feelings held close and locked safely away pushed a pathway into my thoughts. What was the connection that I felt so deeply? It was as if I was listening to my own self, my own thoughts, though they were not recognisable as mine. But I felt them so intensely that they must have come from somewhere.

Another dimension of myself perhaps?

CHAPTER 17
Excitement or Death

EVANGELINA

Each day I missed Donna-Marie more and more. Everything I knew was from her teachings and her loving attention.

I read and re-read every word that she had written and tried to remember everything she had taught me. I made notes of my own and collected more seeds, roots and bark. I cut, chopped, and mixed different ingredients and practised making balms and tisanes. I stored and labelled everything carefully, making precise notes as I went.

I couldn't get out of my head what I knew of the Mandragora. Of all the plants that are grown here, the Mandragora had the most valuable uses, both as an aphrodisiac and as a poison. For excitement or death!

According to Donna-Marie's little scrolls and references, great care must be taken with the dosage as it is useful for pain relief but, as it does not have a strong taste, it is easy to overdose. This could be the most useful of all our collection. I would guard it carefully, as it may take a long time to be able to make use of it as I imagined I could.

Since I had returned to the convent, my only thought has been to go back to Cuenca and find some way to see him again.

How could I gain access to him? How could I become part of his life? I knew I could not if I stayed in Santa Hilda and, even being unsure of what to do, I knew I had to return to the city.

"I cannot stay here, Mother Abbess, I am sorry," I told her when I had decided to definitely leave. "I rejoice in the sustenance and love that this place has brought to my life, but I must leave. To me, Donna-Marie was a living saint and I can no longer stay here without her. There are things I need to do."

I glanced at Abbess Alissa who had calmly folded her hands together and dropped her eyes to the floor. I knew she too missed Donna-Marie.

"I will continue my studies of the plants that God has given us. I will work for the good of others always and fulfil my duty to Our Lord Jesus Christ in humility and obedience." I said this with my tongue in my cheek as I had other intentions for the use of my little store of Mandragora and hellebore roots.

The novice-mistress Sister Magdalena glared at me, her undisguised disapproval making it clear that she believed punishment and prayer would be the answer for this rebellious novice.

With a cluck of impatience, she said, "Our Lord will be displeased to lose one of his future brides. All you need is time to mourn, and prayer will relieve the pain of your loss."

"Sweet Evangelina," Abbess Alissa's voice was soft and gentle. "You will, I know, be feeling the loss of Donna-Marie more acutely than the rest of us. She was a mother to you. Come, let us go to the chapel, pray, and ask for God's advice. We must ask for peace as we live through this together. You will need the support of everyone here."

Her kindness silenced me faster than any rebuke could have done, but my mind was made up. I would leave and find a way to wreak my revenge.

I silently shook my head and turned to leave, but Abbess Alissa put out a hand and held me still for a moment. "Would you like to go to the Convento de Giraldo in Cuenca and learn the art of needlework with Sister Monica-Alma? I am sure I can arrange it, only if you wish, of course. You will not be confined as you are here and you will be able to work in the community and continue with your studies. You must eat, child, and to do that you need a job to earn money. If you go to Cuenca as a young girl without a habit and nowhere to live, who knows what will become of you."

I nodded, delighted at the suggestion. That would be perfect for me. I would be closer to the Inquisitor. I could continue with my plans.

"God bless you and keep you safe," I heard Sister Magdalena whisper.

"I will only ask of you," the Abbess continued, "that you instruct novice Constanza on the care of the garden. She has shown an interest and is willing to take over the responsibility for the planting and harvesting. As you now know so much about the medicinal uses of the herbs and flowers, perhaps you might like to continue to come occasionally and oversee that area of the garden?"

What a delight for me to hear! I could not have asked for more. I would be able to harvest what I needed at the right time of year, so I thanked Abbess Alissa. I knew that I would indeed be better off in the town where I could work in the community and have the support of the Convento de Giraldo where there was more emphasis on local care than the endless, useless prayers here.

I could not express the hatred that was boiling within my soul for vengeance to anyone, least of all Abbess Alissa. Even though I had no idea how I was going to gain access to the Inquisitor's life, or how I could utilise or administer my intent, I was still determined.

I did not believe in the God of love. If He existed, He would help me rid the world of this injustice, I was sure.

"But I will praise Thee, My Lord, with my whole heart. I will, oh how I will, if I can avenge Donna-Marie."

CHAPTER 18
Suffering

LEOPOLDO

As the days passed, my head pains became more intense, so I vowed to visit the El Pillar Basilica in Zaragoza. The feast of Our Lady of the Pillar would be held within the next few weeks, so I decided to go and prostrate myself before the little wooden statue of our Virgin. It had been purported to hold more power than any other shrine, as Santa Jaime had received it from the Mother herself, whilst deeply in prayer. Its powers to heal and absolve were renowned. I would beg for relief from this tiresome pain that assailed me more and more.

I made arrangements immediately, as I would be away for several weeks and wanted my household in order for when I returned. My housekeeper was a surly woman with little control over the household and she had a poor relationship with the cook and the other maids. Little improvement had been made in the house, and the cook was unimaginative and, frankly, unskilled.

I had told Oskar to recruit other staff for me while I was away. I trusted him and he had served me well. It was he who sourced almost all of the ingredients that went into our food from the estate. When we needed meat, he arranged and oversaw the slaughter, the butchering, the salting or the cooking. He personally picked and prepared the fruits and vegetables I ate. He also supervised what the chickens, ducks and partridge were fed on. And, of course, he tasted every morsel of food and drink I was served, no matter by whom.

He did, however, agree with me about replacing the cook and the housekeeper.

"It is difficult to find a good cook who will live in here.

Perhaps our cook would do better with more instruction from a good housekeeper. After all, she is responsible for the menus," suggested Oskar.

"Fine," I said. "Do it."

"What sort of persons should I engage, Sire? The village women are mainly hostile to working here full time. They want to return to town at night, but that you would not allow. Am I right, Sire?"

"We must remain secure, Oskar. Whoever you employ must live here so that there can be no lack of observation of their behaviour at any time."

"Perhaps there are orphans at the Convento de Giraldo who are ready to leave and find employment."

"They would do as maids, but I need a good housekeeper. She must come with good references. See what you can find whilst I am away. I will leave it to you. And investigate the two women in the end cellblock where we kept the little novice. See if you can discover their crimes. It seems they may have been forgotten."

Why am I concerned about two useless old hags? The little novice girl is making me soft. I will not think of her. I must concentrate on redeeming myself in the eyes of our Lord so that my suffering will cease.

CHAPTER 19
Convento de Giraldo

EVANGELINA

I moved to the Convento de Giraldo the following day with a promise to return each month to help with the garden.

I took with me many of the samples of herbs, roots, fruits and flowers, as well as unguents and salves that I would continue to use. I had oils and perfumes too in small, stoppered bottles carefully labelled and dated. In the canvas bag that I carried were Donna-Marie's scripts and scrolls, drawings and instructions. I had promised to return them after I had studied them. There was so much valuable information in them.

As the weeks passed, I was sure that I had done the right thing by being in the heart of the city. The vibrancy and activity of Cuenca instilled in me a new energy and resolve.

I spent a great deal of time trying to master the intricate stitching of the tapestries but succeeded very little, and I often found myself in charge of the kitchens instead. Sister Beatrix had shown me many recipes, so I tried hard to make our meals delicious by adding flavours from the Convento de Santa Hilda's garden.

I also found delight in working with the very small babies that were often left at the convent during the day. Their mothers worked long hours at the mill as weavers and could not take their babies with them. A few wet nurses would come and feed them, but the babies were left alone most of the day in a tiny storeroom. They were at least warm and dry there and would come to no harm. I enjoyed nursing the fretful ones, sang them a few songs and kept them clean.

I ministered to the sick when I could, helped the elderly and improved my skills with my oils and balms.

Three months later, I was no nearer getting close to the

Inquisitor than I had been before.

Then, unexpectedly, one day Oskar came to see Sister Monica-Alma, looking for suitable staff for the Casa Inspiradora. Oskar informed us that the Inquisitor was away and he was commissioned to find a suitable housekeeper.

"Would any of your postulants or novices be interested?" Oskar asked Sister Monica-Alma.

Fate must indeed have been on my side that day because when I stepped forward to be considered, Oskar thought me infinitely suitable.

"You will have to be approved by Leopoldo Sanchez. Report to the Casa in one week's time and he will decide."

That was exactly what I did. I reported myself to the Casa Inspiradora and was met by the surly Inquisitor, returned from his pilgrimage to Zaragoza. I was sure he was going to send me back to the Convento de Giraldo.

Without looking at me he asked, "I need a housekeeper, you need a job and a home. You can come on trial. Is that agreeable to you?"

It was simply stated and he turned, waiting for an answer.

I was so surprised I mumbled, "Yes of course. I would be honoured. I have many skills. I can cook and clean and make your tisanes and poultices. I can do many −"

"You will not need to do anything but obey orders and work with Oskar."

"Yes of course," I breathed.

Before I knew it, I was employed and taken to the housekeeper's room, which was comfortable and newly painted. It had a good bed, a desk and chair, a mirror and a window that looked out to the hills that led to Palomera. For the first time in my life I had a space that was all my own. Even the cook, the cleaners and general maids shared.

I was in his house, under the same roof, and I was elated.

Now, I would wreak my vengeance. I would find a way.

My intense feeling of hatred for him had to be kept hidden. He must never guess that I intended to kill him. But I needed to bide my time and make him trust me. To do a great right, it is sometimes necessary to do a little wrong. Not a little wrong really, but, in the circumstances, perhaps I would be forgiven, for I was driven only by the desire to avenge Donna-Marie.

Whether right or wrong concerned me not one bit!

CHAPTER 20
Opportunity Arises

EVANGELINA
Over the next few weeks, I experienced all the self-defeating pleasures of planning what I was going to do to someone I hated so much. I sickened myself with the thoughts of it, but mourned my beloved friend so much that achieving revenge was all I could think about.

At first, I couldn't sleep or eat as I planned, wondered and turned ideas around in my head. Could I stab him? Keep a knife hidden somewhere? Unlikely, as his henchmen always checked everyone so thoroughly. Could I disgrace him? No, no one other than those close to the throne had any power over the orders of the bishops.

I had to be patient. I would gain his trust first and use whatever opportunity came to me. So, that was exactly what I did over the following months as autumn turned to winter. I was employed as the housekeeper, so I had the responsibility of deciding on menus, work schedules, general cleaning and the laundry. I had to report directly to Oskar so I knew it was essential that he learned to trust me too.

To my immense surprise and delight, Eleanor and Irma had both been given jobs in the Casa Inspiradora. Eleanor was in charge of the great laundry. Irma had been a seamstress many years previously, so was put in charge of upgrading the drapes, curtains and bed linens. I never imagined that Leopoldo Sanchez would release them, let alone give them jobs in his household.

Oskar told them both that they could find no record of when they entered prison or what their crimes had been. Leopoldo Sanchez had suggested they would willingly work well for him if he ordered their release, fed and housed them. He was right. Both women were grateful and happy. Eleanor loved the cleanliness of the laundry after the stink of the cell, and Irma could mostly sit at her work to save her painful legs. She had with her Ora, a fourteen-year-old apprentice whom Sister Monica-Alma had been instructing in needlework skills since she had arrived there nine years previously.

So, Leopoldo Sanchez did have a soft side!

In the meantime, I was a paragon of docility, diligence and obedience. I followed every order with complicity. Each evening, I took myself to my room and slept the sleep of the exhausted, but never so much that I could not plot and begin to conceive my plans of revenge.

One day and night each month, I was allowed to return to the Santa Hilda to fulfil my promise to Abbess Alissa. She was extremely concerned that I had gained employment with a man I hated so much, and warned me about the sin of revenge.

"Nothing can ever bring back Donna-Marie, but you know I will make him pay somehow," I assured Abbess Alissa.

"Then I can only pray for your immortal soul," she had replied sadly.

Although it was then winter, young Constanza was doing well with the garden. She had learned much in the year and had followed my instructions so that everything was running smoothly. The jasmine blossom had been harvested before sunrise and added to the enfleurage that made the unguents and concretes that we were still working on in the planked pits of fat. She had planted some sweet-smelling violets that we decided to add also. They would give the product a relaxing and healing quality as well as a beautiful perfume.

Each month, I took what I needed from the store of herbs, seeds and roots, and Abbess Alissa often allowed me to take some dried fruits back to make Alajú, a dessert that my Inquisitor particularly liked.

I saw little of Leopoldo at first, but he still cringed when I spoke, smiled, or lifted my eyes to him.

I worked hard to gain his favour. Perhaps in time he would overcome his revulsion of me, or himself, or whatever it was that was holding him back. I had noticed his desire, and perhaps if I could remain patient, his need of a woman would overcome his zealous, sadistic nature.

He was a man after all, with needs as nature intended. As it was, he was hostile in my presence. It seemed to offend him, but the strange atmosphere between us was electric and disturbing for him. I knew it. Deep within was a man craving for something from me. I knew not what, but I would use that tiny chink of weakness to draw him toward me, make him lose his shell and his fear of women.

It would take time but I was not in a hurry.

I got to know his routine and found myself deliberately close to him when he was unprepared to see me. One evening, I loitered in a corridor knowing he was nearing me. I stopped and gazed out of the window, pretending not to know of his approach. He came and stood close behind me. I could feel his warm breath on my shoulders. I waited for him to touch me but he did not. His breathing became fast and harsh.

I turned and watched him wince as some sort of pain struck him. I was afraid to touch him, his body folded, his hands clutching his head and he suddenly looked vulnerable and sick.

"What ails you, Excellency?" I asked. "Perhaps I can help you. What is it? Is it pain in your head?"

He nodded, reeled away from me and staggered to the door of his room.

So, he did have a weakness!

I sent him a draft of nettle beer into which I had added a

sprinkling of dried feverfew. The flavour was mild and not unpleasant. I knew that he would get Oskar to taste it and was not really sure whether it would help what ailed him. But try I must to gain just a little of his confidence.

I was overjoyed at the prospect. I would wait.

CHAPTER 21
No Respite

LEOPOLDO

My trip to Zaragoza in October had afforded me little relief from my constant head pains, even though I had attended every Mass and prayed in the private chapel, raising my pleas to the little statue held aloft on its pillar of jasper.

I had also visited the Santa Engracia Basilica, which holds the bones of martyrs killed by the Romans.

Nothing had lessened my suffering.

I had stayed in a Moorish palace by the river Ebro and had enjoyed the folk dancing, singing and feasting of the festival in the Plaza del Pillar. It was a beautiful place. I thought perhaps to return to Zaragoza for a holiday when my duties in Cuenca concluded. But there was still much work to do in La Mancha, so it was probable that I would stay a considerable few years. I liked it well enough there.

Returning to Cuenca, I resolved to spend more time in prayer and meditation. My sins must surely be the reason for my torment.

Finding my household well-staffed, I was surprised when Oskar brought in the little novice girl, Evangelina, as a prospective housekeeper, and although I had thought she would only last a week or so, she was proving to be a great asset. The cook had not only improved her recipes but also the variety of dishes offered. The old furniture shone and several rooms already had new drapes.

Everything in the household was running smoothly.

I had many civil and local duties to perform and several sinners to investigate, so over the next few wintry weeks I was kept busy and away from the house. Oskar kept me informed and told me of Evangelina's hard work and dedication as a housekeeper. He was pleased with her and had certainly learned to trust her.

208

CHAPTER 22
To Begin

EVANGELINA
On a bleak winter's morning I awoke, my heart racing fast.
For a moment I lost my bearings and knew not where I was.
I had been trapped in a forest surrounded by flames.

A thousand candles burned around, within inches of me,
creeping inexplicably forward like an army on the move.
Within the flames were faces full of pain. I was trapped in a
forest, unable to escape as the flickering tongues of fire
moved toward me. From my eyes, nose and mouth streamed
the burning heat. Leopoldo's face appeared, leering and
laughing, holding his flaming hands toward me with a
threat.

I woke crying, sweating, and my throat dry and parched.
It took a few minutes for my breathing to slow and to stop
my body from shaking. That silly recurring dream that
seemed to have no founding in anything I had ever
experienced, but had been a part of my life for as long as I
could remember. The only difference was the faces I saw.

It took me all day to release the fear. My hands trembled
uncontrollably.

"What's wrong?" asked Eleanor as we sorted linens for
the laundry.

"A bad night."

"Nightmare?"

I nodded slowly, unsure of how much to tell, the horror
of it still vivid in my memory. Speaking it out loud might
make it more real.

"Nightmare, yes," I said finally, "I was burning. I kept
trying to shout but each time I opened my mouth flames
poured in or out, I am not sure which..."

"I dream of the prison," said Eleanor as she pounded the

washboard with the laundry brush. "But for you, I would still be rotting there."

I turned to smile at her. She did not look like the same person that I'd met in the cells that evil day. Her cheeks were plump and pink, and although her few teeth were black and rotten, she managed to smile without looking too unattractive.

I was pleased with myself for being instrumental in the release of Irma and Eleanor and for their new occupations. Both worked hard and were healthy and happy for the first time in years. I felt better immediately.

Weeks passed and I had little contact with Leopoldo until, one cold February day, Oskar came to the kitchen looking for me. "Señor Sanchez is asking for you, Evangelina. He is suffering terribly and thinks you might be able to make him something that will help him. Can you? He is in such torment. It must be something stronger than the insipid nettle tea that you made him previously. But it did ease his pain a little," Oscar smiled. "Actually it helped rather well."

I set to work and mixed a combination of herbs; chopped fresh peppermint, lavender and chamomile, together with a little oil to form a thick paste. I wrapped the mix into a double cloth to apply to his forehead where the pain was greatest. I also soaked some willow bark and coriander seeds and mixed the liquid with some wine, crushed feverfew flowers, stems and leaves. It tasted bitter so I added a spoonful of honey until it was more palatable.

Sometime later, Oskar came to collect the drink and I told him how to apply the compress for his forehead.

"Perhaps you will come and apply it yourself. He is not happy about me doing it."

"If he will allow it, I will make an oil mixture to massage into his head and neck then," I replied, knowing this was a good opportunity to get closer to Leopoldo and gain his trust.

As soon as I had made all the preparations, Oskar took me to Leopoldo's bedchamber, where, pale and sweating, he tossed and turned with the intolerable pain.

I took the compress to him and explained that I needed to wrap it across his forehead, and this I did while Oskar tasted the infusion. He wrinkled his nose, but declared it acceptable. With infinite difficulty, Leopoldo sipped and swallowed. Even that took time, as he retched on several occasions.

All morning, his agony and fever raged, and slowly as he took more infusions the pain subsided. I applied the oil I had prepared to his head and neck and carefully massaged him, releasing the knots and nodules around his skull. It allowed him to sleep.

On the second day when he got up from his bed, he stretched and yawned, obviously feeling better.

"I feel so different. The pain has left me. What did you do to me?" he asked.

"I used a compress on your forehead, then with some oils massaged your head and neck. The infusions were simple herbs. You must keep taking them."

"I thought I would die."

I wish you had died, I thought, but instead said brightly, "You didn't. I nursed you and saved you."

"I was saved by God," Leopoldo declared.

"It was not God who nursed you. It was I."

"Be careful, Lina, you come close to blasphemy. You cannot suggest it was you and not our Lord who saved me. We are all in God's hands, you know that."

I clenched my fists and smiled. I was appalled, but said quietly, "Well, sometimes a little help is acceptable, eh?"

I know there is no healing without prayer, and although the power is in the herbs, prayer is in the healer's soothing touch. I had asked, I know not to whom I prayed, but I did pray that day. I needed to be successful so that Leopoldo would trust me. I knew his suffering was dreadful and I did not want that. That would make me as bad as he had been.

Only his death would satisfy me. If there was a God, He could make Leopoldo suffer. I would be prepared to die with him if necessary.

But now I wanted him to look on me well, so I asked, "How long have you suffered so, Leopoldo?"

He flinched as I said his name, but he answered slowly, "I will tell you."

CHAPTER 23
Exposure

LEOPOLDO

What was there to tell? I am what I am. I have earned my respect and I work for God and I live well, do I not?

I was perfectly aware that she wanted to hear about my past, to perhaps hear something that would enable her to understand me better. I could not think why she would want to know about me, after all, I was nothing but a sinful boy castigated and chastised by my mother until I had become a man. I suffer because I sin.

My sins of the past must surely be the reason for my pain and torment. Could I willingly tell her? But reluctant though I was, I told her about my early life.

"My headaches began when I was really young. I was a sinful boy, so I was punished, as I should have been. My masters and my mother helped me become the man I am today with the daily beatings, the prayers and the subjugation that I endured."

"By beating you, you became a man?"

Lina lifted her pretty eyes. They were full of concern so I continued. "It was necessary. Mother had a special whip that she used; three long strands of hardened leather, the centre one had spikes embedded into it. My mother told me it represented the Trinity. 'Accept that you are a sinner, boy. These three thongs will remind you of God the Father, God the Son and God the Holy Ghost.' With each word she lashed me so that my spirit as well as my body would surrender to His love. Some days, when I was especially sinful, she made me kneel in the room with the whip for several hours before she used it on me. The anticipation of the pain to come was part of my punishment."

"Were you such a sinful child?"

"Oh, yes. My scars remind me of my sins. My knees are scarred from walking on them to get to the chapel every day along the stone corridors of the castle, to confess and repent. My hands and wrists are scarred from the spiked binding with which they were tied to prevent my hands from straying in the night. I learned to love my pain. The more I prayed the less became the headaches. I learned to suffer as Jesus suffered. But recently my head pains have increased again, so I must still repent for my sins."

This was the first time I had ever revealed anything about myself to anybody.

Lina's tears had streamed down her cheeks when I told her of the pain my mother inflicted on me with her whips and her words. It was beyond my understanding that she should feel so enraged by my upbringing.

Although I knew little of hers, I did understand that it had not been the happy one that she had described on our first meeting. But all women tell lies, do they not?

I remembered my father's words about women. "They are like a moving mist that shifts constantly to confuse and beguile us. They have so little common sense and cannot keep their natural wickedness in check, and are therefore the downfall of our society."

Indeed they were, but, as I gazed at Lina, I allowed myself to believe that there were exceptions.

She had taken my hand and guided me to a seat, walked behind me and then pressed her fingertips into my head and tense shoulders. For a moment only, I allowed myself to relax to her touch, but suddenly it made me angry that I could respond and that she thought she could do this without my permission.

I felt I was losing control.

Perhaps I should not have divulged so much. I stood and walked away from her touch.

"Leave me alone!" I spat at her.

"I'm so sorry," she said, looking crestfallen by my outburst, "I didn't mean to offend you."

In my head I heard a voice, low and pleading, not the voice of my demons but something softer and gentler. *Don't hurt her.*

"No," I said. "You did not offend. I know I am quick to take offence, but it is hard for me not to. I am not used to anybody caring for me. It provokes a sensitivity in me that I didn't know I had."

CHAPTER 24
I Am Ready

EVANGELINA

So, Leopoldo Sanchez was an abused child. No wonder he felt so strongly about sin, misguided though it was. I could use his vulnerability to my advantage. He would come to me, I knew, and my door would be unlocked.

I had changed into a shift of cotton, left unbuttoned to between my breasts, and I had let my hair down. It was only moments later he came to my door and looked in. As he approached, I lowered my eyes and curved my body towards him very slowly.

He stood watching me as if he was committing my features to memory.

As he stepped toward me, I bowed my head. He laid his index finger on my cheek and slowly traced the outline of my cheekbone and lifted my chin. I did not dare move or lift my eyes as his finger slid down my throat, onto the top of my breasts. I stood frozen, as he stroked and trailed his fingers across my shoulder, this man who had never touched me casually.

I smiled inwardly, but a small voice warned me not to be too daring, as I reminded myself that he was very dangerous. He could send me to the dungeons for the rest of my life, but I had to test my power, so I reached for his hand. Curling my tongue, I licked the ends of his fingers and lifted my lashes. I had watched my mother often enough, lower then lift her lashes and smile a promise.

It usually softened the hardest heart. Now my life depended upon it.

My mother had always told me that it was possible to get the better of any man. 'Use those womanly skills,' was her advice, 'nature has given you the power to train them, and even though they could take what they wanted from you at any time, you could still make them sweat for it, humble them and make them eat out of your hand. Give them the pleasure that they crave. Seduce them,' she had told me, 'and they will do anything for you. It is an art, little Lina.'

But, without warning, he seized me by the throat and I was stupidly surprised. He looked into my startled eyes as if to object but he dropped his hands to his side and turned away.

I waited until I thought it perhaps safe to speak.

"Aren't you feeling any better, Excellency?" I asked softly, daunted by the strange atmosphere in the dark room.

"I am never, ever, really better. I am afflicted with it. It comes without warning and stays lingering for days," he said, pinching the bridge of his nose with his thumb and forefinger. "Christ's bones, Lina, I'm almost never free of pain and it is because I am sinful, I know. God would listen to me if I could only understand better what He wants of me."

"Perhaps I can help. I will make you a tisane that will keep the pain at bay."

"You could do that?" He turned, the expression on his face pale and pained.

"Yes. A simple tisane of feverfew and chamomile taken daily will help."

He moved to me and, putting his hands beneath my arms, he pulled me towards him. I could feel the proof of how much he wanted me.

"You see how I sin?" he said, gazing into my eyes.

"No, that is not a sin, that too is God's gift to man... Why else would it happen?" I let my hands slide down his back and took no notice of the footfalls I could hear outside the door, until I heard Oskar shouting. "Excellency, are you there?"

Leopoldo lifted his head in irritation. I stepped away from

him and with one finger parted his lips. Before he had a chance to move, I pressed my lips to his and he responded instantly, moving his mouth against mine and exploring my lips with his tongue, before leaning back with a quick jerk.

He looked angry and bemused. Holding his hands in front of him, palms toward me as if to protect himself from me, he said, "I have never been kissed before. It's very –"

"Leopoldo, you are needed in the castle," the voice was urgent behind the door.

Leopoldo turned and left, shaking his head in disbelief, either at his reaction or the surprise of it.

I was satisfied!

While he was away, I returned to the kitchen to make the tonic for his pain. I gathered the ingredients as before but this time I added the tiniest pinch of the dried and powdered Mandragora fruit into his favourite wine. I hoped he would trust me well enough to drink it without his taster doing so first, as I had little idea how strong it was or what reaction it would evoke.

CHAPTER 25
Too Much Pleasure

LEOPOLDO

I cannot help myself. As soon as I am in her presence, my guard seems to start to slip away and I find myself with such uncontrollable responses.

On the one occasion during my life when I had formed an attachment to a woman, I had never declared it, but left the town without saying goodbye or even contacting her. I could not waste my time in useless pining and know not whether she did. How then had I allowed myself to fall under the spell of this insignificant girl?

Was it her beauty? No, she was not beautiful, but she charmed me and I recognised in her something else, something different, the first time I had laid eyes on her. I believed in her!

Evangelina's tisanes were indeed reducing the incidence of my head pain and I felt calmer than I had done since moving to Cuenca. As my health improved, other feelings pursued my thoughts. I was waking in the morning with intense desire stirring in my loins and I had started running around the estate early and returning to take a cold bath before breakfast.

As spring approached, the days were warm and balmy. Evangelina had taken to serving me my morning and evening meals on the terrace. She would bring me wine with her concoction of herbs for my head pain. Some days, she dallied, making excuses to watch the sunset or look for the new moon.

"You are an intriguing young woman. A minx I think," I told her one starlit night.

"No, I am not a minx. Why would you say that? I serve you well, do I not?" She kept her eyes averted.

"You should not think that you could coerce me."

Her head shot upright and I could see the violet flash in her eyes. "Coerce you. I do not even know the meaning of the word."

"It means that you use your wiles to make me do what you will."

"To do what?"

She put her hands on the small of her back and bent backward laughing as if to ease a pain. I could see how flat and smooth her stomach was and the curve of her breasts, straining against the soft material of her smock. It instantly excited me.

Yet, a different kind of excitement!

More yearning and pleasurable than the excitement I got from the pain I inflicted. *That* thrill was touched with hatred that made my body burn.

Her words affected me deeply, and I felt as if tears were trying to reach my eyes and spill forth my longing for her. As I swallowed hard to prevent the flow, she smiled and lifted her skirt to reveal her silky thighs. I could bear it no longer and dropped to my knees and pulled her to me. I pressed my head into her body. She caressed my head, her fingers gentle, soothing, as if she understood my pain.

Oh Mother, how I longed for this from you, how I imagined how it would feel to be held and touched. It was unbearable; I couldn't breathe for a moment, such emotion surging through my heart as if I was discovering a whole new depth to myself, but I quickly stood.

Beware… beware… I knew suddenly that my mother was there, under my skin, moving inside my body like a silky snake along my veins and into my thoughts.

I would have to send Evangelina away. She could return to the convent. We stared at each other and I could see that she could read my intent. Her bottom lip trembled.

How pretty she was!

But, no, I could not allow myself to have these feelings.

"Don't send me away," she said as she dropped to her knees, her head between her hands, "I will only serve you and not disturb you again."

How could she know how deeply she disturbed me? I am lost. I must run. I thought desperately and, pushing away from her and bounding up to my chamber, I stripped off my clothes and put on the cilice. By the time I had run the circumference of my estate, my trembling body was covered with sweat. My eyes were stinging with tears and my burning nose was dripping. Every breath rattled like a moan through my clenched jaws.

What is the sense of it all? I should send her away. But should my fear of God be such that I cannot respond? Did being a Propagator of the Faith deny me?

This girl is a simple pleasure and offers me that which men and women everywhere enjoy.

I wanted to feel her gentle touch. I wanted to touch her.

Memories, long forgotten, bubbled through my mind with clarity that could not be denied. Somewhere in the recesses of my mind I felt a thread of longing, unsatisfied and full of regret for this young woman who disturbed me so.

Had I ever felt such a longing?

No, I will not send her away.

CHAPTER 26
Slowly, Slowly

EVANGELINA

Each day I served him, looked after his comforts and his pleasure. I prepared nearly all his food and made things he really loved. Quail stuffed with apple, cinnamon and pine nuts being his favourite. He still used his taster but less and less as he grew to trust me. I set out his clothes for him daily but left his servant to dress him.

I watched his heart melting toward me. Only with me did he drop his guard and I could often see the small, frightened child within him.

He exercised daily, running himself so hard that he came back to the villa with sweat across his brow and running down his neck. He wore the cilice on his arm and his thigh all the time, reminding him daily of his sin so that his body was constantly covered with weeping sores that bled into his clothes. But I could see that the Mandragora fruit was doing its work. He couldn't hide it. I liked it that he desired me!

I had been extremely cautious with the dose to see whether it would work, but now I intended to increase the amount so that when the time came for the final dose he would not notice the different taste.

"I know that you love me now," I said without looking at him. He had come back to the house tired and angry, as his day had not gone well. As he undressed, ready for his run, I covered his face and neck with kisses. He smiled as I continued. "You are just too frightened to take a step toward me and allow yourself the joy of union with me. For now your doubts make a decision impossible."

"I cannot," he said, turning the cilice until I could see a trickle of blood running down his bare arm.

His detached tone caught me off guard. I tossed my head.

"You'll have to admit to it eventually, Leopoldo. Because you know I'm not going anywhere. I will wait."

This time he smiled. He left without another word, and I watched him running down the hill toward the river. But I still needed more time.

Only then would I act out my vengeance. I laughed and ran off to the kitchen where I supervised our supper and hoped that making light of it would help him relax and let himself realise that he couldn't fight his feelings for me.

CHAPTER 27
Don't Hurt Her!

LEOPOLDO
I was not as touchy around her as I used to be, and realised I was feeling an unusual regard for her. My desire for her had increased and the bulge in my trousers told her so. When I pulled her close she smiled and replied, "I think it is a wonderful thing."

I didn't know how to respond or what to say. I stood gazing into those deep violet-blue pools that were her eyes. They were filled with something I found hard to recognise... so soft, adoring and innocent?

I needed to know, so I said, "Then I will try, although I don't know how. I've been trained to be aggressive and assertive and have little knowledge of women. You must tell me."

"I would be afraid to tell you," she replied teasingly.

"Am I so hideous?"

She pushed me away and dropped onto a seat, resting her chin on her hands, her elbow on her knees, gazing up at me with interest.

"No, not hideous... dangerous and cruel. Are you not?"

"Not so much. My er... cruelty...You think I am cruel?" I said the word slowly as if trying to understand it. I needed to explain. "I think it is God's way of using me, tying me to the service of finding the truth, to destroy heresy and corruption. It will save me from the torments of Hell."

I really believed what I said. I considered it a gift, to inflict cruelty and suffering to anyone who I believed stood outside of God's law, but saying it to Lina made it sound hollow and unconvincing.

Her mouth curved in a brief smile. "I am pleased to hear that you will be saved from the torments of Hell, but I believe that only loving action will gain an entrance to Heaven. Your God is so obsessed with sin and the Devil that he seems to have no time for beauty or love. I think whatever your earthly beliefs, God will see the real you. He will know whether you are a good person and look kindly upon you."

I laughed at that, knowing that the good nature that she had stirred within me frightened me too. It took me outside anything I'd ever experienced before. I had no knowledge of love, other than my devotion to our Lord, and that was always tinged with pain and fear. I felt no fear in her presence. I reached forward and entwined her long rope of hair in my fingers. She turned from me and the dark strands of silk slid away. She lifted her fingers to gently stroke my cheek – so loving, so intimate – and the hairs on the back of my neck stood up.

Slowly, not taking my eyes from hers, I eased her dress from one shoulder.

Don't hurt her, came the inner voice. Never before had I felt such a need.

"What is it you want?" she said.

"I am not sure. I think I want to learn to..."

What graceful magic was working on my shuttered soul? What joy and astonishment it brings to me. My icy heart felt it had been touched by the sun. My own mother and father had not touched each other since I was born, and I grew up knowing only of their hatred for each other and for me. My mother had taught me well.

"I'll ask you again later," Lina smiled. "Haven't you felt something, something good? Or is your heart hardened forever against all women?" she asked me, gently holding my face between her hands and looking up at me.

"Is my heart hardened so that it can no longer feel? Perhaps I mistake the pleasure I get from sinners' pain with something that should be there... but isn't?" I asked.

"Your mother beat it out of you with her cruelty."

"No, she wanted me to be good."

"She did not. She forced a vengeful evil God into your soul so that you cannot recognise the God of Love." Lina hesitated and said slowly, "Donna-Marie knew only the God of Love and she taught me too. I know that I had never felt love before knowing her. My mother cared nothing for me and would have let me die of hunger or worse, but she did not beat away all feeling in me, or the spirit that lies within. Donna-Marie taught me about love by who she was."

"I did not know that about you. I thought you came from a happy home."

"No, I lied to you," she told me without embarrassment or regret.

The memory of the pain I had inflicted upon Lina's friend as well as all the other women... no, not just the women, everyone who had come, swept through my heart like an ocean of pain. But it had been mainly the women. It was their pain that excited me and that I enjoyed. How could I be that person anymore?

"Do you imagine that is all that I am?" I said. "Perhaps it is true."

As she replied, she bent forward from the waist and I watched the curve of her hips as she whispered, "No, I do not. You are a man, damaged by the circumstances of your life, as I am a woman damaged too, but brought back to life with love."

I shifted uncomfortably for her words sounded like a flowery poem.

She lifted her face and looked at me seriously. "Don't you believe that two people can be destined to be together, that God may have sent them to learn about love?" she asked. "Perhaps it is meant and I am here for the very purpose of showing you that God will love you even though you are a man with human desires and needs?"

"I cannot talk about a love that I do not understand. Tell

me."

"It's different for men and women. Love for a woman is their whole existence and they cannot be moderate or rational about it. Why indeed should they be? Without the desire of a woman for a man we would have no creation – no real continuation of our race. Man can create of course, but only a woman brings the dedication to love. True families could not exist."

CHAPTER 28
I Have Him

EVANGELINA

As time went by, I could make Leopoldo come to me just by lifting my eyes and smiling at him. I never pushed him, only cajoled and tempted him. I could run my fingers down to his groin and as he grabbed my hands I would laugh gaily and kiss him on the lips.

What fun it was making him dance to my tune. I often left him shaking but would touch him gently saying, "Worry not, Leopoldo, no one can know, nobody is watching us. Do you think your God has nothing better to do? Do you think he sits there dispensing judgment? We did not ask to be created, so owe it to ourselves to live an exemplary life, but one that has within it the pleasures that we were created for. Despite your learning, you are not clever enough to know that we owe nothing to anybody, not even the Creator."

For a second I thought I had said too much, but he smiled. "You *are* a minx, my little Lina."

He often watched me closely as if he was seeking something. Looking for a clue to our extraordinary relationship. But I did wonder if he may guess how I revile him, how I wish for nothing more than his death.

My own desire for him sickened me. Night after night, I asked myself why I could feel such an intense physical longing for someone so vile. For someone who had been responsible for killing my best and only friend in the world? I hated him but I was becoming more convincing as the months passed, and I knew he was beginning to love and trust me.

I was confusing him and weakening him slowly with the help of the Mandragora fruit. Who would have thought a man tortured by guilt could be so much fun? I felt his need, his longing and his loneliness.

I knew that slowly he was becoming enslaved by his desire for me but I was weakening too. How wonderful it felt knowing how I could pleasure him so that he would trust me implicitly and I could carry out my plan of revenge.

I wrapped my arms around his taut body.

I was no longer afraid of him, and my loathing of him had settled low and hard inside me like a frozen lake, solid and unmoving.

CHAPTER 29
Passion

LEOPOLDO

My body is charged with passions of a nature of which I have never before experienced. Do I mind? I am not sure... But no, I think I mind less and less as her fingers ply their miracles. It's a strange feeling because it makes me feel like a man with real desires and needs.

How I loved the feather touch of Lina's fingertips upon my skin. The delicate lifting of her face towards mine and the sweet seal of the kiss that touched deep, dark, soft places inside the recesses of my heart and senses. Swiftly a fire is lit within me that I could not control. I pulled her toward me and could feel her hot breath and her sleek body willing me on. I felt a strange sensation stir within me with scenarios of fear and excitement and a sharp feeling of terror and guilt. She disturbed me, this girl with her soft touch and desirable body.

I am becoming bound to her with chains so strong that even my faith in God cannot break them. I want to gaze into those beautiful violet eyes and kiss her sweet red mouth and let my lips explore... Oh what sin, I will have to confess.

The Devil comes in many forms; he comes with pestilence and disease, he comes in spells and incantations and in the allure of carnal desire. I must purify myself with prayer and punish the flesh, but it was thanks to her that I had discovered the man who had been so long hidden inside.

At first, I had panted and heaved my longing into her and all I could hear were my own fears. My mother loomed above and around me, ready to flay me within an inch of my life for my sin. She stared accusingly at me, her black eyes shining, her wide mouth showing her unpleasant teeth, rotted and gapped. She held no warmth, whereas the woman beneath me was soft, and melting with it. I took a deep breath and pushed my mother out of my mind and allowed myself to be absolved by the pulsating need and the wondrous, soothing softness of Lina. My Lina...

"I love you," I heard her whisper, and all thoughts wheeled away into the recesses of my mind as my body burned again with Lina's closeness. My pleasure sent me into a spiral of ecstasy such that I cared neither for my mother or the love of God while my body was tied to hers.

"Will you stay with me?"

"Forever, Leopoldo. I adore you. I will never leave you," she declared, and I believed her.

CHAPTER 30
Changes

EVANGELINA

I had him! I could sink my nails into his back, my teeth into his breast, and he would moan in an agony of pleasure or pain. But I had him. He came to me every night and my enjoyment of him increased. The physical pleasure of having such power over him made me more and more confident that I could carry out my plans. It would soon be time to wreak my revenge even though a tiny part of me held back. I had to remind myself constantly that he was not a lover but a cruel murderer who would soon know the truth. Perhaps I was a little too confident?

After my next visit to the Convento Santa Hilda I had a small handful of dried roots of the Mandragora tied in my petticoats. I was still not sure how to prepare everything. How much root, how much water, how long would I need to heat them for?

'Experiment is treacherous and judgment difficult.' I could hear Donna-Marie's words. But I did know that the root of the Mandragora would not incite, as the pleasure of the fruits had done.

I made a weak tisane and sweetened it with honey. I knew of many ways to prepare and dry or distil the plants, but I had only ever seen them used to heal rather than harm, so I had to rely a little on guesswork.

What I did seemed fitting. I didn't fear error, just failure. I used my nose, a little judgment and the things that Donna-Marie had taught me. I prepared well.

But perhaps I had overestimated my power over him, because without warning Oskar arrived at my door and told me I was to leave immediately. Leopoldo had instructed him to accompany me back to the Convento de Giraldo that very day.

He had already departed to La Gossa.

CHAPTER 31
My Light, My Love

LEOPOLDO

Lina's absence was like a physical pain. It began deep in my heart, pulsing like an inflamed boil. I had sent her away because I knew that my feelings for her had intensified and I was afraid. Afraid of the hold she had over me. As I became deeply attached to her and our nightly pleasures, I convinced myself that I was the greatest of sinners. Even though my headaches had all but ceased, I could not continue to offend my beliefs.

I heard myself groan and opened my eyes to total darkness. Feeling disorientated, I reached around for my Lina but encountered nothing. Only emptiness and darkness where I would usually feel her body, comforting and always ready to allay my fears and my pain.

In the midst of the searing, scorching pain in my head I wanted only her. How could it be so? With Lina's medicines I had been free of pain for months but I had sent her away!

"Oskar!" I shouted. "Where is Lina? I want her here."

"She has gone, your Excellency, back to the Convento de Giraldo as you instructed."

"Bring her back, Oskar. I need my medication. Did she leave me my medicine?"

"I will find out, Excellency. Shall I call a physician?"

"No. I want Lina here."

"I will personally collect her," Oskar told me, but returned in a few moments with the jar of herbal infused wine that she had mixed before she left.

I sniffed it carefully. "Yes, this is it. It will help, I know. Go and bring Lina here."

I drank the whole jar of wine and immediately fell asleep.

A long spear of agony ripped into me, forcing my innards upward. The force of the explosion through my mouth sent my body backwards against something hard. My bowels threw out the sickening smell of decay, and as one spasm subsided, another began.

What was happening to me? I tried to call aloud for Lina. Before the words reached my lips, another stream of bile poured forth.

Pain shot through my stomach again and I curled into a ball with my arms over my head. Huge flames of agony swept through my throat and skull. My body was hurled upwards, spiralling through the clouds. I was flying toward the stars; cascading colours floated all around me and I felt if I opened my mouth I would taste them. Shooting stars bounced onto my head and I fell, kept falling, until nausea overcame me again and I spewed forth my guts into my surroundings.

Further into the night, I was aware that somebody was swabbing the vomit and the excreta from the floor around me.

I could not speak. My mouth would not open as if fear of another explosion had tied it shut. I could only see a flitting movement around me, and the outline of a crucifix somewhere above me. Through a haze He hung there. He, who understood suffering and pain.

'Saviour, give me the strength and the goodness. You cared enough for the world's sins to take them all. You care for me too. Let me be as strong as you.'

My insides heaved again and the retching hurt my chest and throat, as there was nothing left to force out.

"Where are you, Lina?" My throat was as dry as cork and my voice a mere whisper. "I need a drink."

"I am here."

What mountainous seas of feeling she stirred in me, of love, of guilt and bitterness and some deep anger. It burst upon my soul so that I no longer knew who I was.

"Here, drink this, Leopoldo. It will ease the pain for you."

I felt the warmth of her hand as she held my head up toward the bowl of liquid. The smell was sweet with a hint of apple. I swallowed with difficulty.

She loves me and has pledged her life to me. But I sent her away. How could I have thought I could live without her?

She tenderly caressed my aching head. I was acutely aware of my weakening state but she was there with me. All would be well!

As my insides heaved again and the pain surged through my body, I became aware of her tears.

"Leopoldo, oh, Leopoldo, I am so sorry, but you took from me the most treasured of human beings," she whispered. "You hurt the person I loved most in the world. I cannot, will not, forgive you, even though my heart now bleeds at our parting."

I felt her lips on my scorching forehead. I tried to reach for her but could not lift my arms.

Lina, my love.

"In a different life we could be together. In a different world we could love each other," she told me gently through her tears.

Her words cascaded around in my head and I managed to whisper, "We do love one another." I was so sure of it. I finally understood.

"Yes, I know we do. But we will meet again, Leopoldo."

A rippling barrel of light, shimmering with the brilliance of a sun-drenched rainbow, surrounded and gathered me into a womb of calm and safety. It was only then, with a feeling of detachment, that I realised that I was crossing the divide between life and death. I did not mourn the loss of life, for there, wherever I was, I felt neither guilt nor pain. I knew, beyond a doubt, that existence was eternal. I felt no pain, no fear or guilt.

'We will meet again my love, my angel, my light...'

PART 3
REMORSE

Poland 1640 – 1688

Over the centuries the Kingdom of Poland has played a major role in European history. It was a fairly typical Christian feudal state, eventually developing into 'The Polish-Lithuanian Commonwealth', which encompassed Latvia, Ukraine, Moldavia, Belarusa and parts of Russia. It embraced a wide variety of cultural and religious traditions. Each country had its own Sejm (Parliament), governed by a unique system of democracy and ruled by those who gained power only through election.

It was in the seventeenth century, after much conflict and loss of life, that Poland lost over one-fifth of its territory with the treaties of Oliwa and Andrussow. In the 1650s and 1660s, the balance of power shifted from Poland to Russia. Far more serious for Poland was the loss of her position as the most powerful and wealthiest state in Eastern Europe. Its aristocracy and nobility, the 'szlachta', made up a high proportion of the populous and were wealthy and powerful.

With wars against Sweden in the north, the Russians to the southeast and the Ottoman Empire from the west, Poland had little opportunity of regaining its strength.

It is into these troubled times that French-born **Evina** is thrown, more by circumstance than choice. Her son **Leoska** is born in Warsaw, bearing a residue of the Karmic issues of their previous existence.

CHAPTER 1
Private Mental Hospital/Asylum
Arokja, Poland 1687

EVINA

I remember little of those long years. Whole tracts of time collapsed in on themselves whilst others replayed over and over. The real world retreated and I found myself alone in the agony of dark memories in my head.

When I first arrived I worked mainly in the laundry. I tackled the daily chores with enough energy to feel gainfully employed. I didn't need to think, just to concentrate on moving my body to fulfil the activity required.

Gradually the repetitive routine and languor of the other inmates invaded my being. It was like a sleeping wakefulness that dulled all feeling other than a dark heaviness of my limbs and the slow working of my mind. I was adrift on a poisonous voyage. I had been cast away and for a while I remained in darkness.

It was physically a long daily grind, but it allowed me to fall into a deep slumber when the day was over, something that I had not enjoyed for many months previously.

The high windows gave little light but when the sun was up, small shafts of sunlight illuminated things rarely noticed and caused shadows that frightened some. Shadows changed expressions and shapes of the familiar. Even our own faces illuminated above our heads caused us to look and feel different.

We hung our heads, holding them in our hands or resting them on tables, walls or our knees. On bad days, we slumped on the floor and let the ground take the weight of our fuddled brains.

Many people were so alone and isolated I never knew their names, and tended to speak only to those with whom I worked. All but a very few had to work. It was to keep our brains from devouring us. If we worked well, it was considered a sign of getting better.

There were others, too violent, too mad, who were confined to the padded cages. We never saw them but could hear their screaming and ranting.

Mad people cleaned everything all the time. My hands were raw with cleaning. I asked Marcus why.

"It's therapy. It is better to keep cleaning or the smell would distress some further. Cleaning prevents the rotting that starts on the inside and kills them in dirty ways."

"Ah, is that so?" His answer didn't seem to be relevant to those people I had got to know there.

We scrubbed and polished everything, all the time, but still the stink of mad minds and bodies remained embedded in the very fabric of the place. I could smell my own warm body, but did not think I was rotting from the inside.

My little friend Isolte pushed the linen she was washing forward and backward in a rhythmic motion, and at the same time her head moved from side to side as though she could feel something brushing across her cheeks, her eyes looking for whatever she imagined it might be. An insect? A bird? I could only guess. Her fear was distressing to see as she dodged her thoughts, one bony hand lifting every so often to brush away her imaginary antagonists.

I was carrying a pile of dirty sheets sent from the local hostelry, and caught sight of myself in the shiny surface on the side of the great boiler. I was surprised at the sharp lines of my jawbone and cheeks, my shoulder blades sticking up through the collar of my grey dress. Skeletal! I was unrecognisable from the plump, rosy-skinned woman that I knew myself to have been. But I no longer did know myself, and wondered whether I ever had. My son Leoska would not recognise me. I wondered if he remembered me at all, my beautiful boy who had rejected me.

My life swam around my head like a drunken bee trying to find a spot to land. I was not mad. Perhaps nobody there was mad. Who judges what is mad? It's just being in a different place, a darker place. A place unknown. Places that have too much meaning or none at all.

I had confused what was real with what I knew, and I was here because of it. My powerful uncle, Jan Sobieski, had made me come, had arranged my incarceration, because I was an embarrassment to the family.

I cannot remember what I had done that was so bad, but it mattered little.

I did not know how long I'd been there. Perhaps a year? Two years, or ten? I was not sure, but I had changed. That I knew, for I felt different, relieved somehow. My pained, knotted stomach had released. My anger subsided and my addled brain, although still incoherent at times, was starting to make sense.

Outside, it was the beginning of spring and the light had changed.

"The garden needs some attention," Marcus said quietly. "Would anyone like to work outside?"

Some turned with a changed expression, others cowered or shrank at the suggestion of leaving the safety of their own selves and the comprehension of a structured routine.

I was ready. I wanted a change. So I nodded.

Marcus, our kind attendant, was one of the few people who did not have the absolute and abiding assumption that all of us in this place were subhuman or worthless. He was a gentle man with soft brown eyes that never ceased to smile, even when voices were raised or tempers flared.

He carefully took my arm and led me to the door. We stepped out into the garden beyond, which was surrounded by a high stone wall that sheltered the profusion of plants and trees.

"This garden was established before I came here. We do not know who first laid it, but it has thrived for a long time so we must tend it well," Marcus told us gently.

As he spoke he ran his fingers through the sweet lemon balm. I knew little of what the plants were called, but realised from the reverence with which Marcus spoke that he took great pride in this garden. He said the words softly and reassuringly so that Anna, who had also volunteered to work outside, and I would not be afraid.

I was not afraid. I needed the light.

No one had been outside from our wing since the previous October, and the lack of light and sunshine added to the heavy dread of waking every morning.

I worked all day with Marcus and Anna, another 'mad' person who had spent most of her life confined in this private hospital. She remembered no other life. Anna had imaginary friends who came with us into the garden.

"You stay with me," she beckoned them. "Marcus will tell us what we are to do, won't you Marcus?"

Marcus agreed and addressed his instructions as if to a crowd of people. Anna had bounced and smiled. She occasionally did as Marcus requested but anything could distract her; a butterfly, a pretty stone or a shifting cloud would set her off into another world. Either Marcus or I would bring her back to her task. She sighed dramatically and encouraged her friends to work hard.

It was another world in the garden with the colours, the light and the soft breeze on my skin. I knelt and picked up a handful of dry earth and sniffed it. A good smell. A real smell. It took me away into my memories.

Marcus handed me a small tool and, as he instructed me, I let myself remember other gardens that I had loved: the terraces and soft green lawns of the Warsaw Palace, with hundreds of servants scurrying around, each serving the beautifully dressed ladies and the uniformed sons of the szlachta; the blossoming orchards of the royal houses at Lvov and Żólkiewski; my rose garden in Winnica; but most of all the formal and magnificent gardens of Versailles.

I was born in 1649 into a comfortable and well-ordered life. In my early childhood the gardens of Versailles had been my playground. The manicured lawns and unique sculptured fountains were my everyday pleasures. Created for Louis XIII they were unlike any other in Europe. I was a fortunate child, being born to a family who resided there amongst other nobility of the time.

My mother was Perrette-Lyse de Chartres, and my father Count Vincente de Gaće. Vincente considered himself a diplomat and businessman, but had failed on most of his ventures, although he had distinguished himself in the political arena of the time and was in high favour with King Louis.

Perrette-Lyse had been born into a wealthy aristocratic family, but her parents had no personal fortune or title, her father not having been the first-born. It was a world circumscribed entirely by purity of bloodline. Because of his background, her father became part of Louis XIV's royal cabinet, and they lived in a private apartment within the Palace of Versailles.

The court was presided over by the king's mother, Queen Anne of Austria, who had become Regent. King Louis was still very young and Perrette-Lyse was of a similar age, so she enjoyed the sumptuous world of art, entertainment and the best possible education in court.

As a young child, her closest friend had been Marie Casimire Louise de La Grange d'Arquien, known as Marysieńka, who was five years younger than Perrette-Lyse.

Their friendship was cut short when the Queen of Poland took the five-year-old Marysieńka to train to be a lady-in-waiting in the Warsaw Court in Poland.

Marysieńka's parents were delighted. It was a great honour to be selected for training to a queen such as Marie Louise Gonzaga. Only noblewomen from distinguished families but who were of lower rank than the women on whom they attended were accepted into the royal household. Although they may, or may not, have received compensation for the service they rendered, a good education and a comfortable, interesting life were guaranteed. A wealthy husband was decided for them too if they were lucky.

A lady-in-waiting was always considered more of a companion than a servant to her mistress. They usually travelled and enjoyed the social gatherings and parties together.

Although Perrette-Lyse, my mother, was already being groomed for an early marriage, she had been distressed at the loss of her little friend.

It was over ten years later when the friends met again. Marysieńka returned to Versailles to visit her parents, Henri and Francoise, who were still part of the royal court. Marysieńka was by then seventeen years old, married to the much older man Jan Zamoyski, and pregnant with her first baby.

My mother Countess Perrette-Lyse was twenty-two, married to Count Vincente de Gaće, with a seven-year-old daughter, myself, Evina Genevieve.

We had an excellent lifestyle with many advantages, but being a girl I was only encouraged to develop the qualities to be a good wife. My father Count Vincente de Gaće had already indicated a suitable husband for me; a duke no less, who was due to inherit a large estate in Lyon. I had not met him, but knew that he was seven years older than me and, I was told, reasonably handsome.

My father was not a well man and paid little attention to me or my mother. She was a fair, delicate creature with the pale lavender-blue eyes that I had inherited, although mine were of a deeper shade than hers. She loved drama and poetry, art, singing and dancing. She lived with a quiet acceptance of Vincente's poor health and bad moods, and enjoyed the benefits of being a countess in the royal court.

She also had a secret.

CHAPTER 2
Marysieńka Arrives

EVINA

I remember meeting Marysieńka for the first time. She was stunning, with the sort of dark syrupy beauty that took control of a room with a gesture, a toss of her glossy silken hair, or a single glance. She was a force of nature, which attracted both men and women. She took command of everywhere and everyone she was with, without any obvious conceit, and was considered to be an asset to any social event. She was, however, a strong-minded, clever and ambitious young woman, and my mother adored her.

Together they looked as different as night and day. My mother with her soft, blonde good looks and tiny delicate figure, sweetly patient and kind, and Marysieńka's dark, stunning beauty, always richly dressed in colourful and infinitely noticeable outfits. She was often sarcastic and caustic, but endlessly sought after for her gaiety, wit and intelligence. In my mother's company she was full of fun and laughter but often complained about her husband, her household or her retinue of servants.

During the time she stayed in France, my mother and Marysieńka became firm friends again, spending many hours together gossiping and giggling, attending social events, luncheons and balls.

Marysieńka had come to Paris to visit her family but spent as much time with us as she could. She would sit with a hand resting on her stomach, drinking copious amounts of peppermint tea for her indigestion. Although she had quite an imposing figure, she had a tiny bump onto which she laid her tapered fingers, and informed me that it was a new life waiting to be born.

Lifting my hands, she placed them firmly on her solid little belly. "Can you feel it, sweet Evina?" she enquired.

"No, what should I feel?"

"The baby, of course."

I stood still politely for a moment, but felt nothing. I was far more entranced with the richly woven gown covering the bump, and I let my fingers slide over her beautiful outfit. It was scarlet silk with birds and butterflies of silver and royal blue scattered down the central panel. Her deep blue overcoat of softest velvet was trimmed with ermine and silver ribbons that matched those holding up her astonishing, thick, raven black hair.

When Marysieńka left to return to Warsaw, she promised to keep in touch and to arrange for us to visit her in Poland.

Sadly, just a few months later, the man I had always known as my father, Count Vincente de Gaće, died very suddenly. The future for us at court looked bleak. The count had no estate to leave us and had gambled his remaining finances on a failed business plan to import Italian wine to the court of Versailles.

My grandparents had both died, so the king offered my mother an income for two years only in the hope that she would find another husband to support her. King Louis was more concerned with the forthcoming visit of England's future King Charles II, who was still living in exile in various parts of Europe.

I had hardly known Count de Gaće, so his death had little effect on me until at the end of the two years, with no intended husband for my mother and my betrothal undecided, our life became somewhat critical.

My mother's last remaining relatives were cousins living in a remote urban town in Normandy. Countess Perrette-Lyse de Chartres Gaće was used to living well at court, had her own apartment and retinue of servants.

The thought of living in a small town far away from the buzz, excitement and the social life of a city appalled her. She was, after all, only twenty-four, and I was just eleven years old.

She wrote to her friend explaining our plight. Marysieńka's immediate reply was that we would both go and live in Warsaw where we would serve as ladies-in-waiting to her. She also assured my mother that she would find her a suitable husband.

We were to travel after April in 1660 as an important treaty was to be signed which would bring to an end Poland's war with Sweden, the Habsburgs and their allies. According to Marysieńka, travelling would be safer after the signing.

The journey from Versailles to Warsaw was a long one and would take many weeks. We had a comfortable coach, and another for our servants, of which there were five. Andrei Pontrie our groom, Kristy my maid, Justin Gault our cook, Vilmos our personal bodyguard and Helena my mother's maid. All were happy to travel with us to Warsaw.

Also accompanying us were dozens of packhorses for our belongings, and an armed escort of soldiers in case of bandits or gypsies.

The journey was arduous and necessitated several stops, all of which were arranged by Marysieńka who seemed to be acquainted with every noble family along the way.

We stayed in a variety of places, from castles and lodges, to a convent in Keplow. We were treated well and enjoyed the hospitality offered.

Luckily the weather was kind to us so we often rode, my mother on her white Arabian mare, Selene, and I on my beloved dappled pony, Davriella.

We travelled through beautiful fir forests, stunning valleys and majestic mountains, and through countryside with carpets of spring flowers so stunning that we had to stop and admire them. Many we did not know at all, especially those on the mountain roads. We passed through small towns and villages and big beautiful cities full of noise and smells. It was all rather exciting and frightening, as we didn't understand the language, and had to rely on our escort to keep us safe.

We'd heard of the great mists and snowstorms that could annihilate the landscape in minutes, but we enjoyed blue skies throughout the journey. I had rarely travelled outside Paris, so in the beginning I saw the changes and thought of such an expedition as a great adventure. That was until the reality of the discomfort and boredom of the journey became evident. We travelled seemingly endless miles each day and for many weeks. We rode, sang songs and told stories, played games and slept.

On a few occasions we stayed in the huge tents which Marysieńka had provided. I rather enjoyed those nights when we ate outside under the stars and retired early to snuggle under our fur blankets.

It was during one of these nights that my mother decided to tell me 'the secret'.

I didn't know at the time, but she had imparted her secret to her friend Marysieńka when she had visited two years previously. That was the main reason that we were going to live in Poland.

The secret was about my real father.

CHAPTER 3
The Long Journey to Warsaw

EVINA

On that cold, spring day we'd travelled through Germany, and in the evening we were camped in the mountains outside Lignica. We were still in Habsburg territory, so were being carefully guarded, the treaty only newly signed. Our guards had eaten and were already at their posts. Vilmos was asleep just outside our tent. Justin had been hunting and made us all a splendid meal of wild boar, which he had cooked over an open fire, and we retired early because it was still cold at night. Kristy and Helena were fast asleep on the far side of the huge tent when my mother called me to join her beneath her fur blanket.

I knew that she was going to tell me something important.

As we tucked ourselves warmly together, she said, "Evina, ma chérie, it is time you knew about your real father and why we are going to Poland. I could not tell you while the Count de Gaće lived, although he always knew that you were not his. Now that he is dead I can tell you the truth. The count and I never consummated our marriage. He was unable... I do not have to explain... but he liked people to believe that you were his child."

"And my real father?" I asked, intrigued by this sudden disclosure.

"Your real father's name was Marek Sobieski, a Polish nobleman. He died in battle three years after you were born. That is why we are going to Poland. All his family are there and will welcome us as their own."

"How do you know they will welcome us?" I asked.

"Marysieńka is a great friend of Marek's brother Jan and she has told him of you. He remembers meeting me in Paris and knew of his brother's affection for me. So, you see... we will have another family. You will meet your Aunt Katarzyna and your grandmother Teofila Zofia."

During that evening, tucked up together in a strange place in a strange country and with a future as yet undecided, my mother told me the story of how this had all come about.

"It was 1647 and Jan and Marek Sobieski had completed their education," Perrette-Lyse sighed as she remembered. "They set out from the family home in Żólkiewski to follow the usual activity of the Polish aristocracy. They were expected to go travelling to further their education. They were accompanied by a group of their friends and compatriots and their personal tutor, Sebastian Gawarecki. Together they travelled widely throughout western and northern Europe, mainly studying and getting involved in local art and philosophy whilst doing so. It was during their time in Paris that I met them. They'd joined the 'Musketeers of the Guard' forces, a company of the military branch of the 'King's Household', where they learned to improve their fighting skills. I was only twelve, but already very well educated, and used to socializing with the visitors to Versailles. Marek was so very handsome and delighted me with his wit and stories of his travels."

My mother explained how she, and her group of young friends, had attended the endless gatherings the wealth of society enjoyed at that time. She became entranced with the tall, good-looking Pole who flirted with her and promised to return.

"Marek Sobieski and his brother Jan left Paris and spent the next few months travelling and studying in England," my mother told me. "A series of royalist uprisings changed the political situation in England, so they left to study mathematics in the Netherlands and then lived for a while in Brussels. But you see, Marek did keep his promise to me and returned briefly to Paris. I was by then thirteen and engaged to be married to the count, but I fell completely and madly in love with the handsome Marek. You, my little Evina, were the result."

It took a long while for me to understand the story, but it became clear. I was born in 1649 when Perrette-Lyse was not yet fourteen.

My mother went on to explain how circumstances overcame the situation as events in Poland changed suddenly with the death of King Wladyslaw IV. A Cossack uprising was threatening the establishment in Poland, so the Sobieski brothers returned home.

"Marek never knew of your arrival as I had married Count Vincente as soon as I realised my predicament. I heard that both the brothers joined the military almost immediately after their travels," my mother told me sadly.

I was appalled at this revelation. But, by the time we arrived at our palace accommodation in Warsaw, I was used to the idea, and looking forward, as only a child could, to gaining a new family.

Our house was attached to the Royal Palace, just outside the city, where Marysieńka and Jan Zamoyski lived most of the time. Marysieńka was overjoyed to see us. Her husband was away, staying in his house in Zamosc where, according to the servants, he had a mistress or two.

Marysieńka made it very clear that that was where she preferred him to be!

CHAPTER 4
Court Life

EVINA

To my amazement, I acquired a whole new family and, just as my mother had promised, we were welcomed into the Sobieski family with no hint of prejudice at my being born outside wedlock.

Marek had been a favoured son who had been killed by the Cossacks after the Battle of Batih. His mother, Teofilo Zofia, was old and frail but gazed at me as if seeking a resemblance to her son Marek whom she mourned constantly. Marysieńka told me that his mother had never come to terms with his death.

She was delighted that Marek had a daughter and intrigued that I had a birthmark exactly the same, and in the identical place, as Marek's. It was a small dark cross on the side of my neck and considered a mark of high intellect and spirituality.

I had not inherited my mother's blonde good looks. I was small with dark brown curly hair and rosy cheeks like my Aunt Katarzyna, Jan Sobieski's sister and his only sibling since Marek had been killed. All I had inherited from my mother was my violet-mauve eyes. The family liked my resemblance to them and even though I would never know my father, my new family was rich and powerful and accepted me as one of their own. I could not have been happier. Life was going to be to my liking I was sure.

My mother and I had never been so close. Together we took pleasure in learning about our new family and their way of life. It was all so exciting, and we laughed and giggled at the revelations made daily about the people we met, the customs, the oddity of the language and the food.

We lived so close to the Royal Palace that we soon became integrated into the court society and involved in the frivolous and feverish love of pleasure that was part of the lifestyle there.

Everyone spoke French but I soon learned Polish, with the help of Aunt Katarzyna. She took great delight in her new niece. I found it hard to understand at first, as I thought perhaps we would be considered strangers, but we were welcomed everywhere. I, as Marek's daughter; my mother, as the daughter-in-law that might have been.

We learned that my father had been a man to be proud of, and much loved by his family and compatriots, and even the extensive staff in the palace spoke of him with affection.

The court governess was instructed to include me in her lessons, so I immediately began learning languages, music, history and philosophy, as well as etiquette and court manners.

Before long, my mother became Marysieńka's confidante and comfort as both her baby boy and girl had died at birth. Her little daughter, Katarzyne, named after her aunt, was born soon after we arrived, but was sickly and frail, often confined to her nursery.

I was concerned and afraid for Katarzyne, so one day I asked my mother, "Is not my aunt devastated by losing her babies?"

My mother shrugged. "It happens and it must be accepted. Let us hope that this next one survives."

"I would be so sad if my babies died. I could not bear it," I told her sadly.

My mother was somewhat disdainful of the healthcare in our new country but she explained that most people were resigned to the frequent deaths of children and young adults.

"Marysieńka's children have been born feeble because she is not in great health herself, and I don't think she is really desiring children with Jan Zamoyski."

I accepted that, but resolved to look after little Katarzyne if I was able. She was a good-natured little baby. I loved being with her and helping with her care. Her tiny body was skinny and pale, and her breathing laboured, but her sweet little fingers and toes held me enthralled. So helpless and fragile!

I watched the wet nurse almost with envy as the baby struggled to suckle. My breasts had started to blossom already, and I vowed to myself that any baby that I ever produced I would nourish myself.

Just holding Katarzyne's tiny body close made my insides smile. I loved her.

My mother often confided in me how much she enjoyed our new life and how exciting she found being with Marysieńka again. She told me of the gossiping and laughing they did about the love affairs and intrigue that went on there on a daily basis.

Marysieńka had grown up in the court of Marie Louise Gonzaga, the imperious Queen of Poland, who, by her own admission, had acquired her position by skilful use of her female charms, influence and money. She played a huge part in the political and cultural life of the country and was intent on bringing French laws and customs into Poland. She was known to be meddlesome, and because of it, the aristocracy did not like her.

The king, however, was happy for his wife to influence his political and military decisions as his health was failing and although he was still noble and courageous, he was apt to succumb to despair and apathy.

Marie Louise Gonzaga also believed in consulting the stars and had her own live-in astrologer. Her power was enormous and it seemed that Marysieńka was a royal favourite, so had the queen's ear for all her needs.

It was by Marie Louise Gonzaga's negotiation that Marysieńka had been married to Jan Zamoyski, and been awarded so much of his wealth.

Zamoyski was unfortunately a debauched drinker and womaniser, and there were already whispers of a divorce. The queen was disappointed, but understood Marysieńka's disgust at her middle-aged, drunken husband, and knew that her charms and beauty could be put to better use politically if she were free.

We learned very quickly where the power of the court lay, but being part of Marysieńka's household gave us more leniency than most. My mother and I were very grateful for it.

Most of these things affected me little as I made new friends and enjoyed being educated and indulged in one of the greatest courts in Europe. I was also allowed to attend the grand dinner parties, costume balls and music festivals where I watched the adventures and antics that were part of daily life there, and soon learned the protocol.

Marysieńka was always in the heart of the whispers and innuendos, and I could see that although she was admired, she was not well liked. Her unpredictable behaviour was often due to the fact that she was either pregnant or mourning the loss of her babies. She did, however, have the greatest solicitude for her own personal comforts with little regard for others, except those special to her like my mother.

"I have everything I could possibly want. I don't care about anybody else, so much the worse for them," she would laughingly tell everyone, with total scorn for the opinions of others. No doubt it was because of her selfishness that she was disliked both by the ladies-in-waiting and the servants. They constantly gossiped about her in the most vindictive way, some even suggesting that she had lovers. Marysieńka was indeed free with her many admirers who always seemed to be in attendance wherever she went. Her beauty and charm were her gifts and she used them openly.

I learned to keep the suspicions to myself, as my mother would not have a word said against her best friend.

"There are bound to be stories about her," suggested Perrette-Lyse. "She has after all been brought up in a world of court cabals and political intrigue. She is a wonderful person and others are only jealous of her. Take no heed, Evina. We are lucky to be here and I am so happy to have her as a friend."

"Of course, I know that, Mama. I love her too," I assured her.

"Regardless of all the gossip and intrigue it is a very happy household, and our lives are full of fun, are they not? We have so many parties and endless visitors, all artistic or clever with plenty of riches and wit." She paused with a happy sigh. "Perhaps I will find a new husband."

"Perhaps you will, Mama," I laughed.

It was indeed a happy place, mainly due to Marysieńka's love of the arts, music and poetry. She was a romantic and, although she was ambitious and clever, was a devout Christian. She maintained a belief that she was perfectly entitled to her life and position.

"It is our culture, education and art of conversation, Evina dear, that distinguishes quality from the common folk," she told me laughingly when I had commented on how clever she was, talking to the great philosophers and artists who came to court.

"Every woman knows how to smile and spread her legs, but not everyone has learned how not to be a bore, and men appreciate that. The art of conversation can open many doors."

I knew that she was right. I had seen her charm the most disgruntled old duke with her intelligent and sparkling conversation, watched eyebrows raised as she gave clever answers to political questions, and I'd seen a famous painter flattered by her observation of his art.

CHAPTER 5
Meeting Jan Sobieski

EVINA
One of the most regular visitors to the court was Jan Sobieski, my father's brother, who had recently returned from the battlefields because his mother, Teofilo Zofia, was ailing. He and Marysieńka would talk for hours, and after his visits she was often moody and irascible.

Uncle Jan Sobieski was a soldier, an imposing man, muscular and pugnacious, with eyes that were wide and dark. He was well built and appeared taller than he was, covering his heavy body in long, sweeping, expensive coats. His large moustache was full and fashionable, and the sides of his head shaved so that he looked to have a tuft from his forehead to the nape of his neck.

He carried himself like a peacock, missed nothing, was meddlesome and plotting, but when with Marysieńka he became a lovesick pup. He was also talented, well-educated, spoke several languages and was a patron to poets, writers and painters. He had fought in many battles, been badly wounded in a duel, and was politically and culturally well-informed. He was not a particularly handsome man, but he had a charisma that women adored, especially Marysieńka who flirted with him openly.

Jan brought her gifts, which she accepted with coy disdain. He wrote her long letters when he was away and made his feelings for her obvious to all, even though she was a married woman. Jan Sobieski seemed to completely satisfy Marysieńka's romantic and moral temperament.

She played him well but I avoided him as much as I could because he scared me. His very masculinity was overwhelming to such an innocent little girl like me, and I would scurry away out of sight whenever he was around.

By the time I was eleven, baby Katarzyne had died, a sad, sickly little two-year-old. Marysieńka and my mother went back to France together, ostensibly for my mother to meet a potential husband. He was a relative of the Queen Marie Louise Gonzaga and part of the House of Bourbon. A widowed count, he had recently inherited a vast fortune and was much older than my mother. Having been born and raised in the French court and in need of a husband, Perrette-Lyse was considered infinitely suitable.

Marysieńka went to the spa town of Pau to take the waters and find a cure for her ailments, still apparently unknown, but it was whispered that she had something seriously wrong with her. Many suggested it was the reason for her stillborn and sickly babies.

I was left behind to continue my lessons and was, by now, happily settled. Indulged and cherished, I found I could get anything I wanted quite easily, and followed my aunt and mother's blatant use of our favoured position.

After several months, Marysieńka and my mother came back to Warsaw, Marysieńka looking much healthier. Perrette-Lyse brought with her the French Count Willem de L'Eihrin, whom she was to marry. He was large and handsome, although far too old, but my mother was delighted that she and I would be receiving a comfortable income. The prospect would be even better if she produced an heir for the count.

Teofila Zofia, my grandmother, had died, and Jan Sobieski returned from battling with the Ottomans. He inherited the houses of Sobieski, Danilowicz and Żólkiewski, making him one of the richest nobles in the country.

He also inherited the duty of such great estates, and the tradition of avenging the bloodshed of his ancestors by the Muslims. He was already considered a knightly champion of the Christian cause against Islam, but he now took on the duty of his family.

CHAPTER 6
Marysieńka and Zamoyski

EVINA

During the next few years, life changed dramatically for me. Perrette-Lyse married her count and spent most of her time in France having produced a baby boy, Henri, very soon after her marriage. Because of Count Willem's wealth, I was supplied with a luxurious apartment and several more servants. I retained Andrei to care for my four carriage horses, and also my pony, Davriella. Vilmos remained as my personal bodyguard, and Kristy, my maid, stayed loyally with me. Justin Gault and Helena went back to France to my mother's new estate. Mother assured me that they would all return and set up a household in Warsaw when the borders were safer.

Marysieńka's husband, Jan Zamoyski, eventually left Zamosc and returned to court and to Marysieńka's bed. At first all seemed well, they appeared happy enough until Zamoyski started to drink heavily again.

I heard Marysieńka tell Queen Marie Louise that he had demanded that she return to Zamosc with him but she had retorted, "I will not go back. He is dangerous, disagreeable and drunk all the time."

The queen nodded as she reassured her, "You must not go then. You are still my ward and I will not allow it if you are in danger. I will help you. I will instruct him to stay here with you where we can keep you safe."

They did stay, but very soon the daily screaming and yelling could be heard everywhere they went, and on one occasion I saw Zamoyski chasing one of Marysieńka's bodyguards with a large sabre sword. Zamoyski was shouting obscenities and threatening to kill the poor man. I was on an errand in one of the long passageways and jumped with fright and pushed myself back against the wall as the man and Zamoyski ran past me. Marysieńka appeared just in time and she too was holding a large sword. Zamoyski was clearly very drunk but knew she was capable of using the weapon she held. She was a skilled fencer and extremely strong when she wanted to be. She faced him with determination, her hair awry and face flushed.

"Who are you going to kill, Jan? You... You, drunken bully," Marysieńka shouted. "My man was only defending me against the pain you wish to inflict on me. You will not threaten him. I will not stand for it."

The bodyguard turned and stood at her side.

Zamoyski swayed, dropped the sabre and slurred, "You will obey me, slut."

He sank to the floor in a dead faint right there in the hallway.

I was shaking to my bones, but Marysieńka handed the sword to her guard and with a resigned sigh said, "Come, Evina, he is only drunk. We will get him back to his room."

So between us we took him to his bed. As she dismissed her man, I heard her telling him that Zamoyski was ill and that all would be well. Zamoyski was indeed a strange colour and his breathing laboured and shallow. Perhaps Marysieńka thought he would die there and then. Perhaps she even hoped for it. I think I did. He was a thoroughly dislikeable man who stank and swore and often vomited where he stood.

"I will bide my time," Marysieńka said, as much to his slumped form as to me.

As we left him to recover, Marysieńka turned and said quietly, "Sometimes, Evina, fate will take a hand."

Zamoyski did recover and appeared to curb his drinking, so peace reigned for a few months and Marysieńka agreed to stay with him. It did not last and he returned to Zamosc on his own.

Marysieńka was pregnant again and her health deteriorated in the following months. She gave birth to yet another dead baby and decided that she would never return to her husband.

This time, and with the queen's help, she was going to ask for Papal dispensation for a divorce.

Wars were still raging on the borders and reforms were taking place in the Sejm. An uprising amongst the szlachta who opposed the reforms disturbed the king. Never before had they raised arms against the state. Many felt that civil war was inevitable, but for us life went on much the same as usual, even though we were told that the court would be moved if things got too dangerous.

CHAPTER 7
Marysieńka and Jan Sobieski Wedding

EVINA

I was just sixteen in 1665 when I met my future husband. His name was Otto Adolphus Pasek, a soldier of high rank working with Jan Sobieski. He was young and fit, and dedicated to his life as a protector of Poland. Idealistic and optimistic, I found him entrancing. He lived his life perpetually alert and ready for any eventuality.

I responded eagerly to his charm, seeing it as some reflection of myself. But we were not alike in any way; I was far too young and innocent, unsure of myself, and he was a hardened soldier who knew his worth, had the undivided devotion of his troops, and was aware that he was respected and adored.

Naturally, I fell in love. My life became centred around his visits, which coincided with Jan Sobieski's who came more and more often to visit my aunt. It was obvious to see how much they were in love. Passion flowed about the palaces with many absences and flustered apologies. Marysieńka's health improved when he was around and everyone could see that they were good for each other.

Jan Sobieski had risen in royal esteem and had been awarded the position of Field Hetman for his valiant defence of the homeland.

One night, Marysieńka ordered wine and cake to her chamber. I knew Jan Sobieski was due to arrive so arranged the table in front of a roaring fire and waited to be dismissed. Quite suddenly he appeared and swept into her room, discarding his coat and sword to kneel at her feet.

"I thought you would not come," Marysieńka whispered, taking his outstretched hand. "There is so much scandal."

"What has been said?"

"I'll not repeat it, as it is so vile."

"I want to tell everyone how I adore you," Jan Sobieski said quietly. "All our time apart... I cannot tell you... I miss you so. If only we could marry."

"I am as yet a married woman. But I know we are destined to be together... We must wait. Jan Zamoyski means nothing to me, and the queen will speak to the Pope on my behalf. Also, I know that my husband is mortally ill." Lifting her eyes and noticing my presence, she stood. "Evina, go to bed now."

"Yes... I will go." I flustered, curtsied and headed for the door.

"Say nothing. I trust in your discretion. The queen will not abide any more gossip."

"No, of course, Aunt." I went to my apartment and wondered if indeed Jan Zamoyski was really mortally ill. He was not yet so old as to die naturally, surely?

But, finally, fate did indeed smile on the lovers, as Jan Zamoyski died conveniently in April, whether by his own unfortunate lifestyle or with help from others, no one knew. But he had expired at his house in Zamosc, leaving behind a fortune for Marysieńka. Before she had time to dry her tears or get him buried, she and Jan Sobieski confided to those close to them that they would marry immediately.

The period of one year's mourning was ignored and the queen, who still continued her protection over the young widow, arranged a secret marriage just one month later. Although everyone in the court knew of the wedding, a huge official gala for a public ceremony was arranged for the summer.

The official wedding in July was a grand affair, a testament to the great wealth and the families' fortunes. The ceremony took place in the Royal Palace chapel and the celebrations afterward, a huge banquet at the Kazimierzowski Palace.

It was a joyous, rowdy occasion with impressive guests including the king and queen, the French ambassador, and the Papal Nuncio, Antonio Pignatelli, who gave his benediction to the nuptial ceremony. There were cardinals, high officials and nobility from all over Europe. Poets, musicians, philosophers and high-ranking 'Hetman' all rubbed shoulders with the masses of guests and officials. The day was festive from the early morning service by the archbishop, who made a long speech about duty to Poland and their faith, to the entertainment, the extravagantly furnished tables and the magnificent wines provided.

At noon, the couple had arrived richly dressed in brilliant colours. They came down the river on a decorated barge. Trumpets blew and dancing girls threw flowers. Otto and I watched from the platform that had been especially built beside the riverbank. Wedding songs were sung and the orchestra played; the whole atmosphere was alive and joyous.

I was happy with my handsome soldier's arm around my shoulders, and his smile warmed my heart. I was so excited, for Otto was to stay in court for several months and seek the queen's blessing for our betrothal.

During the lunch, the Jewish musicians came, dressed in their traditional black suits, white stockings, with their black hats over long curls descending about their ears and beards. They played good music: sophisticated dances from Hungary, Ruthenian and Moldavian folk dances, and classics from Italy and France. Dancing was encouraged, and my handsome Otto and I danced until we were breathless.

In the evening there were ten courses of magnificent food, the banquet served on delicate hand-painted platters, the wine from jugs and casks decorated with enamelled and embossed scenes of flowers, birds and butterflies. The servants were dressed in scarlet livery, and the menus devised by Marysieńka herself. She loved to cook, so had prepared cake and bread especially for Jan and presented them to him with a fancy little speech about fruitfulness and love of their homeland. She was dressed like a virgin in a white flowing gown, flowers in her hair. She certainly knew how to captivate her audience. A coquette, certainly, and an extremely skilful one! She had been brought up to be so, and realised at a very young age that her beauty and her charm were her gifts. She used them well.

Very soon most of the guests were highly inebriated, and her loving speech was overlaid with laughter and merriment. Jan Sobieski looked like the happiest man on earth that day. He had finally gained the woman he had loved for so long. It was dawn by the time the couple retired, and many guests fell into a drunken sleep where they sat. All my life I recalled the joy of that wedding day.

Time flew by. My mother and her count had to delay their return to France as there were many areas badly affected by the plague, and movement was restricted in some places. But I was delighted, as I had seen little of my mother during the celebrations.

"As we are delayed, we will organise and prepare your trousseau," she informed me gaily. The queen had given her blessing to my marriage to Otto for the following summer.

"You will come back for the wedding, won't you?" I pleaded. "You must be here."

"All being well and providing the plague doesn't affect our travelling, we will come," she assured me.

Throughout the following week we prepared my trousseau and made the best of our time together.

Perrette-Lyse and her count eventually returned to France at the end of September.

After our wedding, Otto and I intended to go to Italy for an extended holiday before setting up home in Warsaw.

On my return, I would still serve my Aunt Marysieńka when she required, but I would have a different status as a married woman.

At the time I thought that life was just perfect!

CHAPTER 8
The Great Pox

EVINA

Both Jan Sobieski and Marysieńka already had influence, wealth and prestige in the royal court, but being together played a significant role in the country's political life. Their combined fortune made them the wealthiest couple in Poland and Lithuania. Although Marysieńka was rich, powerful and ambitious, her unpredictable personality made her unpopular. We once heard Jan Sobieski lovingly proclaim, "When you choose, you are the kindest of creatures, but, like a garden, you need fine weather to bloom."

It was so true, but those of us close to her knew that she suffered with various illnesses that made her bad-tempered and dictatorial. She frequently had scaly rashes, severe headaches and toothaches. She often complained of chest pains, and it was rumoured that she had the Italian disease – the Great Pox! She had sent to Italy for a remedy called 'Ore Cinnabar', a powder which she put in her bath, and another oily ointment that reduced her sores.

Jan Sobieski and my Otto returned to the battlefields as there were still major areas that were being plundered by the Tatars and Cossacks. At home, some of the noble families were demanding independence and taking up arms against the crown. They disagreed with the election reform that the king was intent on implementing. So, for the first time in his life, Jan Sobieski found himself fighting against his own countrymen, some of whom he had previously fought beside against external enemies.

Marysieńka moped! When they were apart, letters and gifts arrived almost daily. She often read snippets of his letters to us as we sat reading or sewing in her drawing room.

"'*Fairest Aurora, I am suffering a thousand million torments being separated from you,*'" she read aloud, laughing gaily. "He wants to be a flea, not to cause discomfort, but as under that disguise, might remain in adorable intimacy. How wonderful he is, my Jan, my husband."

Another day, with only a few of those closest to her, she read us an alarming letter about her beloved's health. '*I have been speckled from top to toe with thick spots and sores on my arms and body, but the ointment of 'mercury monoxide' that the Italian doctor gave me is helping considerably, so next time we meet it should be better.*'

"Poor man, but I too am speckled," she said, and lifted her skirt exposing her shins, which were indeed scabby and sore. She missed Jan so. She sent him long letters, made him a bracelet of her hair and copied out songs to cheer his lonely evenings in camp. She commissioned a portrait of herself especially for his pleasure, and was amusingly delighted at the thought of presenting it to him on his return. But, while she wanted her likeness recorded, she insisted that the painter capture her beauty with no hint of the reddened sores she had developed around her neck, on her shins, arms and hands.

While she sat, I was brought in as lady-in-waiting and companion to chat and amuse her. The painter was a short, fat Italian with an engaging smile who flirted with us while he worked. I found it embarrassing, but Marysieńka blossomed with the attention.

Jan Sobieski was still far away by September, and Marysieńka had seen little of him following the wedding, so decided she would travel to meet with him. Arrangements were made. I was to accompany her, both of us heavily disguised and with a few carefully selected guards. This was the first of many such clandestine trysts. I thought it was rather fun. We travelled as ordinary ladies in a small coach, only two horses and without any coat of arms or anything to signify our wealth. We kept away from the main highways and arrived at a coaching inn very late in the evening. Jan Sobieski was there, flushed and weary, but swept Marysieńka away without a greeting. I took myself to bed and mulled over our conversations along the way. Marysieńka had read me several French love stories, explained some Greek myths and extolled the virtues of her new husband. We had laughed and played games together. I asked her whether there was a possibility of my meeting Otto on such occasions.

She raised a haughty eyebrow at my request. "No, Evina. But, when you are married, it might be arranged."

"Are you marrying for love, Evina?" she asked later as the coach bumped along a dusty road. "It is so much for the better. We women often have no such choice, do we? We are pawns in the great political games that the men play. Clever, bright women I have known have married men chosen by their parents or by the queen, had children and disappeared into the fabric of family life like a pale thread in a faded tapestry. That will never happen to me. Nor you I would hope. I wonder often about Perrette-Lyse now that she has gone. Is she happy with her count?"

"I think so. He is much better to her than Vincente ever was," I replied.

"Good, and you?"

"Yes, I am marrying for love... I am as sure as I can be. How can I know for certain?"

"If he is good to you, that is the most important thing. I understand that the queen has agreed."

"She has. I am very lucky," I answered happily. "We are even astrologically suited, so she says. He being born under the sign of Leo; self-assured and intelligent, and I under the sign of Libra; respectful and principled, which apparently bodes well for us both."

I was eager to be married and grown-up, and luckily I had no political value, so was not being sent off to some hopeful noble wanting my name or my estates. I was indeed lucky.

Several months later Sobieski had not returned to Warsaw. Marysieńka decided on a further rendezvous, this time at a small country estate cottage. When we arrived, and in her excitement to see her husband, she leapt out of the carriage before the wooden step was put in place, stumbled, and twisted her ankle. I wanted to laugh out loud seeing my aunt so intent on seeing Sobieski that she had forgotten her own safety and dignity, but thought better of it as our coachman stepped forward to help her.

"No, leave me," she responded, pushing him roughly aside. "Go get the horses tended and see to your own suppers. You too, Evina."

She rubbed her ankle and hobbled off through the doorway as fast as she could into her husband's arms. Later, she called me to strap her swollen ankle and laughingly berated herself for her haste. "Truly, I felt no pain until now. My love overrides everything."

CHAPTER 9
Marriage to Otto

EVINA

As time passed, the king himself led his troops against the rebel nobles. As Grand Hetman, Jan fought by the king's side, almost losing his life. He wrote to his beloved wife, '*My death was already proclaimed in the enemy camp, but the Lord has spared me this time.*'

Marysieńka was distraught, but he did recover enough to continue fighting the border wars and civil uprisings.

Otto and I eventually got married in the autumn of 1666. Because of the wars on the borders, my mother and the count could not attend. Neither could we travel to Venice. Nevertheless, I was the happiest I could ever be.

Our wedding was a quiet affair and I wore a white dress decorated with violet and mauve flowers to compliment my eyes. I knew that I was not the most beautiful of women, but that day I felt like a queen. My Otto thought so too and smiled down upon me, his dark eyes glowing. He was very tall and, although he had a few battle scars, one over his right eye that had sliced into his eyebrow, he was very handsome. He wore the uniform of his rank, which had just recently been increased to 'Hetman', and a cloak of black and gold. He had taken to shaving the sides of his head like his commander Jan Sobieski but he looked very good. I tingled with anticipation, for I was still a virgin. I had an idea what to expect on our wedding night because I had had several conversations about it with Aunt Marysieńka.

"Tell me what I should do?" I asked.

"Don't do anything. If you do he will think you have done it before." We both laughed as Marysieńka explained that it was not necessarily good first time and to expect it to be rushed and painful, but Otto was kind and it hurt far less than I had expected. I think he was already well practised. Soldiers were known to have plenty of experience in such matters.

We had a new house and set up home together in Warsaw. Within days he had to report back to duty and set off to yet another skirmish with the Cossacks. We never managed to take our planned holiday in Italy and, although I didn't know it then, we were to be seconded to another part of Poland on his return.

In the meantime, I continued in my service with Aunt Marysieńka.

The following spring, Queen Marie Louise died, and Marysieńka was pregnant with her first child with Jan Sobieski and more radiant than I had ever seen her.

"This time it will be different, Evina. I am overjoyed and I am well, but I'm going to arrange to have this baby in Paris," she explained happily. "I will not lose this one. I know losing babies has always been so, and there has never been any guarantee that conception would lead to a live birth, or a birth at all." She sighed dramatically. "I have already found it so. Indeed, our graveyards show the stories of babies whose voices were never heard because of a fall, influenza, drowning or an unknown finger of death upon them. God's will is to harvest the weakest. More wheat is sown than will ripen. So it is with children. But this time will be different, you'll see."

"Will I come with you, Aunt?" I asked hopefully.

"No, of course not, you must stay here to greet your husband when he comes home."

Marysieńka left Warsaw with a huge retinue of protectors, her own priest and all her servants. She told me that she would remain in France for as long as possible after the birth. I did not want to be left this time. Otto was so far away, my mother was happy with her new family in France, and now that Marysieńka was leaving I found little to occupy me. Being a married woman, I was expected to behave differently and I didn't like it. I did not get invited to the parties, the hunts and dinners that were part of the lives of the younger members of the court. I was expected to accompany my husband to his military affairs when he was home but not on my own. I had not expected to feel so utterly abandoned. I became bored and irritable as the days turned into months, and even found fault with Kristy who had taken such good care of me. I developed a feisty attitude, was moody and depressed. My body changed too and I began to suffer monthly with excessive pain and bleeding. As the months went by, my cycle became shorter and shorter so that I was bleeding two weeks out of every four. I saw the royal court physician who gave me a foul-tasting tonic and bled me, neither of which had any impact on my condition. I was lonely and miserable.

In November 1667, Marysieńka gave birth to a healthy baby boy in Paris.

There were many changes that year. Since the queen had died, it was rumoured that the king wanted to abdicate, as he was unable to cope with the heavy burden of the throne by himself.

He relied more and more on his best generals. It was at this time that Jan Sobieski gave striking proof of his abilities, providing his private purse to raise troops for a new army and planning an operation to secure the borders.

Eventually, with Uncle Jan's enthusiastic rhetoric and prayer, they attacked and defeated the marauding Tatars. They say it was a long battle which caused much devastation, but Jan and his army evoked a public tide of gratitude, and he was acclaimed saviour of his people. He was promoted to 'Grand Hetman of the Crown' and celebrated with an ostentatious parade through the streets of Warsaw.

I heard regularly from my aunt and my mother who assured me that they were both soon going to return to Poland. It all depended on the cessation of the wars and the renewal of the royal court with a new king. I was excited at the thought of having them both back in court, but Marysieńka wrote from Paris. '*Even though Jan wants me to return to Warsaw so that our son, Jakub, can be raised in his home country, I will stay a little longer. I can perhaps influence King Louis XIV in the event to the possibility of a French candidate to the Polish throne. You know that the people must elect the next king. We must make sure that the best possible candidates have French support. There is a distinct possibility that we will be further into the war against the Ottomans. They are gaining much of our land and Jan says they are a greater threat than the Cossacks or the Swedes. Our Christian heritage is in danger. The infidels will not respect us. They bring their own laws, which we could not tolerate. But we are strong and have great commanders like my Jan. They will fight for us and bring us back the glory that we have lost under this present king.*'

My mother wrote of the plague that had swept through Italy and eastern France again, and isolated cases from the north where the great plague of London was just getting under control.

There had been outbreaks in Calais and Brussels, and further north into Scandinavia. She decided they would not travel whilst the plagues still raged.

Time passed heavily but, eventually, Otto returned home. I was so excited to see him but he warned me that things were changing fast. With the Treaty of Andrussow being signed, portioning Cossack Ukraine, there was a strong possibility that he would be involved with the division of Kiev. An agreement allowed the Muscovites to rule for two years and it would then revert to the Poles. In the meantime the army was setting up strongholds and settlements in many of the royal cities around that area to maintain rule.

Very soon Otto and I, with hundreds of others, became part of that programme. Those were awful days. The government was on the verge of collapse and fatalism hung in the air like a black storm cloud. Although it was quite outside my understanding, it was to change my life.

CHAPTER 10
Winnica 1668

EVINA

We were sent to Winnica, many miles from Warsaw and one of the lesser royal cities, to help with the changes. Otto had been promoted and was to take control of a wide area along the borders. I was devastated to be leaving the court, my friends, and family more than I cared to admit, but however much I protested, I knew we had to go.

The weather was still harsh and the journey was uncomfortable and cold. We struggled through frost and snow so it took us days to reach our destination, a large old house where we would stay for the next two years at least.

I screamed and cried my displeasure at Otto, who, after being involved in such heavy battles, seemed resigned to being sent to some faraway outpost. He was weary and querulous and didn't want to be there any more than I did, but he was used to obeying orders.

"Don't fuss, Evina," was all he said as he kissed me on my cheek. "We will be away until the Poles have reinstated Kiev and then we can return to Warsaw, so do me the kindness of not complaining all the time."

The grand house that we had been allocated had a garden and a woodland slope that led down to meadowland and a sparkling stream. When we arrived it was all covered in a deep layer of snow and looked sad and desolate. The days were achingly long. The heavy snow turned to black ice until it was almost impossible to go outdoors. Kristy, Justin and Andrei had come with us, plus Gregor, Otto's man, and another dozen servants. It must have been hard for them too after the bustle and activity of the court and the city. Great fires were built in all the rooms but only seemed to exaggerate the drafts of such a large house. The front of our bodies burned while our backs froze. The hours of daylight were short and dull, and each evening as darkness fell we huddled silently by the fires, wrapped in our furs, sipping warm wine and longing for spring.

When spring finally appeared, it changed everything and, once I got used to it, Winnica turned out to be a very pleasant place to live. As the season blossomed, the land smelled of chamomile, lemon balm and grapevines. With the bright sunshine it was soon possible to appreciate the beauty of the house. Inside, the furnishings were lavish; brightly coloured, oriental rugs and wall hangings, beautiful carved furniture and wood panelling. Our bedchamber looked like a reflection of the garden, all soft shades of the blossom pinks and the mellow green meadows. The kitchen was well equipped with local produce bought from the weekly market. The long windows looked out across farmland and vineyards, and when the sun shone it was very beautiful.

It was so different to living at court. I spent a great deal more of my time outdoors than I had ever done, as the climate was more moderate than in the north. I enjoyed riding Davriella and went hunting and fishing with our wealthy and noble neighbours, the Bidziński and Pieniažeks.

I heard little from Perrette-Lyse, my dearest mother, and I often suspected that she no longer had tender feelings for me. She was so happy in her new life with her Henri and was expecting another baby. Perhaps I reminded her too much of her life with Count Vincente, which could not have been pleasant. Not that I remember it being so bad.

We lived amongst all kinds of people in Winnica, and the local nobility mixed more with the peasants than we had ever done in the royal court. There were many Russians living close by and we were expected to include them in our daily lives, as they would have to honour Poland as their country when the terms of the agreement came to an end.

They mostly kept to themselves but there were a few driven to destitution by the wars that had forced them away from their homes in Russia. Many of them had jobs as gardeners or cooks in the noble houses. We employed several stable lads who worked with Andrei, and kitchen staff who helped Justin, and although I hardly understood them, I found them good enough.

We had a beautiful city church where everyone attended; nobility, the Russian Christians, the local farm workers and landowners alike. It was not large in comparison to the city churches but it was magnificent. The frescoes and icons recreating the gospel stories and miracles unfolded for all to see. The high stained-glass windows sent sparkling light onto the pews, of which we had our own reserved, and our name had been added on a tiny brass plate.

Our Italian priest, Karol Stratavori, encouraged us to worship with him, and his sermons were uplifting and joyous. Once he began his sermons he was compelling, very easy to listen to, as his voice was rich and dark like warm rye bread. He had arrived in Winnica a short time before us and everyone admired him, for he was young and well-travelled and mixed easily with everyone.

I saw little of Otto, as he and his men were kept busy with the many skirmishes and petty battles along the border. He spent most of his free time in local bars and gambling houses when he was off duty, preferring to frequent them with his companions than be with me.

"I am lonely and feel useless. I can't find enough to interest me here," I complained.

"Keep occupied instead of moaning all the time," he told me scathingly when I pointed out my lack of occupation and told him that I was bored. He pulled me close and gave me a long kiss, perhaps to prove to me that I was not as worthless to him as I believed. I laughed at him then.

"Get on with being a good little wife and let's try to get you pregnant. You would be happy then, wouldn't you?"

"Probably," I nodded, and gave him a mischievous grin that ended in the bedroom attempting to make it all possible.

He was a happy, gentle lover, but I did not feel that I satisfied him, as his absences grew more frequent as time passed.

As winter approached again, I found myself becoming resentful of his lack of appearance at the dinner table or in the evenings. The silence in the big house covered me like a blanket, so that often I found myself muttering my thoughts out loud like a madwoman. Otto was not the romantic dream that I had planned. I protested often but he ignored my feelings.

My monthly bleeds were still debilitating and the pain was never far away, crouching inside me. Every month it increased. My underclothes were permanently stained. Kristy did her best, and soaked and scrubbed everything, but my linens were always an ugly colour. The local doctor insisted that there was nothing abnormal and that in time they would regulate. In the meantime I should try to get with child.

"That will be the answer," he smilingly assured me as he measured out a dose of laudanum for the pain. "You will sleep now."

By September 1669 we had a new king of Poland. Jan Kazimierz had abdicated and free elections were taking place. To the surprise of everyone, Michal Wiśniowiecki, a young, inexperienced, non-military nobleman, was elected. However, he had powerful and wealthy friends, and was descended from a royal family who in the past had gained glory and fame.

"Here in Poland, kings are elected," Otto explained. "This is a purely political decision by our ridiculous 'szlachta'. Michal Wiśniowiecki is noble but weak. Jan Sobieski is ten years more experienced, well-travelled and clever, and is still leading the country to victory. Why wasn't he elected? He and he alone deserves to be king." Otto continued to moan throughout dinner but I hardly listened. I was bleeding again and in such terrible pain that I retired early and Otto went out to a local gambling house.

CHAPTER 11
Praying Every Day

EVINA

By the spring of 1670 nothing had changed except that I spent more time in church. Father Stratavori was always welcoming and kind. I enjoyed his company. He became a good friend and I confided to him how much I wanted a child, so we often prayed together.

"Do not despair, Evina. Pray and God will send you what you desire, all in good time. And if it is not His will you must accept that."

"No, I will not," I replied with a smile. "I will keep trying until it happens."

I prayed daily for the baby I so desired. I enjoyed being in the church, not because I was uncommonly good but because I enjoyed the fine words of the prayers and psalms and firmly believed that God would grant me a child if I prayed hard enough.

I had indeed prayed considerably long and hard, but eventually I had run out of words. What could God and I possibly have to say to one another? I was still not pregnant. A childless woman in this isolated place could soon lose herself, and I began to spend time with the children of my neighbours. I would hold them close to me, just to feel their soft little shapes and inhale their smells. It was the babies most of all that gave me such a feeling of longing and need. I fussed and mothered them. I wanted a baby of my own.

Marysieńka had had at least six pregnancies, but most of her babies were dead already. Had she brought that upon herself, I wondered.

The days wore on. I became pale and embittered with my loneliness and disappointment. Otto paid little attention to me, except in the bedroom where he was extremely active, so I could not understand why I was not with child.

It was early May when a troupe of gypsies passed through the province and entertained us for two or three days with their songs and dancing. They brought a little gaiety to our lives, although our priest did not like them or want them around as they were bawdy and irreverent. They sang songs about the joys and perils of sex, big-breasted girls and of skirt-lifting priests.

They came with a laugh and left with a sigh. They had also brought the plague with them. It descended on towns and villages around us where they had camped, and everywhere there was panic. Whole villages were abandoned overnight and burned to the ground. Those who had lost their homes and loved ones wandered desperately through the countryside and camped in the woods. Roadblocks were set up to stop anyone from coming into or leaving the city, and a state of emergency declared. No provisions were allowed into town so that very soon the kitchens were empty. But the precautions were of no avail. The disease crept toward us like a wily fox.

It was one of the Pieniażeks' sons who would be the first to succumb, and from that residence it crept daily to infect half the population of Winnica. During the next month bonfires were lit to cleanse the air, people rubbed their bodies in garlic or massaged themselves with scalded vinegar. Cartloads of rotting corpses were taken to great pits on the outskirts of town, quickly covered before the next load. Households that were unaffected became fewer and fewer.

Each Sunday at church, the growing toll of dead left more and more spaces. The pews sat almost empty. Otto and I brought our servants to the church to pray with us. Kristy sat by my side, mumbling her own special prayers. Between her clasped hands she held a linen bag stuffed with herbs that she kept close to her face. She had given me one also that I held in my muff. Kristy indicated that I should lift it to sniff, so several times I brought it to my nose and inhaled the spicy smell of the chamomile, cinnamon and thyme.

Our priest, Karol Stratavori, looked worn and weary. He was exhausted from tending the needs of the dying and had not slept a whole night for weeks. Before he stepped onto the pulpit, I had seen him push the frown and the folds of sorrow and weariness deliberately from his face. He spoke to us of the love of God, his face serene. His sermon was full of hope. Not until the end did he mention the plague, and lifting his hands towards his congregation said, "Is the plague sent to punish or to cleanse? We know that God is sending us his voice but... is it to test our love for Him?"

Stratavori dropped his voice, his eyes bright and glistening. "Perhaps it is not to punish our sins but to allow us to show him that we too can suffer and be cleansed. We too can bear the pain that he bore for us. Who amongst you would not seize the chance?"

I could only wonder at our priest's courage, for I was terrified and my body shook with un-shed tears. I wanted to leave, to return to Warsaw, to my family and friends. I would be safe. I glanced at Otto who had his head down in prayer. He too looked old and tired. This assignment had not suited him. He was not cut out to keep the peace and control areas that were vulnerable. He loved and needed the excitement of battle, the camaraderie and glory of the rewards gained through his strength and valour. He was also getting drunk regularly with his friends, and lately had not come home at night on several occasions. I was so unhappy, I resolved to leave as soon as I could.

My thoughts were cut through with Karol Stratavori's words. "Friends, some of us have the means to leave, have relatives far away from here who would gladly give them shelter... but we must not carry these seeds of destruction to others. What a great burden we would then be held to carry."

I was startled. It was as if he had read my mind. He looked across at his congregation, intoxicating them with his words. "Do you really think that God would punish us so severely even though we know we have sinned? I am sure there is not one among us who can vouch that his life has been free of error."

Had my life not been free of error? I had not sinned unless I sinned with my moaning and complaining. I knew that I had become resentful and difficult but I had obeyed God's laws. My monthly bleeds had made me so unhappy and I had cursed a little, but not so much as to be punished.

As events turned out, I had no chance to make plans to leave, as the next morning Otto became ill. I had reached out to hold him close, and when his skin brushed my cheek it was so hot that I pulled away.

"Otto, you are fevered," I exclaimed, reaching to place my hand on his forehead as I would a child.

"It is only a cold, Evina. Do not fret. I haven't been out of the city for weeks."

"But neither had the Pieniažeks' son. Get to your bed. I will get the physician to come at once."

"No, Evina, do not fuss," was all he said.

Despite my daily care, he worsened rapidly, and within a short time the raging patches on his neck had spread to the rest of his body. I prayed that the fever would pass, but it did not.

On a bright September morning I went to see him. The sky was a clear blue and the sun was shining but the drapes of Otto's room remained shut. He lay with his hand resting on his Bible, and turned away from me.

"Do you want me to read to you?" I asked as his manservant Gregor wiped a cold cloth across Otto's forehead.

"Some water please," Otto gasped, ignoring me.

Gregor immediately lifted a cup to Otto's parched lips. I did not want to touch him and could only berate myself for not doing so. When he turned toward me and opened his eyes, I was startled. They were like two empty holes, yellow and weeping, his face was flushed and scarlet, and the scar across his forehead glistened. His pillow was drenched with sweat and his pungent smell sickened me. I wanted to run away. He lifted a hand toward me and whispered, "Leave me, Evina. Go away."

I fled, to return briefly the next day, when I stood at Otto's door as Gregor washed his stinking, naked body. Otto was shivering uncontrollably. On his neck, under his arms and in his groin, the pustules had worsened into shiny purple and yellow hillocks that had finally burst and spewed out their disgusting yellow and white creamy pus. Nausea overcame me. I knew I could not attend to him. I gagged and retched, and holding my hands across my mouth, I rushed to the garden where I threw up my breakfast.

Even when I knew he was dying, I kept away.

Karol Stratavori came, staying tirelessly at Otto's bedside as he cried and moaned out his pain. At the end, Stratavori gave him his last rites as I hid in my room, sickened and frightened. I cried at the loss, of course I did, but I was no more alone then than before.

Gregor and Andrei, and one of the new servants, sixteen-year-old Hanya, were the next to sicken and die. I thought that it would only take time before all of us would be gone, but by some miracle they were the last in our household to succumb.

Somehow, as the days passed and the deaths became fewer and fewer, I started to believe that perhaps we were saved. I stayed in my bedchamber, constantly feeling nauseous and weak. Kristy brought me food that I could not eat. She sat beside me and held my hand and whispered her prayers.

It was only when our priest came to tell us that the worst was over that I believed the plague had passed. I allowed myself to breathe deeply for the first time in months. We knelt and prayed together. I heard Karol Stratavori's words as if from far away, but pressed my hands together in thanks that we were spared.

The roadblocks were reopened. I could now go and return to my home in Warsaw. I would not be sorry to leave Winnica but I would miss my dear friend Karol Stratavori.

CHAPTER 12
An Amazing Discovery

EVINA

Several weeks later, as we were making preparations to leave and return to Warsaw, I realised I was pregnant. It was not exactly I who realised, but Kristy. I was complaining that the waistline of my mourning dress had become tight and uncomfortable. Kristy was intent on altering it for me before we finished our packing, so I slipped it over my head and stood as she examined the seams of the bodice to see if it could be let out.

"You have eaten so little in the past weeks I would have thought that you would have lost weight, my lady," she said through the pins she held in her mouth, but, glancing up, she hesitated, took out the pins and patted my tummy. "Oh, my lady," she exclaimed. "I think that you are growing for a reason."

I looked at myself standing in my petticoat and I swear my heart stopped beating for an instant, as I knew that I had not had a cessation to my bleeding.

Kristy was the first to assure me that it could happen. My waistline had definitely changed shape and had a distinctive curve to the front. I did remember that I had had virtually no pain recently but I had not associated it with pregnancy. The constant sickness was not then about a lurking disease, but a change happening in my body that would result in the baby I so longed for.

My immediate thought was how pleased Otto would be, and I dissolved into tears at the realisation that he would never see our child. I cried tears of sorrow and joy all mixed together, but knew that my life was about to change yet again.

I returned home in the winter of 1670 to await the birth of my baby, and stayed with Aunt Marysieńka who had returned to the Warsaw Palace.

It was on a cold February day in 1671 that the first pangs of pain started suddenly. Marysieńka was pregnant yet again and not in good health, whilst I, on the other hand, had been radiantly healthy and happy during those months back at the royal court.

"I will pray for you, Evina. You must be prepared for a loss," Marysieńka said as she got up ready to call the midwife.

"No," I replied. "The baby will be fine, I know. Pray certainly, but do not put fear in my heart. My baby will be healthy."

I was unprepared for the endless pain, and the following day I still had not given birth. The midwife was called Ursula, a diminutive little soul with a cheerful attitude that suited me. She remained positive throughout my screaming and assured me that all would be well. I wanted my mother with me. She had already sent me gifts for the baby, beautiful linens, shawls and a frothy bassinet, and promised to pray for a safe delivery.

Perrette-Lyse's message had included the words, '*Our family are of strong stock, healthy and well nourished. May this child bring you as much happiness as my babies have brought me.*' No word of the happiness that I had brought her when I came into the world. Had she forgotten me?

Another night passed, by which time I had no coherent thought except that surely the pain would stop soon. Marysieńka, bored with waiting, left. Her deliveries had been fast and, although painful, she always recovered quickly. I was not prepared for this endless agony. Wave after wave of pain tore me apart. My screams of protest were met with a smiling Ursula, who reassured me with her soft smile and gentle voice.

"Keep calm, my lady, this baby is going to take its time."
She pressed down hard on my heaving belly. "I think he
needs to turn over."

"He?"

"Oh, it's always the boys who want to come out arse first.
Come, little one, turn around. Come into my arms, your
mama awaits you," she slid her hands between my legs.
"Don't push yet, my lady. He is turning."

The pain swelled again and I couldn't breathe as the baby
rolled and squirmed, slowing a moment, and then another
explosion of agony.

"I don't want it. I don't want a baby at all!" I shouted. I
could think of nothing but the piercing pain that abused me.

"You must be patient. Not long now and you will have
your baby in your arms," I heard the little midwife say
somewhere in the far distance, but by now I felt I was
revolving around the ceiling, taking great gasps of air.

"I can't... Oh my God, I can't," I shrieked as the pain rose
to a crescendo and then subsided as I felt my whole body
opening to release, allowing my baby into the world.

"Push now," urged Ursula. There was no feeling but the
force of the moment as my baby slipped out. I heard a thin
wail, but closed my eyes. I was so tired.

"A fine big boy, Evina, my lady. Everything here, all
fingers and toes counted. I will clean him and you can hold
him." I tried to lean forward but another strong pain forced
me back. I could hear the baby cry, but the sound floated off
into the distance and I could not think why I would want to
know about it. It had nothing to do with me now. I didn't
even have an urge to look at what had caused me so much
pain. It was done.

I slept deeply for the remainder of the night and part of
the following day. When I awoke, my throat was tight and
raw, hammers roaring in my head. I had a bone-shaking
fever that lasted for the next three days. I drifted in and out

of tormented sleep, only aware of Kristy bathing my forehead and the smell of lavender water. Little else registered until one morning I woke and the sun was streaming in. Kristy had pulled the heavy drapes aside and opened a window to let in some freshness. There was a stale, putrid aroma in the room and I realised it was me that smelled so vile.

"Where is he, Kristy?" I managed to whisper, trying to rise. My breasts were heavy and uncomfortable, and a slow trickle of sticky warmth slid down my body. "I must feed him. I am bursting."

"I will wash you first and tell Rosa to bring him, but she will have fed him already, my lady."

"No. Oh no, I want to feed him. Get him for me, Kristy."

As the scent of my son's tiny being filled my nostrils, I felt my back straightening and my energy returning. He was beautiful, his resemblance to Otto startling. Such a giddying rush of tenderness as I could not have imagined filled my heart as I held him for the first time. I marvelled at the perfect little body and pulled him close. He stiffened and screamed. I cooed and rocked and opened my shift to expose my breasts, but the wail increased and his little arms flailed against me. He turned away from me, would not suckle and continued to scream. He heaved his tiny body, widening the space between us.

Kristy took him and laid him in his cradle. Instantly his crinkled red face softened and his screaming became soft snuffling sobs as he calmed and finally closed his eyes. I stood bereft, icy fingers of fear clutching my heart.

CHAPTER 13
Sorrow

EVINA

It was bitterly cold; the liquid from my eyes and nose froze on my face like frosted ribbons. I cared nothing for the weather or that my fingers and toes were burning and numb. My sorrow was overshadowing all other feelings. I'd walked so far away from the palace that the landscape looked unreal, unfamiliar. The leafless trees ahead were solid and unmoving with a frosty mist like a painting with no colour. I knew the forest skirted the huge gardens, but I was unsure how far I had walked or where I was. I had on my thickest fox fur and a hood, strands of which were stuck and frozen to my cheekbones, but I had forgotten my gloves and muff, and I only had on light leather boots. I turned, hoping to see the house, but the misty shifting fog had obscured the distant landscape. I knew I had to go back before I was missed or froze to death. Perhaps, I thought, that would be better than bearing this terrible feeling of loss.

How foolish to think like this. I must fight for my boy. My Leoska. How can it be that I could imagine that things could not change? I knew somewhere in my heart that I would be able and capable again. I would learn to love him. And he would learn to love me!

Already my Aunt Marysieńka would be worried. She still felt responsible for me. After all, it was she who had brought me to Warsaw with my mother. Where was my mother? She should be with me to tell me what to do. I was sure she would know how to deal with my Leoska.

For a moment, my thoughts sped backward to the time when we arrived in Poland. We were so close when we came here as strangers to the family, closer than we had ever been, and I had cherished those moments. Marysieńka had ruined that. She had taken my mother from me, kept her with her, away from me, and I hardly saw her. I spent more time with my Aunt Katarzyna. I hated Marysieńka!

I turned, thinking to return, and realised that I was lost and so cold I could hardly move.

"Evina, my lady, come back, it's freezing." Through the mist, someone was running towards me, waving my squirrel gloves. It was Kristy, the tiny, shrivelled little soul who had loved and cared for me since I was born.

"What are you thinking of, my lady? You should still be in your laying-in period. You will get ill again. The baby thrives, you know that."

As she reached me, my legs gave way and I slid onto the frozen snow. "But without me," I sobbed.

Her strong wiry arms lifted me and forced on my gloves. Wrapping one of my arms around her bony neck, she turned me back and led me through the garden. Slowly we climbed the steps, crossed the terrace and returned to the warmth of the palace.

"How stupid of me to be out here," I cried. "What is wrong with me, Kristy? I felt I was suffocating with my tears and needed air. I never thought about leaving him. I just wanted to breathe. The last thing I wanted was to be away from my baby boy."

But it seemed that everything was preventing me from being with him. The doctor had proclaimed me unfit, too melancholy and traumatised by the birth to be of any use. My 'vapours' were not good for the child, he said solemnly, and I was too exhausted to protest.

All I wanted was to sleep, or to be as far away as possible.

"Where is my baby? Where is Leoska?" I asked Kristy, my teeth chattering. We were in the warm kitchen. She removed my boots and massaged my feet. The pain was excruciating as the blood ran back through them.

"He is not here. Your Aunt Marysieńka has taken him away to be cared for with her boy Jakub."

Panic seized me and I tried to get to my feet. "How can she do that? Her care has already lost her all her previous children. Only Jakub lives. How many now? Three girls and a boy? All dead. Why does she think she can care for babies? I must get him back."

Kristy held me firmly as I struggled to rise. "He is strong, much stronger than hers ever were. Come to bed now or you will get a fever again, my lady. You need to rest. I am sure she will bring him back. Perhaps when he is weaned."

"I don't want to talk about him being weaned. Feel my breasts, Kristy. They are bursting with nourishment for him. I want to feed him." I was sobbing loudly and Kristy held my shaking body as I cried my frustration into her shoulder.

"Hush, my lady. He is being well fed. Rosa is a good wet nurse." Then Kristy added, soothingly, something I already knew but didn't want to hear, "It's not usual to feed your own babies. Not for ladies like you."

For me, all that mattered was that the cot in the nursery was empty, no soft downy skin to caress, no little fingers to hold and marvel at. No wrapping or tucking blankets or shawls. No listening for his soft breathing when he lay asleep. My arms were empty, my breasts heavy with milk that he would not consider, although I had watched him sucking sagely at Rosa's dappled tits.

Now there was nothing to show for the pain, the effort or the need of him. Such grief I had never felt before. I had waited so long for a child of my own and now he thrived without me. Taken from me only seven days after his birth.

They say I shook him and shouted at him. I did. Yes, I did! But he was screaming, he wouldn't let me feed him. He pushed me with his tiny pink hands; he pushed me from him. Just days old and he pushed me away. I cooed and talked to him for hours but he puckered and screamed the whole time. I could no longer look into his eyes as he squawked and squealed at me. I sobbed with utter frustration.

"He needs to feed. Leave it to the wet nurse," said the doctor who had taken the wrinkled, red-faced little demon from my arms and placed him in the bassinet.

"I have milk... I want to feed him myself. Why won't he take it?"

The doctor sighed and lifted his hands in a gesture of 'who knows'.

"How can that be? I am his mother. I have fed him for all these months in my womb and he has rejected me. On sight he rejected me. Why did that happen?" I hesitated as I asked, for the words were now becoming awkward and thick in my mouth. I had not voiced out loud that word 'rejection'... although, of course, it was obvious to everyone around me from the moment of his birth, when he turned his tiny head away from my milk-laden breasts and screamed his newborn wail. In the end they took him away.

CHAPTER 14
A Year of Pain

EVINA

I was sent back to my house in Warsaw, away from my baby boy. That first year changed me so much that it is hard to describe my daily pain and disappointment. I went every day to the palace and begged to see him, but mostly I was refused.

When Leoska was still tiny I was not allowed to see him at all. Eventually my visits were limited, and, no matter how much I pleaded, I could not take him back home. Marysieńka told me she did not trust me not to hurt my baby.

"Please, Marysieńka, how could you think I would harm him?" I had begged.

"Because you shook him and dropped him into his bassinet, screaming and shouting that you hated him. He is a fine healthy boy, and Jan feels that being Marek's grandson he should be taken good care of."

"Did I hurt my baby?" I asked Kristy.

"No, my lady, but you became very distressed, and it was thought possible. He is Jan Sobieski's nephew and that gives him the right to take control and refuse you access to him."

"I can't bear it," I wailed, but as the days passed I took my pain and tucked it away, knowing that I would be able to be with him eventually. I spent hours at home gazing into the street and watched the seasons pass.

The agony of those days without him became a tight knot of resentment and loathing in my heart toward the power that my aunt and uncle had over me. I hated them. Leoska had grown fast in the care of several nursemaids in Marysieńka's household. After much pleading, I was promised that I could return to live in the palace with him if I felt well enough. Of course I felt well enough!

When my Leoska was already one year old, I returned to the Royal Palace.

My own household was secured and I moved back with my small retinue of servants.

I was so entranced with my toddler that I couldn't leave him, and spent hours playing and talking, trying to form a bond with him. He would turn his eyes toward me with recognition, but often moved away from me as if in fear. If I reached for him, he would raise his arms as if to push me away and howl for his nursemaid.

"It will take time, my lady," she told me. "He is a good little soul but he doesn't yet know you as his mother."

"Who then does he know as his mother?"

She said nothing, agitated, knowing of my distress.

"What is it?" I insisted.

"Marysieńka has spent a lot of time with him," she said. "Yes, he calls her Mama, but he calls me that also. He will come to know you."

I was infuriated but kept my counsel, daily encouraging Leoska to call me Mama, refer to Marysieńka as Aunt and the nursemaid as Nanny. But he would not let me love him. I felt a cold stone of guilt in my heart, as I must have created this rejection when he was first born and refused to be near him. But, I could see him every day and make him the focus of my life.

Although I still served Marysieńka as lady-in-waiting, I would never again feel the closeness I had done before. I seethed with jealousy when Leoska rushed into her arms whenever she visited him.

Times were changing dramatically as the Russian Cossacks had occupied more border towns. Jan Sobieski was sent to liberate them and returned again to Warsaw victorious. He was indeed Poland's hero! But not for long!

The attacks were soon resumed. Everyone was concerned, and tension increased daily as we heard of more places that had succumbed to the combined attacks of the Cossacks and the Ottomans. With many battles and much bloodshed, the combined hordes moved westward and triumphed over the undermanned Polish forces. Even though the Tatars were Orthodox Christians they were taking advantage of the triumphs and rode forward like a wave of a firestorm, burning, raping and enslaving those in their path.

The destruction was widespread and pitiful and brought fear to us in Warsaw.

Jan and Marysieńka were together throughout that season, and he was heard to say, "By God, if this continues, there soon won't be any more Poland. Our king does not know how to rule."

"And it is only you, my darling, my beloved husband, who can save our country," Marysieńka was heard to reply.

So, moved by her confidence in his ability, Sobieski resolved to defend Poland against the combined forces and, early the next year, insisted upon action. He called his troops together and gave an impassioned speech against the cruel Tatars and the heathen Muslims. He swore to drive them from our God-fearing midst.

"It is disgraceful and an offence in the nostrils of God that an infidel nation darkens our great homeland," he cried, lighting the noble fire of patriotism in all who heard him. "I am determined to be brutal and merciless against these savages. Men of Poland, I expect you to do the same. We have defeated them numerous times and we can again succeed."

"Death to the infidels," was the excited reply.

We were all so proud as we listened to him. Plans were made to move the court further west as the battles and destruction had reached as far as Lvov, less than three hundred miles away. But within the next few weeks,

Sobieski and his army covered many miles, pushing back the advancing troops and liberating thousands of Christian captives. We were all so relieved. While he was away fighting, Marysieńka gave birth to a baby daughter, Maria, her sixth child with Jan Sobieski.

Meanwhile, the king, without council, had ceded huge areas of wealthy territories to the Ottomans with the Treaty of Buczacz. In the entire Commonwealth, there was not a Pole or Lithuanian who was not indignant at the humiliation of their country. It was considered an affront to the whole nation. All agreed that the Treaty of Buczacz would not be honoured, and so another great army was assembled with Sobieski at the forefront yet again, determined to save his beloved Poland. He wrote to Marysieńka continuously, advising her of his movements, so we all knew much of the battles taking place. He told of a huge army of Moldavians allied to the Ottoman cause who had been convinced to join the Poles, thereby adding to our troops and enabling a defeat of the Ottomans.

'*They have joined us. It is unthinkable that they should fight against us,*' wrote Sobieski. '*It is a source of great mortification and sorrow to my Christian heart. This war is, after all, nothing but a struggle between contending faiths, the followers of Muhammad and those of Jesus.*'

Sobieski wrote daily to Marysieńka, telling her how the severity of the winter had caused the Ottomans to abandon their fight and return to the warmth of their camps.

'*We attacked,*' Sobieski wrote. '*Time and time again we attacked them. From our army, many good men perished because this Ottoman army has been so manly and valorous a force. We were near defeat. But because of our men's extraordinary resolution in our good cause, we held on and defeated them in only two hours. Our men who have had limited provisions finally feasted from the camp of the Ottoman leaders.*'

Very soon the actions of the king were deemed by the Sejm to be nothing short of high treason, but by then Michal Wiśniowiecki was extremely ill and died soon after.

An unfortunate and unsuccessful ruler!

Sobieski was greeted everywhere as a hero, with joy and gratitude that the Muslim hordes had not gained a foothold in the Commonwealth.

We all moved to the old Sobieski residence in Lvov, which was in the process of being extended and rebuilt as a 'Royal House'. It was a lovely place to live, a feast to the eye. A perfect balance of graceful architecture and carved marble figures, full of art and beautiful imported furnishings and a library unequalled in Europe.

During this time Jan Sobieski was intent on fortifying the town of Lvov so that we all felt safer. He had lost concern in what was happening in the Sejm until Marysieńka suggested that it would be in his interest to stay informed about what was being decided with the election of the next king. There were several competitors for the Polish throne including candidates from France, England, Denmark and Transylvania. Sobieski's name was also on the list since the people wanted a hero whose abilities had been proven to protect Poland. Not one of the other contestants could make that claim. But there were some in the Sejm who did not want such a powerful man on the throne. The meetings often ended in chaos, but it was finally decided that Jan Sobieski would be crowned the new King John III of Poland and Lithuania. This decision made my Aunt Marysieńka the queen.

It was a surprise to us all, but Jan had been nominated by the szlachta and the common ranks because of his unending service and his brilliant performances on the battlefield.

Marysieńka's sickly little two-year-old Maria died, and she was inconsolable until she found that she was pregnant yet again. Hope sprang that next time they would have a healthy child. Life regained a little more normality.

CHAPTER 15
Back to Warsaw 1676

EVINA

Leoska was delighted with his new status and exceptionally excited to be included in the grand coronation parade, the biggest celebration that Warsaw had seen in years.

How proud my Otto would have been to see his son Leoska riding in an ornate carriage padded with crimson velour and white satin, and Jan Sobieski being crowned king of Poland and Lithuania. It was indeed a triumphant occasion. A gasp swept through the crowds when Uncle Jan appeared on a huge white Persian horse in a blue cloth of gold trimmed with diamond trappings. He looked magnificent dressed in a blue sable-lined coat, interwoven with gold and silver, and diamond and ruby buttons. Pearls and ostrich feathers completed his attire.

Later, King John as he was now known, addressed the attending members of the Sejm, szlachta and his royal court, with words that brought us back to reality.

"I may look today the prosperous and victorious king but although I have attacked the enemy, I have not slain it. We may feel peace has finally come to us but the Ottomans will not rest until they have taken their revenge. We have now to assemble an army that will defeat them once and for all. Amongst you there are men of great military abilities and who are loyal to the cause of defending our great Commonwealth. I will be honouring with promotions those who have stood with me and who I respect for their military abilities."

King John raised some of his most loyal and trustworthy Hetmans to Grand Hetman of the Crown, and several others to Field Hetman. It meant a great deal more privileges for those whose rank had been elevated, and there were whoops of joy and approval.

Marysieńka smiled her admiration as he continued. "As I speak to you now, I know from intelligence sources that the Ottoman leaders are recruiting and training, seeking allies and raising more infantry, so we must be prepared. I will of course try to find an end to this warring without bloodshed if at all possible, and negotiate rather than fight."

Indeed, over the next few years, King John III proved to be as good as his word and kept the infidels at bay.

In 1679 Leoska was nearly nine years old with a quick temper and an irreverent tongue that often landed him in trouble. He also had charm, for he could convince his great-aunts Marysieńka and Katarzyna of his good intentions, his honesty and integrity. As he grew he began to stoop as if opposing his height. In a space of months it had increased so much and he was pitifully thin, the bones of his wrist jutting out at odd angles. He would not eat and I had become more and more obsessed, watching him grow thin and pale. Every day I tried to encourage him. I could see him fading, and it was as if he enjoyed it. No, not enjoyed it, but enjoyed watching me fretting about him. He seemed to take an unwarranted pleasure in it, so that I would end up crying with frustration.

What could I do? Since he had been born he would not take succour from me.

"You must eat, Leoska. Please let me help you. Don't you care at all about my feelings?" I asked. "You are all I have. I want us to be close."

"You're not the only one who has feelings," he answered in the pinched voice he used when talking to me. "I can't bear you following me around, pushing food toward me. Leave me alone."

"But I only want what is best for you. You are a growing boy. What is it that offends you so?" He ignored me. "Leoska, answer me," I shouted at him. "What is it?"

He turned and spat his reply. "It's the way you look at me. Your eyes pity me and make me feel worthless. I hate your eyes; they are the colour of mourning. They stand out from everyone else's and I can see them even in a room full of people. Sad, mourning eyes intent on disturbing me."

Leoska had walked briskly away, trying to dismiss me, but I followed him into the garden and then along to the stables where his horse was being prepared for his lesson.

Marysieńka had just arrived and was alighting from her carriage as our voices rose. She strode toward us, clearly annoyed at being disturbed. "Why is it that wherever there is a din and voices raised it is you two? You should not argue. You, Leoska, must respect your mother and not taunt her so, and you, Evina, are behaving disgracefully. Leave the boy alone."

My eyes filled with tears as Marysieńka swept away.

"Silly tears, Mother. What are they for?"

Pain broke through me with his words. Although I was always expecting it, his cruel tongue had taken me aback, his need to crush me and to humiliate me with his refusal to allow me to be his mother.

I blamed this entirely on Aunt Marysieńka. We didn't bond when he was born because he was taken from me. I wanted to cry and shout out my pain, but I had learned that it brought no regret from him and gave him more to deride me with.

"Do you really think you can fool me with your tears?" he sneered. "You care only for yourself."

I needed to find a way of closing my heart to his words so I turned my back on him and walked away. It was the only way I could deal with him.

My own private world was diminishing into a tight knot of constant worry.

It was wrong of Leoska to imagine that I was selfish. It wasn't that I didn't care. It was that I cared too much. It devastated me. I hated it, but I understood why he became irritated with me, and his reservations about me. I was becoming less patient and more difficult than I should have been.

The terrible pain and bleeding that had tormented me so returned with a vengeance, but I refused to see the doctors again. They would suggest another child, and for that I would have to marry again. I was unprepared to do that. But in many of my dreams I held a baby to my breast, its rosebud lips searching for me. The feeling was so exquisite that I awoke with sourness at its lack of reality, and cried or snapped at poor Kristy who had no idea why.

The previous year it had been suggested that I have another husband. Because of the border wars we had moved to one of the Sobieski palaces in Żólkiewski. There had been a visiting French count, Francis de Bougé, who wanted a French wife. Without consulting me, Marysieńka had suggested that I would be suitable. The count was exceedingly ugly. He put me in mind of a great toad with his cold eyes and multiple chins. I was horrified and had refused outright. I did not want to leave Poland and my boy.

I begged and pleaded with Aunt Marysieńka to withdraw her suggestion, which she eventually did.

Although I nurtured a deep resentment of my aunt, I was pleased that she had not insisted on me remarrying. I was also worried about her as she had by that time had fifteen pregnancies, with only Jakub, Teresa and Aleksander still living. Her health had always been bad and the pregnancies difficult, but every time she saw her beloved Jan, she got with child again. He still came and went between the endless battles he commanded but, nevertheless, had enough energy to impregnate my aunt on every visit.

I had been ill again with the terrible bleeding, and so I convinced myself that I must have another baby.

Looking back, I know that it was then that my reason disappeared, and I started to live in my unreal reality. During every pregnancy I had attended Marysieńka, felt for her and cried with her as another stillborn came into the world. In my head, I experienced her world with her and, somewhere in the midst of it, I ceased to define what was hers and what was mine. It was on the day that Marysieńka's latest baby had arrived I became somehow convinced that it was I that had given birth.

On the morning I had woken with a start, the pain in my belly was real to me and the movement of my baby was real too. I knew that he would be born soon.

I stood quivering, frozen, unable to remember the simple sequence of the actions I needed next to do. Time vanished and minutes could have been hours or the other way around. I could go neither forward or backward in my head. I felt light-headed and reasonless, dizzily waiting for composure that would not come.

I caught a sliver of light as I turned toward the window. A giant web was collecting the dew, and tiny beads, like sparkling diamonds, were gathering along the wheels of silk. As the sunlight hit the drops, they looked like a row of fairy lights twinkling there just for me. How long it must have taken to make those intricate patterns of such beauty. I had looked for the weaver but could not see anything, so I watched the little beads of light drip towards the earth below the sill.

Was I drifting slowly into madness, I wondered? I feared the line between myself and insanity was as fine as the cobwebs above me.

Eventually, I pushed aside the fear and allowed myself to feel the joy at the thought of the new life that I was about to deliver.

I made up my mind that I would return to Warsaw to the house that Otto and I had when we married. It had remained closed since I was allowed to come back to court when Leoska was a year old. Such a long time ago, but I needed to go back and make a life for my new baby. It would be different this time. My face was wet with tears of happiness.

I had to find Leoska and tell him so that he would understand why I had been so difficult. I needed to show my boy how much I cared for him. Since he had run away from me, I had felt ill again, my head hurting and nausea sweeping through me.

I waited until everything stopped spinning and quickly brushed away my tears. I wanted to find Leoska with a smile on my face so that I could tell him my news. I made my way to his room. It was strangely quiet as I walked the long corridors of the palace, across the landing into the east wing to where the children lived.

As I approached, I could hear nothing, so I tapped on his door. There was no response so I opened the door slowly. I could smell him, my son, so different to everyone else. The bed had been made, the canopy pulled and draped. I picked up a pillow expecting it to smell of Leoska. Instead it smelled of rosewater, which was what the new laundress had taken to adding to her rinses. The bed must have been changed that morning. I left and walked down the dark corridor to the playrooms where Aleksander and Teresa spent most of their lives and then to the schoolroom where Jakub and Leoska had their lessons.

Everywhere was deserted. No sign of the team of nannies or the boys' tutors. I turned, intending to return to my room feeling sad and lonely, the pains in my belly increasing again. I needed to get Kristy to call the midwife.

As I started back the way I had come I found a maid with a chamber pot scurrying toward the back stairs.

"Where is everyone?" I asked.

"Gone to church, my lady." She bobbed and moved away but turned as I clutched my belly again. I felt the grinding cramps that I had been experiencing for the past few days. I was desperate for this pregnancy to end. "Do you need help, my lady? I will find your maid." She scurried off and within minutes Kristy was with me. The pains had then reached such a pitch that I was convinced I would give birth there on the landing.

By the evening all sense of reason had left me and, although I have no memory of it now, I had got up and gone to Marysieńka when she needed me, helped her with the birth of another little dead girl and walked away with the body carefully wrapped, convinced that she was mine. I had locked myself away until Kristy had come and taken the baby away.

Kristy and Doctor Shtevanski had finally calmed me, dosed me and explained that I could not have another baby. How could that be true? I was only twenty-nine.

While Doctor Shtevanski had been kind, Marysieńka was less so.

"Evina, how could you do that? You must pull yourself together. I will not have you behaving like this. You are acting like a madwoman. Unless you get better you will have to leave the court. We cannot allow you here if you are going to be such an embarrassment."

"You took my baby away," was all I could say.

I had never spoken to her of the pain and sorrow I had suffered in that first year of Leoska's life, because I had been allowed back to the palace. At the time I was so grateful to be able to see my son. Every day I let the bitterness toward my aunt stay deeply buried.

Kristy stayed with me through the night, but the pain seeped into my dreams. I thought I woke screaming, though my tormented voice was only in my mind, because when I opened my eyes, it was only Kristy's sniffly breathing that disturbed the calm silence of the house. My skin was wet with the sweat of fear and hatred. All my senses were lost in darkness. What seemed close floated in mid-air, small noises expanded into gigantic sounds. Nothing made sense. Tormented thoughts raced through my brain. Where was my baby?

Now I remember nothing of those dark days or the days that followed.

CHAPTER 16
1680

LEOSKA. Aged nine.
My first memories were all about hunger and the inability to enjoy food, not all food, obviously, but the everyday succour that my mother and family enjoyed brought waves of nausea to me. During my nine years I had seen many doctors who proclaimed that I was a healthy, wilful boy who needed bleeding often and whipping regularly. My propensity to scream loudly when I felt ill, always at the meal table, usually meant I was forced to leave without having eaten a scrap. It wasn't that I wasn't hungry; I could certainly occasionally eat at my Aunt Katarzyna's, and she proclaimed to my healthy appetite every time I stayed there.

This caused my mother to retreat into her tight little space with a look of such despair that, before very long, it was suggested that I should move in with Aunt Katarzyna and Uncle Wladyslaw permanently. I knew that was not the answer. I enjoyed too much the power my rejection of nourishment gave me. I liked it too that my mother was tormented by my lack of cooperation. I didn't know why. Nor did I try to understand. It seemed that was what I was meant to do.

My mother had tried to nurse me, so I am told. It was a memory I cared not to remember, but what did lurk deep in the folds of my mind were her constant efforts to nourish me.

She, and anything she offered, nauseated me. She would bring me special things: fresh strawberries, sweetmeats of soft marshmallow or rose-flavoured posset.

I would feel my stomach clenching, blood pounded through my head, and my throat would burn so that I turned away. As I grew older I tried to assess the feelings but could not. I had some deep fear and a recollection that she wished to harm me, although I have no memory of anything but her passionate regard for my welfare.

"How pale you look, Leoska. You are not eating properly," she would say. "Please eat for your mama. Look, look what I have brought you." Sometimes I would gag. Her face would shrivel and the eyes that haunted my dreams would fill with tears. Her pain at my rejection was clear to see, and even through my own discomfort, I revelled in it.

I did not want anything from her.

I wanted her to know that it was she who had done this to me. Like the residue of a dream, the memory of her doing me harm haunted me.

But what had she done to me? Although I cared for her, I was afraid of her. Of what exactly I could not fully comprehend.

I often studied those deep lavender eyes, like dark ponds, the surface of which was placid enough, but what lay beneath? Treacherous waters or murky secrets?

She deliberately set herself apart and was as surprising as a thunderstorm on a sunny afternoon with her moods. At first glance she appeared a plump, good-looking woman whose age was difficult to define, but she was strong-willed and had the demeanour of stiff, unyielding fabric.

I don't think she liked many people, and her frustration with me cast a dark gloom into her glances. She loathed my stares and would work to catch me out. "What, Leoska? What is it you are looking at with such a disagreeable face? Do you find it so difficult to be pleasant?"

Her tone annoyed me. "With you, yes."

Her expression became more pained than usual; her forehead creased dramatically, her eyes misted and her mouth turned downward in an expression of dismay. She fingered the little birthmark on the side of her neck. "What have I ever done that warrants such disregard for my feelings?" She turned and scurried away, and I could hear her muttering and snivelling like a beaten dog.

I was indulged and happy. My uncle was the King of Poland, crowned in the grandest ceremony that could ever be imagined. King John III, my terrifyingly brave and clever great-uncle, was very good to me. He gave me a new horse to ride, a fine Arabian with a blond mane and tail, and I called him Marek after my grandfather. The royal estate where we were residing at Żólkiewski was vast, and I was allowed to ride and hunt with the men. In fact, I had the very best of everything. I had little time for my mother's fussing.

One day, a year previously, I returned after a day out hunting with Uncle Wladyslaw, and my mother was waiting for me, holding a cake. She had on a pretty gold overdress, opening down the front to reveal a russet underskirt, which suited her well. She was holding the cake above her belly just under her breasts and she looked to have a large stomach. I hoped that I was mistaken and it was her position that made her look thus, because I would be appalled if she had managed to get pregnant without a husband.

It was a fine day and there were tables out across the lawn and a handful of guests enjoying afternoon refreshments. Mother beckoned to me, but when I dismounted I deliberately walked Marek toward the stable yard, and ignored her.

Behind her, the welcoming party celebration for Great-Aunt Marysieńka's parents was being held in the garden. They had just arrived from France. Her father Marquis Henri de La Grange d'Arquien was to help set up a new army for Uncle Jan.

I could see the French ambassador and his family, our priest and several of Uncle Jan's Hetmans. Marysieńka was in the garden with her children and her usual distended belly.

By the time I came back into the garden, the cake had been eaten.

"I made it especially for you, Leoska," my mother declared sulkily. "And now it's all gone. Such a shame! It was your favourite too. I don't know why I bother."

"Did you eat it, Mother? You shouldn't you know, you are getting fat." I turned my back on her and greeted Jakub and Teresa who were calling to me to join them.

Once again my words stopped her for a moment. I could feel the tension in her. The air between us became very still and I moved away.

"Leoska. Don't ignore me, please. Don't you want to know why? I thought it would please you."

"Nothing you do or have ever done pleases me," I replied, not wanting to know about the cake or her broadening shape. "So please leave me alone."

My mother didn't wallow but sniffed loudly and, as if resigned, said, "We stand at odds, you and I, and it is beyond my understanding. I will not bother you again."

"Good. It will be better for me too." I walked away then, the bones of my knees cracking with the tension of wanting to escape her words.

For as long as I could remember my mother had taken to caring for my great-aunt Marysieńka's babies, so many over the years that it was hard to remember them as they nearly all died. This caused my mother constant stress as she blamed her aunt's bad health and neglect of them for their demise. The only three still living were Jakub, older than me by just over three years, Teresa, who was born just before my aunt was crowned queen and would soon reach her fourth birthday, and Aleksander, who was two years old. The very year that Teresa was born, her sister Adelajda, who had just reached her fourth year, died suddenly, and it seemed that history was likely to repeat itself.

Aunt Marysieńka was pregnant yet again, and my mother was beside herself with worry. I didn't realize how distressed she was until last year, when Marysieńka had given birth to yet another stillborn baby and my mother had tried to steal her little dead body. It had taken hours for her to return the baby, and then she had hidden away for several days crying and cursing.

I was not interested in her grief. It seemed pathetic to me that she should worry so, when Aunt Marysieńka seemed so resigned to losing them.

As time passed, my mother Evina became a wraith who scurried around, ostensibly still a maid-of-honour to Queen Marysieńka, but her duties had been curtailed since she had taken the dead baby thinking it was hers. From then on, she never seemed quite the same again and disappeared into her own little world.

Such a ridiculous woman! Some days her resistance was palpable, her angry moods rolling and clashing, and like a thunderstorm she would bang and crash about, the next day he would become hunched and haunted, her body shaking with silent tears. Whatever her emotional weather I had tried to avoid her.

Some days she followed me, asking endless questions. Was I well? Should I be more warmly dressed? Did I take care when I was training? Had I eaten that day?

There were times that I reassured her, but mostly I feigned deafness or ignorance and hurried away, leaving her sighing and ignored. She forgot things and sometimes talked nonsense, and Kristy was always around to reassure her that all was well.

All I could see was the craziness and, as time passed, I was relieved that the pestering about food stopped. When I did see her, she did not bother too much with me, often appearing agitated and distant.

It was a relief, as I was not interested in her problems. Nor was I interested in the feeling of hunger that I carried with me every day, only in the power at being able to control it.

My hunger curled inside my stomach like a great worm.

When bidden to the table, I could find a million excuses for not attending meals, or I would eat a single piece of food, chewing lengthily and carefully hiding chunks in my pockets or sleeves. It absorbed my very thoughts. The only time I forgot about it was when I was studying or asleep. I did not worry or fret about the pangs, but concentrated on the absorption of the act of not eating.

Other thoughts and feelings were pushed to the side and were not allowed to pursue me. I had to concentrate wholly so that all other aspects of my life diminished.

The lack of a father did not hold my attention at all. There was no room to pine for the loss or for the affection or comfort that he would perhaps have afforded me, nor for the seemingly irrational behaviour of my mother and her obsessive longings.

Instead my whole concentration was fixed on how many tiny sips of water I could survive with, how many tiny crumbs of bread I could hold in my mouth so that the saliva softened them to a liquid.

Would I swallow or spit? The decisions were all-consuming.

What a sense of power I had, crushing my own resistance.

There were many ways to pretend, and I was quite able to deceive everyone. I bent low over my plate and then wiped my mouth carefully, concealing what I spat out. I could even transfer food into my napkin before it reached my mouth. It was so easy to chew and smile. I had precious little appetite anyway, but I had come to enjoy the sensation that came from not eating: the fizzy emptiness, the rumbling sensations adding to my feeling of control.

Didn't all the saints live on air alone?

The evidence was gone within minutes as I always walked in the garden after a meal, carefully depositing the titbits of food where the foxes and birds would soon remove the evidence of my deception. That gave me so much pleasure, and I always returned to the house with a satisfied smile as if the fresh air had fortified me.

"Why do you smile so, Leoska? Who do you think you are deceiving? Me?" My mother laughed, her bitter ironic laughter that had no meaning, no warmth. "No, not me. Others may be deceived, but I know you are not eating at the table, and hiding food in your clothes. You are a fool, Leoska, to take your health for granted."

"Do you think it funny?"

She shook her head. "No, what makes me laugh is you, and how you try to make a fool of me as if you don't like me. You, my only and beloved son whom I nurtured for nine long months..."

She stopped as if surprised at the turn of the conversation, and started to laugh again, but this time it sounded hysterical and threatening. Then the look she gave me was cruel, crueller than anger. It was a look of pity.

"You have beaten me. I cannot look at you any longer," she said as she turned and walked quickly away, sweeping her dress up at the sides so that I could see her heels hitting the ground hard as if she wanted to stamp away our relationship.

Even as she left, I could feel how my words had hurt her. For a moment I thought she might return, but she did not. I was saddened in my heart for I had never spoken to anyone else as I did to her. I turned and walked away, feeling suddenly bereft at the loss of my mother.

CHAPTER 17
Dark Days 1680

EVINA

I wondered about the journey of my life, which had taken me from such hope and happiness to so much despair. I had imagined it all so differently; how I would complement my husband by being attractive, clever and witty. Our children would be strong and well behaved so that everyone would be proud and smile, know how well I had done, how charming and well-bred I had turned out to be. How loving and capable.

Marek Sobieski's little illegitimate French daughter.

I did not want to be like that anymore. I wanted to be strong enough to see my son grow into a man. I wanted to live a life not dominated by my pain, my bleeding body and my desire for another child.

Most days I was sure that I was not mad but I doubted my own judgment. Soon it would not be up to me anyhow. I found myself flittering in and out of understanding, in and out of being there.

Otto started visiting me at night. His tender touch opened my heart. He would sing to me and caress me as I drifted in and out of darkness. On those nights I slept badly and woke in a tangled mess of thoughts, my body in a sweat both hot and cold.

Several nights I walked with Otto through the beautiful moonlit gardens.

As we stepped out through the door onto the terraces and down the steps into the garden, everything behind me dissolved into blackness. I held tightly onto Otto's arm whilst crossing the lawns to the fountain. I would leave him there and head down into the depth of the water, my nightdress trailing in the blood behind me. Down so deep, to the dark green muddy depths where peace and happiness flooded through me. I floated in a euphoric dream of contentment before returning.

Otto would scoop me up and, laughing together, we'd head for the downy green lawn where we kissed and made love. Happiness drenched me. Some days I could not bring myself back into the real world and I found just taking a breath difficult. I would hide in my room for days.

Kristy was endlessly caring but, in the end, she too found my moods beyond her ability. She brought me food and often bathed me. She did not understand where I had been or why it affected me so. Some days would be easier. I could smile and work all through the day and evening, eat normally and serve my aunt well, although my concentration was ethereal. Sometimes I would forget what I was supposed to be doing.

Marysieńka's latest pregnancy coincided with mine but I told nobody. I knew I was pregnant because my pains had stopped and the bleeding slowed down. My breasts were tender and my belly growing. I was tired and not quite well. I could not sleep and I would lie for hours in the dark waiting for the dawn when I slept a little, rising late, pale and exhausted. But every day the certainty and joy grew in my heart, and as the months passed I became stronger and determined not to let Leoska anger me.

When the day had finally arrived, I was transcended with joy that I had finally had my baby. I rose from my bed without disturbing Kristy who had taken to sleeping in my room with me. Her gentle snoring assured me that she was fast asleep.

I went down the long corridors and crossed the landing into the east wing. Soft moonlight lit the passageway through the long glass windows along the way. I moved silently as I knew that the guards would be on duty at the far end, where a staircase led down to the kitchens and servants' quarters. I didn't want to disturb them. The nursemaid was asleep behind the door next to the nursery. I waited and listened. I could hear the nursemaid's deep rumbling snores as I paused. Turning the handle of the nursery door, it moved noiselessly and I stepped into the room.

The smell of newborn baby filled the air, and my happiness grew to bursting.

The door was still ajar behind me so I pushed it shut. My baby was there, waiting for me. I couldn't remember why he was there, but it didn't matter. I was here and would feed him when he woke. I stood in wonder and gazed at him as he stirred gently.

No need for him to be here on his own. Should I take him now, I wondered? Should I wait for him to wake? I did not know what would be the right thing to do. Best if he is with me, though, his mother. He needs his mother.

I watched as he stretched and yawned. As I reached into the bassinet he made a soft mewing sound. He was hot and ready for his feed, I felt sure. I would take him to my own room, but first a little fresh air.

I took him through the great hall, out through the main doors into the garden. It was the beginning of May and the weather was fresh and mild. A silky moon was balanced in the warm, windless sky. I stood in my long white nightgown and glowed like a paper lantern in the moonlight.

Happiness surged through me. I had my baby. He slept sweetly in my arms.

Although the moon had risen, it gave little light, but there was a faint glow from the stars that dusted the sky. In the soft luminosity I could only see the outline of his nose and forehead. I rocked and cuddled my little boy close to me. He turned and nuzzled into my breast and my heart exploded with love.

This was how it was meant to be.

Oh, Otto, you will be so proud. Wait until you see our baby boy. Later we will look at him together and observe every aspect of him, his sweet little mouth, the shape of his eyebrows, the curve of his soft pink cheek.

In the distance I heard voices and running feet. My only thought was that my little boy must not be disturbed, so I quietly moved along the bush-lined pathway that led to the back scullery door. It was unlocked and there was no sign of the guard usually positioned there. I looked around for him. I was going to send him to see what all the noise was about. I could hear people surging around the garden so I quietly locked the back entrance and walked the length of the deserted kitchen to the doors that led to the east wing staircases. I locked those doors too.

"We are safe here, my darling, safe and warm. I will rock you for a while until they go away, those noisy people."

I settled onto a big armchair in front of the still warm stove and gazed at my sleeping infant.

I was happier than I had ever been in my life.

Two hours later my aunt sat, back straight, her hands folded in her lap. She had long since perfected the art of her position as queen.

"Evina, I am distressed by this, but it can carry on no longer. You cannot steal my babies just because you want one of your own." Her tone was colder than I had ever heard.

What could I say? I did not know whether she was right or wrong to accuse me. I no longer knew what was right. I stood shivering. If I had not known her well, I would have thought that she was feeling nothing.

"Evina, are you listening to me? I am saddened to tell you this, but Jan has arranged a place for you. We have decided that it would be best that you go away from court for a while."

She lifted her hands as if to prevent a response.

"It needn't be forever, but just until you are well again. Do you understand, Evina?"

"Yes." I stood still, my body encased in a white gown with my arms restricted so that I could not hit out. My anger had made me lose control, and as my baby was taken away from me I had screamed and fought. My arms and body inside my wrapping were sore and bruised, but I had calmed enough to listen to my aunt.

"Jan will find you the very best care, after all you are his..."

"Niece, yes I am."

I had looked across the room at the faces of those before me and all I saw was pity and enmity, but from not one of them could I see compassion or even a reserved judgment. In their eyes I saw only questions and confusion.

I felt suddenly sick, and a dark curtain drew about me so that I could hide. Hide in the dark. Gradually some part of me conceded that there was no escape, and my fear gave way to anger that my aunt could do this to me.

I lifted my head and spat my words. "You should not forget that I am Marek's daughter and my baby is his grandson."

I watched them all staring at me, a mixture of worry and distain in their eyes, and all my conviction and monstrous confidence suddenly leaked away. I was stranded on a bridge between my dreams and reality.

"Evina, you have no baby," Marysieńka's voice had softened. "That little boy is mine and Jan's."

As she spoke I crumpled into realisation.

Oh God, it was true.

What made me believe he was mine? Dear God forgive me. God help me.

What could I say? I no longer knew what was right. Everything that had seemed real, safe and certain had unravelled and left me drifting in a place I didn't recognize.

Arokja Private Mental Hospital/Asylum 1680

The doctor asked me again, "Do you understand why you are here, Evina?"

I shook my head.

"The king has had you committed here for the rest of your life, unless of course you get well again. We will take care of you but you must realise that you can't leave without permission. Do you understand that?"

This time I nodded. I had been cast away but I was in darkness, and they asked me questions I could not answer. My reason had deserted me. It didn't matter anyway. My baby was gone.

CHAPTER 18
1683

LEOSKA

It was years since they took my mother away, screaming and shouting and appealing to God for forgiveness. I had been shocked at what had happened and had kept out of sight, watching silently as her poor, wretched, tear-stained face disappeared into a black coach that took off along the road leading out of Warsaw toward Arokja.

Konstanty, the baby my mother had taken, was now a plump and healthy little three-year-old.

I often asked Great-Aunt Marysieńka about my mother. She assured me that Mama was being well cared for and would be allowed to come back to court when she was better. I vowed to be kinder to her when she returned, regardless of how I felt.

Life for me at court continued much the same. It was full of study and hard physical training, for I was expected to become part of the force that defended Poland from its enemies. I had the best tutors, the best horses, and I was growing stronger daily now that I was feeling less of a need to control what I ate.

It was as my activities and training became more intense that my eating habits were far less of an obsession.

As time passed, I could eat almost normally. I could never begin to understand the reason, but since my mother had been taken away, food no longer seemed a threat to me. I was doing well and was considered to be a fine horseman. In another year I would join Jakub to train for the Hussars. I would learn to use a pike and a musket as well as my sword and dagger. It was essential that my riding skills were above average too, as the Hussars were considered to be the finest riders and the best battalion in the whole army.

Jakub would soon be leaving as he had proved himself and was two years ahead of me with his training, but I was pleased with that. I was already catching up. My duelling instructor was delighted with my progress and sent me tougher and more experienced combat partners, some much older than me.

My body improved as I ate well and trained hard.

Wars continued along the borders, and the Ottomans had taken Vienna and were intent on invading Lvov and Kraków. Uncle Jan had immediately allied with the Holy Roman Empire and with Bavarian and Saxon allies, and formed an army to ward off the forthcoming invasion. First the Ottomans had to be ousted from Vienna so that the war could not escalate. Jakub would ride alongside his father against the infidels, but I was considered yet too young to accompany them.

By 1686 I was nearly sixteen. I had been training hard and knew I could hold my own. My life had taken a new turn. I was now preparing to leave with my battalion of Hussars to fight the Ottomans. I was a strong horseman and a good swordsman. Uncle Jan himself was pleased with my progress so felt it was the time for me to be involved in active battle to help keep our Commonwealth safe. I would fight with him and Jakub under the king's banner. I was excited at the prospect and, although I knew how many men we had lost, was prepared to do battle for our homeland.

My mother would be proud of me now, I thought, as I was issued with a steel and flint musket and fitted with the new lightweight plate-metal body armour, shoulder protectors and a breastplate. I was now tall and well built, and Uncle Jan thought I looked as well as my father had done when going to battle before me.

I thought of my mother often but had had no word from her. It was now six years since I had seen her. I was not even sure that she was allowed to communicate with the outside world, although I knew well enough that both Uncle Jan and Marysieńka wrote to her and to her doctors.

I resolved to ask Marysieńka if she would write and tell my mother that I was going away to fight. I knew she would want to know about me. I had grown up and no longer harboured any fear of her. I wanted her to know that, and I wanted to see her on my return, regardless of whether she was well or even whether she would remember me. I wanted to make my peace.

CHAPTER 19
Arokja 1687

EVINA

Working in the garden in the fresh air, with the sweet smell of blossom in my nostrils, I allowed myself to remember why I was there. As my mind cleared and my memories returned, I gained a deeper understanding of myself.

Realisation of what I had done washed through my thoughts, leaving me to wonder why I had been so tormented and obsessed with wanting more babies.

Perhaps if Otto had not died... perhaps if Leoska had not rejected me... perhaps if my mother had not gone away?

I could not find the answer and decided that indeed fate was involved in everyone's lives, and perhaps accepting that would have been the solution for me.

Surely that realisation proved that I was ready to leave.

I no longer remember the exact chronology of the first months there, only that there were times when the sorrow and drama of what I had done weighed heavily upon me. But soon the monotonous daily chores, the prayers and the repetitive mundane routine dulled my senses.

When I first arrived, it was indeed a sanctuary. There was no reminder of my life previously, no need to express my hankering for a baby or explain my behaviour.

Almost all the women there were those who did not fit into the expectations of the normal, and found themselves like myself, removed and incarcerated, so as not to cause embarrassment.

I wanted to be back in court. I was no longer tormented with longings or desires. I wanted to see my son. But I was in a madhouse, or 'private hospital' as the doctors preferred to call it, with little hope of leaving. I was a prisoner, and there was a world going on outside without me. When you are thus detained, the world shrinks to the stone walls of the building.

There was no entertainment, no gossip or change to the daily routine. Some days nobody spoke for hours, sometimes there was no reason. Some made a point of mumbling or singing, just as one would turn a spindle to make sure it still worked.

Could I get permission to return, I wondered? Would Uncle Jan Sobieski allow me back in court?

I knew I could not leave here without permission, but I did not want to go without knowing that I was well enough. Even though my care and treatment had been kind and patient, the doctors had failed to improve my physical health. Pain and bleeding still assailed me monthly, and I found myself slowly weakening.

A new doctor arrived that spring. He had come to our 'hospital' after studying and practising in Milan. He was called Doctor Romanowicz. He was tall and rather gaunt-looking, but there was a warmth about him that I liked. His company pleased me.

He spent a great deal of time with me, examined me thoroughly but offered me little hope.

"It is a tumour. How it starts we are not sure, but any irritated organ can set it off. In your case it has started in your womb. I have treated many people with tumours and I have seen many recover, but yours is far too advanced. I am afraid to tell you this, but your battle is lost. That which started in your womb is now invading the rest of you. It feeds on your body. It invades everything."

"Please, doctor, I want to know. Can anything be done?"

"No doctor I know would try to cut it out. I cannot offer you hope."

"I no longer need hope, that left me when I left my home and my son. I do not battle to keep my body, only to keep it free from pain. Can you help me with that, Doctor Romanowicz?"

"I will, madam. Before death you will have a few better days when you will be convinced that it has left you. It is the way it goes, you will have unexpected energy and feel better. You must use this time to prepare yourself for your departure."

"I understand. But what happens then? Am I gone from everywhere forever? Is there nothing else?"

"I am not sure that I can answer that, but I believe the soul leaves the body instantly as it can hardly wait to be free. This world offers us pain and grief, and I think the soul releases all as it moves on. Death frees the spirit from earthly suffering. I believe that we can return again to the physical world when we are ready."

"I hope that is true. I have lost myself in this life. I would like another chance. Will I remember this existence?"

"I don't believe so. I think a veil of oblivion keeps memories of past lives from rushing into our present ones. There could be dangers in going back to events or episodes in previous incarnations, don't you think?"

I smiled my understanding. "I wouldn't want to remember some of this life, never mind others. What shall I do now?"

"Pray and hope. You have some time and, as I told you, some of it will be better, so you must make the very best of it. We will double the dose of laudanum and at the end you may have the opium." He did not avoid my eyes as he spoke to me but gazed into my face with an understanding that I had not encountered in anyone else in this place.

"I no longer live in a world of dreams and misconceptions. I used to dream of water, huge rivers and ponds where I looked at reflections of myself. I saw a young happy girl with curly brown hair and purple eyes, always beautifully dressed in silks and satins. But my dreams changed as did my body, and I would walk the moonlit paths where shadows bathed in the velvety darkness of the deep waters. It seemed a fitting place to think of death and leaving the life that was withering me so. In my dream I joined the shadows and headed down to the depths of the lake, trailing my blood behind me and fading into darkness. It felt calm and peaceful until I saw my Leoska, flailing in the distance. I couldn't reach him and I just sank deeper and deeper until all I could see was the drifting weeds and the trail of my own blood. When I awoke, I was crying and unhappy. Now I know what assails me I no longer dream such dreams. I still dream of trying to reach Leoska but I don't dream of blood."

As I hesitated, Doctor Romanowicz took my hand and his forehead creased in understanding.

"Do you think, doctor, that I was afraid of life? That I felt contaminated? Unfit to be a mother?"

He shook his head as he answered. "I do not know, Evina."

"I am not mad, you know. I am melancholic, lost and suffer such guilt that I cannot contribute to the world as I should, but I am not mad."

"No, Evina, I don't believe you are. Madness is seen as a persistent inability to associate ideas correctly, but ideas are not real. They are only the beginning of what happens, the reality is the manifestation of those ideas and being able to sort them out correctly to our experiences. You seem perfectly able to do that now."

"Will you release me then?"

"To what and where can I release you to? Have you a husband?" asked the doctor.

"I have no husband, he died in the plague in 1670."

Doctor Romanowicz shook his head. "I'm so sorry."

"Don't be on my account. I can hardly remember him. It was so long ago and we had little time together. We had been seconded to Winnica and the whole area was infected by the plague. Brought, they say, by gypsy travellers come from Germany. Poor Otto was just unlucky because few people in Poland were affected."

I remembered then, long ago memories of how I had been intoxicated with Otto when we first met. Everything was a challenge to him. His smile had been the most engaging I had ever seen. It was the smile of a man who found the world to his liking. I suddenly felt the loss of him and was saddened by the absence of him in my life.

"When I discovered that I was pregnant with my son Leoska, his father dying hardly touched me I am afraid. I was so happy to have my boy."

Doctor Romanowicz's face showed real concern, and he reached for my hand again. "If you leave here where would you go, Evina?"

"I am not sure, but I do have an income that I can live on, and a residence in Warsaw. If my servants haven't left, I can go there. I can make my peace with my family too if I am allowed to leave, even though, somehow, I feel I have been unfairly judged nonetheless."

"You will need regular doses of laudanum and later pure opium to help with the pain, you know. If you have good care in the city then I will apply for permission to order your release. I will be happy to do that."

"Can you also arrange for me to have a bath? This rotting discharge from my womb leaves me stinking." Doctor Romanowicz smiled. "Does that amuse you, doctor? It must be bad for you always seeing people at their worst, is it not? Next time you come I must be at my best for you."

I realised with some amusement that it must be the laudanum that allowed me to be so apparently flippant, because I closed my eyes and drifted off into my floating delirium of dreams.

CHAPTER 20
June 1688

LEOSKA. Seventeen years old.

Uncle Jan's health had declined so much so that he was forced to resign from campaigning, so under the command of the Duke of Lorraine, our force travelled south for many weeks until we reached Nagyharsány, a huge area of mountainous hills near the city of Darda. It was hot and uncomfortable there, and although we were ready for battle, we had to wait for orders.

The Polish forces had not done well and our generals could not agree on tactics. We were involved in several small skirmishes but could not move forward, as was necessary to restore Mohács, until they decided what to do. The generals had taken several days of planning and re-planning as the Ottoman forces had used their artillery to bombard and destroy the bridges and weirs of the river Drava that we needed to cross to attack their strongholds.

We found ourselves in a defensive position as the Ottomans had set up a fortified position in Darda, split their forces, and attacked us from front and rear at the same time. We had moved forward and then retreated to form again. Orders were finally given, and it was decided to attack rather than defend.

Once started, the battle seemed endless. The horse charge that we led flowed from the deeply forested slopes into the valley below, but because of the steepness of the terrain we had dismounted and charged into the Ottoman army from the side.

At least a hundred of my squadron were ahead of me and, in their frenzy, they had begun to spread and lose their form. We were trained as mounted cavalry not infantry, but the Ottomans, at first surprised, began to absorb the shock, take stock and push us back. From behind us came another charge, but they spread too far apart to cause any damage. The enemy had surged forward, some wielding huge slicing swords with blades so sharp they could take a man's head clean off.

My comrade on my immediate right was attacked and I saw a double-sided curved sabre enter his throat just under his chin and the point emerge at the nape of his neck. I gasped as his blood hit me. I ducked and swerved, taking his assailant with an upward strike into his stomach. My sword whirled out of my hands, out of sight, and, before I could properly rise, I was struck in the back. Turning, I grabbed the assailant by the belt and swung him across me directly into the blade of one of his own comrades.

With agonized screaming all around me, I staggered backwards only to be stabbed again, and felt another sword slice across my calf muscle so that I dropped to the ground. Blood was pumping out of my leg and my back. I turned and tried to rise but passed out almost immediately with the agonizing pain.

I remember nothing more until I found myself being lifted into a rough wooden wagon. As it moved slowly back to our camp, men and women from the destroyed towns and villages ran alongside our wagons, weeping with thankfulness for our victory.

Were we victorious? I did not know the outcome of the battle, but it seemed that we had liberated many towns and villages from the enemy.

I had seen the last breath of so many of my comrades and now I felt that I would soon join them, but I wanted to ask, 'Where have you gone? A moment ago you were right here with me, and now you are somewhere else. I can only see riddled, bleeding bodies, but they hold no one. Empty shells. Where are you?' It led me to wonder whether they were now reunited, all my dead friends. Were they together? Happy elsewhere? Perhaps I would see them soon? I wanted to. It would relieve me of my pain.

The agony in my back and leg was excruciating, and the movement as the wagon jerked to a stop made me cry out. I was moaning and sobbing when I heard a voice asking if I needed water or something to eat. I was instantly reminded of my mother.

How often she had spoken those words and I had turned from her with the pleasure of disappointing her.

A moment of Holy revelation? No, there was nothing divine about my thoughts or what struck me about my relationship with my mother. There was just a slow dawning of remorse. I had thought lately that my mother had done well to put up with me during my childhood, and now it saddened me.

There were times when anything and everything she said seemed trivial and stupid, and it was only natural to goad her. And equally natural that she would rise to it.

Now I realised that she was never trivial or stupid, sometimes wrong in her assumptions of me, but I never gave her a chance.

Lying in pain in that wagon as it rumbled along toward the hospital, surrounded by tears, blood, sweat and suffering, it was a vision of truth. My mother loved me and wanted me to love her.

My most desperate desire since I could remember was about being in control. But for what? As I watched my blood pumping from my wounds, I could see the futility and failure of those desires. A memory stirred that I thought I had forgotten. The guards breaking down the door of the kitchen where my mother was hiding with Marysieńka's baby boy.

Watching her being dragged from the house, her captors trying to prevent her from lashing out and attacking them. Into the yard they hauled her, and I hid behind a wall as they stopped her hands and arms flailing by strapping her into a jacket. Her clutching white fingers disappeared into the folds of the cloth that was tied firmly around her, her stricken face wreathed with distress and wet with her tears.

"Give me my baby, you insolent bastards. I want my baby back. He needs me. Give him back." She had screamed her sorrow as I watched her being dragged away.

I couldn't tell of the feelings that ran through my head that day. So much regret, but most of all of remorse for the contribution I had made to my mother's fate.

As my life was fading and I passed into oblivion, my only thought was the need to see her again.

CHAPTER 21
August 1688

EVINA
I fingered the screwed-up message in my pocket and choked back my tears as I told the doctor about Leoska's wounds.

I had received word from the king himself, my esteemed Uncle Jan Sobieski. He informed me that Leoska had been involved in a battle against the Ottomans near Mohács over eight hundred miles away from Warsaw, that he was badly wounded and there was a distinct possibility that I would never see him again.

"He is not expected to live long enough to get back to Warsaw." Tears welled as I told Doctor Romanowicz how difficult I had found Leoska as a child but also how much I loved him.

I begged him to help me get released.

Many days later, I had a communication that was heartening and terrifying all at the same time. Leoska was still alive and returning from the battlefield to a hospital in Warsaw, so badly wounded that he had lost a leg and the wounds to his body had reduced his mobility so that he could hardly move.

No other information was available at that time, so once again I begged the doctor to hasten my release so that I could see my son. My lovely doctor had appealed to Jan Sobieski and assured him of my sanity. He must also have told him of my tumour because, before the month was up, I had permission to return.

Uncle Jan did not contact me directly, but Aunt Marysieńka had written. 'You know that we will care for you and continue to help Leoska in every way that we can. Kristy and Vilmos will be informed immediately to get your house in order for your return. It will be made ready so that you can be taken care of. We have a doctor from the court who will administer what you need.'

It took another few weeks to arrange, and the day arrived for me to return to Warsaw.

I could still walk well enough, and although my weakened state was increasing almost daily, I determined that I would get back in time to see my boy.

As I said goodbye to Marcus, I told him, "Yes, you were right, I really am rotting from the inside."

He had obviously forgotten his remark and, with a quizzical look, kissed my hand and bade me farewell.

Little Isolte had hugged me tight and swept her hands across her face as if I was a swarm of flies.

I said goodbye to Anna and her many friends, whom she assured me wished me well.

When my coach arrived to take me back to my home in Warsaw, Doctor Romanowicz and I stood on the top step of the front entrance of the hospital, blinking into the bright morning sunshine while our eyes adjusted.

We'd had a long summer without rain and the colour had been bleached from the surrounding hills and valleys, giving the landscape a look of an old watercolour painting.

Although I wore a brimmed hat over my hair, I could feel the heat of the scorching sun.

The doctor took my hand and told me to whom I should apply to for care when I returned home. I would not see him again so I thanked him and wished him well. We knew this to be the end and I turned to say goodbye but couldn't speak. I trembled at the thought of a future without his care and kindness. But, without another word, he handed me into the coach, which sped off down the dusty road toward a short, unknown future and hopefully a reunion with my son.

The yard outside my house smelled of horse piss and muck. I carefully lifted my skirt as Kristy limped toward me, her eyes full of apprehension and tears. She wrapped her arms around me. I must have looked so different to her, but she welcomed me home as if I had been her own child.

She too looked old and tired, and I wondered at the troubled times I had afforded her. She had been steadfast and loving to me always and had cared for the house whilst I had been gone, praying daily, she told me later, that I would return.

"Where is Andrei?" I asked, "this yard is a disgrace and the horses need tending."

"He is dead, my lady. Don't you remember? The plague. We only have the boy to care for the animals at the moment but we will get a new groom soon."

Of course, how could I have forgotten? But it did all seem such a long time ago. I smiled reassuringly. "I do remember, yes, I do. Don't look so worried, Kristy. I am well and everything will come back in time. I feel as if I have been on a long journey. Is Davriella here?"

"Yes, my lady. She has been well cared for, but she is old now. You will not want to go riding, surely?"

"Perhaps, who knows?" I teased, but I knew that it would be unlikely.

Kristy did not yet know of my prognosis, although she understood that I was ill. She was fearful for me, remembering those days and nights of my madness when nothing could convince me that I was not able to have another baby. She did not ask until we had climbed the steps to my old home.

The familiarity was reassuring and everything was spotless and gleaming. My bedroom alone was different, as the old linens had been replaced and the drapes renewed. It looked beautiful with no residue of the dark days I had spent there in the year before my return to court.

"Our queen herself, Marysieńka, has arranged it," Kristy explained with a smile at my look of surprise.

There was also a question in her look, so I told her exactly what Doctor Romanowicz had explained. She sobbed loudly and I made my voice calm and gentle, just as she had done soothing me to sleep when I was a child. "You must know, Kristy, that I will sometimes feel better but my sickness will take me soon. I will need your help." She nodded and sniffed so I continued. "And Leoska is mortally wounded but he still lives and is in a hospital nearby. I need to see him as soon as it can be arranged."

"My lady," was all she could manage as she wiped her face with her sleeve and attempted a smile. She tucked her bony arm around my waist and helped me to the great comfortable armchair by the fire.

"What will I do when you are gone, my lady?"

As she removed my hat and my boots, I reassured her. "You will stay until I need you no longer. But, be assured that when I am gone you will be taken care of. You will be free to go back to France if you wish." That, I knew I could arrange, for my mother still lived there and would be happy to help Kristy if she so required. "You will also be free of any obligation to me or my family, and I will undertake to have an allowance arranged for you so that you need work no longer. Now, Kristy, get me comfortable and bring paper and pen on a tray as I wish to write some letters."

To our king and my esteemed uncle, I wrote:

'Thank you, Uncle Jan, for your generous help when I needed it. I know that I challenged your generosity sorely when I was distressed and I also know that I caused you and Marysieńka trouble and heartache. I am eternally sorry, but I wish to assure you that I am now well in my mind and returned to my home, which you have generously allowed me to keep. I will live quietly for as long as I have left. You know from Doctor Romanowicz what he has diagnosed and I trust his judgment wholly. I wish firstly for your forgiveness and ask that you will allow my Aunt

Marysieńka to call on me. I would ask you also to please honour the arrangements that I make for my servants, mainly Kristy and Vilmos, whom we brought with us from France. I also need your permission to see Leoska, who I believe is still in the military hospital close by. I beg you, Uncle, that I may be able to go to my son whom I love beyond words. I could not bear to die without him knowing this.

Evina.'

To Perrette-Lyse:

'It is so long since I saw you, dearest Mother, I wonder at your life now. I hope and pray that you are happy and safe and that your children are healthy. I know that Aunt Marysieńka will have told you of my progress and I am now well in mind if not in body. The years have passed almost without my knowing, and now I find my life drawing to an end. I know that perhaps my life would have been entirely different if we had stayed in France and I would not have had the benefits of such an amazing family and the care that I have been given, but still remorse drags at my heels. Could I have changed things? I do not know. I want you to know of my continuous love and respect for you. You brought me into this world through love and kept me safe throughout my childhood, and my only sorrow is that you have not known your grandson Leoska, who has fought valiantly for Poland and is now mortally wounded. I am waiting for permission to see him.

With fondest love to you, Mama.

Your daughter, Evina Genevieve.'

Marysieńka came to visit me. She had not brought any of her children and watched me warily throughout our conversation. "I am surprised at how well you look, Evina. Thin, yes, but surprisingly well. Are you really so ill that you could soon die?"

"I have been told so, but today I feel fine." I did not tell her that each day I needed more time and help to do the simplest task, and I was now on maximum doses of laudanum.

She too looked different, having lost two more daughters since I had been away. Although she was as always beautifully dressed, she had become plump and mottled. She was after all nearly forty-six and had given birth to eighteen children since she was seventeen.

She had four healthy children and planned, she told me with a twinkle, to avoid having any more.

Our conversation was short and stilted but I told her how sorry I was about my behaviour when Konstanty was born.

Marysieńka's reaction surprised me. She replied with tears in her eyes, something I would never have expected as I had always thought her hard and uncaring when her babies were born dead or died early. I know she mourned them, but with each birth it seemed to me that she became hardened to their loss. I suppose that was inevitable. I did know that she loved her children and had made great plans for them all.

"You really frightened me, you know. Konstanty was such a healthy baby and I thought that he would be the last." She sniffed and straightened her back. "Jan is no longer a well man and I fear for him, but my children are my life now. Politically we are still in danger from the Cossacks and the Ottomans, but in time my sons will retain Poland for us, you will see."

I could wait no longer. I had to turn the conversation to Leoska. It seemed to me that she was avoiding mentioning him. "I hope so, Aunt," I said. "But my son lies dying and I need permission to see him. Can you ask Jan to arrange that for me?"

She lifted her dark eyes, saddened now, as she too had been fond of Leoska and had watched him grow into a man whilst I had been away.

"It is already done. You may even stay with him if you wish, as the doctors have given him little time. Evina, dearest, I know of your love for him but he has little chance of any sort of recovery. You do know that?"

"I do."

I prepared carefully, and by the end of the year my own health had deteriorated dramatically and I now needed the opium. It sent me into a delirium of visions and dreams but relieved the incessant pain that now afflicted most of my body.

Kristy helped me take a carriage to the hospital and I managed to walk easily into the great hall and up the stairs to a quiet room where Leoska was being cared for.

Leoska's doctor told me that he was comfortable and assured me that everything that could be done had been.

"He is wounded so badly but he has survived the long journey back to Warsaw. We can only pray that he will recover enough to enjoy more of his life. He will probably never walk again, you understand, as he has severe spinal injuries. If he continues to bleed we will not be able to do more than keep him sedated."

No longer my little boy, but a grown man, he had lost all the softness and boyishness of his youth. His face was smooth and tanned but tougher, his dark brows heavier. His hair was long and smelled of black earth and burning, and needed washing. He lay without moving.

I could no longer control myself. My hands of their own volition lifted and caressed his cheek. Those same hands that had wanted to love and feel him as a tiny newborn. Those hands that had been pushed away more times than I could count. Those hands that had trembled with the need of him, but had been afraid of the feel of him, were now steady and loving.

I traced the line of his jaw, still as angular and sharp as ever, but in it I saw my own face as it looks now. Tears leapt to my eyes, spilling in a fast stream over my cheeks.

He opened his eyes. I swear I saw pleasure there. I watched him close them again but he had a whisper of a smile upon his face. "Mama," he breathed.

I took a deep breath. "I am here, Leoska. I will not leave you. You are not alone."

He was heavily sedated and the doctor told me he would probably sleep for most of the day. I sat close by his bed, gazing at the bulky outline of his body, a gap in the curves of the blanket below his knee where his leg had gone. Every so often he moaned and his face creased with pain, so I held his hand and spoke softly, telling him of my love for him.

He woke in the early evening and was given his medication, but he would not eat and sipped only tiny amounts of water, swallowing with difficulty.

He smiled at me and a surge of happiness overcame me. My tears would not stop and I wanted to tell him how I had missed him.

"What happened to us? I loved you so, but we lost each other somewhere. I wanted so much to care for you," I whispered.

Leoska spoke slowly. "Mama, I cannot explain why I felt so strongly against you... I could not take what you offered no matter how I tried. It was as if you were offering me a poison with your love. I felt so repelled I made them as one." He gazed at me as if trying to remember. "My early memories of you are tinged with fear and pity. Also of longing. Longing for a trust and love that I couldn't feel from you."

He paused, as if the effort of so many words overcame him, his pain obvious in his eyes.

"Hush and rest, Leoska."

"No, I need to tell you while I can. I feel such remorse at the lack of my ability to show my love for you. You were absent in my heart. I don't know any way to explain it. It was too deep for me to understand or undo. I can only say that I am sorry, and as I look at you now, I see how I was responsible for tearing you apart. Although it was not meant."

"I'm worried that I did terrible things to you as a child, that I hurt you very much."

"No, you didn't. It was I who hurt you. I disliked you, I was always cruel to you."

"I can't remember what I did... I wanted to ask you to forgive me, because if I did hurt you or was a bad mother, I'm sorry."

Tears formed in Leoska's eyes. "Let us forgive each other and ourselves. Perhaps it really was out of our hands and some unforeseen forces were at work." With laboured breathing, he continued. "Or perhaps some unfortunate pre-planned fate from before our understanding awaited us and saw this life as an opportunity to create this strange relationship."

"Did I reject you?" I asked. "I don't remember that... not at first... All I wanted to do was love and nurture you."

"No, I have no real memory of it being so. I do know that I rejected you. I led you to question your own sanity by my actions and words..." Leoska said as he tried to lean forward to take my trembling hands in his. "And now, Aunt Marysieńka has told me that I could lose you. Is there nothing that can be done for you?"

"No, it is spread too far. I have only days left. We will lose each other."

"We will die together then, as it seems I too have little hope. The internal haemorrhaging will not stop and I cannot move from my chest down. We will be reunited I am sure." His voice wavered but he lifted a shaking hand to press his fingers onto my birthmark. I took his hand and held it to my lips. I wanted to tell him what Doctor Romanowicz had told me, so I said, "When you were born, I tried to show you my love but time passed and somehow we grew apart. Now, we have no more of this lifetime. Doctor Romanowicz believes that we are reincarnated. I hope it is so and we can come again in a different light. Perhaps in another lifetime we could understand and love each other unconditionally."

CHAPTER 22
Reunited

LEOSKA

I watched my mother smile, aware of her love. Her face was aged, and getting it into focus was difficult. Looking at her soft greying hair pulled back from her now-bony face, her fine Sobieski looks inherited from her father, and her soft lavender, sometimes purple eyes from my grandmother, Perrette-Lyse, whom I had hardly known. My mother's eyes were hard to look at but they no longer repelled or tormented me. The familiar sense of feeling that she wished me harm had gone. She was still quite a handsome woman, straight-backed, and she had something patient and regal that had developed in her. The tiny lines around her eyes, the tired skin, the sweet smell of chamomile and soap; I felt I was coming to life after a protracted frozen winter of hibernation. I knew it was not so and that I was dying, but I trembled as my mother soothed me. She held me and would not let go. It was a gift beyond recompense.

All I could give in return was my acquiescence. For the first time ever. I felt my strength slowly draining away, the blood on my dressings weeping my life's blood. I knew that this was the end. It was time. I felt my breath slowing and I had to tell my mother. I pushed my final words upward and whispered, "I have to go, Mama. Hold my hand, stay with me. I love you."

CHAPTER 23
Together at Last

EVINA

I pulled him to my breast, my sweet boy. I knew that he had gone and that I would join him in days if not moments. In the meantime, I held his body and lived my love through the feel of him.

Leoska had taken his last breath in my arms. The room was silent and still. A moment of loss too deeply felt to comprehend.

I lifted my body onto the bed beside him and wrapped my arms around him. I promised myself not to fall asleep, as my pain had lessened with the last dose of bitter opium, but I could feel my own life force diminishing.

Had we wasted this lifetime?

Had we been set a task to learn through each other in this incarnation, as Doctor Romanowicz believed? I hoped so.

I stroked my Leoska's face as I too drifted into darkness, happy that we were joined together for our final parting.

It is over. For now…

PART 4
UNDERSTANDING

Musqat, Oman 1800s

For thousands of years the traffic in slaves from East Africa, India and the Mediterranean to the Persian Gulf and the Middle East was considered equally with any other type of commodity. Wealth was derived from the number of slaves owned and indeed was generally ignored by the British, who for many years saw it as a price worth paying to sustain the ancient societies upon which British rule depended.

Slavery has been accepted under Islam since the beginning of time, and it was normal for slaves to be taken as plunder from where there were disputes, but only if they were non-Muslims.

Rough estimates state that from the 8th to the 19th Century, between eight and seventeen million slaves were taken out of East Africa to the Oriental and Arabian slave markets. Several thousands more were from Eastern and Western Europe, Southern Ireland, Greece and North Africa. Many died or were disposed of along the way. Unlike the Atlantic slavery, most taken were females and young children: the boys destined to become slave soldiers or eunuchs, the girls household slaves or concubines.

Thousands of young boys were castrated to provide the eunuchs that every wealthy household depended upon, without any concern that they could die in their thousands by bleeding to death or with terrible infections.

Descendants of slaves in Arabia do not identify their origins with Africa, India or Europe because often they were given their freedom or earned status within their household. A contract/mukātaba gave them a legal status with an income providing they became Mohamedans. They were then allowed to marry and keep slaves themselves.

Our travelling souls, this time as **Leonard** from Zanzibar, and **Eveanya** from Mysore, India, meet to live out their lives as slaves in and around Musqat in Oman, where their love for each other in difficult circumstances leads to **Understanding**.

CHAPTER 1
Musqat, Oman 1825

EVEANYA WODEYAR

When the rain came, it came fast. It was very hot and the sun disappeared into the desert floor behind the huge clouds. Within minutes the water levels in the gardens had risen. The dry, parched earth, baked hard by the endless heat, was unable to absorb the torrent. Of course the gardeners would be pleased, but it made the pathways hazardous and slimy.

It was May, and rain was unusual for that time of year. I was heaving and straining, dragging a huge basket of cleaned pans through the arched walkway.

Stopping for a moment, I stood and watched the central fountain overflowing, and pools of glassy water spreading around its base. A pretty hoopoe bird landed close by, its black and white feathers and orange crest sparkling with raindrops. He spread his stripy wings and enjoyed the coolness of the unexpected rainfall. I too lifted my sleeves and smoothed the cool droplets into my sweating arms and wrists.

"Eve, will you get in here now," shouted Imanki, her arms folded across her enormous breasts. "I'm waiting all day, I need the pots. And straighten your veil, you are showing your scars."

Standing at the door of the outside bake house, Imanki, the tall kitchen slave from Zanzibar, beckoned for me to hurry. I grabbed the handles of the basket and pulled with all my might. I had been working since five that morning and my exhaustion was evident from my weak efforts.

I would dearly love a little rest. I had never been so tired. For months I'd done nothing but the crudest, filthiest manual labour, no rest at all, scrubbing, cleaning, then more and more. My back hurt all the time from lifting and bending. I was so exhausted that I wanted to cry, but I would not. I knew I was lucky to be alive.

Imanki helped me pull the heavy cooking vessels into the bake house. "I hope you have scrubbed these well," she frowned at me, "the last lot you did was still crusted."

"They are scrubbed, just look at my fingers, they are bleeding from the lye. I can't do better than that," I spat at her sourly.

Imanki pressed her lips together, flicked her heavy towel in my direction and inspected the pans I had brought. With a nod she dismissed me.

Adjusting the heavy black burqa that covered my face, I returned along the corridor back to the main kitchens where another batch of china and serving dishes were waiting to be cleaned. My mind was not on my task, but on the fact that I was still alive and would be given my freedom in less than half a year.

Those past few months had been hard to bear, and if it hadn't been for my beloved and dearest friend Leonard, I would have wanted to die. I was of little use to anyone with my distorted spine and my ugly, scarred face. It was only due to him that I was still living at all, albeit with difficulty. But I knew it would not last, and although the work was hard, I was no longer expected to perform in any man's bed.

I say I was of no value, but Leonard loved me and valued me, I knew. He understood my pain, and I his.

Soon we would be free and together. I knew he would take care of me.

As I hurried back to the washrooms my thoughts drifted backwards. It was hard for me to remember my life before I was like this. Before my disgrace.

Some of it has gone forever from my memory. I know that I was valued; I wore beautiful clothes and jewellery, and slept with the other concubines in fine silk sheets in warmth and comfort. My days were languid and indulgent, spent in the Turkish bathhouse learning new dance routines, massage techniques, singing and being pampered as one of Sakarbin Said al-Busaidi's favourites.

It was not always so. When I first arrived I was so young, but I had worked hard in the Sheikh's house and the harem. After the first few months I was assigned to serve Chole, the Sheikh's bad-tempered principal wife.

So much happened after that and my life was changed so dramatically.

It is passed now, but some nights I cannot sleep at all. Occasionally my father's words hum in my ears. 'You must be proud, whatever happens remember who you are, what you are, and let no one forget that you are of noble blood from a long line of leaders and princes.'

I no longer remember all of what or to whom he was referring. In fact, I can hardly recall his face. I know he was much older than my mother, kind to me, and I do remember that he was very tall. His name was Nalvadi Wodeyar and he was related to the Wodeyar dynasty of Mysore.

His second cousin Krishna Raja was four years old when he was anointed Maharajah, and so when I was born in 1805, the British still administered because Krishna Raja was too young to take over his duties.

I saw Krishna Raja only once when we went to a family gathering but he didn't speak to me. I was very young and so very different to the rest of the family. I didn't look as if I belonged to the Wodeyars at all. But then neither had my mother, who was never included in family invitations. It was my resemblance to my mother with her blonde good looks and violet eyes that had been the reason that my life had taken the turns it had, and why my stepmother sold me when I was six.

I remember that day well enough. My own mother I can hardly remember at all, as I was only two years old when she died. I am told she was a very beautiful blonde, taking after her Dutch father, Jacob Debeke. She was named Vani Eveanya and had married my father when she was just fourteen. My grandfather, the widowed Jan Debeke, returned to Holland when his daughter died, so I had naught but a vague memory of him.

It wasn't until my father married Rhana Kumarita from Kathiawar that I had any sisters or brothers. I remember my excitement when Nanja arrived in 1809 when I was four.

Until then my stepmother had been kind to me, distant yes, but she was young and living in a strange house surrounded by my mother's beautiful Dutch pottery and the carved furniture that had been brought by her father. All of which Rhana disliked.

She became more verbal about her tastes after Nanja was born. By giving birth to a boy she had established herself into the family and became more demanding and domineering.

There is still so much I cannot remember, but I know I was a happy child. We lived in a large house close to the town. My father was a keen gardener and we grew our own crops, flowers and fruit trees. My happiest memories are those that were spent with him in our garden, planting or harvesting the beans, nuts and mangoes. A little strip along the outside wall was designated to the rosebushes that my father adored.

He would sniff and smile. "Little Eveanya, there is nothing on earth that smells so beautiful."

He was right. There were few flowers anywhere that I had lived since. A few jessamine and orange blossom, but nothing smelled as sweet as the roses that my father grew. It was a shame that more of his time wasn't spent in his garden, because Nalvadi Wodeyar was a gambling man. He gambled every penny he earned and more. He borrowed, he lost, and his debts grew.

By the time Sani, my sister, was born in 1810,

moneylenders were pursuing my father, and we left our lovely home to live in a small brick house in town with no garden. Our lives changed dramatically and Rhana, my stepmother, complained bitterly all the time.

"There is no money. What am I to do? My babies will starve." Endlessly she had screamed at my father. He had become thin and haggard, and one day disappeared from our lives forever.

It was early morning when my stepmother woke me with her wailing and screaming. "Your father is dead. He is dead... he is dead. We have nothing left. Nothing. We have to leave."

She hauled me from my bed and shook me hard. I was sobbing too. How could he be dead, my lovely father?

Rhana dropped me and grabbed my hair. "It is the festival of Ugadi tomorrow and I have nothing." Sweating and dishevelled, her voice was cracking with emotion. For all her youth and beauty, she was reduced to bitter ugliness in her distress. "That he should do this to us. The wicked, wicked man. I cannot look after any of you. My sister's family will take Nanja and Sani, but they will not take you. You... you are a half-breed."

She pulled me to my feet and threw my cotton puthia and sulhanki trousers toward me.

"Get dressed, Eveanya. No jewellery, only your shoes," she instructed. "I will have to sell everything."

I could not then imagine that she would sell me as well!

CHAPTER 2
Exported

EVEANYA

I cannot remember the exact events from that moment, but within hours I was taken by Rhana's brother, my Uncle Dev, to a house on the outskirts of town. I was shaking and terrified, and after some haggling about how much I was worth, Uncle Dev handed me to an ugly, black-bearded man and left without a word.

The man held me tight. He wore a dishdasha and a coiled cloth on his head, so different from the Indian dress. He dragged me along a passageway and pushed me through a dark doorway into a tiny room with twelve or so other children of varying ages.

No one spoke, each wrapped in their own misery, some sobbing and sniffling, one small boy shouting for something. I didn't understand him so I could only imagine what it could be.

My tears were for the loss of my father and my family and everything I held dear. I was only six years old after all, and had been indulged and happy. I had no understanding that we could lose everything with what my father described as his little weakness.

Now he was dead, by what means I had no way of knowing. Neither could I imagine why I was in that place. When I begged my Uncle Dev to tell me why I was being sent away, his only reply was, 'To keep Rhana's children alive.'

The days and nights faded into each other. I discovered that the other children came from far and wide in India. Many only spoke Tamil, Urdu or Hindi rather than Kannada as we did in Mysore. Within the space of a few days, others joined us, some as young as three or four. The terrible sobbing and begging eventually became all I could recall.

I have no memory of eating, drinking or bathing, or being spoken to. I lay shivering and crying and praying to our god Ganesh to bring me good fortune.

We were there for many days. The bucket into which we relieved ourselves was emptied daily, but the younger children often wet and soiled themselves, so the stench became foul. We huddled together in our misery, not knowing or understanding our situation.

One early morning the door opened and a group of men with ropes entered. They started to tie us together. The eldest, a boy of about eleven, yelled and fought, so was secured first. His hands were tied behind his back, a strip of black cloth wrapped around his face and mouth. I could only shiver with terror as it came to my turn.

Where we went from there, I cannot recall, but we travelled in a wagon all the next day, tied and with our eyes and faces covered. When finally our blindfolds were removed, the biggest boy read the sign that stood in front of us marked 'Karnataka Port'.

"This place is where my father brings his spices to go to faraway countries. They are going to export us." He started to cry and we retreated into a sad, sobbing cluster of despair.

He was right. It was so, and within hours we were on board a large dhow and heading off into the Indian Ocean.

Soon we started to feel the nausea of seasickness as the seas rolled and raced. We were no longer tied, but in a filthy hold with other exports; huge bails of cloths and cases of what smelled like leather goods.

"You'll soon be better," declared the burly sailor who was responsible for keeping us together. "It's the last bit of the monsoon so stop wailing and clean ye'selves up."

Even the smallest of the children had curled up in their own filth and were mainly silent and shivering. I only remember being ill and frightened, the days and nights fading into one.

On arriving at a great port we were taken off the ship. Altogether we were only about twenty children, all from India. The eldest boy, who I now knew to be called Sadru, told us we were in Musqat. I knew it was a different country as the smells, the language and the air had a different quality. Only Sadru could understand what was being shouted at us as we were taken through the town to a big house that backed on to the slave market. The room where we were held was dark and cold, and we huddled together exhausted and confused. The older children remained tied, and some of the smaller ones were taken away. Two middle-aged slave women came and brought us bread and water. They were kind and gentle as they washed the worst of the grime off us, but only Sadru could understand their speech. By gestures they told us to sleep and gave us a blanket each.

"We are all to be sold in the Musqat market in several days' time, when other ships full of captives will arrive," Sadru informed us. "Some are arriving today from faraway lands, and one is due in from Zanzibar."

I had never heard of Zanzibar until then.

CHAPTER 3
The Musqat Slave Market 1811

KATUNGI/LEONARD

By some miracle I had survived the long sea journey from Zanzibar, even though I was covered with sores and bruises and was half the size of when I was boarded onto the ship. The loss of my family and home, the misery and loneliness, was to be my guideline for my life ahead. But I'd survived so far. Although I was terrified, I held my tears and distress and remembered my mother's words. "Always be proud and honourable, and behave well in whatever circumstances you find yourself, Katungi. Trust that things will always improve."

With hunger rumbling in my belly, my hands trembling at my side and in the stench of that filthy ship, I stood tall and tried to be brave.

From birth, my home had been in Zanzibar. I lived on the Bet il Moni plantation, close to the sea, an estate that stretched inland for many hectares and grew mainly sugar cane and spices. My mother Kitu had been taken from the Zanj area of Africa into slavery when she was very young, and had worked there all her life. We were lucky, as our Master Haissam bin Ahmed had been good to us, and my mother had raised her seven children there. She was a gentle and obedient woman, lacking in spirit and conditioned to her situation of hard work with little return. She considered herself fortunate as she had been allowed to marry Buntingu, my father.

"Too many children, Kitu," Master Haissam told her when I was born. "Any more than six is too many, so those who come later will stay only until they are seven and then they must be sold. I have more slaves than I can contend with." My father was rarely seen after that, as he was sent to the farthest fields to work, and live.

Therefore, from the moment I was born, my family knew that I would be sold when I was seven. Until I was three winters I lived with the rest of my family. After that, I was moved to live with the kitchen slaves in a small wooden shack away from my family. I ran errands, cleaned vegetables and washed dishes, for even the youngest had daily tasks.

Kitu would visit me often but explained that she could not afford to get too fond of me. She had, of course. I knew she loved me just as much as the others but, knowing that I would be leaving when I was seven winters, she kept her affections for moments when we were alone together.

"Wherever you go, you are to be obedient and well behaved, so that you will have a peaceful life. I will pray daily that you get a good master, close by, so that I can continue to see you." Kitu had told me from the moment I could understand it that I did not really belong to her. So I spent most of my young years working alone, mainly in the kitchens or on the plantation, but I was not mistreated and had become just what my mother wanted, a well-behaved, hard-working slave.

When my seventh birthday arrived I was sold and everything I had known was ripped away. Even the isolation and lack of family bore no resemblance to the pain I felt in my young heart when I was boarded onto that ship, not knowing where I would be taken, or to whom I would belong.

It had been a long and difficult journey as we had hit the monsoon and had pulled back several times. Many had not survived and had been casually dumped overboard.

We had run aground on a small island, and took several days to recover. When we did eventually arrive in Musqat, the adult slaves were brought up onto the decks and pushed out into the sunshine. Some screamed in pain, their sores and whipped bodies bleeding, their eyes so crusted they were blinded by the bright morning sun. Others sank to the decks in exhausted states, too emaciated to walk. There were far more slaves on our great ship than I had realised.

Although skinny and filthy, most of the children had survived, but they had not been chained below decks in the slops and slime like the adults. We, the youngest, were offloaded first, and then those who had been imprisoned in the holds were brought ashore.

Out came the whips, and slowly the shackled men and women were tied together. Those who could not walk were abandoned like the feral cats and dogs that were left by the seashore, to die alone in the blistering heat, or to be swept away with the tide.

We stood in the hot sun whilst the sugar cane, spices and coconuts were unloaded.

It was hours later that we were moved toward the centre of town, to the souq, where we were to be sold. Along the way the guards prodded us forward with their sharp sticks and waved their heavy whips, shouting about the forthcoming sale to the crowds.

The slave market was enormous, rows of buildings with barred doors, pens and fences just like the animal markets in our towns at home. There were already many people there, tied and shackled to posts, and some with gags and blindfolds.

Although one or two of the men fought and shouted, most of them were shut down and cowed into a pile of stinking no-hope, shuffling along with no idea of a destination, or a life of any sort. Never did I imagine that my life could get any worse.

CHAPTER 4
Recognition

KATUNGI/LEONARD

On arrival at the main market enclosures, the men, with their heads shorn, were led away. The women, their bodies filthy with vomit and excreta, were kept with us children. Buckets of water were poured over us and stiff brushes pushed up and down our bodies. Blood and muck poured from us all. What was left of our ragged clothing was pulled off and swept away so that we all stood naked, wet and glistening in the afternoon sun. A sweet-smelling balm was plastered onto our sores, and we were all given a cloth to cover our nakedness, women and children alike.

The best-looking young women were taken away to a separate area. Later, we would see them perfumed and adorned, ready to be sold as concubines to the wealthy Sheikhs, Imams and their ministers.

Hollow-eyed and dumb with shock, we crouched together in the compound for several days. We were fed, and our sores were treated with the smelly white cream. There were children of all ages and colours, most with tear-stained, haggard faces. Many were dark coffee brown like myself, others with varying shades of brown and olive skin, and a small white boy with red hair, skinny as a snake and ugly as an iguana. Where he had come from, I did not know. He had not been on the ship that I had arrived on. His eyes darted from place to place as if he was watching a butterfly, but he said not a word.

By the day of the sale, I had no feelings, other than fear. We were taken out into the morning sun, and into the small compounds, where twenty or thirty of us were crowded together.

There were at least ten pens, and to one side raised

platforms surrounded by the obviously more wealthy Arabs. There, the young females were being paraded up and down, and being fully inspected.

It was then that I saw the girl with the golden hair and wide violet eyes. Her skin was a soft honey colour and, even though she was dressed in clothes that looked like the other Indian children, she didn't look like them at all. All of the others with her had dark hair and eyes that made them easy to identify as coming from India.

The girl's face was grubby and tear-stained, her eyes wide with fright, but I felt a surge of something in my chest that I found hard to describe.

She stood by the wall, her eyes darting around in fear and trepidation. I felt it then, something so profound and deep. I wanted to move toward her. I thought her beautiful.

As she turned to look at me, an extraordinary feeling of warmth and knowing overcame me. It reminded me of the feeling that my mother gave me late at night, after I had woken fitfully from a dream or with a thirst. It comforted me. For a moment I felt Kitu's gentle touch and sweet love flowing through me. My mother would come to me in the dark of night and lay her hard-working little hand on my head, and I, with the knowing of recognition, relaxed back into my dreams. I felt it then; something, so profoundly deep that I could not explain, but connected it to the feeling of a mother's love.

The little blonde girl too made an involuntary movement toward me, as if she recognized me and thought our paths should come together. Her violet eyes shone for a moment, but were quickly extinguished as she was moved away by one of the guards, busy lashing out at an older child who had attempted to leave the compound. A very young child who sat snivelling on the ground had taken her attention. She lifted the child and gently patted her back.

I wanted to catch her eye again but she was swept away

in the mob of small bodies moving away from the guards. I tried to hold on to the feeling, but the reality of my situation overcame me again and I shivered and huddled fearfully back into a corner.

As the crowds collected in the market, I held my breath and covered my head with my hands.

A fat Arabian with a whip hovered around us, snarling and threatening us if anyone moved too far. Not that there was far to move, as the compound was small and all the older children were tied to the posts.

As people gathered it was plain to see that they were mainly Arabs, their curved khanjars and knives tucked into their embroidered belts. I had seen plenty of them in Zanzibar and knew that there were as many different tribes as there were in Africa. Each tribe wore slightly different clothing, but I didn't know enough about them to be able to distinguish.

My only prayer was to find a kindly master.

The noise was intense, and as the day wore on and the heat increased, the stench got worse. Many of the buyers held cloths across their noses as they moved around the compounds, pointing and shouting.

Even though I was so young, I had heard of the slave market in Musqat because Haissam bin Ahmed was originally from Oman. He had taken slaves with him when he went to live in Zanzibar many years before. I had not imagined that I could be sent there.

Besides the Arabs in the crowd, there were a few white faces. Others from the Far East with slanting eyes and embroidered coats, and strangely dressed Indians with their hair and beards wrapped in big coloured cloths. The already-owned slaves and servants stood around waiting for orders from their masters.

Shivering with fear, I put my head down and prayed the only way I knew how, to the great spirits that ruled the earth.

On requests from the buyers, our guards lifted or pushed us forward, one child at a time, shouting for a bid. Rough hands lifted me several times, examining me as if I was a piece of fruit in the bazaar. I was dropped again and again, as others were taken.

Some were hauled to their feet and passed around, examined closely, their mouths opened, their hair parted. Even their genitals were inspected as the haggling began. The auctioneer shouted above the din. The hysterical cries of the children made the noise unbearable.

The traders, who were looking for slaves to sell on, pulled and pushed until they secured what they wanted, tied them together and marched them away. I held my hands across my ears and watched the crowd.

As I scanned the bodies and faces of those around the compound, I noticed a very tall, fair-haired man. Dressed so differently from the rest, he stood out, pale and refined against the swarthy Arabs and Indians. Even in the heat, he wore a cravat and a white shirt, tailcoat and high boots. He was pacing along the perimeter of the enclosure, scanning all the children with a worried frown. He spoke to our whip-bearing guard. The conversation was fast and heated. I could not understand what they were saying, but their conversation was halted again by the continuation of the sale.

I was aware of the white man shouting and gesticulating as several children were taken to him and passed to other men, who carried them away. He pointed to me and I was lifted to my feet. He put his index finger under my chin and spoke to me in Swahili.

"How old are you?"

"Seven winters," I whispered.

That was all he said, and he passed me to another tall white man who hoisted me over his shoulder.

I lifted my head to look for the girl with the violet eyes, but she was being moved to the area where the decorated females were being sold. She had her arms wrapped around the tiny black-haired baby, who was barely old enough to walk. The golden-haired girl was being pushed toward a fleshy, dark-eyed Arab with an embroidered coat and several servants attending him. He was watching her closely, and it looked obvious that he was about to purchase her.

I wanted to call out to her, but I was being carried through the crowd away from the noise and stench. Behind me, an Indian servant carried the lanky red-haired boy, who was vomiting over his shoulder.

As we were dropped into a wagon, the white boy sank onto the rough planks beside me and groaned.

Eventually we were six children: three boys and three girls of varying ages, of which the red-haired boy and myself seemed to be the eldest. The tall white man had bought us, and within minutes we were passed a water flask and a blanket each. We lay where we had been put, without a word, and eventually we slept.

On waking, the wagon had stopped outside a small two-storied house. One by one we were carried into the dark interior, the smallest first and lastly the ugly redhead and myself.

It was a dark starry night and I was cold.

Inside, in the gloom of the oil lamps, a gentle white lady exclaimed and cried out at our state, touching each of us as she spoke. I didn't understand her words then, but she was concerned and kind and I felt that we were safe.

The tall man was frowning and distressed and spoke quietly to her as he removed his coat and immediately began to wrap us in blankets.

The only child who understood their words was the red-headed boy, who smiled for the first time and indicated to me that all was well. Although he had been severely sick before the journey, he was the first to enjoy the thick soup that we were offered by the Indian servants.

The lady and two others of our rescuers fed the three little girls with small wooden spoons. Then they were carefully bathed, their ragged hair brushed, and dressed in an assortment of pretty clothes. Wrapped in warm blankets, they were laid on pallets of camel hair in the corner of the room.

The red-haired boy and I watched each other warily, and although he was smaller than me, I reckoned he was older. He grinned and chatted happily to the woman as his face was scrubbed and he was given a blanket.

Turning to me, he said, "Me, Patrick. Who are you?" He poked himself in the chest and then pointed his grubby finger at me and asked again. "Who are you? Do you have a name?"

"Katungi," I replied at last.

So it was with Patrick's help we all learned the names of the others. The girls were from somewhere in the northern Mediterranean and called Louise, Lana and Meria, and were four or five years old. The other boy was black like me, but smaller. He didn't speak at all.

"Who are you?" Patrick went through the same gestures. The boy did not respond but surveyed us all with large, frightened eyes, and then sobbed until he could hardly breathe. The gentle white lady held him to her breast until he quieted, and then she soothingly stroked his head until he fell into a deep sleep.

We never did learn who he was, or where he came from, because he never did speak. Emily and Cecil Leonard, our new masters, called him Sam, and they looked after him the best way they could.

Each of us was given a space to sleep and, although the room was small and strange, I felt at ease.

I slept without fear for the first time since I had left home.

CHAPTER 5
Sold to Sheikh Sakarbin

EVEANYA

I stood as still as I could with my back against a wall. I was trembling with fear when a different emotion overwhelmed me. I stopped shivering as my eyes were drawn to the pen next to us. I had noticed the boy watching me. I felt immediately that I must know him. Our eyes met and he almost smiled, although I could see that he too was scared and bewildered by what was happening around us. He was very good-looking, dark-skinned with soft brown eyes surrounded by long lashes, and we appeared to be about the same age. His intense gaze had, for a few brief moments, felt reassuring and uplifting. A wave of comfort moved through my body, an intense feeling of recognition. It was only for a few seconds that we connected in a way that I cannot explain, for suddenly a little baby girl, sitting on the ground close by, distracted me. She started crying loudly, tears and snot covering her terrified face. She lifted her skinny arms to me for comfort so I picked her up and held her close.

Feeling her soft body as she clung to me reminded me again of my lost brother and sister, Nanja and Sani, and tears flowed afresh down my grubby cheeks.

Before I had a chance to turn again to the boy, I was pulled roughly out of the pen towards another part of the sale. A group of men were inspecting some of the younger women. One man in particular was beckoning the guards to bring me closer. I was pushed toward him and the baby was taken from my arms and passed to one of the merchants.

The man who was inspecting me was quite young, overweight with a hooked nose and a dark beard. He had a cruel, handsome face and he was beautifully dressed in a long dark coat, embroidered with gold trim, over a sparkling white dishdasha. On his head was a silk turban with a gold tassel.

He looked me over very briefly, turning me this way and that, until with one long brown hand he lifted my hair from my face. I noticed that the other hand worked his prayer beads. He gazed into my eyes for a second or two and a broad smile hit his fat mouth. He had noticed my mark and was stroking the tiny cross-shaped birthmark on the side of my neck. I did not understand what he said but his expression showed his approval.

I had closed my eyes in fear and, before I could understand properly what was happening, had been carefully lifted and carried away from the crowd to a horse-drawn wagon.

Two black-skinned African girls, older than I, were placed alongside me. Both were exceedingly pretty, and I later learned they were called Ora and Adell. We now belonged to Sheikh Sakarbin Said al-Busaidi, a wealthy breeder of horses and camels, and trader of dates and pearls. I later learned he was a sixth or seventh cousin to the Sultan of Oman and Musqat.

We travelled only for a short while and arrived at a house that was unusually large and beautiful, in a village just outside Qurum. It was close to the seashore, surrounded by mountains and a great wadi that spread into an open bay where boats and dhows were moored.

When we arrived we were immediately taken to the harem, and put under the guidance of the chief housekeeper, Fatima, a black African with a face like a squashed fig. She was responsible for the household cleaning, laundry, and all of the young female slaves, of which I was probably the youngest. On that first day, a hijab was tied tightly around my head, supposedly to cover my light hair, but all the other girls were similarly restricted. I was given a plain dark dress and trousers. My pretty embroidered shoes were discarded and now I went barefoot.

That night Ora, Adell and I were locked in a small room and instructed early in the morning to our duties, of which there were many. We only stopped for a drink of water and a bowl of rice and beans. If we were lucky we got a slice of spiced bread. Fatima carried a hide whip with her and used it often. Ora and Adell were quietly acquiescent and quickly accepted their new way of life, but not me. I had always been a good, obedient child and could not have ever imagined being restricted from movement when I wanted to play, laugh or run, or sleep. But from the moment of my purchase, I had no choice but to obey without question. I found that every minute of my day was ordered and controlled. I was whipped regularly for the faintest disinclination. I was six and a half years old, afraid and bruised all the time, and terribly homesick.

After the first few moons, and when Fatima thought I was duly obedient, I was instructed to serve the mistress of the house, as and when she required. I was moved into a tiny room with another girl, Jilfidan, who I had only ever seen from a distance.

Although still inside the walled harem, our room was attached to the main apartments of Chole bint Hari, wife of the Sheikh. Next door, wife number two Deilah, and further on, wife number three Zuena.

Jilfidan was a Circassian, taken by Ottoman rebels and brought south with hundreds of others over a year before. She was a blonde, like me, rosy pale-skinned and much fairer, with soft blue eyes that twinkled mischievously. She told me that she was nearly nine years old. Standing tall, she proudly announced that she had been told that she would become a concubine to the Sheikh when she was thirteen or fourteen.

"He likes fair girls and I am the fairest here," she told me. "You will probably be selected too, as you are fair and rather pretty, and you have unusual eyes. I hope you will, then we can stay together."

"I'd like that," I said, as she took my hand to guide me on our first mission for our new mistress. Not that I understood exactly the meaning of her declaration, but I admired her already.

Jilfidan had a charming wit and a naughty laugh that constantly got her and me into trouble. She told me that she was to start her training to become a concubine with Lumaria, the mistress of the concubines, when she was eleven or twelve. At the time I had no idea that I too would be sharing her training.

Chole, our new mistress, was the principal wife of H.H. Sakarbin Said al-Busaidi.

"We have to address her as 'Sayyida' – Highness, although she is nothing of the sort, only being married to a Sheikh and not a Sultan," Jilfidan told me knowingly.

Inside the harem, Chole was hated and feared by young and old. She never smiled or gave an encouraging word to anyone. She knew everybody and everything that went on and had ultimate power over the inhabitants. Chole had her own bathhouse and spent some time every day being washed, oiled and massaged.

Being wife number one, she had the biggest area of the house inside the harem and the most highly ornate bathhouse and terraces. She was the daughter of another Sheikh from a different tribe, and had become bloated and unattractive. She had been married to Sakarbin through a trade deal between two tribes many years before. She had no children of her own, but expected the Sheikh's twenty-eight other children to defer to her. Toward the Sheikh's other wives and concubines she behaved with a domineering haughtiness.

Most avoided her, when they could, but all were expected to call upon her for instruction and advice at least once a week.

Chole was a bad-tempered woman who shouted her wants and needs at us, kicked us when she could, and pinched our arms and legs whenever we went near her. She called Jilfidan 'Cat-eyes' and myself 'Grape-eyes', as if we were dirt on her shoes.

I constantly hid myself from her if I could, but Jilfidan laughed and said, "She is just a sad, fat old lady, jealous of anyone who is younger and prettier than she. Take no notice. Just never lift your eyes to hers, she will beat you to a pulp if you do."

We were expected to perform our duties as if we were invisible. I quickly learned that was the way to avoid being kicked or pinched.

I followed Jilfidan's lead and we became firm friends. It was she who helped me, showed me around and told me where to find things. The estate was enormous and hundreds of people lived there beside the Sheikh and his family.

CHAPTER 6
The Harem

EVEANYA

The walled harem was an imprisoned life, a segregated complex of buildings populated by all the females in the family plus a few unmarried or widowed sisters and aunts, but mostly by captured foreign slaves.

There were at least seventy females of many hues and manners of dress, various ranks and ages, plus lots of small children, who tore about squabbling and shouting and clapping loudly when they wanted attention from their mothers, the eunuchs or the servants.

Boys and girls were permitted unrestricted companionship until the boys were eight or nine, when they moved in with their father. They were mostly the offspring of the Sheikh's wives, Deilah and Zuena, and the numerous concubines who often stood or sat in gossipy groups, talking and laughing.

They were all the wives of one man, for that is what the Sheikh called them all, even though he only had three real wives.

There were of course a few jealousies and rivalries, and two of the most beautiful concubines, Thalis and Scylla, were never included in the groups of joking and chatter. They were Circassians, as was Jilfidan, and current favourites of the master. They were both pale-skinned and had dark eyes and hair the colour of dates. They stayed sullenly together, mostly ignoring the others. Even when meals were served, the brown Abyssinians and Somalians sat apart from the lighter European and Circassian women and children. There was a tacit understanding that this was how it should be.

The eunuchs and serving maids also lived in the harem, so there was always activity and endless noise. There was one main entrance and only the Sheikh was allowed entry. Even the male children who had reached puberty were excluded.

All of the Sheikh's older boys, personal staff, the male servants, advisors, managers, scribes, tailors and the cooks lived in and around the main houses. High walls surrounded the whole complex. The doors and entrances were grand and pillared with ornate and decorative covings. I thought it was a beautiful place.

"This house was built many years ago by the Persians," Jilfidan explained as we made our way through the gardens, past the fountains and along the arched walkways to the big storerooms.

We had been sent to collect fresh towels and bath sheets from the main laundry for Sayyida's bath.

"The Persians were here for a century, I think. There are other similar houses in the village. Not as grand as this one, though," Jilfidan told me proudly as she skipped along. Grabbing my hand, she veered off onto a side path, indicating another walkway, and led me behind the main house.

"We have to walk around the back here. This is where the Sheikh lives with his personal attendants and his army of slaves. It's the biggest wing of the house. We all have to walk around the back." She giggled. "But come, I will show you a little peephole where you can see what is going on in the big house. You must tell no one, though." She pressed a finger to her lips as we slid past the senior eunuch's quarters to behind the wall of the master's wing. A narrow alleyway took us to an area of climbing plants that had made their way halfway up an ornate wall. It was the outside of the main hall and the huge reception rooms.

"No, I won't tell," I whispered, already fearing that we might get a whipping if we were found out.

Jilfidan reached up, and pulled a small area of plant that

had obscured a long slit in the wall, probably part of the air ducts, and pressed her nose to it.

"Nobody there now," she informed me. "This is where they sit and gossip or devise strategies of trade or war or domestic problems. All the ministers and visiting Sheikhs, Imams or their families meet here in the master's quarters. Take a peek."

She stepped back and lifted me so that I could peer through the dusty slit, my nose pushed against the wall.

"This is where we will dance and sing for the Sheikh when we are trained. We will have our costumes made and be covered with jewels. What do you think of that?"

I giggled quietly at the thought. It was indeed grand inside, with silk hangings and beautiful Persian carpets of red and gold. All the seating was decorated and padded with plush material in shades of yellow and ochre. The tables looked like gold with marble tops, on which stood great lamps of ornate and intricate designs. I had never seen anything like it before. I also doubted that Jilfidan's words meant anything at all, and could not imagine that I would ever entertain the Sheikh.

We pushed our way back onto the main pathway, and soon had collected the towels and returned back into the harem. I could see that the main building was joined to the other wings by more paths and walkways, many of which were covered, and some had climbing plants that secluded areas where there were tables, cushions and rugs.

Time passed, and within the next year Jilfidan and I had become good friends. I told her about my family and why I had been sold, and she told me of her old home in Gilan close to the Black Sea. She'd had a carefree and happy life until the Ottomans came, beating the Russian troops sent to defend them. The Turks burned everything and took almost all the inhabitants as slaves, transporting them into the Arabian states where they were considered more valuable.

She told me that the rest of her family had gone to Egypt and, with a shrug, dismissed the conversation.

I was still homesick for my family and also for the gardens, pastures and lakes of my hometown, but Jilfidan seemed resigned to her fate.

"Don't you miss your family, Jilfidan?" I enquired.

"Not anymore. There is no point. I know I will never see them again and I am going to make the very best of it here. If I have children with the Sheikh I will be well looked after and will not have to work. Far better than being the wife of a poor man."

I laughed at her. She amazed me with her logic, but I was too young to understand what she meant. How could she think of having children; she was only a child herself?

As night fell in the harem, coloured lamps were hung along the arched pathways and up the stairways, which lent the house a dreamy magic. During the early evening, voices and sounds mingled. Nurses could be heard relating stories and traditional tales to their little charges, mingling with the endless swishing of the sweepers trying to keep the desert from the house and gardens, and the stream of water carriers hurrying to the kitchen. Often too, arguments between the wives, the eunuchs or the servants mixed with the general melee of sounds. The noises were not only from the variety of people but also from the mixed bag of cats, small deer, the shrill peacocks and birds that were free to wander around the gardens. The noisy fighting cocks that were penned at the back of the kitchen were often brought into the main gardens on contest nights.

Although we had little spare time, we managed to play with the numerous small offspring that lived in and around the big house. We generally kept our distance from the Sheikh's many children, who ranged from sixteen to a newborn. Three of his daughters were of a similar age to Jilfidan and I, but they were not allowed to play with us.

Sometimes they joined in the general fun and games in the courtyards, but they were carefully guarded by eunuchs and female slaves and were not often seen outside at all.

The Sheikh's daughters were all darkly handsome and haughty with different mothers in the harem, mainly the concubines, who did not venture into the main gardens at all and were rarely seen. I wondered if this was Jilfidan's fate, never to be allowed outside except when they were needed to dance or attend the men in the bathhouses. I soon learned that, as soon as we reached the age of twelve, we could only leave the harem with permission and heavily masked.

But, at that time, we had as much freedom as we were ever going to get, and we made the best of it. When the wagons delivering fish or fruit arrived, servants and eunuchs and the kitchen staff would be summoned to unload them, giving us the opportunity to slip easily past them and out into the surrounding shrubs. Sometimes we saw two of the Sheikh's older sons, Jahangeer and Musab, who were allowed to ride the horses and camels. Both were fifteen or sixteen, and they were always accompanied by guards and instructed by Hamid the horse manager, who had been in charge of the animals since he was a small boy himself.

The stables were a long way from the main house and completely out of bounds to us, even though we often sneaked down behind the ornamental bushes to watch the riders and the beautiful horses.

"I used to ride my own horse in Gilan," Jilfidan confided as we crouched watching a group of trainers breaking a young colt. "I loved to ride along the shore with the wind in my hair. Shall we try it one day?"

"How?"

"Perhaps we will ask one of the Sheikh's sons to take us."

I laughed at her, but realized she was serious.

She pushed out her chest and said boldly, "I will seduce

one of them," and added, "when I get a bit older, of course."

I didn't believe her, but, in truth, had no idea what she meant.

CHAPTER 7
A Real Family

KATUNGI/LEONARD
It is hard now to describe the kindness of the Leonards as so much time has passed, and so many things are changed, but none of us had expected such gentle concern as we were given that first night.

The following years were like a dream. We were living in a village south of the ancient city of Qalhat, several miles north of Sur where the great boats and dhows were built. It was a beautiful place with soft sandy shores, palm groves, small plantations and strips of cultivated land, all surrounded by a background of mountains.

We were told that we were not slaves but that we were free and would be taken to the British Isles when the Leonards themselves returned. We would be their children for as long as was required, and they would personally take responsibility for our education so that we could make a way in life for ourselves. Patrick and I understood what they meant, but the little girls were only too pleased to have a mother and father again.

The Leonards already had two baby boys in their care. A Bedouin woman, purported to be crazy, had abandoned them when they were tiny. She had disappeared into the desert and never returned. Gone mad, they said, with hunger and despair.

The small boys were twins, so Emily and Cecil named them Albert and Andrew, and even though they had been with the Leonards for nearly a year, they were both so small that we called them Pebble and Pip. Their background was a mystery, although they were, undoubtedly, tribal Arabs.

We were all treated so well and expected to contribute to the household and to learn as much as we could.

"Any sort of skills will hold you in good stead," Cecil had encouraged each of us. "You will need to support yourselves at home. I know that each of you will have a talent. Learn what it is and develop it."

Our daily work included working in the garden where we grew beans and kept chickens, sand grouse and a few goats, and we learned to build a beehive made out of hollowed palm trunks. Very soon we had our own honey, and it was so good that it became another source of income. We were laying the foundations for a good, productive life.

Patrick wasn't keen on the garden or the stock, but was an excellent swimmer and fisherman so happily provided crabs, shrimp and an assortment of fish.

Although the girls were still young, they learned to cook and weave, and sewing became part of their daily lives. The two servants who came from India were also highly qualified and adept at alterations and tailoring, so we started a good business.

Emily brought us all together every afternoon for an hour when Pip and Pebble had their afternoon nap. She taught us to read and write in both English and Arabic. We all had our own camel shoulder bones to use to write on. They were scrubbed clean each night so that we could start afresh the following day. Sam scribbled on his, but Emily would hug him and praise him for his efforts.

Cecil was not only a clever diplomat but a practical man too, and could turn his hand to almost anything. He intended to give us all the skills that he could so that we could be free and independent, a concept that I had never before considered. Having been brought up a slave, self-confidence and dignity were not attributes that I expected, so a whole new world of exploration and learning was given, not only to me, but to all of the Leonards' children. We all learned to understand English, the language of our new family, mainly due to the efforts of Patrick, who already spoke in a similar way.

In our new life Patrick was the happiest, and he never stopped smiling.

"Never had it so good. Back home I was never fed, but here I feel like a freakin' king. I love the endless blue sky and the soft warmth of the sea, and even the desert. Twas always cold at home!" he declared.

Although he hadn't, as yet, experienced the heat of the summer, and was surprised at the lethargy it brought to us all when it came. His home had been in a place called Baltimore, right in the south of Ireland where, apparently, it was not unusual for slaves to be taken by pirates or Ottomans, and even when captured by the British were often sold to anyone who wanted them. A small ship that had raided Ireland, Cornwall in England, the south of Spain and Italy for slaves to sell in North Africa and the Middle East had taken him to Musqat to be sold.

Over the next year or so I learned that Cecil Leonard was a high-level diplomat who worked for the British government and was responsible for negotiating deals with the Sultan, the Sheikhs and Imams.

When I asked Cecil to explain to me what he did, he laughed. "It's pretty difficult to explain, Katungi, but I will try. My capacity is for ensuring diplomatic agreement between the tribal factions. There are many disputes amongst them, and discord in the Sultan's own family, chiefly about who should rule Musqat. These differences have slowed down and negated the development of issues that are important for the British to maintain their influence in Oman. As it stands, there is a Sultan of Oman and Musqat, but the tribal factions want an Imam to rule, one whom they would consider to be the elective authority of the Ibadi Muslims. They want a ruler who would retain religious purity. They, most of the tribes of the interior, consider the coastal area too predominately involved in mercantile trading, too deeply embroiled in foreign relationships and commercial activity, to maintain their true religion."

"Is it so?" I asked.

Cecil shrugged, "Yes, I guess it is. The coastal area is the wealthiest part of this enormous land and there are many countries that have an interest in trading here. There's a lot of rivalry between the tribes too. I try to help, but I am afraid I am unable to reconcile the differences. I would dearly like to change many things here, especially the trading of slaves and the human misery it creates, but I don't know the answers. It is only my job to try to keep the peace. I can't tell you how distressing I find it. It will have to be stopped."

"I will help you when I am grown," I told him with all the confidence of an eight-year-old.

Cecil laughed. "Of course you will, Katungi. You will come to England and be an emissary for change, by telling your story."

"I will," I promised.

How could I have known then what the future would hold for me?

Cecil was a haughty, well-bred, caring man who vowed that on his return to the British Isles he would present his objections about the slave trade to the government, and implore them to help bring it to an end. I had no idea at the time whether other countries so far away would, or could, have any impact on the traditions of centuries.

It was the first time I had ever heard slavery being condemned and, although it meant little to me at the time, I listened carefully when he talked of being educated, having a free life and what it meant. I was eager that I would live the life of freedom that he had described.

The Leonards were determined to provide all of us with a good future and were spending every penny they had saved to organise plans to take us with them when they left. I felt we had been blessed. A great deal of documentation was needed, but Cecil was convinced that it would be worth it to see us become free, contributing citizens, to the great British Isles. Life for us all became peaceful and secure, and the Leonards cared for us in the best way imaginable. If only I had known then how our circumstances would change, I would have urged him to leave there and then.

CHAPTER 8
Dance Classes Begin

EVEANYA

By 1814 the weeks passed quickly and our routine became easier. It was late summer, still very hot and no one moved very far. The rasping sound of the mules, and oxen operating the water wheels at the wells, filled the humid atmosphere, while the afternoon naps became longer and longer each day. The water carriers worked double time, transporting from the wells that were fed by the great mountains that surrounded us.

The heat was so oppressive, and the only relief was by the shore. Jilfidan and I would try to escape after we had carried the food dishes away and washed them carefully at night.

Although we were still young enough not to be totally confined to the harem, we were not supposed to leave the estate at all. Of course, we did so whenever we could and on many occasions got caught, and received a light whipping from Fatima.

Even though Ora and Adell, my first companions when I came to Sakarbin's estate, were still confined to the kitchen, they often joined us for a night-time swim. We had found a tiny secluded cove where we could not be seen. Jilfidan swam better than any of us and would disappear into the depths, squealing with delight, so I would wade and dip, float and straddle my legs as the waves pitched and rolled. Ora and Adell splashed about but never really attempted to swim.

When we returned, our salt-encrusted bodies and horror of tangled hair gave us away, but it was not considered too great a sin, especially when it was really hot.

Slowly through the next months I almost learned to please Chole and, with Jilfidan's help, found many ways to get out of the house and the work when we could.

We spent time learning the Quran and were expected to attend lessons. Endless repetitions, droned daily, that meant little to either of us, but were expected. Once, when we managed to escape after a gruelling session of Mohammed's laws, we crept along the riverbed to explore the hidden pools of water in the wadi. The great boulders, swept down from the mountains at the beginning of the year, created pools which were wonderful to swim in. But we got lost. We had wandered so far along the wadi that we couldn't find our way back.

It was always a surprise to find that darkness descended so quickly and with such drama so early in the evening. There was no gradual change from day to night, and that night was as black as soot, with little moon to show us the way home.

It took us until the early hours to reach our little room. We'd been climbing, exploring and swimming in the great pools of water, and we'd lost track of time. We had been bitten by leeches and mosquitos but we'd had so much fun that we didn't really care. It was not often that we escaped the dreary work, but we had not been missed at all. We were so tired the next day that we struggled to stagger through our duties.

Chole had shouted at Jilfidan when she had spilt the water jug, "What's wrong with you today, Cat-eyes? Are you sick?"

"No, Sayyida, I am sorry. I am just a clumsy girl." Jilfidan bent her head in a deep bow, to hide her amusement, and quickly left the room with me trailing behind, trying hard not to laugh out loud.

That night we slept like exhausted kittens.

Over three years had passed. Jilfidan and I had developed so strong a bond that we felt like sisters. My memories of my life in Mysore had faded, so that I no longer wondered about my family. Jilfidan never spoke of hers, and insisted that our lives would be better as we grew into women and would become the Sheikh's favourites.

"Just you wait and see. We'll be pampered and adored, dancers of extraordinary skill, and we will probably travel with the Sheikh when he goes away, just like Bellia and Ester used to do. They are ancient now and are always arguing, so very soon they will be discarded." She told me this with the utmost confidence that I believed every word. Only occasionally, when I had seen some of the other girls crying, often bruised or having been whipped for some misdemeanour, did I wonder what being the Sheikh's favourite entailed. I did not understand until much later.

Bellia and Ester were both from Abyssinia, in their twenties and had four children each, so their life would soon revert to motherhood only, as more and more often the Sheikh chose the younger concubines to entertain him. The youngest, Thalis, was only fourteen and pregnant. Scylla, although the most beautiful, couldn't dance well according to Jilfidan, who had watched her through the secret crevice in the wall of the main hall.

Our services to Sayyida became less taxing, and when we learned that the Sheikh had instructed Chole to let us start attending the singing and dance classes, we were overjoyed.

"Eve too?" enquired Jilfidan excitedly when we were told. "She is only ten whereas I am almost nearly fourteen."

"Yes, Eveanya too," our sour-faced mistress replied. "You will dance as a pair because of your unnatural colouring. You will probably enter the master's bed together. He has strange tastes, so you will have to learn to please him too."

With a half-smile Chole added, "I won't be sorry to see the back of you. Neither of you have been good servants. You should have been more grateful for having such an easy mistress. You will see, life will become harder for you now. You will need to develop some of the things that will be required of you. You shall learn etiquette, culture, sexual skills and how to behave properly. Lumaria will be in charge of you from now on and she is a hard taskmaster. You will be expected to be proficient enough to entertain the Sheikh. And very soon I would guess, as he has no boy at the moment. And he has tired of Thalis and Scylla."

Jilfidan looked amused, but I had no idea what anything she had told us meant.

"It will be more fun than working for you," Jilfidan muttered.

Chole lifted her hand to strike Jilfidan, but her weight reduced her speed and both Jilfidan and I moved quickly away and stood waiting to be dismissed.

"Learn that slaves who cannot control their tongues may lose them, Cat-eyes," Chole shrieked at us as we giggled behind our hands.

"Yes, Sayyida. I know," laughed Jilfidan.

"You can go now, but there will be no escaping off to the seashore or the mountains anymore. You think I don't know? I know everything that goes on here," she warned us with a smirk. "The guards have been doubled because of the tribal uprisings down in the south. Many have been slaughtered and there could well be bloodshed closer to home as our Sultan has failed to subdue them. So, don't expect to get any freedom from now on. Go on, away with you. Get off to your dance class. I will be pleased to see you gone."

We raced down the corridors to join the class in the practice room, having no more thought about uprisings or tribal battles in our excitement. There were six of us who started classes together, including Ora and Adell who had now been relieved of their kitchen duties. I was the youngest and not expected to do as well as the others, but I was determined to keep up and be the very best I could.

It was in fact Jilfidan who stood out in class. She was a

natural. Her high-spirited dancing came wrapped with a sexy undertone. She moved easily with natural grace to the rhythm of the music. Her body was fluid and loose-limbed, so that each move drifted into the next, whereas my movements were stilted and stiff at first, never having attempted to dance before.

For hours we practised the steps and rhythms, in a comedy of errors and bad judgment. But because of Jilfidan's patience with me, I ended up performing a good imitation of her wonderful fluid movements.

"You just let your body go with the rhythm, Eve." Jilfidan took my hands and placed them on her hips as she started to roll and rotate. Her upper body undulated to the music. Although she was older than I, she was only a little taller. She was maturing fast, whereas I had a straight up and down body with no sign of breasts or hips.

"Just follow me," she instructed.

With her arms extended she pushed her budding breasts forward and shook her shoulders. She looked amazing. Tambourines, drums and flutes accompanied us. The roundup of instruments was rich and diversified, and one small eunuch tapped two conch shells together in harmony with another boy who swung a cane covered with brass cymbals. Often, those attending would sing as well as dance and practise for celebrations, weddings and festivals.

Classes became part of our week, and before long we could perform several traditional dances and started to practise a dance from the north of Arabia, the Khaleeji hair dance. We had to comb out our long hair so that it hung loose and, with a series of special steps, swung our hair in rhythm.

It was exhilarating and dizzying, but Jilfidan and I stood out from the other girls because we were so blonde. Coordinating our shoulder and hip shakes, we faced each other and swished our hair together, round and round, laughing and singing to the music.

By the time Jilfidan was fourteen and I was coming up to my eleventh birthday, we were no longer expected to serve anyone or perform any menial tasks. We were immersed in the intricacies of being there to please Sakarbin, besides just singing and dancing for him.

There was much competition for his favours, so we started training with the mistress of the concubines. Lumaria herself had gained this elevated position after years of pleasuring the Sheikh in the most intimate ways. She had borne him no children and was destined to live out her life teaching others to please him.

We learned very quickly that to gain the rewards of a good life we would be expected to satisfy the Sheikh, however painful or disgusting we found our duties to be. Lumaria whipped good sense into us whenever we complained, so we closed our hearts and minds to what we knew we would have to do and enjoyed the positive aspects of our lives. Each day we wore pretty clothes, our hair was brushed and coiled and decorated with ornate silver and beaded headdresses and veils. We were cosseted and perfumed but allowed no freedom outside the harem. Nevertheless, we did occasionally find ways of escaping and got used to the hidings we got if found out. Our singing and dancing lessons were our delight, and Jilfidan and I created our own happy little world. Life had improved, or so we imagined.

CHAPTER 9
October 1815

KATUNGI/LEONARD

We had been with the Leonards for over three years, and Patrick and I had learned to read and write both in English and Arabic, how to calculate distance and time, and how to row and fish. Patrick, already adept, became a fantastic navigator, fisherman and swimmer.

We also learned to cook, and Emily would allow us to take over the kitchen from time to time. She was an extraordinary lady who loved us all equally, and the eight children in her care blossomed, except Sam who never spoke, smiled or showed any emotion at all. He was the only one of us that did not thrive. He was of little use except in the kitchen, where he would solemnly stir the soup, clean the fruit, or stack the wood collected from the shore into neat piles. We never heard him make a single sound after his sobbing on our first night there.

We lived in an area where many foreigners had settled; Dutch merchants, Portuguese businessmen, freed African slaves, and Indian bankers were our neighbours with different traditions, beliefs and backgrounds. We all got on well, respecting and learning from each other's differences. Some families like the Leonards were Christians, others Hindu, and there was even a Buddhist named Po Long, a quiet lonely man who attempted to teach us about prayer flags and thoughtfulness.

In the house next door lived another mixed family, the father Andre, the Portuguese owner of a ship and dhow building company, also ran a fleet of fishing vessels. He had been living in Oman all his life and had married Ialea, a freed slave from Sudan. They had two boys, Fatu and Ahmed, who were about the same age as Patrick and I. We all gained immensely from each other's friendship and learned a great deal about tolerance and acceptance. Of the many children in the village, Fatu and Ahmed were our greatest allies. We took our Bible reading lessons together as they were being brought up as Christians, as were we.

Patrick was an inspiration to me as he stolidly pronounced me his best friend ever. When he could, he followed me like an adoring pup and chose to use comedy as his way of dealing with life. I was a willing audience. When he chose to be serious, my role was to play the admiring fool. I loved him like a brother but he could be annoying, as he didn't take anything seriously. I would sometimes deny him any sort of closeness and scowled at his efforts to make me laugh. Nevertheless, Ahmed, Fatu, Patrick and I were an intrepid group of friends and often went hunting or fishing together. Life was exceedingly good for all of us.

It all came to an end when, on a scorching day in the autumn of 1815, Cecil arrived home sweating and distraught. He had been away for over a week on a long campaign, meeting and negotiating with Wahhabis and affiliated and influential tribes, who had been causing trouble in the south. Fighting had broken out between the tribal followers of the Imam and the Sultan's forces, Sheikhs and the wealthy dealers and traders along the coast. A British family in a nearby town had been slaughtered by a group of marauding tribesmen, and the houses of others set on fire.

"They are insisting that the foreign influences should be purged and the Sultan deposed," Cecil was distraught as he explained to Emily how he had failed in his mission. "I have travelled miles to meet with them, talked with their leaders and promised to help, but they will not listen. They have gathered many tribes together so they are large in number and are looting and burning all the coastal villages and towns where the most wealthy and prominent live. I can see no way that civil war can be prevented. I fear for you all. You and the children must be prepared to leave as soon as possible. They are but a few miles down the coast. Please hurry, Emily."

We had never seen Cecil so distraught. He was usually so calm and in control, but he was pale and shaking, trying to decide what to do. He turned toward the door. "Firstly, I must warn the neighbours of the threat. Get everyone ready now."

As he was about to leave, Emily caught his arm. "Are you sure we have to leave, Cecil? Surely they will not come here. We cannot just leave our home."

"They will come, Emily. We must get you all away from danger," Cecil's voice betrayed his concern. "You must get the children to somewhere safe. Get them to the port at Musqat. They will not attack there as it is strongly fortified. I will stay here and try to talk to them."

"Will there be a ship to take us? Will the Sultan's army protect us? Can't we stay? Hope it will settle?" Emily asked as he pulled away.

"No, Emily, I'm sure this time it will not settle. Please get the children prepared, you must all leave immediately. I will ask Andre to bring his boats to take you north, to Musqat," was his reply as he departed.

Panic ensued as Patrick and I helped Emily gather the children and necessities together. The girls squealed and fussed as we dressed them to travel. Sam just gazed at us with his usual unconcern, and Pip and Pebble yawned and complained. The Indian boys were instructed to bring the mules and harness the wagons.

Andre returned with Cecil, who announced that they had roused all the neighbours who were preparing to resist any attack.

"We will stay and try to negotiate, but we will be prepared. Please, leave now, Emily, and get the children down to the shore and wait for the boats. Andre has sent word for them to be made ready. Ialea and the boys are coming with you. Take as many as you can. I will talk to the rebels and try to persuade them that these people are not their enemies."

We rushed out of the house behind him. Everyone was shouting orders, and the crowds of frightened people moved toward the main street.

"The women and children must get to the boats until we can overcome these rebels," shouted Cecil above the din, trying to organise the terrified.

"We'll be prepared," Andre told us. "If we stick together, we can keep them at bay."

The wagons gathered together outside of our house as Patrick carried Pip, and I took Pebble. Emily herded Sam and the girls into the wagons. Ialea, Ahmed and Fatu soon scampered in with us.

Before long, the men and many of the women who had decided to stay were gathered in the streets, armed with any weapon they had to hand. We had no time to bid them farewell for we could already hear the approaching hordes.

Within minutes we were on the shore watching the boats line up to take us north, but we were not fast enough.

As we started to run across the beach towards the boats, they came in their hundreds with their muskets, knives and long curved swords, whooping and screaming. "In the name of Allah, we dispose of the infidels that destroy our lands. Allahu Akbar."

The muskets fired, the khanjars and knives slashed, killing and wounding as they surged onto the beach. We fought so hard but there were too many of them.

They could not be stopped, and within the hour all of the men, our Indian servants and most of the women were killed. The beach was covered with screaming, bloodied bodies. In horror, we had seen our adored Emily cut to death before our eyes. Ialea had run with the boys towards one of the dhows but they were caught as they tried to board. Ahmed and Fatu were dragged to where myself, Patrick and Sam were being held, their mother a pool of blood at the water's edge. All of the children were herded and tied together and taken back to the village where the piles of bodies were being cleared away and the triumphant tribesmen were celebrating. The bigger children, including Patrick and I, fought as best we could, but we were tied and separated. Fatu and Ahmed were with me, but Sam, Patrick, the girls and the twins disappeared.

The pain and terror of that day was intense. I find it hard to tell of our ordeal after that night. Cecil and Emily Leonard gone, my brothers and sisters disappeared, and I with Fatu and Ahmed was sold to a company of men who transported us with dozens of other boys, somewhere into the interior.

To the place where we were castrated.

CHAPTER 10
The Desert

LEONARD

We'd travelled for days, but how far we'd gone or where we were I did not know. Eventually we were unloaded in a large encampment with mud brick buildings, canvas tents woven of goat hair, and small, palm-covered enclosures. It was an oasis somewhere deep in the desert. We were prisoners there for several weeks, locked into a small smelly room, fed and given camel's milk to drink. Until the day we were told that the 'surgeon' had arrived.

I could never explain the horror that our lives became. One by one we were tied to a narrow bed, our bellies and thighs strapped tight and our penises and scrotums cut off with a sickle-shaped knife. Hot oil was poured onto us to cauterize our wounds. It is impossible to describe the torture of those days or how I nearly bled to death as my friends Ahmed and Fatu had done. How a reed the length of my foot was inserted into each of us before we were buried in the desert sand up to our armpits, fed on alternate days with pieces of doughy fetir softened with camel's milk. For five days we stayed there, and even though we were beneath a palm-covered shelter we could still see the surrounding camp. During the day, the yellow-faced Egyptian vultures circled, and at night shooting stars careered across the clear sky. When the wind blew we were covered with sand and had to endure our captors scooping the sand away from our faces and pouring buckets of water over us.

We did not even speak to each other, so immersed we had become in our individual pain and terror. We had also become nameless, addressed only as 'you'. 'You eat'. 'You lift your head'. 'You keep still'. When we were dug out we were allowed to walk around, but were tied to our beds at night. Our torturers came each evening and slapped a thick paste onto our wounds, liberally laced with Luban. It was an antiseptic taken from the bark of trees in the desert and had a strong, pleasant odour.

I had not been able to pee, and my belly was painful and bloated. It was only after the reed was removed and in an agony of suffering that I relieved myself. We could hardly walk when we were released, but we were expected to exercise after our confinement.

Once the scabs started to appear, I had no infection, unlike so many of the others who had scalding mounds of pus at the site of their cuts. In the following weeks the pain was excruciating and the sorrow intense, as I watched my friends screaming and dying. I too wished for death.

In my worst moments I would pray to Cecil Leonard, but not to the God he believed in. How could I believe in Him? I was eleven years old and my genitals were gone, leaving me in that terrifying state of pain and distress. Cecil's kind, merciful God would not have allowed that to happen to me. I tried every day to pray for relief, but my pleas turned to dust.

By the time winter was over, we were reduced to about seventeen from the forty or so who had been captured, and we lived together in the mud brick buildings with our captors; greedy, ugly men with no compassion or feelings. The desert had become our prison.

As the weeks passed we had to tend the livestock and camels that were in the encampment, and grow strong and therefore more saleable. We were naked most of the time as our wounds were still uncomfortable and raw.

Looking back, I realised how it changed me, not in a physical way. That was painfully obvious. From my uneventful and mainly easy childhood, my world had become morbid and useless. It was not just the awfulness of my body that unmoored me, but the realisation that I was so completely worthless, that my body could be hacked to pieces at the whim of another.

My will to live had all but left me. As I had begun to heal and learned to pee through the painful hole that had been kept open with the reed, I found myself unable to do anything without instruction, and I performed each task dutifully without question or feeling. I felt that I could never make any sort of life again, and had sunk into the unclear depth of myself.

Nothing could absorb or move me in any way. A measurable touch of madness entered my heart and I was unaware that there could be any spirit left within me. In the worst times, I lived in isolation, would not speak unless spoken to, could not find anything beautiful or amusing, and my life turned sour and cold. I was a different person. I went into complete numb blankness that left me without any feelings, hopes or dreams for any sort of happy future. Most of the other boys were the same as me.

We were now called 'eunuchs'.

One day I heard our captors talking about what they would gain from our sale, and stories of many eunuchs who had become influential, who ran whole households and those who had gained their own wealth and freedom.

They discussed openly who would buy us and what they would pay.

Another night I heard Kiros, the cruellest of our captors, gleefully telling our guards, "We will make a fortune from this lot. We have two or three pretty boys who we can offer to Sheikh Sakarbin al-Busaidi. He has been begging us for something young and tempting since his bed-boy has grown up. The Leonards' boy is the most beautiful and he has learning. I believe he can read and write. He is our most valuable."

So, I had also become a valuable commodity, more able to become rich and powerful, more able to become part of a rich man's ministry. I had more learning than most at my age, thanks to the Leonards, and as I understood, would therefore be more valuable. I knew that having mastered the skills that I had, I would soon master others, if necessary. And freedom? Was there some hope then?

It was in those days of solitude and pain that I became 'Leonard', no longer a little African boy but a young man with a potential that I could not yet understand.

When Sheikh Sakarbin's agent came in early March, he immediately picked me out from the rest of the boys.

"Yes, he's the one. The master will be pleased with him, I know. How much is he?"

The sum that was quoted was enormous, and after a certain amount of haggling I was purchased.

Was I worth so much? If I really were so valuable, surely that would be to my benefit. Those were the only thoughts that kept me going.

"Do you have a name?" asked the agent before he left.

It was at that moment that I decided on who I would become. The boy Katungi was gone forever. I would be Leonard after the Leonards I'd admired so much.

"Leonard is my name," I replied.

There must be a good reason that I had survived. Whether I knew it or deserved it, I was only sure I would make good use of it.

So many months had passed since losing my family and friends. I remembered the dead as best I could. I mourned them, yes, and I missed them badly, but my heart had hardened to such a point that I no longer believed or wished for anything but the freedom of which Cecil had told me.

I could not change what had happened to me, or the things over which I had no control, but I resolved that one day I should indeed be free.

What is done is done. But…

CHAPTER 11
The Sheikh's Favourites 1815

EVEANYA

Although it was still wintertime, it had been a hot, hot day, and now that the sun was setting it cast crisscross patterns on the shiny marbled floor of the great hall. The room was soupy warm and stuffy. Jilfidan and I stood, quietly waiting as instructed.

We'd been told that morning that we were to entertain the Sheikh that night. Preparations had taken all day and we were both excited and nervous. Although we had been instructed by Lumaria for many months on how to please the master, not only on the dance floor but also in his bed, we were not prepared for the reality of what that entailed. We were both still so young and had not dreamed that we would be called upon so soon. In our innocence we had given it little thought, other than that it would happen one day in the future. But that day had arrived, and we thought we were prepared.

At sundown Sakarbin swept in with a group of friends, his retinue of servants and slaves carrying boxes, a carved casket and a plate of dates, halwa, fruit juices and jugs of water. He glanced our way without a smile or a greeting so we stayed pressed to the wall, holding hands and hardly breathing. We were both wearing full-beaded veils with decorative bells over our ears. Our blonde hair was coiled and adorned. Our outfits were diaphanous, prettily coloured and overlaid with gold mesh. Standing like two little ornamental statues we waited and watched silently as they ate, drank, gossiped and laughed without taking any notice of us or the two little flute players that had been summoned to accompany us.

It seemed like hours later that the friends left and the servants were dismissed.

Once alone, Sakarbin beckoned Jilfidan and I, and the flute players, to follow him into his private chambers. The rooms were highly decorative and colourful, the walls decorated with trophies of valuable weapons, mirrors and clocks, the outer room with couches and tables, cushions and soft oriental carpets. At the far end, a door led into his sleeping quarters.

Our master turned to look at us and stood stroking his dark, bearded face. He appeared to be pleased with what he saw, as his fat mouth stretched into a smile.

"Well, my little fair ones, Eveanya and Jilfidan, you are indeed both very beautiful. Are you ready for me at last?"

Jilfidan was more confident than I, and smiled for his approval. He walked behind us, firstly touching the little cross-shaped birthmark on my neck and then sweeping his fingers across our bare throats and arms. We were wearing very little and our shoulders were glossy and pale with oil and perfume.

"Dance for me now and then we will see what else you have to offer. I will reward you well if you please me." He licked his lips and drew his index finger across the tops of our budding breasts.

"Do we please you, Excellency?" Jilfidan asked lightly.

He leaned toward her and spoke softly into her ear, then laughed, his fat lips curling.

"What did he say?" I whispered.

"He says we do, but if we obey him, we'll please him more."

Sakarbin moved around us as Jilfidan lifted her pretty blue eyes to him. She was so sure of his favour.

"I have gifts for my little ones," he said as he lifted the carved casket from the table. He stood behind me, removed my heavy veil with its strings of bells, and took hold of my ears, one at a time, and carefully fitted an earring into each.

"Jewels look better on milk-white skin. Both of you should wear your veils outside all of the time. I fear you have had too much sun on your faces."

Jilfidan's face was alight with pleasure. "Oh look, Eveanya, they are beautiful," she sighed.

He removed them and laid them carefully on an embossed table by his enormous bed. The golden earrings glowed in the lamplight.

"These are the finest workmanship in the land, and I have had them made especially for you to welcome you to my bed." He handled them with reverence and respect. "You will have matching chains and headdresses. They are for my little golden princesses. The Sultan will be visiting soon and I will want you to look your best."

Jilfidan's eyes were shining. "You are most generous, Excellency. Will they be our own? To keep?"

"Indeed they will, and the more you please me the more you shall have. Now dance for me and take off your clothes slowly whilst you do."

With a smile he reclined on an amber couch and instructed the musicians to play. We danced as never before, we sang with the flutes and smiled throughout everything that followed that night, just as we had been instructed.

Of course, I had known what to expect, but it hadn't made it any easier. Lumaria had instructed us to oil our openings every day and stretch them as much as we could to reduce any tearing. We had both done so, and laughed at the thought of what would happen, but the reality was nothing like I had expected.

The night stretched towards dawn. I could not sleep. Neither could Jilfidan. I could hear from her breathing that she was wide awake. Sakarbin on the other hand was snoring gently with one arm wrapped around each of us. I wondered if Jilfidan was as sore as I was. I felt bruised all over, and between my legs was painful and sticky. I dared not move.

CHAPTER 12
Springtime in Musqat 1816

LEONARD

I was collected early one morning in April by the agent who had purchased me on behalf of Sheikh Sakarbin and, after travelling for two days, was delivered to the Sheikh's house in Musqat.

The agent told me Sakarbin's estate was elsewhere, but until I was deemed acceptable I would not be allowed to join the main house. He also told me that I was indeed lucky to be going there. He said many of the other boys would not have such a wealthy owner as I.

I was handed over to a very black, smooth-faced, bald man with a soft voice and a gentle manner, who escorted me up the stairs to the second floor. I was guided through an ornate doorway into richly decorated rooms. One of the rooms was lined with shelves full of books and manuscripts. There was a bedroom and a bathroom with a bathtub and running water, the likes of which I had never seen before. The large, barred windows looked out across a street of buildings, mainly storerooms, but I could see a forge, a tailor's shop and a row of houses with ornate balconies and fretwork panels, obviously occupied by the wealthy.

But I didn't really care where I was. My future, still unknown, meant nothing to me.

When my keeper came with a tray of food, he tried to ask me about myself, but I did not speak unless I had to. I ate and drank what I was given and turned my face from him whenever he came near.

On the third day he brought me fine garments to wear and a kummah, the traditional embroidered cap that all Omani boys wore, and said quietly, "I know you are suffering, but you must help me take care of you. You must bathe daily and eat well. Life will be better for you if you do. My name is Jem and I am the chief eunuch of Sheikh Sakarbin's estate. I am here to look after you."

"Indeed?"

"I have to instruct you. There are certain things you should know."

"Really? Things I should know? For what?"

"Sheikh Sakarbin is now your master in every way. You would do well to remember that he is rich and powerful, and it is up to you whether you benefit or not. When you are ready, I will be here."

The nights were still cool, but I had a large warm bed, heavy silk drapes and carpets, and once I allowed myself to relax, I explored the cupboards and shelves in the room.

There were many books and scrolls, maps and paintings. I had, of course, learned to read at the Leonards'. Mainly I'd read the Bible, but they had owned old copies of dictionaries and works by a variety of European writers. There in my prison I found treasures beyond description. Books about culture, satire, pearls, medicine, history and many diaries including one autobiography by Usamah ibn Munqidh who wrote about fighting in the Crusades. There were writings and essays from Basrah and Kufah, a group of plays from Egypt and Lebanon, and many versions of the Quran written in several languages.

Cecil Leonard's words rang in my ears. "The trouble with learning, Katungi, is that it unlocks the gates to vast and unsuspected deserts of ignorance. But without it we are all slaves."

My freedom therefore could be in learning. I decided that I would improve my skills and my knowledge whilst I could. Slowly, in the comfort of Sakarbin's house, my anger dissipated and I absorbed myself in the bounty that I had at hand. I spent my days reading and exploring the poetry and songs traditionally used in Arabia.

I also studied the Quran so that I could understand better the concepts and ideologies. I found some European philosophers who wrote about social conscience and equality. Rousseau and John Locke made me question my life and circumstances and, although there was much I did not understand, I determined that I should learn to.

Jem came daily, and I slowly saw him for the gentle soul that he was. He genuinely seemed to care about me. I asked him about the collection of books and manuscripts.

"Some are part of Sakarbin's father's collection. He travelled widely and was somewhat of a scholar."

"And Sakarbin?" I asked.

"No, not so much, but he does appreciate and respect knowledge. He will be pleased that you are reading."

"What about you, Jem? Are you a scholar?"

"I am the master's scribe and sicritir, so I am good with figures and writing, but I have not read this lot. I have not studied philosophy or poetry. I content myself with learning the Quran so that I may eventually gain my freedom."

"Do you believe it?"

I watched as Jem smiled and lifted his eyes upwards. "I have to. You will too if you ever wish to be free."

I listened carefully to what Jem was telling me, so I too studied the Book. I read and re-read trying to understand, for although many of the chapters seemed like common sense, I did not believe that the words in the Quran had been given by a messenger of God.

I decided to discuss it with my gentle keeper.

The next day I asked him. "Why do the Mohamedans believe that everything that happens is by Divine Will? It was not Divine Will that cut off my genitals. It was the will of evil men for gain only. It has naught to do with God, Allah or Divine Will."

"You will have to ask a wiser man than I, young Leonard," he declared. "I can only advise you to learn it, not to understand it."

"What about Akhirah – life after death or the day of judgment? As thinking and reflective beings, can we not ask ourselves what is the meaning and sense of life on earth if that is all there is? If there is nothing else that we are living for, except for the promised paradise in the afterlife, how can we accept that there is only the here and now and that we will not get another chance? Does that make sense to you?"

Jem shook his head slowly, "None of it makes sense to me."

"I read in the Quran that good deeds will benefit the soul after death and bad will cause eternal suffering. But the deeds of violence and sin perpetuated in the name of Allah cannot be found to be acceptable on the day of Akhirah, the last judgment. I am living, breathing proof of suffering caused by *good* Muslim men, who must know in their hearts that they have sinned. Can they therefore be judged to go to eternal suffering, or are they justified to be judged worthy of paradise because they have believed themselves to be working for Allah?"

"That is not something that I am able to answer," Jem replied solemnly.

"I will read some more. How long will I stay here, Jem?"

"Until after the Sultan's visit. Your arrival came at a bad time for Sakarbin, as he will be expected to present his women and his children, but it is not considered wise to have boys, although all of the wealthy men do. Probably the Sultan has his own boys too, but it is not considered acceptable for people to know."

"Hypocrisy then?" This was a new concept for me, but something I had learned through my reading of several diaries and observations of great philosophers. "Claiming to have higher standards or more noble beliefs than others. It seems to me that religion is about what one is most interested in and what allows control."

"You are becoming quite the philosopher yourself, Leonard, but use it. Use your pain to fuel your journey and you will do well," Jem assured me.

CHAPTER 13
Riding at Dawn 1816

EVEANYA

On becoming the Sheikh's bed mates and concubines, Jilfidan and I were restricted as never before. We learned very quickly that to gain the rewards of a good life we were expected to please Sakarbin, however painful we found our duties to be. Lumaria whipped good sense into us whenever we complained. As bed slaves we had to be grateful for what life offered us, but it was a long time later, when demands on me became less, that I did appreciate that my life as part of his harem was better than most of the other slaves who lived there. We were assigned our own servants and eunuchs, and were now expected to stay inside the walls.

Harem life was a life in a snake pit and not easy. All of the girls had an interest in their own survival and, according to their capacity, wove conspiracies to topple others. We were now expected to compete for the Sheikh's favours. I had little idea why, for I found the experience agonising, and disgusting.

"If we don't stay his favourites or get pregnant fairly soon, we could be short-lived," Jilfidan explained. "We could get discarded and be sold on, as others have been in the past."

I felt myself shudder at the thought. Being a mother did not appeal to me.

"I haven't yet had a bleed, and Lumaria says I won't get pregnant until I do."

"No, it's unlikely."

"I don't want to get pregnant anyway. I cannot see myself as a mother. Perhaps I wouldn't like *it* at all or *it* wouldn't like me. The whole idea revolts me. No, no, not for me. Poor Thalis nearly died pushing that baby out last month and she never feeds or cares for him. She doesn't want him and she is crying all the time. I am sure I would feel the same way."

"But," laughed Jilfidan, "she is guaranteed a home here. Now that she has his baby, Sakarbin will take care of her even if she doesn't go back to his bed at all. We have to guarantee our future."

Other than being occasionally bruised, and constantly sore between our legs, we had little to complain about when we were away from the Sheikh. We were well fed, perfumed and pampered, massaged and adorned in beautiful outfits. We were to be prepared at all times for Sakarbin to visit the harem and possibly choose us to spend the night with him.

Scylla still went occasionally, and the two black African girls, Ora and Adell, spent an odd night with him too, but mostly it was Jilfidan and I who were called upon to pleasure him. We had become used to his disgusting needs and mostly never discussed what was expected of us and, indeed, had to do. It was as if we both entered another world when we were in his bedchamber, that we became different people.

During the following months we danced and smiled and acquiesced. Once we had left him, sometimes in pain or with sore marks on our bodies where he had tied or whipped us, we never talked to anyone else or indeed with each other about those nights spent with him. We pretended that the scars and tears were somehow part of a forgettable dream, tucked away and hidden from our real world or ourselves. We blocked all the unpleasant memories and closed out conscious thought to those things that happened to us when we were with him.

He gave us gifts on every occasion, pretty silver bracelets and anklets, chains and headdresses, gold coins and pretty purses or perfumes. We hoarded them in private places so that others didn't see them and stir up jealousies.

News came that the Sultan of Oman and Musqat, Sayyid

Said, would be visiting in May and we were all to prepare. We were expected to take special care of ourselves and never be seen without appropriate clothing. The dancers were to have new outfits, veils, shoes and jewellery, and would be expected to entertain the Sultan and his large retinue. Sakarbin's wives, concubines and their children were to be presented to the Sultan, who was apparently still quite young and attractive, although he had a reputation of being ambitious and cruel.

He was coming to buy horses from Sheikh Sakarbin for his vast army of troops that he'd had to increase because of the tribal uprising over the past year or so.

Lumaria told us that Sultan Sayyid Said admired beautiful women as well as beautiful horses and would probably take concubines whilst he was in Musqat. He was already married to a Persian princess of great beauty and had a son, but he was a travelling man and had residences in Oman, Bandar Abbas and Zanzibar, where many of his concubines lived full time. He would stay in Qurum for two days and nights, and there was to be grand feasting in his honour, with singing, dancing and poetry performed.

Chole was in her element instructing and orchestrating the banquets and entertainments.

To our relief, Sakarbin went off to his Musqat house and would only return the day before the Sultan's visit, expecting everything to be ready and prepared.

After a particularly busy day, Jilfidan was sulky and tired. She slumped onto her bed.

"Let's get out of here, everyone is busy with the preparations and the Sultan is not coming for another two days. We've done all we can. The boys are going to set up the cockfighting in the courtyard today. They think it's entertaining watching the poor, bloodied things claw bits out of each other, but it's disgusting and I hate it," she pouted, "so no one will miss us if we slip away for a while.

We can go see the horses."

Always cautious, I said, "Jil, we'll be flogged if we get caught."

"I know." She took a quick glance around to make sure no one was watching. "Put on your veil," she ordered, and, grabbing my hand, she led me toward the harem door. We stood still behind one of the pillars, adjusted our veils and watched for the senior eunuch who was always on guard. However, that evening he was nowhere to be seen, so we slid quietly out into the main courtyard. We kept our heads down but everyone was too busy to take any notice of us. Jilfidan pulled me quickly through the outside gates to a clump of prickly bushes. The land dropped away into a natural ditch and we dropped down into it like a pair of desert rabbits, as we had done on previous occasions. Fists of thistles pushed upward through the sand, catching at our bare ankles.

"Come on," Jilfidan said as she scrambled along ahead of me, pulling off her black veil.

Keeping our knees bent until we judged that we were out of sight of the main house, we covered a good distance.

Stopping for a rest, Jilfidan squeezed my arm. "We did it and nobody spotted us."

"We will probably get caught on the way back," I thought morosely.

Seeing my sullen face, Jilfidan said, "Trust me, Eve. Don't I always take care of you? Come on, let's see what's going on at the stables."

CHAPTER 14
Discovered

EVEANYA

We followed a barely discernible path that led past the entrance and toward the far end of one of the biggest paddocks, where huge fences surrounded the training grounds and stables. In the distance we could see a group of slave soldiers mounted on camels heading into the desert. There was no sign of the armed guards that were usually patrolling the boundaries. Everyone was preparing and training for the Sultan's visit.

"That's a bit of luck. They are all off practising for the camel races. Come on, there's nobody about."

We climbed over a gate and headed toward the stables. Usually we had to stay hidden because of the guards, grooms and stable boys, or even the Sheikh and his sons were often around. Entering the big gates that led to the stable yards we could see where the broodmares were penned, and there were a couple of newborn foals.

"Oh, Eve, just look at these babies. Aren't they adorable?" Jilfidan pulled herself up onto the wooden gate. I followed, and we were so entranced with the pretty foals that we didn't see or hear the approach of Jahangeer and Musab, the Sheikh's sons.

"Well, what do we have here? Are you two allowed out of the harem?" Jahangeer asked, reaching out a grubby hand and catching Jilfidan's elbow. She nearly jumped over the gate in alarm.

They had obviously been out riding themselves, as they were both sweaty and smelly.

I was speechless with fear, knowing that we should not be seen without our veils, and stayed rooted where I was.

Jilfidan turned, stepped down, smiled sweetly and said in

a breathy voice, "You won't tell, will you? We were just so bored with the preparations for the Sultan's visit that we had to get out for a while."

They both laughed. In general, females were not permitted to speak to grown males, other than the Sheikh himself, and we would be severely punished if found out.

"No, we won't tell will we, Musab?" Jahangeer still held Jilfidan's elbow. "Will you be nice to us if we don't?"

"Of course. Will you show us around now that we are here?" Jilfidan asked coyly.

"Why not, although I would suggest that you have probably been here before." Without waiting for an answer, he continued. "I've seen you two dancing for our father. What are you named?"

These boys didn't seem to mind that we were breaking the rules by being here, and were both grinning at our embarrassment. Jilfidan's eyes were sparkling as she introduced us, although she did include a slightly deferential bow as she addressed them.

Other than the occasional eunuch, we had never had a chance to speak to any of the boys who were of a similar age to us. The eunuchs never showed any interest in us at all, whereas Jahangeer and Musab were eyeing us with very male appreciation.

I climbed carefully down from the gate as Musab held out a hand to me. He looked so much like his father that I felt myself shiver. He was probably not much older than I, but he was already tall and muscled. I was not sure who their mothers were, but I guessed that one must be from Deilah and the other from Zuena. Both of these sons had lived under their father's care ever since I had been brought here.

Jahangeer took Jilfidan's arm and led her across the compound, through the grooming sheds to the stables, and showed us the best stallions and broodmares. Musab and I trailed behind them.

Jahangeer was confident and well-informed. He told us he intended to become an agent for his father when he was old enough to travel on his own.

"The al-Busaidis' horses are the best in the country, and I will sell them all over the world. I will make our Arabian horses famous," he informed us as he strutted around telling us the names and backgrounds of his favourites. He was showing off to Jilfidan and she was enjoying his attention, oohing and aahing at his jaunty flirting.

Approaching another set of stables he pointed out a pale silver stallion. The horse snorted a greeting. "This one is called Alqamar and he is mine. I will show you," Jahangeer told us proudly as he opened the stable door and led Alqamar out. He was indeed beautiful.

"I used to ride before I came here," Jilfidan told him as she caressed the horse's muzzle. Tears came to her eyes, and she breathed in deeply and said, "This reminds me of my home and family."

So, Jilfidan did have a sentimental side after all!

The image of my own childhood appeared briefly in my memory, dissolved and reformed. I stood silently as Jahangeer and Musab watched Jilfidan, who sniffed and flicked away a tear.

"Can I ride him?" she asked.

"No, not him," Jahangeer said, shaking his head. "But we will take you out riding if you want to, won't we, Musab?"

Musab nodded. "We often get up before dawn and ride. Do you want to come? We can take you with us."

I was not sure that we should take such a chance. Indeed, we would receive a good whipping if we were caught, but Jilfidan nodded excitely. "Yes, yes, tomorrow will be our only chance before the Sultan arrives. Can we really? Will you take us with you? Really... really?"

Both the boys were almost as excited as we were at the prospect of an illicit early morning ride. They, of course, would not be punished for such bad behaviour, but we certainly would be. Before I had a chance to offer my objections it was agreed. We would make our way there before sunrise and meet at four a.m.

The boys would have the horses ready.

"I have never ridden before, Musab," I whispered.

"That's no problem. We have just the perfect mare for you. Sadiqa, she is old and patient and totally reliable for an absolute beginner," Musab assured me. "Your sister can have Donil. She is spirited and fast."

"We will have to go now, Jil," I said as she nodded to Musab. "It's getting dark and Lumaria will be looking for us."

We made our way back to the harem and to bed, but neither of us slept well. I was scared but Jilfidan was excited at the prospect of our early morning ride.

At four the next morning, while all but the servants were sleeping, we crept out of our room, through the corridors and slipped out. The old black eunuch who was on guard at the harem door was fast asleep and snoring loudly.

We took the usual route along the ditch, over the fence, and made our way to the stables just as Jahangeer was bringing out the horses. It was still dark but we soon realised that Musab was not the only other person there. They had brought with them two of their younger brothers, Ahmed and Gusiffa, the youngest of the Sheikh's boys, who were allowed to ride out with their older siblings. We already knew them as they had only recently been taken from the harem to live in the men's quarters, as was the custom.

"They knew we were up to something," said Musab, "so we had to bring them with us. They won't tell, don't worry."

They were probably about the same age as me and they greeted us with cheeky grins, and laughingly told us what sport it was to be out with two of their father's concubines.

Jilfidan and I waited while the horses were saddled and

readied. I was given a small pretty white mare, Sadiqa, and Jilfidan the long-legged grey mare, Donil. The boys rode their own spirited stallions.

Although I had never ridden before, I found it exhilarating and comfortable. My horse was patient and gentle, and Musab quietly instructed me on how to hold her steady or guide her with my knees and feet.

It was still dark as Jahangeer and Musab led the way along the shore and then turned inland into the wadi. Jilfidan and I followed behind with Ahmed and Gusiffa. The horses obviously knew their way as they confidently stepped around the great tumbled boulders that had narrowed the wadi entrance. A stream of water continued down toward the sea in restricted channels, leaving a pathway that we could follow. The water was still fresh and sparkling despite the dryness of the season. Our horses picked their way through the narrow gullies and then took us onto higher ground as we got deeper into the wadi. The boys told us that they would normally be accompanied, but today all the servants were still preparing for the Sultan's visit the next day. We all knew that being away from the house could get us into trouble, but there was so much activity going on there that we were hoping we would not be missed.

Jahangeer was in particularly good form and flirted with Jilfidan as she drew her horse alongside his. I kept my distance from Musab, as I could see the same look as his father had when he fingered his penis, particularly when we were dancing. I stayed with the younger boys.

By sunrise, we'd left the stables far behind. We had encouraged our mounts to climb up the rocky slopes, along the pathways hewn out by centuries of wild goats, foxes and donkeys. Below, the pools of water flashed and beckoned as the sun rose. As it grew hotter, the idea of undressing and slipping into a pool was so immediate that I could almost feel the cool water on my sweaty skin, but I knew that we could not disrobe and swim as we had done when we were younger. As we ascended we could see the whole extent of Sheikh Sakarbin's estate. To the east, the long stretches of ornate buildings, surrounded by the gardens, courtyards and walls, and the bright blue dome of the mosque, which sparkled in the first light of the morning sun. It changed colour according to where the sun shone on it, from pale blue in the morning to a deep violet as the sun set. In the distance, the wells and the stables with the training grounds, and further still the penned camels at the oasis.

Across the flat, sandy plain that lay beyond the estate, we could even see the coastline where the pearl fishers had their huts along the shore, shrunk now to the size of a toy village.

Climbing was exhilarating, and we watched the sunrise casting orange and yellow rays across the desert landscape to the west. As the heat increased, a cloudy vapour rose from the rocks.

For the first time since being here I felt genuinely happy and free. The sensation of being high up, away from the rules and confines of our life, was exhilarating. I loved the feel and smell of the horses, and a resolve to do this again wormed its way into my head. I knew that Jilfidan would feel the same. I admired her adventurous spirit because without her I would never have been brave enough to have such an adventure. In fact, without Jilfidan in my life, I would not be able to deal with what was expected of us. It was only her enthusiasm and positive attitude that made life bearable for me.

It was still very early when we made our way home, knowing that we had a busy day ahead. Sakarbin would be returning and we had final rehearsals and fittings for our dance costumes.

We thanked the boys and they promised to take us again after the Sultan's visit, but we were to tell no one. Jilfidan was aglow from the ride and the attention she had received from Jahangeer.

As we hurried back along the ditch, she whispered, "That was the best ride ever, wasn't it? And Jahangeer, he is so nice, kind and attractive too. Nothing like his father."

"Musab is, though," I said. "I can see that we will have to avoid him before he is much older. He gives me the creeps the way he watches us. He looks at us just as his father does and I don't like it."

CHAPTER 15
May 1816

LEONARD

It was two days before the Sultan's visit to Musqat when Sakarbin arrived at his city house. Jem had warned me that he was coming to inspect me, and that I should be deferential and obedient. It was important to my future that Sakarbin should like me. I'd been at the house for over four weeks and had learned a great deal from the wonderful library there. I'd become more aware of my ability and value, and thought perhaps, if I was clever enough, I could earn my freedom.

I had gained a toughness and confidence that I never knew I had. The docile little slave boy was no more. But I was afraid, for I had no idea what my role in the Sheikh's life entailed.

Sakarbin came with a retinue of servants, and immediately sent for me to be brought to him.

I was dressed in a white silk dishdasha with a gold trim and tassel around the neckline. I had never worn such a garment before and surveyed myself in the great gilt-framed mirror. My hair had grown and Jem had cut and oiled it so that it framed my face. It was rather long so it looked straighter and glossier. My dark skin against the milky silk robe was flattering, and what I saw cheered me. I was still small and skinny but had a healthy, well-cared-for glow that I'd not had when I arrived. On my feet I wore leather, embossed sandals, and on my head, the embroidered kummah. I was ready.

"This is only a brief visit because we will stay here until after the Sultan leaves Qurum," Jem told me as he escorted me down the stairs to the reception room. "You do know that he will want to look at you, every part of you, including your cut. He must approve of you if you are to stay?"

"I know, Jem. You have already told me. Stop worrying." I knew that I sounded more confident than I was, but I was determined to make the best of this, whatever it turned out to be. Jem had told me that it was my body and obedience that Sakarbin was most interested in, so I must play my part.

As we entered the vast reception room, I dropped my eyes and bowed low, but not before I realized that I had seen this man before. It was not until he lifted my chin to look at me fully that I knew it was the man who showed an interest in the little blonde girl at the slave market. I swallowed hard and kissed Sheikh Sakarbin's outstretched fingertips.

"What a beautiful boy you are," Sakarbin said as he peered at me. "I usually prefer pale skin and blue eyes but... I must say, Jem, we have done well this time. Is he obedient?"

"Yes, he is, Your Excellency, and clever too. He's been reading your father's library."

"Indeed. What is your name?" he said as he circled me.

"Leonard, Your Excellency. That is my name now."

"Do you speak Arabic well?"

"Yes, Excellency, I do. I also speak English and Swahili."

"Excellent. Let me see your cut."

I was surprised, and shivered at the thought of exposing my mutilation and took a step backward.

"Let me see," he insisted.

Jem wrapped an arm around me reassuringly and slowly lifted my dishdasha. Sakarbin bent, and his fat mouth lifted into a smile. He reached to touch me, and I steeled myself not to move as his finger traced the area where my genitals had been. There was still tenderness but the scar was now pink and smooth. He let his fingers explore my upper legs and hips. He reached around me and felt the small curve of my bottom. As he stood, I noticed his hand go to his penis and slowly he rubbed it up and down, but he turned quickly to seat himself on a large blue sofa. "Perfect, I will look forward to you coming back to my home, Leonard. I will welcome you. Jem, keep him safe and don't let him out of your sight."

He dismissed us with a wave and Jem turned me away from him and quickly steered me back up to my room.

I was angry and felt a dread that I could not then explain.

CHAPTER 16
Losing My Best Friend

EVEANYA

The day following our wonderful early morning ride with Sakarbin's sons was the morning of the Sultan's visit, and I woke with terrible stomach pains and blood on my sheet. I screamed to Jilfidan who wrapped her sisterly arms around me. Her only concern was that I would have to go to the 'women's waiting room' and wouldn't be able to dance with her for the Sultan.

It meant three days in isolation, so I wouldn't even *see* the Sultan, nor be able to take part in the feasting and fun. I was overwrought and cried at the unfairness of life. Lumaria came and escorted me to the bathing area where I was washed and a felted pad pushed between my legs. I knew what was expected, of course. Many of the girls enjoyed being in the waiting room as they didn't have to work and were not even expected to read the Quran or pray. Some would sulk and snivel because they hadn't managed to get pregnant. But I was devastated at the unfairness of missing out on all the fun.

My first menses was to be celebrated, Lumaria informed me. So, on the morning of the Sultan's visit, in between all the preparations, the women, girls and female children danced and sung around me in a circle, creating a small celebration of my step into womanhood. I, on the other hand, was not impressed, and knew that this would mean that I could get pregnant at any time. So far, Jilfidan had not done so, and she had been having her bleeds for over a year, so I was hopeful that I too would not do so. Arrangements were made for Adell to dance with Jilfidan. Jilfidan being so fair and Adell so dark, they were to depict winter and summer and perform their dance with coloured veils from the darkest blue to the palest lemon. We had danced this before as a group, but it had never been done as a pair. Jilfidan and Adell were sent off to practise as I sat bereft in the women's room. Ora, who usually danced with Adell, would not be excluded but joined into the group with Scylla and Thalis and three of the other younger girls. How could I be so unlucky?

So it was that, when the Sultan arrived and the festivities began in the evening, I had to wait for the girls to return and relate all that they had seen and learned from the visit.

The following day, whilst the girls practised their singing and dancing, the Sultan went to the stables to negotiate for the horses and camels that he wanted to buy. I hoped that Alqamar, Sadiqa and Donil would not be sold, as Jahangeer had promised to take Jilfidan and me riding with them again. They had devised a plan so that we would not be recognised. They would hide a set of boys' clothing and turbans for us in the saddle room. At least I had something to look forward to.

It was late when Jilfidan came to tell me all about the first evening.

"Oh, I missed you so, Eve, but Adell danced well with me and Sakarbin is pleased with us. He has promised that we will be allowed to dance together for the Sultan again in the future."

I put on a sulky face. "Really?"

"Don't look like that. You and I will always dance together. In reality I doubt we will be asked to dance again." She laughed as she hugged me tight. "You and I could dance springtime and summer next time."

Off she skipped to bed, leaving me vexed and sulky.

My stomach still ached and now so did my heart, thinking how easily I could be replaced!

By the time I was allowed to leave the women's waiting room there were four of us there. Old Fatima, Ora, who had missed the last evening's dancing, and Bellia, who was the Sheikh's favourite singer and storyteller. She didn't mind the rest, as one of her children was teething and causing her and everyone around a lack of sleep.

The harem was alive with talk and gossip about the Sultan and his retinue of advisors and ministers. He was leaving that afternoon having bought forty of Sakarbin's horses and fifty of his camels.

Other news was more disturbing!

He was also to take several of the servants, and two concubines.

No one yet knew who would be going but everyone was worried, some of the girls excited that they might be picked. There was also a rumour that part of the deal the Sultan and Sakarbin had made was that, in an effort to unite the rebel tribes, Sakarbin would take a fourth wife. In the hope of preventing the endless skirmishes with them, an agreement had been reached. The seventeen-year-old was the daughter of a Sheikh from one of the powerful inland tribes that had been responsible for many of the uprisings over the past few years.

Before the day was over we were informed of who would be leaving. To my horror, Jilfidan and Adell had been gifted to the Sultan, and would be leaving that night with one of our cooks and two young servant girls.

'No, no, how could this happen?' I was beside myself with grief, and Lumaria had to lock me in my room as I screeched so loudly when I heard the news. We were not even allowed to say goodbye to each other and, by the time darkness came, they were gone. I cried and screamed hysterically. My one and only real friend had disappeared so unexpectedly out of my life. I wanted to die. I had no idea how I would cope without her friendship, her sisterly love and her sweet naughty laugh.

Ora, too, was devastated as she and Adell had been

together and close friends since we had been bought in the Musqat market over five years previously.

I could hear her sobbing as I was locked away with a warning from Lumaria that she would give us something serious to cry about if we didn't stop soon.

Callous old woman with no feelings at all! How could she not understand how we felt? Were we expected to have no regret at losing our best friends?

The following week I was ill with grief and refused to go to Sakarbin when I was called. I feigned a fever and lay in my bed, sobbing and distraught.

Life would never be the same again.

CHAPTER 17
Meeting Eveanya Again 1816

LEONARD

As we approached the estate, I could see the great walls that surrounded the stables, paddocks and training rings. The camels were penned in the far distance where tall palm trees created a small oasis.

"Armed guards are always on patrol," Jem explained as we passed by. "Some of the horses and camels are very valuable. They are the main source of the Sheikh's considerable income. Further on is where the slave soldiers live." He pointed to the small mud brick houses that spread off into the distance. "There are several hundred soldiers. Over there, close to the camel pens, Sakarbin has some of the best warriors in the land. The entire male slave population, regardless of their status, is expected to be competent to defend the property and lands of our Sheikh. I expect you will too, in time. I am afraid that tribal feuds and power struggles are part of everyday life here, although I think there are some new decisions being made to unite the tribes of the desert," Jem grinned at me. "It looks as though our Sheikh will be taking another wife, his fourth and final one, from an opposing tribe. It will help the Sultan keep them in order."

The walls and gates that surrounded the huge complex of the Sheikh's estate were high and impressive. Once inside, I could only exclaim at the vastness of it. It was like a small town with pathways, gardens full of palm trees and fountains, courtyards, and carved stairways up to the ornamental rooftops.

Jem led me to the largest house and through the vast hall, explaining the layout as he did so. Showing me into my new room, he explained, "You will initially be confined here. It is very close to Sakarbin's rooms and he will expect you to be ready for him at all times. Until he feels he can trust you to be discreet about your relationship with him, he will not let you mix. Only those close to him will know that you are his bed boy. The position will allow you many advantages, but only if you behave in accordance to his wishes."

"Will he explain what he desires me to do?"

"He will," said Jem. "Do not be alarmed and do not fight him. There will be much that you dislike about your duties. Just say, 'May Allah take my soul into your service. I am entirely at your disposal,' and he will be pleased. Even so, he will hurt you at first. Be patient and gain the Sheikh's trust, then you will be allowed some freedom. Remember always that this life will not last forever, especially if you are wise and clever. I am sure that you are, Leonard. If I had been more so, I would not still be here. But I have learned to be patient, and now I have the Sheikh's promise that I'll soon be free, so I will return to what is left of my family. Now, I must go to morning prayer."

I was left alone, but Jem had brought many books from the Musqat house so I could continue reading and studying. I had already improved my Arabic spoken word but still needed to improve my script. So I set to work. When Sakarbin came, I repeated what Jem had told me and he beamed. "That pleases me greatly, Leonard."

I understood very quickly that Sakarbin was a conceited, egotistical man, who could be flattered and cajoled, but I would take my time and get to know him better. I knew I had to be obedient to whatever he demanded.

He made it very clear to me what he wanted of me. The first time he restrained me, and it was so unexpected that I fought, but to no avail. He enjoyed his power over me and smiled at my suffering, which I could not hide. He hurt me so and, although he had lubricated me, I was sore and bleeding for days.

He did not send for me until the following week, but I knew others had been in his bed, as I heard a cry or a plea coming from his bedchamber on several occasions. I spent my days reading the Quran and strengthening my desire to be free. In the meantime, I would put aside all thought of freedom and ingratiate myself with this man, who had complete control over everything that happened to me. I was still so young. I knew I could not survive on my own, but in time I resolved that I would learn to.

When Sakarbin sent for me again, I quietly acquiesced, smiled and allowed him his revolting pleasures. Although he fussed and stroked me, he always smelled of cruelty. It emanated from him like a stream of bad breath. He missed nothing. His eyes would pick out the smallest fault with my body or my manner toward him. He was sly, and when he was excited he licked his lips continually with his thick pink tongue. Sometimes I had to sleep in the same bed as he, and I hated it.

I was called regularly to his room over the next few weeks. I learned to be obedient and polite, would bow and smile and allow whatever he chose to do to me. He liked to lick me, particularly my scar, his fingers poking and exploring. I had to oblige with the same. Then he pushed himself into my body and took his pleasure. Afterwards, sweating and sighing, and saying how satisfying it was, he withdrew and wiped me clean.

Holding the cloth before him, he smiled. "See how gentle I am? No blood today, my beautiful Leonard."

He beamed his pleasure and held me close. "I will reward you for the delight you give me, you know."

"How will you reward me, Excellency?"

"In many ways, my little Leonard. You will see. I am an honourable man and Allah's goodwill shines upon me."

"Of that I am certain, Master." I smiled at him and he stroked my cheek.

Within the following month I had ingratiated myself enough to be allowed some freedom. At Jem's request I was allowed to go and help with the distribution of wages while Sakarbin was away to Musqat on business.

It was a bright summer morning when I first set eyes on the beautiful girl that I'd first seen in the slave market. She had not seen me. She was busy watching the mistress of the concubines, who was on her knees arranging a pile of Indian silk materials, pulling out bales of cloth, and holding them out toward the girl for discussion or approval.

It was the day of my introduction to the harem, and Jem was showing me the dormitory of the harem eunuchs. He was explaining the rules and protocol, where the wives lived and the status of the various concubines and other inhabitants. Although I was assigned to my own room close to the Sheikh, I would occasionally be expected to guard or work for the women.

It must be almost five years or more since I had first laid eyes on the pretty little blonde Indian girl. I was struck anew by her soft, fair beauty. She had grown tall and her body was only just beginning to show the curves of a woman. She stood in a provocative posture with her hands on her hips.

My heart almost stopped. The same feeling of warmth and recognition that I had felt in the slave market overflowed within me. As we got closer, the girl turned. I could see from her body language that she was angry and distressed. Her face was red and she was frowning.

"I don't want anything new," she wailed. "I'm not going to dance for him or do anything else. I thought we were *both* his favourites? How could he be so cruel and heartless?"

The mistress of the harem stood, stepped in front of her and slapped her hard across the cheek. She turned and ran past us, sobbing loudly.

"Looks like we've come at a bad time. Poor girl. The Sultan took two girls from the harem and one was Jilfidan, her best friend and dance partner," Jem explained, moving quickly past, "and she is inconsolable."

I watched as the girl disappeared into one of the concubines' shared dormitories.

"What is her name, Jem?"

"She is called Eve."

"Like Eve in the Christian Bible?"

"That I wouldn't know, Leonard. I have not read the Bible. Eveanya is her name but her friends call her Eve. She is one of Sakarbin's favourite girls."

So, she too was a sex slave to our master. I wondered for how long she had suffered, as she had been very young when he bought her.

I longed to speak to her.

CHAPTER 18
Misery June 1816

EVEANYA

It had been over four weeks since the Sultan had taken away my best friend. I could still summon no reason to get up in the morning. I'd managed to feign illness for two weeks after she had been taken, when I had sobbed until I could hardly breathe. I would never forget our time together and how much fun she had brought into my world.

Eventually, Lumaria had dragged me out of bed and insisted that I return to my duties. I hadn't been summoned by Sakarbin at all since Jilfidan had left. I hoped that I never would be again. But the thought of being sold frightened me too. I might not find myself in such an indulgent and wealthy household.

A group of visitors from Musqat came, and dancers were required. Even though I felt weak and sick, with Ora's help I managed to learn a dance, and was fitted with a new costume. I could work up little enthusiasm. It must have shown as I gave a poor and lacklustre performance. Leaving the main hall to return to the harem, I heard a whisper from behind one of the supporting pillars at the entrance.

"Eve, come here a moment." I stepped away from the group of girls and slipped behind the column. It was Musab. He and his brothers had been with the audience in the great hall where we had danced. Although I had noticed them, I could never acknowledge them, or address them in public.

"You look miserable, Eve."

"I am, Musab. I miss Jilfidan so."

"I can tell. Do you want to come riding with us in the morning? It might cheer you."

Why not? I nodded my assent before returning to the others.

The following day, I began my extraordinary double life. I knew I would not be able to get away during Ramadan in August, so several times over the next few weeks I rose before dawn, found ways of slipping past the guards, and raced along the ditch to a gap in the fence.

Head down, I ran as fast as I could in the dark to one of the saddle rooms where we kept my change of clothes. In my boy's riding outfit I strode across the training ring to the stables, to all intent and purpose looking like one of the stable boys. The tight turban kept my blonde curls in place, and I learned to swagger like a boy.

The Sheikh's sons would have the horses ready and we would ride away as quickly as possible. Sometimes the guards would be sleepily aware of us, but they knew the boys well and never stopped us.

We kept away from the open spaces that could be seen from the houses, and headed into the scrubby desert where we raced and played. On very hot mornings we would ride inland through the wadi and up into the high plains, seeing no one other than an odd goat herder or the wild mouflon and gazelle.

For me, these mornings of freedom brought a little light and enjoyment back into my life. It was in fact my only pleasure. Even without Jilfidan I felt exhilarated and free.

Only once was I nearly caught, but had managed to convince the sleepy guard that I was a new stable boy on my way to saddle horses for the master's sons.

Other than my early morning rides, my life had become listless and dull. I had never had any friends other than Jilfidan. Now, I found I was unable to summon any sort of enthusiasm for making new ones.

CHAPTER 19
Making Friends 1816

LEONARD

It was soon after my first sighting of Eve that I saw her again. I'd been sent by Jem to collect some information about purchases made by the housekeeper. Just as I entered the harem courtyard, I saw her sitting alone, staring into space. As I approached she looked up at me with a vague interest, so I smiled and said, "Hello, Eve."

Her mouth dropped open and a startled puzzlement crossed her expression. Almost immediately she recognised me. "From the suq... you? Yes, it is you. How is it that you are here?"

"I came last month. I have been bought by Sakarbin and I am here to serve him."

"I had heard that he had a new boy... Are you he?"

"I am."

"Is it difficult? Being here I mean... allowing him, letting him... I know what that's like."

"Yes, it's difficult. I have to submit to everything but that doesn't mean I consent."

"I know that too."

She hesitated, her brow creased in a moment of understanding. "Where have you been all these years? I have been here since... a long time now. It seems so long since I saw you."

I knew then that she felt it too, the familiar knowing, some special connection that seemed to go beyond the simplicity of conventional understanding.

I told her how lucky I had been, how the Leonard family had adopted me and how well I had been treated. I told her of the rebels who had killed them. I did not tell her what happened after their death, only that I had been imprisoned and sold to the Sheikh.

I told her of my time in Musqat and my studying, and how I hoped to use it to earn my release from being a slave.

"Ha, is that even possible?" she laughed. The chance of freedom had obviously never crossed her mind. She lifted her head so that I could see her full face, and I was once again intrigued by the wonderful colour of her eyes. Those eyes, that hinted at a mystery I could just not fathom. They knew me well, of that I was sure.

As she tipped her head to the side I noticed the birthmark.

For a brief moment I felt as I had done in the slave market; a wave of my mother's love swept over me.

'Mother!' shouted a voice in my head.

My mother Kitu had no such mark, but again I heard it clearly… 'Mother'. A tidal longing to touch her and bring her close swept through me. I swallowed hard. I was flooded with an emotion I could not comprehend, and for a moment was overcome with a wave of terrible remorse. For what, I knew not. She was still gazing at me, waiting.

"I understand, it is so, but it will take time," I said slowly, watching her carefully, aware only that I felt something I couldn't explain. It was as if I had found someone whom I'd lost, and a feeling of relief swept through me. "It will take a lot of time," I repeated, trying to hold myself steady. "I am determined that I will be a free man…"

She sighed, pursed her lips and lifted her brows in disbelief. "If only I could feel that too."

I had to ask her. "Is your life that bad? You look so sad?"

Tears immediately filled her eyes, and she said, "My best friend has been given to the Sultan and I miss her so. I hate it here now, whereas before she made it bearable. Being with her made everything worthwhile."

"I was told about Jilfidan. I'm so sorry."

We sat quietly side by side without speaking, and she was

slowly comforted whilst I was confused.

"Can I tell you something?" I asked as she sniffed her tears away.

"Yes, of course."

"It's odd but I feel I know you. Do you ever feel a connection when you meet someone for the first time and don't know why? It's like some distant memory lurking in your head. You think it's mad but you know that you have known them before. It's as though they are glimpsed on the edge of your vision, and when they come into full view all sorts of deep emotions surface. I felt like that the first time I saw you."

Her face brightened as she replied, "Oh, definitely. You and I have met before, haven't we?"

"At the slave market, yes, but didn't you feel a connection even then? As soon as I saw you, I felt I already knew you. I still do."

"But we haven't met before, before the market, have we? Maybe it was in a previous life," she laughed. "In India we believed that reincarnation was natural, and it was accepted that we must build good karma in this life, because in our next one we might meet others that we have known before. Perhaps it is so."

"Do you believe we have lived before?" I asked. "Perhaps in another place, another century?"

"Possibly."

"I think it's more than possible, but wouldn't it be great to be able to remember?" I thought for a moment and then said, "Perhaps it's better not to remember. It is pretty scary. If our lives have crossed before I could've been your slave or your master."

"Or I yours," she laughed.

I had cheered her, I knew. There was a look of such amusement on her face.

"In Zanzibar I was always a master, or thought I was. In

reality, I was a slave there too, but I had friends and was treated well. My mother worked hard and she was a valued member of the household."

We talked for hours. Both of us comfortable, as if we had known each other for a long time and, even though our backgrounds were so totally different, we quickly developed an understanding. I told her again of my dream of freedom and how I had learned so much more than I had ever imagined, both from living with the Leonards and from my studying. I asked her what she felt about her life.

"I have no control over my life, Leonard. I am nothing. I am at the will of Sakarbin. He treats me how he wishes. I can't change anything."

"Does he hurt you?"

"He does often, and he tells me it is Allah's will that I am here to please him. He says Allah would not have brought me here if it had not been what He wanted."

"My first master here in this land, Cecil Leonard, always told me never to trust anyone who makes the excuse of their bad behaviour that they are serving their God. He would say, 'They will use sweet words on you and sound clever, and convince you with the argument that they know because they are more educated than you. They seduce your reason and your conscience. They will make you believe that you are animals, people who can't understand, that you deserve to be treated badly and only understand with the use of force. But, young Katungi...' That was my name then," I explained. "Cecil promised to give me enough education so that I can make my own decisions and not be subjugated to others' ideologies or illusions of superiority. We are all born equal."

"Do you believe that is true?"

"Yes, I do. But I will have to wait for my freedom. I will earn it with my service and my skills, and if, in the meantime, they wish to believe me an animal, so be it, but I will prove it differently. I have heard some of the older slaves talking and explaining to each other how they will gain their freedom. Apparently if your master agrees, you can apply for something called manumission... only after years of honoured service, and conversion to Islam of course."

Eve nodded along as I talked, and breathed an agreement of my words, "If it is so, I too wish to learn how to earn my freedom. Though I have no idea where I could go or what else I could do."

I did, at that moment, realise how much more difficult it would be for a girl.

"Shall I bring you a book and teach you to read? That could be your first step to learning new skills."

Eve nodded, not sure of what use it could possibly be to her. "If you think so. Yes, please."

In my innocence I said, "Perhaps I can marry you and take you with me."

"Insha'Allah," she replied, and we both laughed at the absurdity of my remark.

CHAPTER 20
Leonard My New Friend

EVEANYA

From the moment I saw Leonard again that day in the garden I was bewildered by the way he made me feel. Our conversation had unnerved me slightly, and I was now convinced that we were brought together for a reason.

Perhaps it was because I had lost my only friend, but whatever it was I was glad of it. I dismissed my feelings as crazy even though they had been so vivid and disturbing. The comfortable sensation with him that seemed so natural made me feel safe. I almost felt that I wanted to take care of him. Little by little, there had been a gradual erosion of my shyness with him, and I found him easy to talk to. I was baffled by it. I had never before spoken of my sadness of being a slave, and I kept my inner thoughts contained and hidden. Even with Jilfidan, we never talked about what our fates could possibly be or if we had any other wishes besides being fed and housed. I had long since resigned myself to the prospect of motherhood or being sold again.

No one really knew each other. Real feelings were kept deeply hidden in the harem!

I found myself watching Leonard without knowing why, studying his expressions, the curve of his shoulders, his dark eyes. He was so slight, smaller than I, thin as a reed but handsome in a way I cannot describe. He had smooth, deeply brown skin, a full mobile mouth, his kinky hair was shiny and long, and he stood so straight and proud. He was always beautifully dressed too.

I had been interested in what he was saying and tried to concentrate, but was becoming increasingly frustrated by that insistent itch of familiarity. If reincarnation holds any truth, I thought, our paths must have crossed many times!

Leonard had appeared in my dreams once in a while, and in my thoughts whenever I remembered the horror of that day at the slave market, but I'd never had a sense of wanting to see him again until the day after we had opened our hearts to each other.

I looked forward to our next meeting, and started to go about my duties with renewed enthusiasm. Nothing, other than my horse-riding mornings, had previously cheered me. I had been so lonely and downhearted since Jilfidan had gone, but Ora missed Adell too, so we often consoled each other, took our dance classes together, and developed our own version of the winter and summer dance routine.

But now I had met Leonard! I began to think that after all, a life without a close friend was not inevitable for me. I saw him again the following afternoon walking through the harem courtyard toward the eunuchs' dormitories. I guessed he was bringing them their evening instructions from Sakarbin, who had just returned from Musqat. I was on my way to the bathhouse and I waved across the garden.

"Hello, Leonard."

His face lit up when he saw me, and seeing how pleased I was to see him, said, "I can come back later if you are free."

"Come during Asr, the afternoon prayer, I will be here then."

He waved a 'yes', "Insha'Allah, fair Eve."

"Yes, God willing, Leonard," I laughed.

And so our regular meetings began and our friendship developed. Each time we met was better than the last, and slowly we got to know each other. An intimacy bloomed between us and he became the truest friend, my closest confidant and my happiness. One day he brought me a book and started to teach me to read. I promised him I would practise when I had the time.

Ora and I had been summoned to Sakarbin only once during that month. We all knew that it was because the

Sheikh had his new boy in his bed.

Now, knowing it was Leonard, I often wondered and worried about him.

It was a blessed relief when Ramadan arrived in August as none of us were called upon to attend our master.

Ramadan was a time for spiritual reflection, and normal activities slowed down. Sakarbin made a great show of being pious and good, inviting local villagers and tribesmen to the night-time feasts, opening his coffers to distribute gifts to everyone. All the servants, eunuchs and concubines were given gold coins, the wives expensive jewellery, and all the children had presents of toys, pets or outings.

I hated the fourteen days or so without food or drink, especially during the hottest month in the year. From the moment of its beginning, no healthy adult could take any form of nourishment from sunrise to six at night, and then only after Maghrib, the sunset prayers. Sleeping during the day was the only answer, so I did not see Leonard often during the month of Ramadan.

At night, during the feasting, stories were told, religious songs were sung, and endless prayers intoned to bring each and everyone nearer to God. That was the intention, but for many it was an excuse for laziness in the daylight hours and gluttony at night. I was not convinced, but like everyone else I wanted to be seen to be pious and good, even though it was something I considered myself to already be.

In truth, those not of the faith were not compelled to fast, but Sakarbin insisted that all who did not have heavy labour were to abide by the 'teachings', and so everyone had to. That included all the wives and concubines except those who were pregnant. Luckily, neither Ora nor I were, but Zuena, wife number three, was due to give birth again at any time.

During Ramadan I could not go riding either, and I missed it. I told no one about my secret dawn rides with Jahangeer and Musab, not even Leonard. It was a way of stepping outside my real life for a short time, and I couldn't wait to go again. So, I practised the reading that Leonard had taught me, although I had to admit it didn't come easily to me. In truth, I couldn't see how it could help me change things, but Leonard insisted that it would give me some skill for a different life in the future, whatever he perceived that to be.

The day of Eid al-Fitr, when everyone was celebrating the end of Ramadan, I got a message from Jahangeer that they were riding at dawn the following day, when everyone would be tired and relaxed. If I wanted to go I could join them.

I had attended the Sheikh in the bathhouse, as was the custom, with six of the other girls early in the morning, and had been dancing most of the day as part of the entertainment, so I was tired when I got the message. But having not been riding during Ramadan, I was excited at the prospect and decided I would go.

CHAPTER 21
September 1816

LEONARD

On the last day of Ramadan I watched as the Sheikh and his personal staff, the converted slaves, and eunuchs headed toward the mosque for morning prayers. The call to prayer had become part of my life and often interrupted my work.

"When we are told to do a task, do we stop for prayers, Excellency?" I asked the Sheikh.

His reply made me smile, "For me, yes, I must, of course, but for you it depends on the task, and how important it is. If it is urgent to complete, you are expected to do so. If not, you can pray, but it will be of no credit to you as you are not yet a Muslim. You are an infidel with little use to Allah, who watches and knows what you are. If you learn the Quran and abide by its teachings you will be able to pray with us, eventually. Insha'Allah."

"I will, of course, when the time is right."

"Good boy. After Eid tomorrow I want you back in my bed. I have missed you. I have gifts for you."

I hoped that the gifts included money as I already had a small sum collected and carefully hidden.

I smiled my assent. I had to stay in favour with Sakarbin.

CHAPTER 22
Ride with the Boys 1816

EVEANYA

The morning after the Eid celebrations Musab, Gusiffa and Ahmed met me at the stables. Jahangeer had been called away. I was concerned that he could not join us because he was the one who led us safely, was sensible and careful.

Musab was not much younger than Jahangeer but inclined to be reckless and would easily lose track of time. Without Jahangeer around, Musab flirted and teased me. I didn't like it at all. He was growing fast and would point to his penis in a suggestive way when he caught my eye. I ignored him and enjoyed the wind in my face as we raced along the deserted beach, almost reaching the pearl divers' huts.

However, that morning, I decided that I wouldn't go again without Jahangeer and told Musab when we arrived back at the stables. He screwed up his nose at me and made a wanking gesture.

Oh, no, I thought. I couldn't bear the thought of him even touching me. I changed quickly and managed to get back without any problems.

Nobody had risen in the harem and since Jilfidan had gone I had a room to myself so I tucked myself uneasily into my bed.

Perhaps I would tell Leonard about it when I saw him next.

CHAPTER 23
1817

LEONARD

I had become less disgusted with my role as time passed; I disassociated myself, closed my mind to what was happening to my body and forced a show of affection to Sakarbin when he demanded it. It sickened me through and through, so that the resolve to attain my freedom increased.

He became more demanding, and some nights there would be two or three of his friends who would pleasure themselves with me, each exclaiming on my soft skin, my beautiful body and my devotion. On those occasions, I was sometimes given a bitter drink that made me sleepy and a little dizzy, but it made the ordeal more bearable. There were also a few times when I was restrained, which I didn't like. I became frightened at first, but I soon learned that if I struggled there would be blood and more pain. The master said it gave him pleasure to watch other men with me. It showed how proud he was of me!

Cecil had told me once that God holds a greater love for his hurt and suffering children than he does for the wealthy and privileged, but I questioned the truth of that when I was being abused. Why would He allow such pain to manifest in the world, and to the people that He had created?

It was a long time later that I learned that my fate could creep up behind me unexpectedly and disguised. Sakarbin told me I was beautiful, clever, to be treasured and cosseted, and that he would always look after me. He enjoyed my body almost every night, but increasingly enquired about what I was reading, and listened to my opinions about the writers and the great philosophers. The price I paid was high, but with my growing approval of myself I developed a greater determination to learn, to explore my mind and to understand and free myself of the limits of my world.

I knew that it was time to use my attraction to my own advantage.

"What will you give me, Excellency?" I asked many times as I kissed his fingers.

He was a vain man and he enjoyed my feigned worship of him. At first I asked him for trinkets, a little spending money, new clothes or a trip out with him when he went visiting, although he didn't often allow that.

On other occasions he would say to me, "Whatever you like you can have. I am a wealthy man."

"You are so good to me," was my sarcastic reply, although the inference I did not allow to creep into my remark. "There are many things I would like to do, but mostly learning how to be useful to you, to improve my skills so that I could help you in your business. Perhaps some more books from the Musqat house?"

I would do anything to achieve my goal of freedom, so I continued to gently instil the idea of making myself useful to him, in other ways besides in his bed.

"Firstly, I need to learn to better read and write. That would enable me to help you with your contracts and accounts. I know Jem does it now, but he is getting old and his sight is not good and I think he'll be leaving soon. I could take his place for you. You know I can read and write well already but I still need to improve." I watched Sakarbin carefully so that I would not annoy him or let him think I was asking for too much.

His smile allowed me to continue.

"I would love to learn to ride a horse as well as you, Master, and to be allowed to mix with the other boys. I would like to be able to swim and fish as I did in Qalhat."

"So it shall be, my boy. You can swim and fish as much as you like, but always have someone with you so that none can take advantage of you. I will let you learn to ride, but you will have to be discreet, as it is not usual for me to be so tolerant with a slave. I will even give you your own horse. How do you like the sound of that?"

I opened my eyes and my mouth so that he could see my adoration for him. I was becoming a wonderful liar, and said, "I will be forever grateful, your Excellency."

Encouraged, he continued, "I do need another sicritir, to improve my accounts for the export of the pearls in particular. We will set you up with a mukātaba so that you can save money for your retirement."

"What does that mean?" I enquired innocently, although I already knew of this type of contract, and I had heard that the eunuchs Hamid, Jem and Yanni already had them.

"It means you can save what I allow you to earn or give you, and when, and if, you become free you can use it to buy a house or return to your home. It will be your savings that give you a choice. Serve me well and I will arrange it. Learn the Quran, my boy. By the grace of Allah, you will be free. Allah is 'All Knowing and All Wise'. But, my precious, beautiful boy, it is a long way off. In the meantime, learn mostly to give me pleasure."

He stroked my skinny arm.

I lowered my eyes, pleased with the results of my pretended adoration of him, and I smiled demurely. "You are so good to me, my master. Can I join the soldiers and learn the sword skills... and the fighting groups too... to improve my muscles?" I knew that would help develop strength and stamina, quick responses, flexibility and persistence. In addition, the soldiers enjoyed healthy and well-shaped straight bodies. I was determined that I would learn to fight and defend myself even though I was small in height.

"You may, my sweet boy. I will arrange everything, but don't get too muscle-bound as that will spoil your body."

"No, of course I won't." If only Sakarbin knew how I

hated him, but I was careful. I never allowed my feelings to show, nor spoke against him. He had his own army of surveillance slaves who would report anything and everything back to him. Any attempt to deceive him, change or thwart his power, was immediately dealt with in the harshest possible way.

I had heard of the dreadful whippings that some had received for minor sins, and on two occasions slaves had had their tongues cut out for spreading gossip. I was very careful. Within days Sakarbin had arranged with Hamid, the horse and camel manager, for me to visit the stables, not only to work there but to receive some riding tuition.

He also enrolled me with Crasi, the trainer of the fighting men, who would educate me in fencing and sword and knife skills.

Hamid, a small wiry Zanj slave like my mother, looked at me with a smirk when I arrived at the stables.

"You will be useful, no doubt," he smiled. "When you are properly trained, of course. We need the riding horses exercised daily. If you become competent you can also help with the broodmares. In the meantime you can learn to clean the tackle."

He pointed to a room full of saddles and equipment, and added with a grin, "It'll put some meat on you, moving that lot around."

I loved the smell of the horses and couldn't wait to be allowed to ride. But I was happy just being there, polishing the tackle, grooming or cleaning out the stables. I would soon prove my worth.

I could see that Hamid found it strange that such a small, insignificant slave had Sakarbin's blessing. It was unusual, I knew. Any sort of riding tuition was reserved for the family or for the horse soldiers that were part of the private army. None were small and skinny like me, but Hamid would not question the master's decision. Sakarbin retained ultimate authority on all important domestic issues, and no criticism of him was tolerated. Everything down to the distribution of wages, funds, gratuities and who should ride his horses was at his whim.

Soon after, my training with Jem began.

"About time I had some help," Jem declared good-naturedly. He knew of the study I'd done, and was delighted that I could already read and write so well.

I worked long hours with Jem, who had been in sole charge of the household accounts for many years. He dealt with all the export and import documentation for the horses, camels and the pearls that were part of the business, and the payments to slaves and servants who had contracts with the Sheikh. He was also intent on gaining his retirement the following year. I learned fast, watching Jem make simple lists of financial transactions, laboriously compiled and scrupulously updated every day, bills of sale and invoices catalogued and filed. I very soon knew a great deal about Sakarbin's businesses.

I met with Eve whenever I could as I found talking to her endlessly fascinating. She was chatty and vivacious and happier than I had seen her previously. Her expression as she grinned, frowned, pouted, and wrinkled her little turned-up nose made me smile with pleasure. She always asked me what I was learning. Her interest inspired me, and as our friendship grew I helped and encouraged her with her reading and writing.

Before long I was enrolled with Crasi, who would educate me in fighting skills. He was a good teacher and a hard taskmaster, heavily muscled and scarred from his battles. I watched as he ran his thumb down the edge of his big, heavy sword.

"A good fighter keeps his weapons clean and sharp," he advised.

I checked my own weapons. Mine were clean and sharp,

but I felt they were far too big for me. Perhaps I would grow into them. The sword was heavy and the curved khanjar knife in my belt lay uncomfortably against my hip. As he demonstrated I watched carefully. Crasi held the sword in his right hand and his knife in his left. He snapped into position. "Begin. Feel the weight and balance of your weapons and move with them." He danced forward and thrust his blade ahead and across, swishing it through the air with practised smoothness.

"With this move your opponent will lift his blade as you move away," he instructed. "While your foe's blade is high up there, and just before it comes slicing down to split your head in two, you swing your sword diagonally upward and forward with your right hand and from your left hip. Your right arm then fully extended, thus cutting the front of his throat with the tip of your blade."

It looked easy, but it wasn't, and we practised until our shoulders ached and our hands were blistered. I discovered my short stature to be an advantage because I could dodge and move faster than most, but I was so tired with the exercise and the weight of my weapons.

That night I moaned with pain as Sakarbin pulled me this way and that. He cared nothing for my aching muscles and pressed a pile of coins into my hand the following morning so I cared not. Gold coins for my freedom.

CHAPTER 24
The Wedding 1817

EVEANYA

It was December, and Jem called us all together for an announcement.

"We are to prepare for a wedding that will take place in February next year," Jem told us solemnly. "Our Sheikh has promised the Sultan that he will take Halima bint Almasi, the daughter of a Salafi Sheikh, for his fourth and final wife. The hope is that the marriage will unite the peoples of Musqat with the Wahhabi border tribes of the interior that have been causing trouble. We must start making preparations. Halima bint Almasi and her retinue will arrive here shortly. There will be no dancing or music as she obeys a strict religious conduct and will expect all her slaves and servants to do so too."

"How can we have a wedding with no celebration or entertainment?" asked Deilah, who herself had enjoyed a whole week of dancing, singing and partying when she married Sakarbin many years previously.

Zuena, Sakarbin's third wife, was particularly scathing about the announcement, and refused to be involved with the wedding preparations at all. Zuena loved festivities of any kind and was not so pious as some, so was scornful of Sakarbin's proposal for a fourth wife. She had a good excuse not to be involved in the wedding preparations as her new baby girl had been born at the end of September and she was happily involved in motherhood.

When Halima bint Almasi arrived at the end of December, we were all intrigued. She was seventeen years old, slim and pretty with dark hair down to her knees. But she was serious and pious, used to having her own way, and arrived with a collection of cowed slaves. She came with a set of attitudes and behaviour derived from the teachings of a particularly severe religious reformist who lived in central Arabia a century past.

As was the tradition, the betrothal time was a month, and Halima's days were spent in confinement and prayer, with only her personal slaves in attendance. During the last week the bride was to be confined without pretty clothes, perfumes or jewellery, so we had some time off.

The last batches of henna and aromatics were mixed ready for the following days when the bride would be decorated and perfumed. For three nights before the wedding the henna was applied to her palms and the soles of her feet. Once the henna was carefully painted on, it had to be fixed into place, which meant her hands and feet had to be bound for the night. A really uncomfortable procedure, and I was pleased that it was not me subjected to so much discomfort.

When the morning of the wedding arrived, we were up at four for prayers, dressed and perfumed, each trying to outshine the other in the splendour of their finery. As the festivities normally last for three days, we all needed several changes, but our lovely dresses and veils were wasted as we all had to wear the niqab. No singing, dancing or jollity was allowed. Only a monotonous drumbeat and readings of the Quran were included.

Halima's acceptance into the harem was slow, and the easy attitudes of our lives were changed as she insisted on separating her own household from the rest of the harem. We did not reach her expected standards of piety and constraint. Most of us were pleased, as being confined in the harem we had little enough entertainment. We soon reverted to our usual pleasures of singing, dancing and playing games.

I met Leonard the day after the three-day wedding celebration, although none of us would have called it a celebration. It had been a sombre affair and we were glad that it was over.

It was the end of February.

"Are you relieved that Sakarbin has taken a new wife?" I asked him.

"Oh, yes. And you? We will not have to go to him. We can spend more time together and on your learning. Yes?"

"We will," I said happily.

During the next month, Leonard and I met as regularly as we could. He was learning to ride, and Sakarbin had promised him a horse of his own. For a moment I was so jealous. I had only been out riding once of late, and had avoided Musab whenever possible.

I still had not told Leonard about my escapades with the Sheikh's sons. Perhaps it was better that I did not. I wasn't sure that he would approve.

It was about that time that Zuena became ill. No one was sure what was wrong with her, but she became breathless and feverish and her leg and foot inflamed. Lumaria told me eventually that they thought that a scorpion had stung her, but she wasn't getting any treatment. Her young baby Razia was fretful and demanding, so Ora and I took over her care as best we could.

CHAPTER 25
1818

LEONARD

It had been such a relief that Sakarbin had taken his new wife and was intent on getting her pregnant. It meant I was moved to the eunuchs' dormitory and could concentrate on my studying, my body training and horsemanship skills. I spent as much time as I could with Eve too, and was surprised how well she was learning to read. Our short times together were such a pleasure, and I appreciated her for her sweet nature and endless patience, especially with the plethora of children constantly making demands on her. She told me that she and Ora were looking after a five-month-old little girl as the mother, Zuena, was ill. When I knew that it was one of Sakarbin's wives suffering from a scorpion sting, I said, "I have a medical book that might give some indication as to treatment. Shall I bring it for you?"

"Yes, please. In India we would use Kathaligidi juice."

"What is that?"

"Here I think it is called Sabr. It grows in the gardens and in the wadi. If you could get some for me, I will make an ointment for her." Taking a piece of bamboo, she drew a long spiky leaf shape in the sand. "This is what it looks like. It is a desert lily and has healing powers, but there is none in the harem garden. I have looked already and I ... I shouldn't leave here, should I?" she asked with a grin.

"I'll get you some." I went immediately and cut six of the outer leaves as she had instructed and brought them to her.

"I have to leave them standing upright to drain before I strip and press them," she explained, and took them away, returning in a few minutes, this time with a small brown boy who had banged his head and was seeking comfort.

"Do you want to have children of your own?" I asked as

she cuddled her little charge.

"No, I do not. With Sakarbin? No. I have been trying to find a way of preventing pregnancy as Bellia did. After she had had her fourth baby, she decided that there would be no more but she won't tell me what she did."

"Perhaps it was the lemon trick."

"What's that?"

"A small half a lemon tucked up inside. Stops it, so I believe."

"How do you possibly know such things?" Eve laughed at me as her little charge scampered off happily sucking his thumb.

I tapped my nose and told her. "I read a lot. It's amazing what you can learn from books."

"Really?"

"If you learn to read you will open your mind to all sorts of wonderful things. Subjects that you have never even thought of before," I explained.

"I suppose you're right. There must be so much more to the world than the little space we live in here. I do sometimes wonder if there is more to life than growing old in the service of the Sheikh."

A profound worldly sadness showed in her eyes as she leaned toward me, holding her face in her hands and resting her elbows on her knees.

"Hah, doing the Sheikh's bidding is going to make me wealthy and I will someday be free, you will see," I told her.

"Really, is that so? I'll need to study more so that I can understand. Bring me the medical book so that I can learn something useful."

Eve laughed, but I did know that the hope or the possibility of freedom was something that had never occurred to her.

I couldn't get her sad face or her violet eyes out of my mind. Those eyes that hinted at a mystery I could not fathom. They gave me a window to other feelings, deep unknown feelings of love, pain and guilt. They appeared to know me well, to know so much. I felt again as I had in the slave market – overwhelmed with emotion.

Surprising her, I reached forward and stroked the birthmark on her neck.

She smiled happily, her spirit lifted. I departed with a promise to meet her again the next day.

Almost another full year passed. We had some bad storms that winter and I'd spent a great deal of time studying and working with Jem. I knew that if I earned the same every month it would take seven or eight years to get enough to leave. I would then have to earn an income to maintain myself, but I was already working with Sakarbin's accounts and could calculate margins of profit and loss, fractions and percentages. Perhaps I could get work in one of the new banks that I had heard about, or with a professional moneylender. In the meantime, I would work on being physically strong as well as clever and well-read.

The fourth wife, Halima, was now pregnant, and I was summoned back to my room next to Sakarbin. I knew that he had recently tired of her, as Ora, Eve and I had already attended him on odd occasions. Now he wanted me every night again. He welcomed me with gifts and affection, remarking that I had not grown too much or become fat. He admired my strong, lean body.

I'd asked Jem why I was not growing as fast as the Sheikh's boys, who were of a similar age to me. Jahangeer at nineteen was a full-grown man and ready to marry. Gusiffa and Ahmed, both younger than I, were at least a head taller, with deep, masculine voices and the beginnings of a beard. Musab, who was two years older, had a full beard and a broad, hairy chest like his father.

"Will I catch up do you think, Jem?" I'd asked as we collected the invoices of the latest batch of exports.

"No. Look carefully at me, Leonard. I should have grown taller, my voice should have become much deeper than it is, and I have a soft body prone to flabbiness. I've no beard and little hair to speak of. It has always been so, but it is not just because I am old. I know I am fat, but that too is one of the disadvantages. Look around at the other eunuchs, none have grown properly." Jem carefully explained that the effects of the castration were permanent, and that I would never develop like an ordinary man.

"You'll have noticed it more as you see the Sheikh's sons grow into men. They will be bigger and hairier than you, with deep voices that you will never have. They will have the women to satisfy them."

"What gives them the right to deny us, Jem?"

"I will tell you this in the utmost confidence, Leonard." I nodded. Jem knew me well enough now to trust me. "We are nought but commodities to the Mohamedans, Leonard. Utilities. Useful. For purpose only. They've made us like this so that we are no threat to their women or their dynasty. Because we're unable to perform sexually, we cannot father any children. We cannot challenge them. We must remain only interested in carrying out the duties expected of us. We can waste no time lusting or wanting or indeed needing sexual gratification as normal men do."

"But they've taken from us a vital part of our bodies, to deny us the pleasures of the flesh, fatherhood or any normal masculine growth. How can that be right?"

"We live in a world where right and wrong do not exist. To them it is only right if the Quran says so. Their holy book lies about what is right or wrong. It must be wrong for one human being to own another and to do the things to us that they do. To the Mohamedans we are only animals. I used to fight it, but the fire that I had in me as a young man is long quenched. I am now old and my life has been what it is. I know of nothing else. Not you, though, Leonard. The master loves and desires you because you are so beautiful and you have the intelligence and learning that he admires."

"He's trying to stop me going out on my own because he thinks other men will desire me too."

"That is true. You could come to harm. We all have to be careful, but you're smaller than most. You could be at risk because you're so good-looking. Are you learning to defend yourself?"

I nodded as he added, "Build up your strength and don't get fat like me." I took notice of what Jem told me and decided straight away that I'd increase my daily exercise. I went swimming and running. My training and fighting routine became an important part of my daily life. Although my legs were strong and muscled, my upper body needed building up too, so I asked Crasi the troop trainer what I should do.

"Get some rocks and lift them," he told me. "Anything will do really, but repetition is the answer to get you strong. Start slow and build up to bigger weights and you'll soon see a difference in your upper body."

I collected two equally large rocks from the wadi that strained my arm muscles as I lifted them. My muscles developed slowly at first, but I could clearly see a difference as the months passed.

Sakarbin smiled at me, his hand caressing my rear as he leaned forward and licked my earlobe. "You are growing firmer by the day."

I was irritated and pulled away, but he held fast.

"I've neglected you, so I have something special for you. Do you want to see?" He indicated a coloured box at the foot of the bed. "Get it," he instructed.

I crawled to the end of the bed and opened the present. It was an embroidered, expensively decorated coat. I stroked the beautiful material and smiled.

Sakarbin lifted his sausage fingers to my cheek. "I had it

made especially for you. Do you like it?"

"I do."

"You must only wear it when you are with me, of course."

"Yes, I understand."

But I didn't want to. I didn't want to be like this. I wanted to be a real man.

CHAPTER 26
My Love for Leonard

EVEANYA

I'd learned so much from Leonard that I was now able to read simple things in Arabic and English. I'd learned to speak in English too, so that we could converse without others understanding. As time passed, I began to feel more confident about my ability to improve myself. Our friendship was now deep and strong. Little changed in our lives as another two years came and went; more babies were born; more slaves were bought and sold. My body had changed alarmingly as my breasts and hips had blossomed, but I hadn't become pregnant thanks to my little lemon trick.

Sakarbin was disappointed. He told me I was still one of his favourites and, although I still danced regularly for him, my night-time visits became less, for which I was grateful.

Leonard and I had found a quiet place with a seat alongside one of the hidden pathways inside the harem and we met when we could. We would talk for hours, and we composed songs and poems, read aloud and promised to be friends forever. He had a special song that he would sing to me about gaining his freedom. He wrote it down so that I could learn it too.

"Do you believe that we all have a soulmate?" I asked him one morning.

"What do you mean?" Leonard enquired.

I quoted from the book that I had been reading. "You know, someone who is more than special, a person who has shared other lifetimes. Perhaps an ideal partner in understanding, wit and intelligence. Destined to be together in perfect harmony."

Leonard raised an enquiring eyebrow, as if he'd misheard me, so I continued.

"Have you ever thought about reincarnation? Meeting

again, perhaps someone loved and lost in a previous existence. But awakened sometimes by a fleeting memory, a look, a dream, a feeling which parts a veil between the worlds to glimpse the journey of souls. Destined to be together. Someone not remembered exactly −"

"What have you been reading, Eve?" he asked with an amused smile.

"The Plato book you lent me, where all the men discuss the wholeness of relationships. Aristophanes talks of the purpose and nature of love. I don't understand most of it, but it has made me wonder about true love and what it really means. If it carries on through lifetime after lifetime."

"Yes, Eveanya, I do believe it," Leonard said with a gentle expression on his face, "we have met before, and we are meant to be together now. Of that I am sure."

I had a sudden and intense urge to touch him. I'd never felt like that before, not with a man. Affection between the girls in the harem was normal, but I'd never had any *desire* to touch a man. Perhaps the forced intimacies that were part of my life had made me believe that I couldn't feel anything. Knowing that it was possible to have such feelings and that I was not dead inside made me feel euphoric and wretched at the same time. Realisation of my growing love for Leonard changed the way I saw him.

He suddenly wrapped his arms around me and pulled me close. I became deeply aware of his physical presence. The sensation of his skin on mine was overpowering, almost too much to bear, wonderful and scary at the same time. I longed to press further into his body. My heart was racing. The strength and warmth of him was electrifying, unlike anything I'd ever felt before.

"I love you," I whispered into his chest. He leaned forward and kissed me on the top of my head, and said, "Let us not speak of love. This moment is the only thing we can believe in."

CHAPTER 27
Understanding

LEONARD

Her declaration had made me uncomfortable, but the truth was I'd grown to love her too. But it made me nervous.

When our gazes met, Eve flushed and looked down, but I could tell from the way her breast lifted that she was nervous too.

She'd brought to my life a renewed desire to live it to the full. She was the only person who I could talk to openly about my feelings and myself. Our friendship held richness and completeness that I wouldn't risk losing.

I shook my head but suddenly felt the panic of exposure – she was so close I could hide nothing.

I wanted to feel her nearness, her weight and her breath on my cheek. I liked it. Her body emanated comforting warmth as her breasts pressed into my chest.

I loved her, of that I was sure, but the stirring was in my heart, not in my loins. I knew that I would have to explain to her soon, as our relationship was becoming so close and I loved her so dearly. She would need to understand that physically I could give her nothing more than this moment of intimacy. No one had explained it to me until Jem had told me, that my voice would never break, that my muscles would not develop in the same way as a normal man or that I could never enjoy the physical intimacy with a woman as other men did. I thought I should try to explain to Eve. "You do know that I am a eunuch?"

"Yes, I do. Of course I know. I don't know how or why, but I am told it is the will of Allah that some should be so."

"No, no. The Mohamedans believe that everything that happens is by Divine Will. It was not Divine Will that changed me into what I am now. It was evil men, with their need for power, their fear and their carnal desires. It has nothing to do with God, Allah or Divine Will."

"I never thought about it like that," Eve leaned away and gazed at me. Her lovely violet eyes were wide open. "But I do know that you won't grow and that you have no... None at all?"

"No. None at all."

I started to speak again but she placed a finger on my lips. "Don't try, dearest Leonard."

"You know I can't give you... don't you, Eve?"

"I do know. I know that we cannot... It doesn't matter at all. I love you, that's all that matters to me."

CHAPTER 28
1822

EVEANYA

Although my life had changed little, I was still summoned to Sakarbin's bed on occasion. I was nearly eighteen and still one of his favourites. Sometimes Ora accompanied me. As with Jilfidan, there was an unwritten law that we never spoke of our experiences with our master with anyone. I hoped that it would come to a natural end, but could see no future there unless I got pregnant. I was still taking the precaution that Leonard had told me about, and I knew it would not be long before I would have to make a decision or be sold. I could not bear the thought of leaving the only place that I thought of as home and my beloved friend.

Ora was the next to become pregnant, and she was pleased. Her baby would be born later in the year.

Halima's baby boy, now a noisy three-year-old, had calmed her influence on the harem, and they stayed in their own quarters more and more. I was pleased to hear that she too was pregnant again. Her baby would be born at much the same time as Ora's.

There were some of the girls in the harem who were not happy mothers, and Thalis was one of them. She had no natural maternal instincts and already had five children; she was not yet twenty-five. I thought I should tell her of my secret, but was very wary because I knew that it would be frowned upon.

I had been reading the medical book that Leonard had lent me. It was a huge undertaking, written in Arabic, and called *al-Qanun fi al-Tibb*, by Ibn Sina.

It was difficult for me to understand, but several parts of it caught my attention. It had a whole chapter on avoiding pregnancy. I was determined to learn all I could.

"Do you know, Leonard, that besides the lemon trick there are many herbs that could be used to prevent conception?" I told him wisely the next time we were together.

"You really are reading the medical book then?" he laughed.

"I am, slowly… it is hard, but I am learning a great deal. There are some strange ideas in it, but I am determined to find out more and help others who don't want more babies. Under the heading of *'restoring the menses'* there are herbal concoctions to abort one already started."

"Take care, Eve, that could get you into trouble."

"I know, but I am worried about Thalis. She suffers so with her pregnancies."

Leonard was amused, but said he understood my concern and made me promise to keep my new knowledge to myself.

"Perhaps one day it will be useful," he told me quietly, "but don't get into trouble, Eve."

As the year progressed Jahangeer moved away and was planning to marry the following year. Musab, Gusiffa and Ahmed still took me for an occasional ride. My transformation into a stable boy was well practised, but by then I had to bind my breasts. Some of the guards had got used to seeing me, they even greeted me on occasions. I was careful to keep my distance from Musab, who was now a large, hairy young man and three years older than I. He constantly showed off, slapped my horse when he could, and made lewd noises with his mouth when the others were out of hearing. He reminded me on occasions that I was a slave and he could do whatever he wished to me.

"Oh no you can't. Not if your father finds out," I'd spat at him after our last ride.

"Father says I can have any woman I want," he scoffed as I marched away. I had noticed that Gusiffa too had become suggestive and laughed when Musab was taunting me. I decided that I wouldn't ride with them again, but I would miss it so. I wondered whether to ask Leonard to take me, as I knew he too had become a competent horseman, but I imagined that he could get severely punished if we were found out. I wouldn't risk getting him into trouble. He still didn't know about my early morning jaunts.

Several weeks passed and eventually I felt confident enough to consider taking a horse out on my own. I decided I would take Sadiqa, who was reliable, sure-footed and knew me well.

I could easily avoid the boys if I went early enough. I knew where to ride out of sight of the estate, and was good at judging time from the rising sun. I decided that it wouldn't be difficult, especially now that the perimeter guards had become more relaxed. Since Sakarbin's marriage to Halima, the interior tribes had ceased their raids and attacks and we had had a few peaceful years. Early the following morning I followed my well-known route to the far end of the stable yard.

Taking great breaths of the cool morning air to rouse my courage, I reached the saddle room where my clothes were kept. It was going to be a beautiful morning, but now it was cool and there was a light breeze from the shore.

A perfect day for a ride!

CHAPTER 29
The Fire

LEONARD

My strength was increasing and I was pleased that my body was becoming toned and strong. I could run fast and I was confident that I could defend myself if I was ever set upon, something which Jem had warned me could happen. I had seen the possibility occurring when I had been training with the troops, some of whom made suggestive remarks about my smooth skin and lack of body hair.

My ability with the horses allowed me to ride most days. I was even involved in the training events, which I loved. I had got on so well, and Hamid had learned to trust me and relied on me more each day.

It had been a hot night and, being unable to sleep, I had risen exceptionally early and decided to go for a morning ride. I would take out Flavia, my new, beautiful bay mare. She was my latest gift from Sakarbin, after a miserable night with him and one of his *honourable* friends.

Even though Sakarbin had forbidden me to go out on my own with her, I was not concerned. I would take her to the shore and race along with the incoming waves and chase away all memory of what that filthy night had entailed, and I would sing my song of freedom.

Sakarbin had been entertaining another new girl that night and would probably not rise till late. I was sure that I would not have to explain to him where I had been. I started to sing as I walked.

Freedom lies within my grasp, regardless of my journey
No pain or sorrow will hold me bound
No rules and ropes will still my yearning
Unlock the gates that close my mind, let me free
The keys lie in my learning.

I was approaching the stables, humming and softly mouthing the words of my song, when I saw a small dark figure ahead of me and hesitated to see where he was heading. It was obviously one of the stable boys, but from where I stood I could not identify him.

I thought to call out, but the figure was bent low as if to hide, so I followed at a discreet distance and waited. He arrived at the big stable doors where the private mounts were housed, including my Flavia, the Sheikh's favourites, the sons' horses and the valuable stallions.

I was still a distance away and I lost sight of him. I took my time as the sun had not yet risen and it was still dark.

Just as I reached the double stable doors I heard a muffled shout and the sound of laughing and scuffling. I thought perhaps one of the stable lads had a servant girl in the hay at the back with him, but the noises became rougher and more insistent. It was only when I heard a scream and Musab's voice that I became concerned.

"Don't fight me, pretty girl, you know how I desire you... thought you could get away on your own did you?"

A slap and another muffled scream, and I stepped inside. Someone was being hurt but I had to be careful. Musab was a big, dangerous and powerful young man, and I was only a slave.

I moved slowly along the wall and noticed an oil lamp propped above Sadiqa's stall. No one ever brought oil lamps into the stables. The danger was obvious. My thoughts were racing. If I could make my way around the other side I could perhaps identify what was happening. In the dim light I could see a body on the floor of the stable by the wall. Sadiqa was prancing, and although tethered her feet were clip-clopping close to what I thought to be the stable boy who was kicking and scrabbling to rise. The noise was spooking the horse. Musab put his hand on her flank and shoved her to the other side of the stall, then stood with his back to me, obscuring the figure on the floor. He was releasing his riding pants, and as he stepped back I could see instantly that it was Eve struggling to get to her feet. A long coil of her blonde curls had escaped the turban that she wore. I leaned forward far enough to see that her mouth was bound and she was trying to push herself to her feet. Musab was restraining her with one outstretched arm as he pulled down his pants.

I stepped forward and opened the stable door fully so that Musab could see me. I was seething with rage, and as he turned I saw his enormous penis over the top of his leggings.

"Get away from her," I said as menacingly as I could.

He dropped his shirt and laughed. "It's Papa's little bed boy. Come to watch have you? Or do you want a turn? Hey, hey, you're a eunuch, you can't can you?" he taunted. "Gusiffa, come and see this."

Gusiffa appeared suddenly behind me, and with a hoot of laughter rammed me in the back so that I lurched forward into Musab and we careered into the shaky wooden walls of the stable. The precariously balanced oil lamp was dislodged, and it dropped to the floor and rolled. Instantly a flame lifted into a single golden glow, and before anyone could speak, a dribble of oil spewed out and a blanket of flames spread across the floor.

Sadiqa was neighing wildly, her eyes wide with fear.

Eve had managed to stand, tied her trousers, and pulled off her gag. She was intent on releasing Sadiqa, while I grappled with Musab and Gusiffa.

Musab hit me hard across the side of my head, and I punched him in the groin so he bent with a howl and screamed at Gusiffa to grab hold of me, but he had already fled outside and was shouting for help.

Eve released Sadiqa, who galloped past us into the safety of the paddock, and Eve ran back to release others from the adjacent stables.

Regardless of the seriousness of the situation, Musab kept after me. He was so much bigger than I, but I was fast and strong. We wrestled and fought whilst the flames grew higher and the noise of panicked horses filled the air. Musab managed to punch me several times before I hit him square in the jaw and counter-punched him in the stomach so that he fell with a thud, a sliver of flame catching one side of his shirt. He was dazed and panicked and about to get severely burned, so I grabbed him, dragged him outside, and rolled him into the sand. The flame was extinguished instantly but he was coughing and winded. He managed to push himself up to examine his arm which was red and raw, one side of his beard and face badly scorched.

"You'll pay for this, you little runt Leonard," he shouted, blazing with anger.

I could see over my shoulder that the flames were rising quickly, but Eve had released several of the other horses, which were galloping away from the danger. I noticed that my bay Flavia was amongst them.

Guards and a few stable boys were appearing from all directions, and the great water trough outside was already in use as I made a dash for Eve, knocking Gusiffa out of my way.

"Help with the fire, Gusiffa," I shouted as I ran toward Eve, who was leading Donil to safety. Released, the frightened horse set off at a gallop to join the others. The mounting army of men and boys were already getting the flames under control. Before Eve could run back again, I grabbed hold of her and I held her close. She was shivering with shock. "Get that turban on properly and get away from here now," I said, as I pulled her behind the saddle room and pushed her out of sight. "No one must find out that you were here. Go quickly before anyone recognizes you."

She opened her terrified violet eyes and whispered, "Oh, Leonard, what will happen to us?"

"You have not been here and you know nothing. Those boys will not admit to their father that you were here and what they intended to do to you. Do you understand? Get changed and get away from here as quickly as possible. Promise me that you will deny any knowledge of what has happened. The fire is under control and the horses are safe thanks to you."

"I didn't know Musab and Gusiffa were at the stables."

"It matters not, Eve, but you must not be recognized. Go now."

I left her then and went to see what I could do to help. Luckily the fire had done little damage, and all of the horses were safe. Musab had a bad burn on his left arm and his face looked sore, and he was swearing that I would get the blame.

I had already come to that conclusion and was ready for the consequences, whatever they would be.

It didn't take long!

CHAPTER 30
Questioned

EVEANYA

We were all questioned. It was routine that if a slave disobeyed, all would answer for him. Our master believed that a slave would not tell the truth without torture or the whip. Of course, it is never enough just to punish the guilty. An example must be made to all who cooperate or even have the slightest inkling of what had happened.

I was so distressed at the thought of being found out and knew the penalty would be high. But how had Musab and Gusiffa known that I would be going to the stables that morning, and why was Leonard there? I was mystified. I had thought that I was on my own as I had hurried to change and crossed the stable yard without a thought of being seen. As I entered the stable I whispered a 'hello' to Sadiqa. She whinnied a reply. "How do you fancy taking me along the shore?" I had whispered as I started to untie her lead rope.

Intent on what I was doing, I heard nothing, but a moment later I glimpsed a movement out of the corner of my eye. I turned quickly and saw Musab behind me.

He was carrying an oil lamp. In the dim light he looked like a menacing ghost. He kicked the stable door shut behind him.

"Good morning, Eveanya," he said as he moved toward me. There was a strange look in his eyes. At first I could not read his expression, then, after a moment, I understood and was frightened. He put the oil lamp on the wall of the stall and stepped toward me, wrapped an arm around me and tied something around my mouth. I lashed at him but he pulled the cord of my riding trousers and they slid down to my knees. I fell with a thud against the wall of the stable and was struggling to rise when Leonard had appeared.

Everything happened so fast, but the minute I saw the blaze my only thought was for the horses. I moved quickly, untying and releasing them. I was aware of Leonard and Musab fighting and shouting, but I saw only the fear in the eyes of the horses. It was only when Leonard grabbed me that the realisation of what had happened hit me. Leonard's warning had scared me so. I ran as fast as I could back along the ditch. I was terrified but I returned to the harem without detection and lay shivering in my bed until Lumaria called us all at dawn to attend the inquiry.

A message must be sent to all who might be thinking that they could get away with any misdemeanour, so Lumaria questioned everyone in turn.

One of Zuena's offspring had seen me leave the harem but had gone back to sleep so didn't know when I had left.

"Can you explain yourself, Eveanya?" Lumaria glared at me. "You were seen leaving the harem. Is that true?"

I swallowed hard and stood tall. "I know of nothing. I have slept until we were woken this morning. She must have seen me last night, when I was summoned by Sakarbin," I lied. It wasn't true of course, but I hoped that she would not ask me about the previous evening. Lumaria knew that any of us could be called at a moment's notice, so she didn't pursue the previous night's activities but continued with what she knew.

"The boy Leonard has been caught and is accused of causing the fire. Do you know anything about this? If I call in the questioners, young Eveanya, you will tell all you know. You will be hard to recognize by the time they have finished with you. Is that what you want? To be made an example of?"

"How can I tell anything when I know nothing?" Fear pooled in my body, and my quickened heartbeat coloured my cheeks, but I lifted my eyes with an appeal to Lumaria. "Leonard is a friend but I do not know his thoughts or his motives to what he is being accused of." I dropped to my knees. "Lumaria, please, do not let them question me. Please. I know of nothing at all."

"Very well. Get back to your bed, child." She lifted her right hand and slapped me hard across my cheek. "You had better be telling the truth, or it'll be I that pays."

I hurried away, my face smarting with pain and a sigh of relief as I pulled my soft covers over the top of me. All I could think of was poor Leonard, who would be cruelly whipped. I was the only one, other than Musab and Gusiffa, who knew the truth, but Leonard had warned me to keep quiet. No one had been badly hurt and the horses were not harmed, so why would anyone be punished? If anyone should be, it should be me.

"I must go to him," I said to Ora, who had come to ask me about the situation.

"No, you shouldn't," she cried. "You don't know what will happen."

"All I know is that Leonard is going to be punished."

CHAPTER 31
Punished

LEONARD

"You are a slave," Sakarbin pronounced the last word with slow deliberation, as if speaking to an imbecile or an animal. "You will be punished with the whip as that seems to me to be the only way you will understand. I cannot have you undermine my discipline. It is the will of God. Allah be praised."

"No harm has come to the horses, Master."

Sakarbin stared at me, quivering with fury. In a hard voice he acknowledged that indeed the horses were unharmed, but he stressed that it could have had a different outcome, and he would need to punish me for my disobedience. It mattered not that his son Musab was to blame for bringing the oil lamp to the stables. It was he who bore the scars of that morning and, although I was innocent of any crime, I had to take the punishment.

"I will make an example of you so that none of the others think that you are exempt from my anger or that they can take advantage of what you have done." He turned and shouted to Jem.

I truly did not think that he would carry out his threats. I had after all been his favourite bed boy for over six years, and he was a long way from being tired of me, but I could see that his anger was so intense that there was a chance I would lose his favour.

In comparison with my castration, the whipping had been easy to bear. I was tied to the whipping post as Crasi administered the twenty lashes, and had been swiftly dismissed. Sakarbin had watched, his eyes cold, his teeth clenched.

"This pains me almost as much as it does you, but you

must never disobey me again," he said as he untied me and I staggered to my feet. "Do not ever dare to question the actions or words of your superiors. My son is scarred because of you." He spat at me as he turned to leave, but I saw a tinge of regret in his eyes. "You are now disfigured and no longer beautiful. I will not allow you back in my bed. I have made other arrangements."

Through my pain I felt a relief that I could not hide. It was worth the beating then! That news alone made the pain easier to bear. It was later that same day that I was aware of Eve caressing my cheek and sobbing softly. She changed the dressings on my back that Jem had applied after my beating, and after kissing me softly left with a promise to return. I could feel her tears on my face, but my wounds, although still painful, had eased considerably with her ministering.

CHAPTER 32
Feeling Guilty

EVEANYA

I'd tiptoed along the corridor to the eunuchs' dormitories. I knew where Leonard slept when he was in the harem. I crept into the darkened room without knocking as I'd done on a few previous occasions.

He lay on his stomach in semi-darkness, bloodied bandages covering his back. Tears pooled in my eyes and my stomach clenched. This was my fault, entirely my fault. If I hadn't been there on my own, he would not have fought with Musab.

My instinct was to slip under the sheet with him and cover his lips with kisses, to pretend that he was not really hurt at all, but I knelt at his bedside and touched his cheek with my fingertips instead. His eyes opened and he started to push himself up, but the blood began to flow from his shoulders. The bandages were soaked. I crouched beside him and gently motioned for him to be still.

His eyelids fluttered and closed. He lifted a hand toward me and whispered, "Go away, Eve."

I sighed and leaned forward just a little to press my lips on his. I wanted to wrap my arms around him and heal the places on his shoulder that the whip had scarred. I wanted to soothe away his pain. There were no words to say how sorry I was, how much I cared for him or how I wished it were I that had been whipped instead.

"I have brought you some salve for your wounds," I said simply.

Leonard had always been quiet, silent almost when others were around, but his silence was different after the beating. The anger, the accusation in his face was palpable, and I thought they were directed at me. Everything had changed since our encounter in the stables and his punishment. I was distraught. Although Leonard still felt I shouldn't admit to being at the stables that morning, I felt I should tell the truth, clear his name and take the blame for my disobedience. I had not seen Musab, but of course I now remained in the harem. Leonard could move freely and he told me that Musab's beard was growing back and he had a long red scar on his upper arm. He was claiming it happened when he was bravely putting out the fire that Leonard was responsible for.

CHAPTER 33
A Happy Discovery

LEONARD

One week later I was still sore but the cuts had stopped bleeding and were beginning to heal. I felt better but I was still so angry at having been accused of causing the fire. I resolved that I would make Musab pay somehow.

Sakarbin sent for me. Gone was the cold stare, and he spoke to me with affection and a tinge of disappointment. He leaned toward me and stroked my cheek. I did not smile or respond as I had done before, but he knew that everything was now changed. He gave a resigned shrug.

"A lesson learned, I hope, Leonard. You will agree I am sure that I have been extremely good to you, and although I am deeply disappointed in you, I will not dismiss you. I need your expertise in my businesses. I know that you are valuable to me, and Allah be praised that you have learned from your disobedience."

"It's true, I went to ride Flavia and I should not have disobeyed you, but I did not take the oil lamp into the stables," I repeated. "I did not cause the fire, Excellency. If you choose to believe Musab, so be it, but Allah will know the truth. Allah be praised."

"Allah be praised indeed. It is my son who has the scars, but no one else was hurt and you have taken your punishment. I wish to hear no more on the subject. You will take over from Jem, who is leaving very soon. He has gained his manumission, so now you will be my sicritir. You will no longer receive gifts from me, only a wage, and I expect absolute loyalty and dedication. We have expanded our pearl business as you know, and I want you to handle all the negotiations. Can I trust you to look after my business?" Sakarbin hesitated long enough to watch my reaction.

"Of course, Excellency." I did not want him to see how delighted I was. I already had almost enough money and jewels to furnish my future, and I was still going to earn a wage and never have to get in Sakarbin's bed again. I wanted him to know the truth about the fire, but I was more than happy with the outcome. At some point in the future I would make sure that Musab was disgraced.

"You will make yourself known to Ahmar, the manager of the divers. He has been a good, reliable servant for the past eight years, something that I could not have known when I bought him. I thought him extremely valueless, but he has proved his worth many times over," Sakarbin continued, obviously happy with my feigned look of regret.

I listened carefully as he told me about his pearl fishing manager.

It was only when he mentioned that he was called the Ahmar smak, which meant 'red fish' in English, that I wondered if it could possibly be Patrick. At the Leonards' he was often referred to as 'Ahmar dualifin' – red dolphin – because of his red hair and amazing swimming ability. His name had never been mentioned to me before, so I couldn't wait to find out.

I'd heard nothing of any of my family, and knew only that Cecil, Emily, Ahmed and Fatu were dead, as I had seen their deaths with my own eyes. What had happened to the other children I did not know. Could it be possible that Patrick had been just a few miles away all these years without me knowing?

The pearl fishers' houses were about two miles along the shore, and although I had often ridden past them, I had never seen any of them. I knew they worked long hours and slept when they could. It was a short, demanding life, as the pressure was intense. Jem had told me about the business side, of course, and I knew that Sakarbin had made huge profits from the pearls. I vowed to find out as soon as I was able, although I did ask Jem what he knew of the manager.

"Indeed, yes, he does have unusual colouring and is tall and skinny. The most exceptional swimmer we've ever had."

"How come you have never mentioned him to me?"

"Why would I? He was here before you came. He was bought from somewhere south is all I know of him."

"Could it have been after the uprising when the villages and towns of the foreigners were fired and the merchants and traders killed?"

"Most likely," Jem replied. "But you came later, from the interior, did you not?"

"I was living in Qalhat when the tribes came and destroyed my family, but I was taken to the interior for the cutting and stayed there for many months before I was taken to the Musqat house."

"He came with another, a deaf and dumb black boy who works with him, diving mostly. Ahmar takes care of him."

"Sam, it must be Sam!" I was overcome and screamed with joy, already believing that Patrick and Sam had survived and were so close by.

"I will ride down today, Jem. I am sure they are part of my family. Sakarbin has told me I can use Flavia, but I am to have a guard if I leave the estate."

"I will arrange it for you," Jem looked happy for me, and I wondered again at his life in the service of Sakarbin and his father before him. He would soon be free to leave and I would miss this good, kindly eunuch who had taught me so much. Neither he nor Sakarbin knew how old he was, but he knew where he came from and was ready to return the following month.

While I was waiting for permission to leave the estate and ride to the pearl fishers' houses, I rushed to tell Eve my news.

CHAPTER 34
My Future at Risk

EVEANYA

Little Razia was still in my care, and I was entertaining her when Leonard came to tell me that he thought two of his adopted brothers were close by, at the pearl fishers' establishment down the coast. He could hardly breathe in his excitement, and I had never seen him so happy. His scars had barely healed, but he had already been given permission to take over the administration of the pearl business and was preparing to visit.

"I will come and tell you later. Oh, Eve, so much is changing for the better." He departed as quickly as he had arrived, and left me wondering what he could mean.

Even though I wasn't sure exactly to what he was referring, his happiness and excitement cheered my day even though I was beginning to worry about my own future.

The previous night I had been summoned to Sakarbin but he was in a poor mood, satisfied himself quickly with me and asked me to give him a massage. As I was preparing some scented oils, he moaned and grumbled that his servants and slaves should appreciate him more.

"I take care of everyone, do I not, Eveanya?"

"Indeed you do, Excellency." I knew it was true, but there were conditions; complete obedience to his rules and wishes.

Sakarbin continued to mutter and pray whilst I poured the oil across his back and carefully pressed into the tight muscles of his neck and shoulders.

"Why am I not obeyed? In the name of Allah, Most Gracious, Most Merciful. Whatever good a man doeth on earth must declare the Praises and Glory of Allah. To Him belongs dominion, and to Him belongs praise. He has power over all things. So it must be. I should be obeyed. Allah be praised."

Eventually he relaxed, but continued to complain. I was sure all of this related somehow to Leonard. He had punished him severely, and it occurred to me that he must regret it. I thought again that I should confess so that Leonard could regain the status he had lost. When Sakarbin rose he was quiet, but surveyed me with a quizzical stare.

"Why have you not borne me any children, Eveanya? I want some fair children, and now Jilfidan has gone you are the fairest. You have been here a long time, have you not?"

"Since I was six and a half years old."

"And you are now?"

"Nearly eighteen."

"So?"

I didn't know how to answer. He had never questioned me before. I knew Sakarbin usually disposed of his girls if they proved to be barren. Although, of course, that was not the case with me, as I was taking great care *not* to get pregnant. I had been lucky so far.

"I am sure that it will happen when Allah wills it to be so," I replied carefully. I smiled and dipped into a bow as I retreated, hoping that he would not expect me to stay all night with him.

Sakarbin allowed himself to be satisfied for the moment and waved his fingers with a dismissal. I knew he would sell me if I didn't get pregnant soon. The thought terrified me, but then so did the thought of bringing a child into this unfair world.

Leonard's talk of freedom over the years had encouraged me to look at families in a completely different light, and if I ever had a child it would be in a world of equality, where no one owned another, where both boys and girls were valued and I could be a happy mother. I was becoming more and more disenchanted with my life, and constantly wondered whether it would ever change. Lately I had been thinking a lot about what freedom meant, and resolved to ask Leonard to tell me more of what he had learned at the Leonards'.

CHAPTER 35
Reunited

LEONARD

My guards and I had ridden at full speed along the shore until we reached the largest of the pearl fishers' huts. We passed the great pits of discarded oyster shells, each with a strong stench and a million hovering flies. Jem had told me to go to the far end of the houses to where the pearl fishers' manager lived, and I would find the man they knew as Ahmar.

I had convinced myself that it was Patrick, so as I arrived at the furthest house I leapt from my horse and shouted as loudly as I could, "Where are you, Patrick?"

The surprised red-haired man who rushed outside at the sound of his name literally whooped with delight at seeing me again. He was more than a foot taller than I, but still as ugly as ever, although now he sported a scruffy, rusty-coloured beard. Even gaunter than he had been as a boy, he had a tanned, skinny face that beamed with delight.

"By all the glories," he exclaimed. "Can it truly be you, Katungi, my brother, my friend? I thought you were dead."

We wrapped our arms around each other, and tears of joy wet both our faces.

As I wiped my soggy cheeks, I became aware of a figure beaming at me from the doorway. A small man with a handsome, very black face. It was Sam! I couldn't contain my delight. I grabbed him and hugged him tight.

"Sam has been with me since the beginning," Patrick explained. "He's good… he still doesn't talk and he is deaf, but we communicate like this." He held up his hands and made a few elaborate movements that meant nothing to me, but Sam responded with some of his own, and Patrick announced that Sam was happy to see me again.

It took hours together to relate what had happened on that fateful day so many years previously. The tribesmen had taken both him and Sam to the slave merchants, back in Musqat, where they were sold again. It was by sheer chance that Sakarbin was looking for boys who could swim and dive as his pearl business was expanding. Patrick had insisted that Sam was included in the deal, and had kept him close and protected him ever since.

"They thought he was worthless but he has proved to be a good diver and he is my brother, the last one I thought I had left," Patrick said with a happy smile.

I could only wonder at the good man that Patrick had become. I asked him what his plans for the future were.

"Sakarbin has given me permission to apply for manumission next year, and I am going to take Sam back to Ireland with me. Katungi, what about you? What will you do?" Patrick had asked after he had listened in horror when I told him my story. "You must apply too and find a way to come with us. In Ireland no one will know that you are any different."

I thought how unlikely it was that Sakarbin would release me and told Patrick so, but knowing that I had him close by was the best gift I could have wished for at that moment.

I rejoiced that he would gain his freedom and go home, back to Ireland, and I told him that I would enquire of my chances of applying to the Qadi, the local judge, for the papers that would give me freedom.

CHAPTER 36
Thalis's Ordeal

EVEANYA

The next day Leonard came with his wonderful news. Not only had he been reunited with two of his brothers, but also Sakarbin had acquired another bed boy and had no further use for him in his bed.

He laughed as he told me.

"You must not confess that you had been in the stables on that fateful night, because I do not wish to be restored to my former position of favour."

He was so happy. I could not dispel it with talk of what might be or the chance of freedom.

I was busy reading the big book of medicine that Leonard had lent me when Thalis and Scylla stopped by my little room. Thalis looked distressed and haggard, her copper hair tousled and unwashed, so I gestured for them to come in.

Over the past few years everyone in the harem had been concerned for Thalis. Motherhood had not come easily to her, and her five children were used to seeing her distressed and unhappy. We all knew how she suffered throughout her pregnancies and births. Even though the two eldest boys had now gone to live with the men, Thalis couldn't cope. In fact, she had never been able to cope. Mostly other mothers in the harem cared for her children.

Scylla was trying to comfort her, and pulled her into my room so that they could close the door behind them. Thalis sank to her knees and sobbed.

"What is it, Thalis?" I asked.

"Thalis thinks she could be with child again, and she can't face it," Scylla said as she held Thalis and tried to calm her. "She had five days' labour with the last one. She is threatening to kill herself if she is pregnant again. What can we do, Eveanya?"

"I don't know, Scylla. I've read of many ways of preventing pregnancy from this book Leonard has lent me, but I've not yet discovered what to do with an unwanted one."

Scylla was impressed that I could read at all, as none of the other women could. I hadn't told anyone, as it was not really acceptable for women to be educated.

"Please don't tell anyone that I have it," I said, indicating the book, "but I promise that I will see if there were any recommendations. In the meanwhile, look after Thalis. I am convinced that there is something we can do..."

A glimmer of hope lit Thalis's worried face as they left.

For the next few days I studied the book and found several suggestions to 'restore the menses'. Should I tell Thalis? I was not sure at first, but eventually decided that I must. The following day I beckoned both the girls into my room. Thalis looked as though she had been crying again.

"There are things that you can do, but you must tell no one. Thalis, you will need Scylla to be close by as I think what is suggested is initially painful. Some of the ingredients may be hard to find too. I cannot guarantee that any of this will work, but it is worth a try. Remember that Lumaria must not find out or we will all get into trouble."

Thalis's eyes filled with tears again. "I'll try anything, Eve."

Scylla promised to maintain secrecy and collect the ingredients and make whatever was necessary.

I explained the problems slowly, for I knew from the book that careful dosage was necessary. "You must make a purging drink with either castor oil or water, to which you add small amounts of dried mosquito plant, pomegranate peel, lupine beans, hibiscus flowers and cardamom or cinnamon. This is to be taken in small quantities over several days, and you must take care that it only induces diarrhoea and vomiting, and not convulsions or paralysis. Also, insert into the vagina the same mix mashed up with garlic, and paste to make a pessary. It must be changed every two days. Keep away from the other girls and pray that it works."

"Thank you, Eve, I will." A small light of hope lit in Thalis's sad face.

There was so much more to learn, so I returned to my study and hoped that I had helped.

As time passed I saw little of Leonard, as he was busy renewing his relationship with his brothers and learning about the pearl fishing business. He was so happy, and I loved to see his broad smile whenever he told me about Patrick and Sam. They spent many hours together, and Leonard related the tales they told of the seven-plus years diving and living such a remote and extraordinary life. The divers' life was hard, a demanding and exhausting activity, and they could usually only work for a few years. I resigned myself to seeing less of my friend as he now spent a great deal of his time away from the estate.

So it was that Thalis regained her menses after a week of vomiting and bouts of diarrhoea. Such was her relief that she brought me a gold bracelet and thanked me profusely.

Within a week or so her dark features regained their former prettiness, and she assured me that she would not get pregnant again. Her visits to Sakarbin were few and far between, and she would use one of the many ways we had discovered so that pregnancy could be avoided.

In the meantime I learned how to cope with cuts and rashes, sweats, palpitations and coughs from the *al-Qanun fi al-Tibb*.

CHAPTER 37
Patrick and Sam

LEONARD

My introduction to the pearl fishing business was a revelation. I had no idea what torture these men and boys endured to pull those beauties from the sea. Both Patrick and Sam had permanently squashed noses from the wooden nose-pegs they were forced to wear when diving. Patrick told me how their days were filled. It was an incredibly taxing life. He told me of the areas where they had to wear leather boots and gloves because the rock and coral were so sharp, how they oiled their bodies and plugged their ears as many became deaf after their stint of diving. They worked in cramped conditions and got little rest. He explained how they dived for three to five minutes at a time, and only allowed themselves five minutes' rest between each dive.

There were days when they couldn't work on the boats and spent their time opening the oysters, a dirty, smelly job that often had little reward, but also the joy of finding a rare pearl.

Patrick's stories told of a hard life of cramps and coughs, exhaustion and storms at sea. One particularly bad storm had nearly taken their lives. A strong wind had blown up, accompanied by torrential rain. The raging sea had taken them by surprise, and they lost many of their men and boys, while the survivors who managed to return were sick and traumatised. He and Sam had held onto the pearls and the mast and clung together.

They had achieved the reward of manumission because of the work they had done to increase Sakarbin's income.

Patrick wanted me to apply for it too, so that we could leave here forever. I knew that I would have to have Sakarbin's favour to do so, and that I did not yet have.

Jem prepared to leave, and like the fine friend he was, left me with some good advice. "Work on the honourable will of your master. He is a man who wishes to be seen as pious and good, although he knows not the meaning of the word. Work your knowledge to create the opportunity and you will gain your freedom while you are still young enough to make another life," Jem had told me earnestly.

He left soon after, and I was sorry to see him go. His whole life had been spent here in the service of the al-Busaidis, and although he was probably no more than forty, he was tired and worn. But he would go home, and for that he was grateful.

CHAPTER 38
Disgrace

EVEANYA

Early one morning, one month after Thalis's relief, Sakarbin summoned me.

"It has come to my notice that you are a trouble-maker, Eveanya. You have been meddling in something that is no business of yours. Teaching my women things they do not need to know, and giving them ideas above their station. You are a disgrace."

"No, I am not," I lifted my head in surprise and defiance.

Sakarbin glared at me. It was not the first time I had noticed how old and fat he was becoming. I had served this man in his bed for nearly seven years, pandering to his cruel sexual appetite, his whims and his domination. I suddenly felt that I could take no more. He repulsed me.

Had he perhaps heard how I had helped Thalis? Or how I had managed to avoid getting pregnant?

"You are to be sold," he declared, "you have failed to provide me with any children. It is a matter of honour, Eveanya. You have not enhanced my standing. You are a pretty young woman and I'll still get a good price for you, Insha'Allah. Even though you are a trouble-maker."

I felt sick, and stood unbelieving at what I was hearing. It was true then, what Jilfidan had told me, that we were only kept for breeding, his disgusting pleasure, to accommodate his lust for power, and we meant nothing more to him. How could he use people and then dispose of them like an old rug. I stood staring at him, and could not hide the disgust I felt.

"We will wait another half-year, and then if you cannot provide me with a child you will have to go. Allah be praised if you do. You have been here a long time now. Have I not treated you well?"

I hesitated only a moment before I gained the courage to reply. I was angry, and I could see no way of avoiding being sent back to the slave market. I would not breed with him. I would not!

Taking a deep breath, I said, "No, I do not think you have treated me well. Yes, I am well fed and I am at your disposal like a horse or a new garment. Yes, I have a family of sorts, but no freedom."

Sakarbin stood before me, his brow creasing and his face reddening with anger, but I continued. "You don't even know me, you don't know any of your women… your wives or your consorts. You have no idea whether we want to be here or not, what we like or dislike, whether we want to breed with you, whether we even care for you. Whether we are happy or unhappy. You are an egotistical, cruel and unjust man, and I hate you. You punished poor Leonard for your own son's stupidity. Yes, it was Musab who took the oil lamp that caused the fire into the stables. I know because I was there."

He laughed in my face. "You stupid girl. How could you know what happened?"

"I was there because I have been riding out with Musab and Gusiffa, but they are like you and wanted to make use of me, so I went on my own. Leonard saved me from your disgusting son and took the blame to protect me."

Sakarbin shook his head, but I could see that I had set him thinking. He said quietly, "No, it could not be so. I loved Leonard. It was to maintain my honour and my standing that I punished the boy."

"Your honour and your standing means nothing to me or anyone else."

He lifted his fist and struck me on the side of my face.

My head swam and I staggered but did not fall. I pulled myself upright, ran at him, and banged both of my fists hard into his body, reaching for whatever I could strike. I clawed at his face, screaming, my own anger exploding. The life of degradation, the loss of Jilfidan, the beatings, the humiliation of being a sex slave rose like bile in my throat. I thrashed and thumped my rage into his fat body, the body that had abused and used me for so long.

Within moments his guards had come and roughly pulled me away from him. I was crying with rage and spitting like a wild cat.

Sakarbin, his intense anger manifesting in swift pulling and shaking movements, straightened his clothes as he spat the words that were to change my life forever.

"Take her up to the point and cast her into the sea. She has no place here. Get rid of her, she is a disgrace to Allah. Praise be to Allah. She will be punished and face her eternity in disgrace. It is the will of Allah," he shouted as I was dragged away.

"No, no… Don't throw me into the sea," I was incoherent with rage and hysteria; fear had such a complete hold on me, then I could only scream.

Within minutes a crowd had gathered. I was tied and hoisted onto the back of one of the guard's horses that had been tethered outside the walls of the house, and Abdulla, the roughest of men, raced with me towards the point, which was high up and on the other side of the wadi. A group of guards, soldiers and servants followed, and as I was hauled from the horse and pushed toward the cliff edge I could only think of Leonard. I screamed his name, but he was not there.

As I was dragged forward I could see the cut of the cliff curved around on either side of the tiny, pebbled beach, but this morning the tide was high and there was no sign of the bay. A surging mass of water roared below, and I felt myself resigned to the death that awaited me.

Better now. Better this way. I could not imagine a future away from here, away from Leonard. I would embrace death if I had no other choice.

CHAPTER 39
Eve Thrown to Her Death!

LEONARD

My skin was crawling as I listened to the soldier relating what he knew of the rumpus that I could see ahead of me. When I heard that it was Eve, I threw down the ledger I was carrying and raced out of the gates across the scrubby desert and up the pathway that led to the point.

I felt a great surge of anger welling up inside me, a seething molten rage pushing me into action. What had she done? Was this down to Musab again? I would find a way to kill him if it was. I could see the horse carrying her ahead of me. There were others running too to observe the disobedient slave woman who was to be thrown to her death.

I sprinted ahead, determined to prevent what was happening to my beloved Eve.

Usually whatever I did was a mere whim, hardly affecting me at all and utterly subject to the power of others and the vagaries of chance that I could never control. I had become a person no longer of any free will, controlled and subjugated so that all my real self was buried so deeply I could only obey. But my life was suddenly yielding up an instant courage.

I had to save her!

I could sense within me a gathering of power, and even as I started to run upward toward the edge of the cliff, I increased my resolve and my muscle power to propel me as fast as I could. She was screaming my name but she had not seen my approach.

Before I could reach them, Abdulla and Hamid had propelled her forward and stood ready to throw her over the cliff.

I shouted to them to wait, but without delay they pushed with all their might, so that she sailed toward the sea before I could get close enough to stop them.

I had no clear idea how far she had fallen, whether she was dead or alive. I hesitated just long enough to gauge the drop and how fast I could get down it.

Abdulla and his cronies had started to move away, laughing, as I galloped passed them and the gathering crowd along the cliff top until I could see Eve below. She lay atop a large rock about ten feet above the sea. Her head and shoulders hung backward and she did not move.

I lurched toward the edge, and seeing a way, steep though it was, I began to descend. Rocks and stones clattered seaward as my feet pushed for footholds. A small shrub slowed me enough to take a breath and reduce the momentum of movement that had taken me halfway toward where she lay.

"I am coming, Eve, don't die. I will get you and take you home. You are everything to me. I beg you, Eve, don't die. I am coming for you. I love you."

The rock face got steeper, and the ocean roared below me, but in those moments I was not afraid for myself.

It took me several more minutes of careful descent before I reached the huge rock onto which Eve had fallen. It angled toward the sea, so I crawled slowly forward on my hands and knees until I could hold her waist, and gently began to pull her towards me. As her shoulders came across the rock, I could see how crushed she was. One side of her right shoulder was a bloody pulp, and as I lifted her head onto the rock, that too was smashed and bleeding hard. The right side of her face was cut to ribbons, and part of the skin on her scalp had lifted so that her hairline had all but disappeared.

"Eve," I pleaded.

She looked limp and lifeless. "Eve, I am here. Please open your eyes."

For the first time since my castration, I cried, great pools pushing up from the burning pain in my heart.

CHAPTER 40
I Want to Die

EVEANYA

I was exhausted from the pain, worn down, and I lay in the darkness in despair. The pale moon that shone in the tiny window cast soft shadows around the room.

I didn't want to be there. I didn't want to be anywhere.

I couldn't move my back or my shoulder without a stabbing pain. My head was aching and my face sore. The room was hot and still and I was sweating, the bed felt damp beneath me. No matter how I tried, I could not move. Nor did I want to.

I had no future now. I was damaged and useless, and Sakarbin would never forgive me for what I had said.

I wanted to die!

All I had to show for this life was a broken body, an ugly face and the pile of carefully hidden jewellery and coins collected over the years for my services.

But for what?

None of it would be of any use to me now. I would never wear any of it again.

"I will keep my eyes closed and wait to die."

CHAPTER 41
She Will Survive

LEONARD

The lamplight picked out the white of the bandages around Eve's head. Nothing else of her face was exposed. I carefully lifted the grey blanket, but she was deeply asleep.

It was now over ten nights that she had lain there, and she still did not move more than a few inches. Her matted hair with the chopped tufts on the right side lay across the pillow like a handful of dried grass. She would not open her eyes or take any food. I had gently forced a few drops of water through her swollen lips each day as she moaned softly.

It was several more days before Eve carefully and very slowly pulled herself up into a sitting position. I could see how painful it was for her. She pushed her hair back, her fingers lingering on the bandages across her head and right eye and cheek. She squared her shoulders and looked me in the face, her one violet eye full of tears of frustration.

"Why did you save me, Leonard? I want to die."

I reached for her hand, which she allowed me to take from her bandaged head, but her eye still blazed its anger at me. "What could I possibly do without you, my Eve? You will live and we will have a free life together."

"You are being ridiculous, Leonard. Life for me is over, and I cannot accept that Sakarbin tried to kill me. I am worthless and now I am hideously deformed. There is no going back for me." Her voice dimmed into a whisper.

"There is, Eve. Please listen. Many people at some point in their lives feel darkness around them as if they had fallen into something, slipped through the fingers of reality into an unknown place, but there is always light. Once, I was lost so deep inside myself I thought I would never feel that anything was good ever again, but there is a reason to go on living. I met you and you made me smile again, gave me back my will to be happy. I have found my brothers and they are to be free. There is always hope."

She scowled at me. "No, there is not."

"Let me tell you what I have arranged before you shout at me."

"I don't want to live like this, Leonard." Her voice raised and her fists clenched. "Don't you see? Survival here depends on beauty and desirability. You are beautiful. I am ugly and disgraced."

"We are to be free, Eve. I have discussed with Sakarbin, and as an act of piety and if we commit to Islam, he is prepared to allow us to apply for manumission. I have enough money to buy us a house, our own bayt. We can stay here or move away, or go to India or Ireland with Patrick and Sam or to the British Isles if you like." Eve was shaking her head and frowning dismally. "What?" I demanded, knowing exactly what she was going to say, but I would allow nothing to prevent us this chance of freedom, and both of us must be seen to be sincere.

"We have to commit to Islam?"

"Yes, we do."

"I cannot, I've seen how cruel it is, how little regard it has for those who are different, to women and those outside the faith. There is no love in it at all."

"We already have love in our lives, do we not, Eve? What I must do is help, advise you, and remind you of the words of Allah and the words of His Messenger. Peace and blessings of Allah be upon him and call you to repent from this disbelief. If you repent and turn to Allah, it will be for the best." I let the words slide off my tongue exactly as Sakarbin had said them to me on many occasions, but I was smiling. Eve knew instantly that I was only making a point. "We must both be seen to be totally sincere."

In truth I had always known that Eve was not as wise as she was beautiful. She was generally obedient as she had been taught, but she was also quietly silly and headstrong, showing off and playing games. It was because of her bad judgment that she had been so hideously punished. Now, I must teach her to be wise, and although I was aware that she had learned huge verses from the Quran, she must pray and be seen to be converted.

"There is one God, and Mohammed is the prophet. Pray to Allah that you may see this truth," I used my eyes to convey my meaning. "Five times a day we will bend our knees to God. Our days will be regulated by our religious devotion."

She understood me well enough, but asked, "Will that not make me a hypocrite?"

"For our freedom it will not matter. Our time on earth has been naught but pain. It can be no worse in the hereafter for our immortal souls, can it? We deserve some liberty and happiness, and if converting to Islam is the way out, I will be seen to be the very best," but I added, "only while I have to be. And so shall you. If Allah is merciful he will indeed grant us our years of freedom."

"Is it true that we will really be free?"

"It is so, if Sakarbin abides by his promise. I am sure he will. He knows the truth about the fire and his son's involvement, and because he proposes to go to Mecca soon, needs to show his goodwill and piety by his actions."

"What is piety to a Muslim?"

"Piety goes beyond the actions of the body. It has to do with the heart, with the intention behind actions. He has told me that piety is one of the most important concepts in the Quran, and the criterion by which people are ranked before God. This is why I believe Sakarbin will honour what he has said. Even Sayyida Chole has agreed to our release."

Eve gave a faint, disbelieving smile.

I recalled my proposal to Sakarbin. He had been informed that I had brought Eve back, and had not summoned me immediately to explain. Eventually I begged an audience with him.

He was discomforted at my insistence on seeing him during the day, when I would usually be working or attending to his accounts. Nevertheless, he sat and listened as I spoke as quietly and as reverently as I could. I knew he was still angry with me for rescuing Eve, but I found him in a different frame of mind. Clearly what had happened with Eve had impacted on him, for he said, "I now believe that it was not you who caused the fire, and Musab has admitted that it was he who took the oil lamp into the stables. I do not care what their intentions were toward Eve, but I can assure you that Musab will be punished for putting my horses under threat. He has been sent away and will not return until I see fit."

Sakarbin must have considered that that was what I had come to hear. I stood resolutely before him.

"Well?" he enquired, his fat lips pressed firmly together.

"Master… when I first came here and you instructed me, it was hard for me to bear, but I promised that I would be good, and I have been. I have served you loyally and without complaint. When you were too rough or unkind, or allowed your friends to enjoy me, I did not complain. In return for my discretion and loyalty you made a promise that you would take care of me – perhaps not forever – because times change. I understand, but you have generously given me the opportunities to improve my knowledge and my skills, to earn so that I could eventually take care of myself. Allowing me access to your father's library you gave me the means to lift myself from ignorance to capability in many fields."

At that point I knelt, took a deep breath, and reached forward to take his hand. "I thank you sincerely. You are an honourable man, and in return for my willing cooperation and love for you, I wish to ask for a manumission, for both Eve and myself."

Sakarbin stared at me, opened his mouth as if to refuse, and I continued, "Is it not a gesture of piety and strength that Allah asks of you before you take the Hajj? The reward for freeing a slave is immense, is it not, Master?"

Slowly, he released my hand and I stood. I kept my head bent in silent hope.

"You are right, Leonard. It is time I released you. You have served me well. And, Allah be praised, I have seen you become a believer. You must give me your assurance that you will obey Allah and His Messenger, fall into no disputes, lest you lose heart and your power depart, and be patient and persevering, for Allah is always with you. Allah is strict in his punishment."

"Of course, Master."

"The girl too must follow the laws of Allah and no other."

"She will, Master. She understands it is only because of the will of Allah that she has been saved. She will be with me and I will insist upon her devotion. I will need no support as you have been generous and I have earned enough to feel confident that I can support both Eveanya and myself."

"I am pleased to hear that. What made you want to protect her, Leonard?" he asked me quietly.

"She is my friend and I love her," I told him simply. I watched him carefully. Whether he understood or not I could not tell, so I continued, "We have both served you well, Excellency, and will honour your wishes, but we wish for a life together now."

"I will give it some thought. But, for both of you, it will take some time. In the meantime, I expect you to continue your work, and Eveanya too will continue to serve me. Put her in the kitchen with the cook, Imanki, and let her be humble and obedient. I never wish to lay eyes on her again.

She is disgraced."

I had spent a long time with him, and now that the truth about the fire and his son's intentions on that morning was out in the open, I knew he had resolved to make amends. He quickly turned, never mentioning the fire in the stables again or his son Musab.

"Allah be praised," were his final words that day. And as he walked away, I heard him instruct Hamid to bring the boy to his quarters. Latif Rashid was a newly acquired slave who looked surprisingly like I did when I arrived. I wondered if he too had had his genitals removed and his spirit broken.

Eve cried when the bandages came off, for she would never completely lose the scars that covered the whole right side of her face, and, as her finger traced the welts, she looked to me for reassurance.

"They will gradually fade, but you are still the same person, Eve, and I will love you always," I told her, but she continued to cry.

CHAPTER 42
Freedom, Perhaps?

EVEANYA

To me, the greatest surprise was that Chole had endorsed our application for release. She did have a heart after all! Perhaps she too would like to be free of Sakarbin. It was more than likely that it was due to her that Sakarbin had agreed. He took a great deal of notice of his principal wife.

Daily, when I was able, I washed and ate, readying myself for the life that I had been offered. Sleep had given me the clarity to realise that I did have something to live for. If what Leonard had told me came to pass, we would both be free in a few months' time.

Learning to stand upright was the most difficult, as my spine was so distorted that I leaned to the left, and so my right shoulder seemed higher than the other. Towelling myself carefully, I looked in the mirror. I found my face too repulsive to contemplate, the scars were still red and raw and covered the whole of my right cheek, from my wobbly hairline to the long scar from my chin to my ear, where the impact had been greatest, leaving a finger-length cleft which distorted my jawline.

The veil gave me something to hide behind, a mask that preserved a sense of detachment, if not anonymity. Previously, I had always seen it as an insult, hiding what I considered my beauty.

I pulled out my new prayer mat, and with the help of a walking stick joined the many in the courtyard for Fajr, the dawn prayer. Leonard had convinced me. I would intone and bang my head as many times as required to get away from here. With the prayers over, I reported to Imanki who would rule my world until we could leave.

I could no longer mix with the girls from the harem, and

was given a tiny space at the back of a cupboard where I was to sleep. My rations and wage were pitiful, but Leonard assured me that it would not take long and we would soon be gone from here forever.

I willed myself daily to believe him. Each day I became stronger, not just in my physical self, but in my belief that if I could endure what had happened to me, I could cope with anything.

CHAPTER 43
Waiting

LEONARD

Six months had passed. Sakarbin kept his promise, and had sent a written application for both Eve and I.

Manumission had been granted, and our application to leave the country accepted. We had to wait. But freedom was really going to happen at last!

Patrick and Sam and five of the other pearl divers were also to be freed before Sakarbin set off for the Hajj.

We found that we were wealthy beyond belief. Both Eve and I had so much jewellery, given to us by Sakarbin, and none of it meant anything to either of us. We were going to sell it all, except the one gold bracelet that Thalis had given to Eve in gratitude for her help. She also had gold coins to add to my own wealth that I had built slowly over the years. There was no doubt that Sakarbin had been generous with us.

Patrick and Sam had less money, but they did own a few priceless pearls, secured honestly, Patrick told us with a smile.

CHAPTER 44
Escape

EVEANYA

It was as I returned from my kitchen duties that Leonard came racing round the pathway, skidding to a halt on the slippery wet stones in front of me. Two little palm doves that had been enjoying the unexpected rainfall lifted themselves up and flew over us. Leonard reached out and wrapped his arms around me.

"Eve, we are to be released immediately. Sakarbin is setting off for the Hajj in two days' time and he wants us gone. His piety and goodwill must not be in doubt," he added with a laugh.

I could only gasp. Moments before I had been steeling myself to stay positive about the possibility of leaving.

"I will arrange everything, and all I need is for you to collect your things from the harem and I will pack them for you. Meet me tomorrow at dawn at the harem gate," Leonard laughed and sped off.

I hastened back to the kitchen, my heart beating fast but with a new resolve to get through whatever I had to do to be ready. Excitement and worry about our future completely overtook my thoughts. I had been a slave for so long. How would I cope with freedom? But Leonard was so sure and confident. We'd agreed where we should go and spent a great deal of time making plans, but now that it was happening, I found myself looking backward.

My life had followed an extraordinary pathway: losing my family in India and being that frightened little girl, sold like a bag of beans in the Musqat slave market to a wealthy, cruel man. The heart-breaking loss of my best friend, Jilfidan, who had given me a reason to laugh and dance. I wondered about her so often, but had never had any news of her. My training in erotic sex for the enjoyment of a man I hated, and my disgrace for saying out loud what I knew to be true. I had gained so much confidence from Leonard. I knew that I was prepared to fight for what I held dear, for otherwise sooner or later it would be taken from me.

Even if my freedom had been in death it would have been better than being sold again, perhaps to an even harsher master. And to be without Leonard was unthinkable.

CHAPTER 45
Freedom 1825

LEONARD

The clouds had overshadowed the sun, and we knew that we would have to soon return to our cabin.

Patrick and Sam stood watching the waves whilst Eve and I rested on the bench, set against the side of the cockpit where our master seaman and captain was plotting our course. We had been assured that even though it was a long, difficult journey, we would reach our destination as planned.

Our ship had a well-drilled and obedient crew who kept away from the passengers. There were three others: an elderly widower and his two sons. They had been living in Musqat for several years, working for the East India Company, and were now returning home. They kept very much to themselves.

"Do not leave the young lady on her own," advised our kindly Captain Peak, "nor you, sir, if I may be so bold, you are too good-looking, and some of our men have been away from home for a very long time."

Patrick and Sam kept a sharp eye on us both. Except for this short time on the deck at sunset, we had made a point of remaining in our cabin or staying close together whenever we ventured forth.

It was the second week of our journey to Ireland. We were on a British East India Company merchant ship, calling into several ports along the way to restock our food supply. Our eventual destination was Cork, in southern Ireland, where we would disembark.

Eve was beginning to relax and smile again. The past few months had been hard on her, and she had left looking grey and tired, still unsure that it was truly happening.

We'd all had our doubts, but our manumissions were approved, and a passage away from Arabia booked. In our cabin we had all the documentation needed to prove that we were truly free.

It became a reality as we left the Musqat port. We waved farewell to the pearl fishers, the long sandy shore of Qurum, the wadi and the Al Hajar Mountains, where much of our riding had been done. Sadly, I had to say goodbye to Flavia, but Hamid had promised to take good care of her.

Sakarbin had been generous as usual, and we were each handed a bag of gold coins and two copies of the Quran, and to our surprise he offered us his good wishes.

"Allah will look upon me kindly. I will earn my place in Paradise. Do you not agree, Leonard?"

"Indeed, Excellency. Allah be praised," I replied.

"May the light of faith shine upon you."

"Of course," I said as sincerely as I could manage.

Sakarbin could believe whatever he wished, but in my heart I believed that what we do in life, how we treat others, and not what we believe, will be our ultimate reward.

We left without a backward glance, the vast, beautiful, confining and hypocritical life of the al-Busaidi household, with its harem of enslaved individuals, most of whom had been denied their freedom and their families.

We passed the great Fort Al Jalali as the ship sailed out through the old harbour.

We felt we were a family now. Probably the oddest-looking family ever: Patrick tall and skinny with his red hair and rusty beard, little Eve with her violet eyes and her long blonde curls now freely cascading down her back. Sam, although not tall like Patrick, was tough and strong and coffee black. He had learned to smile even though he could not speak or hear. He was secure in the knowledge that we were his family. He knew that we would care for him, and I knew that he was happy to be with us.

I'd had my long hair cropped short and dressed simply. My complexion was still smooth and hairless, but I was fit and strong. I knew I would always look like the youngest member of our group, but it could not matter less to any of us, as we were contented and could not wait to start our new life together.

We'd talked endlessly of the possibilities. Where should we go and what should we do? We agreed from the start that we would stay together. We would live close to the sea, buy some land and some stock, including horses, and build a comfortable house. Patrick wanted to return home to Ireland. He had finally had enough of the endless sun, the desert and the overpowering temperatures, and talked of the soft green rolling hills, and the seasons that gave a variety to life. So it was agreed.

Eve had nothing to return to in India, and I did not wish to go back to Zanzibar, for I had enquired about my family and both Kitu and Buntingu had died.

We agreed that it would be wonderful to go somewhere completely new. We envisaged a life where we could have some children, not our own obviously, but there were orphaned and unwanted children everywhere in the world. According to Patrick there were many in Ireland, and he agreed that we should adopt a few, so that we could give them the opportunities in life that the Leonards had given us.

Such plans! But now that we were free and with the riches that we had earned, we would make our dreams come true.

Eve's back slowly improved, and as we walked the deck in the evenings she would perform a few dance moves, moving her hips and shoulders. It was her only daily exercise. Being confined to the tiny cabin that we shared was difficult for her. We amused ourselves trying to learn a few steps. The captain had been stern in his warning that passengers must not be on the deck during the day when the sailors were doing their duties, but each evening, before sunset, we were allowed to walk and exercise. We took Eveanya's hands and lifted our feet, swung our hips and sang my song of freedom, changing a line or two.

Freedom lies within our grasp, regardless of our journey
No pain or sorrow will hold us bound
No rules and ropes will still our yearning
We'll prove that we are worthy now
To live untethered by others' desires
Freedom beckons and a new life starting
In the Isles of Emerald.

Patrick proved to have a good singing voice, but trying to dance was beyond his means. He was long and skinny, tripped continually and found himself flat on his back several times, enjoying the fact that he was making us all laugh with his clumsiness.

A great surge of happiness ran through my veins as I watched Sam's face as we cavorted about the deck. Nothing could persuade him to attempt to dance, but he did smile a great deal which made my heart glad.

It had been a soft, balmy day. Patrick and Sam went to their bunks, so Eve and I sat together as the sun set.

Eve whispered, "I'm cold."

I pulled her on top of me. "Come, I'll keep you warm. We can stay a while longer."

She fitted her little body, curving, folding her knees, so that she sat warm and weightless in my lap. We were welded together, floating in the dark perfection of the moment.

Eve laughed and wriggled and snuggled close. I kissed the top of her glossy golden head and wondered at the feeling it stirred within me. We had an understanding. We'd both lost our families when we were so young that our pasts were a dim memory. We'd lost people we loved. We'd battled some of the same demons, searched for love in the same shadows, and been confronted with the same master, the darkest of men.

I'd saved her life and she mine. We had given each other succour when we needed it most, and our only real ties in life were to each other. Hopefully we would be bound together for the rest of our lives. We would attempt to see if we could still love and understand in the simplicity that brought our fates together as children, to measure ourselves against the innocence of those children who found themselves imprisoned from such a young age.

The future beckoned and we opened our hearts to it. We could only wonder that fate had catapulted us into lives that led us to be brought together.

"How did we find each other?" Eve asked.

We locked eyes for a long, intense moment, and her violet eyes swam with tears.

"We will always find each other," I answered, holding her tightly. "Always."

PART 5
FORGIVENESS

North Yorkshire, England 1990 - 2005

Is it the end of their journey when our travelling souls find themselves in northeast England? Their lives are no longer dominated by religion or creed. Freedom of speech, movement, activity and sexual preferences are paramount to the modern democracy that prevails, and there are long-standing laws that protect the society and maintain a modicum of order.

Equality between the sexes has been slow, but women have taken the lead in so many areas that men have found the new breed of well-educated, successful women hard to define in terms of their masculinity, and the roles that they have to assume in a new society.

Domestic violence due to alcoholism and drug addiction is nothing new, but women's rights have changed, and laws exist to support and to protect them.

Although attitudes have changed considerably in the twentieth century toward premarital and consensual same-sex relationships, attitudes toward extramarital sex have not become more permissive in the same way. Situations that cause deception are not part of the general relaxation about sexual activity, so affairs within committed relationships are viewed with less tolerance.

Sexual addiction is now recognized as a genuine complaint of the modern generation, and some could say that it is encouraged by the easy access to pornography on the Internet, etcetera.

In this, our overly tolerant society, men, and sometimes women, assume that the more sex you can fit into your life the better. Perhaps like Leo they come with a Karmic memory of being unable to have a normal sexual life in a society and situation that didn't allow it.

Our travelling souls meet again to test each other, and learn about **Forgiveness** in a modern society of freedoms and choices.

Leo, with an addiction to sex and alcohol, and **Evelyn,** who needs to learn that not everyone has been as fortunate as she, having been born into a happy family where love and affection were paramount, never needing reassurance or pretence.

CHAPTER 1
Paris May 2003

LEO DAVISTEIN

Wrapping my scarf tightly round my neck, and leaning away from the incessant rain and sleet, I turned a corner and there she was.

I'd suddenly noticed the slight, familiar figure hurrying along in front of me. I would know that walk anywhere. The way she placed her feet so carefully, her toes hitting the ground first like a catwalk model or a ballerina. Her shoulders were hunched against the weather. I could just see her glossy mane of chestnut hair pushed up inside a thick, black velvet beret.

There she was, Evelyn, my wife.

Every time I thought of Evelyn − which I did frequently − I was reminded of her determined spirit and her positive approach to everything and everybody. This was the woman whom I'd loved and admired ever since I first set eyes on her thirteen years previously.

Although our separation must be two or three years now, we'd still not divorced. I had ceased to wonder why. When we first parted it seemed inevitable that the marriage was finished and would end officially. But, somehow, neither of us had taken the step to start the proceedings, even though at first we had talked about it often enough.

I had just had my thirty-fifth birthday when we first met in 1990, and Evelyn fascinated me. We were at a friend's dinner party and the attraction was instantaneous. From the moment she lifted her violet blue eyes, I was entranced. She exuded the sort of confidence that I wished I had.

No one knew about my feelings of insecurity around smart women because I smiled a lot, nodded knowingly and kept them guessing. I was a past master at hiding my real self. Whatever they saw in me was what I wanted them to see.

But somehow from our first meeting Evelyn was wary; she knew instinctively that I was playing a part.

I hesitated to ask her out even though I really wanted to. I knew she would raise an enquiring eyebrow, smile and decline because she saw through my practised facade.

I wasn't used to being turned down by women. I might be low on morals but I was high on charisma and I wasn't sure that I could handle it. Part of me reasoned that I would bide my time and find ways of seeing her in social situations. After all, we moved in the same circles, and Stokesley and Great Ayton, the side-by-side villages where we lived, were small and socially confined. I was sure that in time we would meet again.

I really wasn't that sure, so I vowed to make it happen somehow!

I suppose in a way I wanted to test myself and see if I really was still as intrigued by her as I thought.

Even though she was confident and attractive with her soft red-brown curls, lovely eyes and her unusual looks that instantly demanded attention, there was an undercurrent of sensitivity that I found hard to understand.

Both of us had been previously married. I was divorced from my first wife, Jill, whom I could barely remember. It had been a short marriage, but definitely not sweet; a totally unsuitable union based on which of us could drink the other under the table first. Luckily we hadn't had any children, and the divorce was final at least three years before I met Evelyn. She too had been married and had two beautiful children; Lily, who was nearly four, and a boy, Daniel, who was seven. Her husband, Matt Joyner, had been an engineer and had died tragically in a work-related accident three years previous to our meeting. Evelyn had inhabited my dreams ever since we first met. Now here she was again.

Another chance meeting? It had happened so often before. In fact, ever since the very beginning it seemed that fate was drawing us together. Everywhere we went we bumped into each other. We weren't even particularly suited. She was well-educated and well-read. I'd heard that she had recently qualified as a psychotherapist. When we were together she was studying to be a nutritionist and reflexologist, and making a good living as a freelance writer for a national magazine. I was a mediocre architect, who had clawed my way into a well-paid job by being persistent and hard-working, and perhaps knowing the right people at the right time. A stroke of luck, when I particularly needed it, allowed me to work in Milan and Barcelona, and now in Paris.

I hesitated only a moment. Against my better judgment, as my heart was beating fast, I hurried forward until I was close enough to speak to her. She half turned and her face lit at the sight of me.

"Hello, Leo," she smiled and seemed somewhat unsurprised at our meeting, as if we had only spoken yesterday. In truth, it had been possibly over fifteen months, and then only to discuss an issue she was having with the bank.

Did she expect to see me? Did she know I was here? Her smile seemed to suggest she did. "What brings you to Paris?" she enquired.

"Come into the cafe out of this appalling weather and I'll tell you all," I replied, taking hold of her arm. I was immediately aware of the electricity between us, the startling thrill of contact. It was still there, exactly as it had always been, and I could see that she felt it too.

We pushed our way quickly into the warm cafe and inhaled the smell of the coffee and croissants.

"Good heavens, is it really you, Evelyn, or am I dreaming?" I asked when we were seated. "Such a surprise!

I've been working in Paris for three months negotiating a deal with our competitors. It's all about a housing project in Suffolk. Long story, rather boring. So, what are you doing here?"

As she replied, she lifted her beautiful eyes that sparkled like polished amethyst to watch my reaction. A small smile played on her lips. "I'm here on holiday with Pierre Renard."

I could feel my stomach clench, but smiled and said, "That ridiculous French buffoon? The one we met at Sylvia's wedding who upset everyone with his chauvinistic remarks and offensive manner?"

I know I sounded peevish and sarcastic, but I was instantly deeply jealous, and all the emotion of our long relationship stirred within me again.

I smiled to cover my feelings; I wasn't prepared to be hurt. I saw the look of satisfaction on her face. Could she be pleased by my pompous outburst? Did she enjoy making me jealous? Of course she did.

"We are engaged," she added. "And there is no need to be offensive. I can see you haven't changed one iota."

"Don't be ridiculous, we're still married."

"That can soon be sorted."

"Possibly, but how can you even contemplate marrying that garlicky, French what's-it... Just what is your problem?"

"I'm not aware I have a problem. I'm living life to the full, just as I guess you are, Leo. No, I don't have any problems." Then she laughed and said, "You're the one getting cross."

I had calmed sufficiently by then to remember how often I'd been hurt by her flippant remarks. Instead I said, "You can't marry him."

"No?"

"No."

"And why not?"

"We're still married," I floundered. "I miss you... I know

I messed up but I miss you." She glared at me, raising a cynical eyebrow, but I carried on. "Is this what you really want, Evelyn?"

She took a deep breath, and I knew she was going to berate me. "No, Leo, you know full well what I really want, or wanted, I should say. But you denied me, let me down, and now I'm free of you and I'm going to make a new life with Pierre. You and I have been three years apart and... you miss me? I don't believe you."

I couldn't find the right words, had never been able to do so. I sat silently and stirred my coffee.

I was aware of her looking at me, her eyebrows raised. "Tell me, Leo," she said slowly. "Who are you screwing now? Having sex with?" Why would she ask me? I wondered without replying. "Well?" she said. "Anyone I know?"

What could I say? I wanted to be truthful but I stuttered a reply. "People have sex for a million reasons, Evelyn. Often it has little to do with the person involved. I've always enjoyed sex. You know that. It's my weakness, but I am curious to know why you should concern yourself about what I'm doing after so long?"

She winced at my words. "I'm not concerned."

"You are. Is it because you might be a bit jealous?"

"Oh, come now, Leo, I used to be jealous and distressed every time you cheated on me, but I'm not a bit interested now, if you really want to know. You have such a... a... Oh, for heaven's sake, I'd have to be ten shades of crazy to be interested."

I felt like a repentant sinner at the confessional, overcome with guilt, but this time I was going to tell her. I might never get the chance again, especially if she wanted to marry someone else.

Over the past year I had changed. I had decided to contact her the moment I got back from Paris to try to explain *and* ask her to come back to me. I really believed that we should be together. I needed her. It was more than I'd ever dared to hope that we should meet by chance. I felt somehow that fate had brought us together yet again. We were meant to meet now, before it was too late. I watched her carefully. Although she must be nearly fifty − I should remember, but I couldn't − she looked fabulous.

"I want us to be together. I love you. You're not seriously going to marry someone else?"

"I might," she replied teasingly, ignoring my declaration of love. "Are you going to get us a drink or are we going to sit here arguing?"

Relieved, I tipped my head back and laughed. "Then you might possibly *not* be getting married? You can't be serious, Evelyn? About being engaged?"

At that point the waitress asked for our order, and as she moved away I asked her again.

"Are you really going to marry him?"

"No, I think not, but he is much nicer to me than you have ever been. He treats me as though I am special, worthy, desirable..."

"*You* are special, and *I* have always loved you."

"Ah, but you didn't show it or make me feel it."

"I don't understand how you can say that."

She was gazing at me, her dark eyes serious. "No, I know you don't. That's the saddest part of all."

I felt I should say something, but she continued, "*That* was the trouble, darling, you never did understand. And there was the drinking too, of course. Anyway, time has passed. I've had help to get over my obsession with you. It's taken a while, but I do know now that you couldn't help it, and I've got over our... misunderstandings... or whatever. Anyway, what have you been doing with yourself?" she asked lightly. "You've obviously missed me then?"

"I always miss you, you know that."

"But you've never called."

"No, it only upsets you when I do."

"Not anymore, darling. I'm fine now, but it would've been nice to know that you thought about me occasionally. After all, we were together a long time." Then she added with a grin, "On and off."

"It upsets me too, you know… remembering all that happened. I still think about it all the time."

"Still full of guilt. Well, so you should be." She said this with a smile that made me feel even more determined.

"I still love you, Evelyn. I want you back."

Her expression changed instantly, and she said, "Don't let's go down that road again. You love yourself more and that's not good enough for me. You know that, so stop saying it, Leo."

"I want you back."

She was getting angry. I could see the furrow across her brow and her eyes filling with tears.

"Shit," she sniffed, "you're making me cry. How is it you can always make me cry?"

"I can only really live when I'm with you, without you I exist, I get on with life, fill it with the women who like me. Without you in my life I…" I wanted to tell her that my affairs with Mo, Sheila, Nina, Dorothy and Julia were shallow and sordid in comparison to what I knew I felt for her. Why the hell had I always been so obsessed with satisfying my own sexual needs? It's not as if Evelyn and I hadn't had a completely satisfying sex life. I don't know whether I'm any different to other men, but my preoccupation with my genitals and sexual gratification has caused Evelyn to think me weak-willed and obsessive. Alcohol has usually been involved, although I no longer used that as an excuse. I knew I still needed to address my demons and had decided to make some changes and finally get some help, as Evelyn had suggested years before.

"So what if I was a pain to live with? We're married. We love each other. Sometimes things happen and we make mistakes," I pleaded.

"Here we go again. There is no understanding between us."

"I *have* learned my lesson, Evelyn."

"That'll be the day," she muttered, still really cross with me.

CHAPTER 2
Paris May 2003

EVELYN JOYNER/DAVISTEIN

I couldn't believe my eyes when I realised it was Leo calling my name. Nevertheless, I wasn't going to give him the satisfaction of knowing how my heart leapt and my insides quivered.

It was totally ridiculous that, after so many years apart, he could still impact on me. We had such a long and chequered history of passion and betrayal, anger and joy, that I wondered at my reaction to him that day in Paris. It felt like a moving programme of events that had already started long ago, and the momentum was reigniting again with our unforeseen encounter.

Or was it? As I turned, I could see how pleased he was to see me. It was unexpected. I was so sure that he would have found another partner. Several, I would have thought. As well as plentiful sex, Leo liked to be looked after, and women responded easily to him.

I'd never really recovered from our separation, although I'd always had the ability to immerse myself into whatever took my fancy, whether a man, a job or a hobby, so I had kept busy. I'd also had some good therapy, which had made me realise that I had to forgive him. I had been driving myself crazy with bitterness and resentment. But go back? I didn't think there was any chance of that!

I was still endlessly busy, and even more so now that I had qualified as a psychotherapist. In the past Leo had often belittled my achievements, especially after he'd been drinking. I usually succeeded because what I did, I did as well as I could. I always felt worthy and satisfied with myself, something Leo seemed totally incapable of, and he found himself irritated with my successes. Although he excelled in most sports, he showed little ambition to design prestigious pieces of architecture, or create a reputation for himself. When we met he'd accepted a job at our local council and dealt with building compliance documentation, ensuring adequate access to public buildings and car parking spaces. Whatever he did seemed to me to suggest that it wasn't particularly inspiring or notable, and I was sure that it was more to do with his indolent attitude to life than his lack of skills. Things changed for him when he moved to Milan in 1999 to a prestigious job that inspired him to better himself. But it hadn't saved our marriage, as we thought it might at the time.

That day in Paris was so unexpected. Although everything about Leo was familiar, he looked different somehow. He was still good-looking in a rough sort of way, still wearing mismatched shirts and ties. He was pale, but more than that, his eyes had lost their sparkle, his skin seemed sallow and I noticed he held his hand against his chest as if in pain.

I felt myself flush recalling the pleasure of his body, his scent, his soft caresses – I wanted to touch him. I wanted to lean against him, wrap myself around him, and yet the act of doing so was so scary, like leaping off a cliff into a sea of unknown depth and danger. That was the sort of feeling that I'd had when I first met him on that fateful evening. I had managed to keep away from him at first, often wondering at the strange reaction he caused in me, but to no avail.

CHAPTER 3
Meeting Leo

EVELYN JOYNER

It all began at a dinner party in 1990.

Looking back to our first meeting at a friend's house, I was sure I'd already met him. It hit me like a brick. I was drawn to him with such an immediate gut-wrenching feeling I couldn't explain. There was definitely some sort of connection. I knew him. Without voicing what I felt, I watched him carefully, trying to assess whether we had in fact met before. But... No. I was sure. Yet, I felt myself drawn to him like a magnet. I didn't even really find him attractive at first. He had a slightly northern accent that I couldn't identify and, although he looked clean and reasonably well dressed, there was something rather scruffy about him. His hair was too long and he wore a remarkably ugly ring and bracelet. I didn't like men in jewellery. It gave an impression of him as being tasteless, flashy, a bit of a lad. Yes, that's how Doreen described him later when I asked her about him.

"That bloke, Leo. On his own, divorced I think. I asked him if he wanted to come as he's just moved here from Manchester. We met him in The Swan last week. A bit rakish... A bit of a lad!"

"Mmm. I think you could be right, but there is something about him..."

"Yeh, he's very charming, so watch out," said Doreen with a smile. "Could be just what you are looking for."

"I don't think so. Not at all what I'm looking for. You know me, Doreen. Don't need any aggro in my life."

I'd been on my own almost since Lily was born. It was about three years, struggling sometimes, but I'd come to terms with working hard and being independent. My children were my world, and most of the men I'd met had either been immersed in their own fatherhood or messy divorces, or too selfish to be considered as stepfathers. We'd enjoyed the company of several over the past few years, but Dan and Lily knew that I had no intention of bringing anyone into their lives on a permanent basis. Unless, of course, he was an absolutely special one. That didn't mean that it couldn't happen, just that it was unlikely.

That dinner party changed everything! Whatever it was, it felt like an absolute certainty of an ongoing connection, something so already fixed, already destined to happen.

My friend Judith laughed at me when I tried to explain about how I felt when I met him, and the certainty that we were somehow linked, but I could only add, "You can think what you like, but he *is* familiar, connected to me in some way. Like he's someone I know, have known before, in a dream or in another life perhaps. I've often wondered about that."

"Wondered about what?" asked Jude.

"Whether we've met people before in previous lives."

She laughed again, "Don't believe in all that shit. Perhaps you were at school together or something."

"No, we couldn't have been. As far as I know our lives have never crossed before. It's quite scary. I feel that it's essential that we *are* together. As if there is some sort of ordained plan for us. I've thought about it a lot, and I've really tried to avoid him, but I can't. He turns up everywhere I go. Even outside playschool the other day. I was collecting Lily and he just happened to be driving past. You know how far out of town the school is? He said he was looking for a place that was selling second-hand fridges."

I was surprised at my intense feelings. I wasn't sure why, but I didn't give him my phone number when he asked for it, or make any plans to see him again. But within a couple of weeks I bumped into him twice, once shopping in the local supermarket where I had almost completely ignored him, and then at the village fair when we said a brief hello and, in an attempt not to spend time chatting, I said I had to go as I was taking the children swimming.

"Do you go every week?" he enquired.

"Yes, they love it."

"Is it a good pool? I like to swim but haven't had the chance yet. I've only moved here recently."

"Mmm. Yes, it's a very good pool."

By that time I was walking away, aware that he was having an unnerving effect on me. I think, looking back, that I was having an effect on him too because he stuttered and smiled a goodbye.

The following week at the swimming baths, there he was, wearing a particularly gaudy pair of swimming trunks, and grinning as if surprised at seeing us there.

"So, which are yours?" he asked, surveying the pool full of small people splashing and shrieking.

I beckoned Lily and Dan to come out as our time was up and the pool was reserved for serious swimmers for the next hour. Lily surveyed Leo with interest, but Dan ignored him, more interested in the fizzy drink and packet of crisps I allowed them after their swim.

"See you," I waved a goodbye as we headed for the changing rooms, knowing full well that I would see him again. I liked him.

How our lives so quickly became intertwined was a mystery, but everywhere I went I managed to bump into Leo, even at times when I was deliberately trying to avoid him. The children got used to seeing him at the pool, and every time we went shopping or to the local park, there he was, smiling. And oh so surprised to see us. Jude reckoned he was stalking me, but he never suggested we should meet or contact each other, although he now knew where we lived, having walked home from the village sweet shop with us one sunny afternoon.

He lived in Great Ayton and the shop was in Stokesley.
He just happened to be in there buying a newspaper!

CHAPTER 4
December 1990

LEO

So it began. Even though I'd been deliberately trying to get to know Evelyn, it was really by a lovely coincidence that we met again socially. We'd both been invited to a Christmas fancy dress party by mutual acquaintances. I worked in the same office as Vic, and Evelyn had been a neighbour of him and his wife Cathy years previously.

I'd found an old Indian outfit and a pair of worn moccasins, and Evelyn was dressed as a cowgirl. We laughed as she pulled her gun on me when I arrived, and I acted a dramatic death, to the amusement of Vic and Cathy. They were surprised that we knew each other.

For me it was a strange evening in many ways as Evelyn knew everyone, was familiar with their children and all the local gossip. I was the 'new' boy and was soon introduced.

I'd scanned the room for any totty but decided there was no one as gorgeous as Evelyn. She caught my eye, she knew what I was doing and she gave me one of her knee-trembling smiles. I decided it was time to ask her out, and to my surprise she said, "Okay then, where shall we go?"

"Anywhere you like."

"Shall we try the Thai place?" she suggested. "It's new and I haven't been there yet."

"Great, I love Thai food," I said. In truth, I'd never ever tried it!

It was a lovely evening and we learned a little about each other, our families, our holidays, our hobbies and such like. We talked with all the enthusiasm that couples do as they get to know each other, looking for compatible subjects and shared interests. Over the next few weeks we saw each other regularly. But she kept me at arm's length!

She was obviously hard-working and resourceful, as her life appeared to be organised and happy. Her little semi-detached house was neat and clean, full of pretty colours and shiny hardwood floors, and her children bright and gob-smackingly frank. On an outing to the local park one Sunday, Lily asked me seriously, "Are you Mummy's new boyfriend?" Without waiting for an answer, she continued, "She only keeps her boyfriends for a little while. They come and they go. Gets bored easily, I think."

"Is that so?"

"Yep," she said, and skipped off to challenge her elder brother to a swinging contest. I could only smile, but I did understand the sentiment. Evelyn had no truck with fools or time wasters.

It's a shame, looking back, that I didn't take more time to evaluate exactly what that meant, but I was not the sharpest knife in the box. I thought my charm would melt her eventually, and although I was becoming increasingly fond of her, I had my eye on a little blonde piece that I had met on one of my pub crawls in Guisborough.

Research, I called it! Being new to the area meant sourcing suitable drinking holes, preferably somewhere where I could meet women. I liked a drink or six, and regular sex was essential. Having a local was important to me, and I'd already sorted several good ones close to home in Great Ayton where I had recently bought my own home. It was the first house that I'd owned since my break-up with my ex.

Evelyn was lovely, intelligent and good company, and I was constantly drawn back to wanting to see her again. She was a brilliant cook and was interested in the environment, nutrition and food production, especially animal welfare. Things I had never given much thought to. Evelyn had strong views about most things, she was well-read and well-informed, but would willingly admit if she didn't know anything about a subject. She never pretended to be interested in things she wasn't, was truthful and entertaining, and I liked her company immensely. I fancied her too, but I had a clever little warning light that told me she would not be an easy conquest, so I never attempted to seduce her into my ever-ready bed.

In the meantime, over Christmas and well into the new year, my blonde-haired barmaid Amanda was enthusiastic and willing, and lived far enough away from Evelyn that I thought we wouldn't be seen out together. But it's sod's law that we were. Several times blokes from the cricket club came out of town to the Guisborough pub, and then one night, Vic and Cathy came in. They were out celebrating Cathy's brother's engagement.

Little Mandy was everything I could possibly have wanted under the duvet, freezing on the beach at Redcar or behind the pub car park wall. She was far too young to be going out with me, but she was satisfying my preoccupation with sex and I got half-priced drinks in the pub that she worked in. She probably thought I was quite a good catch, having my own house and a reasonable job, and when she asked me how many children I would like, I smiled and said, "How many would you like, Mandy?"

"Oh, three perhaps. Not just yet, though. I need to grow up a bit. You won't mind waiting, will you? I know you are older than me, but it doesn't matter so much for men, does it?"

"No, lovely, it doesn't matter at all," I told her sweetly. She took that as a confirmation that we were actually heading toward a long-term relationship, but I didn't want children at all and had no intention of heading down that path.

CHAPTER 5
Spring/Summer 1991

EVELYN

Over the next few months I became totally intrigued by Leo. I suppose not so much *by* Leo, but by the extraordinary feelings he stirred in me. He'd made no obvious advances to me in the early stage of our relationship, and it was only after Cathy and Vic's party I decided I liked him enough to have dinner with him.

We found ourselves in a friendly relationship. He was good with the children and they found him easy-going and fun. Dan particularly liked talking to him about football, something that was completely beyond my conversational capability. The times spent with Dan and Lily were easily more relaxed than when he and I were alone together, mainly because his alcohol intake increased when the children weren't around.

Years later I discovered how intimidating he found me, even though he was instantly, if somewhat unwillingly, drawn to me on our first meeting.

He was a sexy flirt, but was careful to avoid being pushy or vulgar with me. I liked his company. He was quietly spoken and humorous, initially appeared good-natured and helpful, willing to lend a hand or join in parties and outings. Having joined the cricket club, he was soon a dedicated member of the team as well as giving up one evening a week to coach the juniors in the club. Locally he became well known for his drinking excesses, and I understood from his friends was well tolerated as he only very occasionally became aggressive or argumentative. His newly acquired mates at the cricket club were always willing to get him home safely, and knew he would be back with no hard feelings and no hangover.

Leo never ever had a hangover!

"You drink too much," I'd told him at a dinner party where he had flirted and embarrassed me with his excesses.

"No more than most," he sniggered at me.

"Much more than most," I replied angrily. "Don't you dare let my children see you like that."

I did find his excessive drinking hard to tolerate, but in those early days of our relationship it was his unreliability that often caught me off guard. I was not used to being cancelled at the last minute, or promised phone calls that never arrived. He was unpredictable most of the time. Sometimes he'd say he'd cook dinner for us or call in, and not do so. His excuses were usually lame, and had to do with getting involved in a football, cricket or tennis match, when I often found out that it was because he'd just had too much to drink or was elsewhere.

He always apologised. Saying sorry slipped off his tongue so easily. He was charmingly reticent and humble and often bought me flowers. I liked that, and found him easy to forgive.

I was aware that I fancied him like mad, but I was wary. Friends had told me of seeing him out with other women or flirting in the pub, or not being where he'd told me he was. But, hey ho, we lived in a world of liberated sexual activity, and I had no doubt that he was doing exactly what most men of his age were doing. But we'd been seeing a lot of each other, and as the months passed I'd got used to having him around.

We often walked in the park with the children on a Sunday, and he'd mowed my lawn and cleared a blocked gutter for me. I cooked for him at least once a week and he would help me. He would bump around in the kitchen, cutting the lemon for the gin and tonic, knocking things over and getting in the way, but I liked having him near, the comforting bulk of him.

"How's your day been?" he'd ask, sipping his drink.

"It's been all right, I've done two important articles today, but I'm a bit bored with it all. I don't want to do this forever. As soon as Lily starts full-time school I'm going to start studying again. I want to do something a bit more worthwhile," I told him.

Leo was busy pouring himself another drink. "Like what?"

"Don't know yet," I replied as I whipped the gin bottle back into the cupboard and gave him a gentle dig. "We've got wine."

I didn't like to nag him, but I was not going to allow him to get drunk in front of Lily and Dan, who were waiting for their supper.

The first time we spent the night together was at my invitation. The children were staying with my mother in Scarborough, and I hadn't had sex for quite a long time and unexpectedly I'd asked him to stay. I'm not sure what possessed me, as I'd found myself becoming more and more selective about who I slept with. I'd got into the habit of relieving myself when I had the need.

Living in a society where having sex on the second or third date was the norm, I had felt slightly uncomfortable about taking so long, but I'd long since given up playing sex games with men. Leo and I had avoided getting into bed because basically I wasn't ready to, and I was grateful that he didn't push me. We'd kissed once or twice; gentle, soft, friendly kisses that had slightly alarmed me with their tenderness. I had an unnerving feeling that there would be no turning back once we took another step.

I was right!

Leo's eyes lit up when I suggested he stay the night. He hadn't had time to drink too much and had been amusing and sexy all through dinner. He reached for me and without a word led me to my bedroom. We stood for an embarrassing moment next to the bed as I unbuttoned my blouse. With an engaging grin he pulled off his shirt, and I relaxed as he said, "I've been waiting for this." Then his mouth was on mine, and I was surprised at how easily and comfortably we kissed. Usually the first few snogs with any man were exploratory and sometimes awkward. A deep sense of dread as well as excitement pulsed through me the moment our bodies came together. I knew he was trouble and I knew I was falling for him. It puzzled me because, even though I was aware of these things, it was what I wanted.

Leo was a rather well-set, soft-bodied man, and as I wrapped my arms around him I felt comfortable, and we drew ourselves together so easily. His hands were softer than I had expected. Kind, gentle touches, he explored my neck and naked spine, his fingers lingering on my birthmark.

The taste of his lips and his delicious scent intoxicated and excited me. 'Oh…' I felt myself moan softly as he lay me on the bed, and again he pulled me close. His tongue took possession of my mouth and it was more delicious than I could ever have imagined. He held me, pressing the length of his body against me, murmuring softly.

I hardly heard his words. I couldn't think clearly at all, I was dizzy with lust for him. I kept telling myself that *it* was wrong. *He* was wrong, but it didn't seem to make any difference.

It wasn't the most sexually exciting experience I'd had with a man, and certainly nowhere near the passionate, emotionally charged sex that my husband Matt and I had enjoyed when we first met, but it was wonderful. We sort of fitted together, and it felt right. Afterwards Leo lay back and fell asleep instantly.

It won't last, said a voice in my head.

CHAPTER 6
Bad Behaviour

EVELYN

Over the next few months I saw Leo frequently and, providing he hadn't drunk too much, we spent nights together whenever the children were away. I always responded on a really deep level to his body. It seemed like the most natural thing in the world, as if I'd been practising and responding to these moments for an eternity, perhaps even, I thought wistfully, in another lifetime.

We morphed into a couple. He'd told me on several occasions that he adored me, but I had laughed of course, mainly because it was usually after a couple of bottles of wine.

I liked the fact that he was a simple man. I found it refreshing that he didn't read the Times or talk about emerging Latvian poets or talented musicians, as Clive, my last long-termer − seven months to be precise − had done. I'd always felt that I should be more sophisticated than I was with him.

I didn't feel like that with Leo at all, and when we were doing ordinary, everyday things together, we laughed a lot. The same things amused us and we got on well.

I was so physically drawn to him. I do remember that touching Leo for any reason gave me pure pleasure. I'd wipe his chin, straighten his collar, bump into him or massage his shoulders for the sheer contact that I needed.

"What are you doing? What's that for?" he'd ask, laughing at my flirting.

Although I never touched him when he'd had too much alcohol, as he would respond in a sloppy, leery way that made me feel foolish.

I hadn't been out with anyone else since that first night

with Leo, interpreting our relationship as something special. I soon discovered that Leo on the other hand had not, and it wasn't long before I knew that I wasn't his only sexual partner. Men think women don't know, but my instinct was absolutely right. So many little signs, his absences when he'd told me he was home, the lies about the matches at the weekend, his responses when I asked him what he had been doing.

So, with this feeling, the unreliability and the excessive drinking, our relationship became a rollercoaster, and it wasn't long before I knew that his intentions were different to mine. I'd long since lost the ability or the inclination to put up with bad behaviour from men, so I decided it would have to end.

I had a good job, lovely kids and a reasonable social life for someone who had no immediate family close by. I also had good, supportive friends who looked after Dan and Lily if I needed a night out.

Somehow, though, Leo always crept back into my life, and we were drawn back into the fray, no matter how extreme our differences. Sometimes a month would go by without seeing him, and then the phone calls began, usually late at night, when he was always cheery and bleary, telling me of his love for me. I often put the phone down on him but it didn't deter him at all. Eventually he would turn up with his little boy look, flowers and promises.

"You either cut down on the drinking or I'm finished with you," I told him after he'd turned up an hour late, completely wasted and with a singularly stupid excuse. He stood in my doorway unperturbed and disregarded how upset I was.

"Okay, I will. See you later," was all he said. He threw up in my front garden, and without a word disappeared into the night. At least he wasn't driving.

He didn't call and I wasn't sure whether I was relieved or

disappointed. Yet again I resolved to put a swift end to any further association with him, especially when I found out that he had been at the cricket club that night with a young lady who he'd introduced as his girlfriend. I was incredibly upset and cried myself to sleep a couple of nights before deciding it was all for the best.

A week later it was Lily's birthday, and Leo appeared at the door with a present for her and a bouquet of roses for me.

"I love you," he said simply.

"Come on in, Lily is having a party. You can give her your present." I was ridiculously pleased to see him, but said firmly, "I think an explanation is in order, Leo. I don't understand what's going on with us, but I would like you to try and explain."

The birthday party was in full swing, and Aunty Sally was organising a pass the parcel game. While Leo presented Lily with her gift, I whispered to Sally, "Give us five minutes, Sal. Need a serious talk with this bonehead."

We retreated to the kitchen. He lifted his arms to embrace me but I stepped quickly away. He already knew how easily I was swayed. But I had decided not to be.

"Well, explain!"

CHAPTER 7
Betrayal 1991/1992

LEO

How could I explain when I didn't understand myself what motivated me to cheat on her? What I did know was that I'd met a woman I wanted to impress. I wanted her to love me. I longed to live up to her faith in me, to be the man she needed and deserved. Evelyn and I had something special, and it was never just about sex. It was much more than that. Whatever it was that drew us together was different to the other women in my life. I admired her – her ability to look things in the eye, analyse and address them, the way she related and understood people, her passionate and caring attitude to those less well off than herself. There were no hidden agendas with Evelyn, and her depth of feelings was immense.

I guess that's what scared me most. I could feel it when we made love, an outpouring of emotion that I knew I should be responding to, but somehow it distanced me. Nevertheless, our relationship was very special, and the sex was wonderful. She had a smooth, soft body, which had several little birthmarks. The first time I saw the dark little cross on the back of her neck it stirred in me such a protective feeling that I couldn't explain. I caressed it when we made love and sensed it deepened my tie with her. It felt like coming home, and some nights I would let my fingers linger on the little cross as we drifted into sleep.

I knew that I pleasured her physically, but there was always a feeling of not quite achieving, not quite satisfying her. I wondered whether it was that feeling, not really fulfilling her, that sent me elsewhere. It wasn't even that I needed variety, but I found myself easily responding sexually to any woman who showed an interest in me, even though I had to admit that they never really got the real me.

Some, of course, never even wanting it, preferring, as women do, to read whatever they needed into a relationship. But they never got past my cloak of pretence. I made sure of that.

I liked all kinds of women, posh girls and rough girls, fat or thin. Bright girls were a challenge, and dumb ones a bit of fun. What did it matter? I was able to fold myself instantly into the shape of whomever they thought they wanted. I was a blank page for every woman to write her fantasies on. If they wanted love, I gave it... or the actor in me did. Sometimes I played the part so well I believed it myself. If it was a body they wanted I became the fuck-artist they longed for, but I obviously couldn't fool Evelyn and I didn't really want to.

I knew that I'd made promises to her that I never kept, played around and often assured her that I wouldn't drink too much when we were out together. Yet, within a social environment I'd be powerless, overtaken with the pleasure rush which swept away all the guilt, the promises and the knowledge of my growing love for her. Slivers of memory would return the next day, and the build-up to blocking out the guilt would start again. The need to drink would creep in, as I watched the unhappiness that I caused Evelyn with my unreliability and drunken behaviour.

I wasn't exactly unkind to her but an obvious embarrassment sometimes, and a damn nuisance when I fell asleep, disappeared for days or collapsed where I was. I allowed the guilt and humiliation to give me another excuse to blot it out with a bottle or two. It gave me a way of pretending it didn't happen. But there was a rage growing inside me, getting stronger each time I retreated to the bottle. I could almost feel it building, an anger that could not be stopped. The terrible truth that I'd admitted to no one was that I often greeted this inner fury with relief. I don't think at the time I could have admitted it, but my ability to satisfy a woman was totally confined to the bedroom, where I was a past master at keeping my emotions absolutely detached from my penis.

Emotions were painful, so I avoided them if I could, and whilst I could enjoy a woman's body without any inhibitions, I could not release myself from that tight, safe little box that I had shut myself into at an early age.

It's not that I didn't love Evelyn. No, I did, I know I did. But I questioned my capacity for the commitment she needed, or to love her in the way she expected. I don't think I'd ever developed the ability to love fully. I never received love from my mother. My father, Solomon Davistein, had gone back to Israel the week after I was born. We had no idea where he was after that. Consequently, I always felt unwanted, so I protected myself by limiting my expectations, and therefore emotions became unnecessary. I played a good game, though, but in truth I didn't really know how to respond to women's needs, except sexually.

"I know you've been seeing someone else. Why? What can't you explain, Leo?" Evelyn challenged me.

"It's not what you think. Mandy... the girl..." I started again, although not denying what she already knew. "It's nothing... nothing serious."

Evelyn's mouth tightened. "So that makes it okay? Does it? Please explain."

"It's not that I don't want to..." I stumbled into incoherent speech, only to lose my way before I could explain. "I just can't," I said at last. "I love *you*."

"Do you? How can I take you seriously? If I really was the love of your life, then tell me why you need to have affairs." She held up her hands. "No, don't tell me... you had too much to drink. You were lonely... you don't like being on your own. You wanted a fuck more like. You're a selfish, unfeeling prick."

She glared at me.

"I know you love me too −" I started.

"You're a cheat and I'm sick of you... sick of not being important enough... of putting up with your shit behaviour and..." She turned away from me, tears springing to her eyes. "Yes, I do love you, though heaven knows why, but I will not be two-timed, I want you out of here now."

I let out a long sigh before the words would come. "It's the getting close, I back away. I know how it must look but I am doing my best." How pathetic I sounded. I could hear the shrill tension in my voice and I stopped. It was no good. I could only apologise yet again, and hope that she would see that it was my own weakness and nothing to do with her.

"I'm so sorry," I said miserably. Yet, I did know why I played around. I needed to feel wanted. Self-satisfaction and pride. I was appalled to think my own vanity was the thing that could sever our relationship.

Evelyn was the most fascinating, most wonderful woman I'd ever met. I wasn't able to make her understand how I really felt. I stood, looking like a fool, but her expression had softened.

"Leo, love is about feeling. It's like standing in the sun. When you do, you can feel it. You allow it. It's also about commitment. It's that simple. If you can't feel it, it's not there, or you are standing in the shadows. It's not difficult to understand."

I'd never really talked to anyone about how it felt to grow up in a home where there was no feeling of affection or love. I didn't expect it, because I didn't know what it was. How could I miss something that I'd never experienced? What happened? My mother didn't love me. Was there something wrong with me? I was a lonely child. Even as a five-year-old I had a key hung around my neck. I used to finger it as we sat and drank our milk in the mornings, hoping that just for once my mother would be there when school finished.

Sometimes I tried to believe I was wrong. Surely my

mother did love me, she clothed and fed me, made me go to school. True, she wasn't there when I got home, neither was there any warmth or food in the house. I kept my coat and gloves on in the winter until she came in and lit the tiny gas fire that heated our flat.

I pictured myself in the silence that happened when she did finally arrive at around six o'clock. She would come in the door, just glance at me, not make any attempt to hug or greet me. Throwing her shabby coat over the armchair, she would slump and close her eyes for a moment or two and I would stand still, wanting and waiting. Without looking at me or touching me, she would sigh and heave herself off the chair to unpack her shopping bag.

'Put the radio off. Read a book or something. I'm tired so don't make a noise, and don't look at me like that. I have to work. Do you understand? I have to work to keep us? If I didn't have you, my life would be different.' Images came of her hurriedly applying her lipstick or brushing her hair in the morning in front of the old, pockmarked mirror by her bed. Watching her massaging her tiny feet after a day's work, or pushing a plate towards me when she could be bothered, swam through my memory. She would roll her eyes if I made too much noise, tut-tutted if I cried, but never once asked me if I was okay, what I'd been doing, how I was getting on at school or how I felt. I ate everything she gave me because I was never sure whether it would be enough. She always had biscuits and apples and beans. I had lots of biscuits and beans as a child.

Waves of emotion overtook me as I recalled a moment when I caught her eye and she stopped what she was doing, pursed her lips and said, "Well?" as if I'd asked for something or needed to explain. It must have been a response to the look on my face. One day I summoned up the courage to ask, "Don't you like me? Am I ugly or something?"

She laughed. It wasn't meant to be funny, but in the absence of any affection her laughter was the next best thing, and it had at least been a response. But she did say, "No, you're not ugly, you're all right as kids go."

My mother had taught me well. All my life I held everything tightly to my chest, smilingly getting on with my work, feigning interest in topics of conversation and silly jokes at parties or dinner tables but, when it came to it, the truth was that I cared for no one or anything, except the next drink and the next fuck.

Often, as I lay in bed at night, my head was full of thoughts of my mother, trying to capture a memory of her that would bring some comfort. Once or twice after having enough to drink, I allowed myself to feel the pain of being an unwanted child.

The first time Evelyn met Jeanette, my mother, she picked up instantly the clever way my mother always kept me in check. Her constant appraisal of anything I did, belittled with a single scornful remark.

CHAPTER 8
1992

EVELYN

Leo said sorry again and, if he was, it didn't change anything at all. For a month or so he would be the perfect partner, sober and loving, but without warning he would disappear and the slurring drunken phone calls would begin again.

Dan and Lily got used to his comings and goings, and I always made sure that they only saw the best of him. I didn't make an issue of his drinking or his unreliability in front of them, although I often blubbered to my friends Jude and Sally as I tried to explain.

"I think he is just emotionally immature. He can say the words. 'I love you' comes easily enough to him, but that's it. They're just words. I do believe he loves me, in his own way, but he has an impenetrable shell around him that prevents real involvement. If he let anyone get too close he'd have to talk about what those words really mean, or at least think about them. He'd have to expose what is really hidden away inside that box he hides in."

"Sounds like some sort of sociopath to me," said Jude as she sipped her tea. "It's not like you to be involved in complicated affairs. You're the most sensible of the three of us."

Jude had been married twice already. Both had been successful, likeable men, but once over she closed the doors on them, got divorced, and eventually found Frank, another equally successful and likeable bloke, whom she now lived with. Anyway, that's how it looked from the outside, but people have different needs, and Jude was quite distinct about hers. She had no trouble moving on from anything that dissatisfied her.

Sally, on the other hand, had been almost permanently

548

single and was really okay with it. She was a successful journalist and reporter who travelled to remote hot spots and got involved with men, usually on a temporary basis, but who went their own ways after assignments. It suited Sal immensely, as she never wanted to settle down or have children of her own. She came from a big family and had a bucket load of nephews and nieces, all of whom adored her. She was Dan and Lily's favourite babysitter.

"Get rid, Ev," she advised. "He's a 'no-go' area. Bloody hell! Evelyn, why do you keep letting him do this to you? I've never known you to be a pushover for any guy."

"I know."

"What are you going to do?"

"Don't know. It's like an illness. I decide it's over, chuck him out, and he comes back every time *and* I let him. It's like having an infection I can't get rid of. There is no cure," I answered dramatically.

Jude closed her eyes briefly, before replying, "There is, you know. He's a worthless, two-timing git and you need to move on."

I felt my eyes pricking with tears. "You're probably right. I'm behaving like a thwarted heroine in some awful cheap novelette and I can't seem to pull myself out of it."

I felt a flush of fear as Sally asked, "Did you ever feel like this with anyone else?"

"No, never. I've never been involved with someone I didn't understand. No, I've never felt like this before. When I'm with him I know it's different. It feels real and necessary. I don't feel safe or happy. I just feel it's right and inevitable, somehow, that we are together. When I'm not with him, something is missing. I know that sounds crazy. We're not really even suited at all, as a couple. I don't know how to explain it."

Sally gave me a sympathetic look, smiled, and said, "Okay, but I don't get it."

"I really thought that Leo's coolness, with his laid-back, unflappable nature was a sign of stability. Now I see it as a weakness. He doesn't seem to have the inner strength to explore his feelings or make a real commitment. For him it's easier to say sorry for his cheating, and expect me to accept that he won't do it again."

"He will, they always do," Sal said sagely.

I nodded, "I know you're right."

"What does he have to say for himself?" Jude asked.

"Nothing, he can't give me any reason. I think it all stems from his relationship with his mother somehow. She's the coldest woman I've ever met, very bright and a whizz at the bowls, I understand, but Leo seems cowed by her somehow. Don't know. It's all beyond me. I came from such a warm, loving family myself."

Of course, my friends were right about him. But in hindsight, I really did believe that there were dynamics from previous lifetimes, and that was a feeling that I couldn't shake off.

I often dreamed about him. Some dreams or memories really matter and illuminate something in our choices, or reveal some intuition that is trying to push its way to the surface, but I couldn't fathom it.

In one of my dreams I was searching for something in a garden full of herbs. In the background the sound of female voices singing a prayer or a holy psalm. All around me leaves and flowers swayed and gave me their voice. "Pick me, I can kill or cure. I can make you love each other, join an erotic dance, or fly to the stars." Leo was there too, laughing and running, singing a song about freedom.

In another dream he was my child. I was holding him so close, my arms wrapped around his body, our breathing synchronized and we were lifting slowly up towards some outer universe. I would wake with my heart hammering and feeling that I had wandered into another life. Once, I had asked Leo if he believed in reincarnation.

"Dunno, what do you think?" he asked.

He didn't seem to have any strong opinions about it or anything else really.

"I think I do," I told him, "I have felt that I already knew you since our very first meeting. Maybe from a different life and being somehow bound together in our journey through eternity."

Leo raised his eyebrows, laughed, and kissed me on the top of my head. "Right. If you say so."

He obviously thought me foolish, but I continued. "Perhaps we have arrived together in this life, at this time, just to be with each other and work out some Karmic mystery. Surely one life together is too short to achieve complete understanding and unconditional love. It must take many lifetimes to know someone well enough, so that nothing more could be achieved in that relationship. What do you think?"

"I think you lost me there." Obviously Leo was already losing interest.

"I am sure many lovers feel this way, but I really believe it's true," I continued. "How else could feelings be so strong with you and with no other man in my life? If we only see things in terms of this life, all is ultimate tragedy, because death will part us forever from our love. It is scary, though, isn't it? Just imagine if you remembered being really evil, a torturer or a murderer. Could we really concentrate on being here if we knew that? How could you live with the knowledge? It's hard enough getting it right now, isn't it?"

By then Leo was completely ignoring me, but muttered, "I guess." He disappeared off to watch the tennis.

I wanted him to communicate, to discuss what I was talking about, but he often seemed closed in, unapproachable, not only about meeting with me intellectually but sometimes physically too. When *he* wanted sex, he was full on, and although it was highly erotic, he was never particularly loving or romantic, whereas I felt it deeply.

As soon as he was satisfied he would sleep, whereas I was left emotionally frustrated. On the occasions that our lovemaking brought us together, I loved him with such intensity. I found it difficult to explain.

Leo saw my reaction as emotional and feminine, but as the months passed I began to understand that he didn't really fill my emotional needs at all. I would make up my mind to call it all off, but somehow fate dragged us back together. On one such occasion in the summer of that year, Sal decided to cheer me up with a trip away for a long weekend. I had been feeling really low, my work had petered out and I was on my own. I had not seen Leo for over a fortnight because we'd had a fiery argument.

Dan and Lily had gone to spend a week of their summer holidays with my mother. The weather was gorgeous and Sally had friends who had a brilliant little hotel in North Berwick, so that was where we headed. We planned to visit Edinburgh the following day.

We couldn't believe that on our first evening out in Berwick, and randomly choosing a pub along the road, there was Leo, pint in hand, surrounded by a group of guys from one of his local pubs. I saw him as soon as I walked in.

His face lit up when he saw me, and before I knew it he was buying us drinks. My heart was catapulting around my chest as he said softly, "I knew we were meant to be together and here you are."

He was there on a golfing holiday. I didn't even know that he played golf!

But I had made a decision and told him clearly that I didn't want to see him again. He was amused and said, "Perhaps you might have to, if your theory is right about me and our past lives. Perhaps you don't have a choice."

"I always have the choice," I told him confidently.

For nearly six months I dated other men, enjoyed my children and enrolled in an anatomy and physiology course. I had decided to train in some sort of holistic practice, and so my studying became my focus.

CHAPTER 9
Another Mistake

LEO

The summer over, I'd finally tired of Mandy's childish twittering about love and marriage, and left her convinced that I was desperately sad about our parting, but told her that I would be far too old for fatherhood when she was ready to make babies. She cried, of course, and I was duly sympathetic and caring.

In truth I missed Evelyn, I knew I loved her, and as I swallowed down the feeling of self-loathing at my behaviour, I decided to make it all up to her and not mess about again. What had become blindingly apparent over the course of the last few months was that I really was the most total idiot, playing about with young girls or married women so that I could always find an excuse not to commit to them. I decided it was time to put things right and show Evelyn how much she meant to me.

Time passed, and seeing her in Scotland that day had wound me up. I knew that she had been seeing another bloke. Jeff from the cricket club had told me that his friend Andrew was dating a lovely woman from Stokesley who had two children and was a successful freelance writer. It was obvious that he was talking about Evelyn, and I was as jealous as hell.

By the time it was nearing Christmas again, I took a day off work because I knew she worked from home on a Monday. I spent a great deal of the morning deciding what I was going to say to her. At lunchtime I had a couple of strong Martinis.

Wrong thing to do!

"What in heaven's name do you want? Why are you bothering me again?" she asked as soon as she opened the door to me.

"I need to say something to you," I swallowed. I could already see the tears springing into her eyes, so I continued, "You see, I think –" I stopped and corrected myself. "I know, that getting married and being settled would blow my need to tart around and drink myself stupid."

"You're drunk already, Leo."

"Am I? Well, what do you say?"

"Absolutely nothing, except that when you drink you say things you don't mean. Stupid things. Now go away."

"I do mean it. I love you."

"Yep, I know. Fuck off, Leo. That's not good enough." Evelyn walked away, but I caught her arm and turned her toward me.

She rolled her eyes when I said, "I want you to marry me."

"Really. It's suddenly hit you has it? Go ask silly Evelyn to marry you? How come after all these weeks without me you suddenly want to marry me? Why?"

"I just know that we should be together, but I didn't feel as if I was important to you before, but mainly the fact that I thought you were completely out of my league."

"What?"

"Clever, smarter, better-looking, better dressed, better educated, saner in every way."

She raised her eyebrows. "Well, I am, aren't I?"

"I had no idea how to compete with your children to get your attention."

"Don't be so fucking ridiculous. You do realise that is the stupidest – the most stupid thing you could say to a mother. Nothing, nobody competes with my children for my love and affection."

"Will you marry me, Evelyn?"

"No, I won't. You've got a drink problem. Go away, I don't even like you anymore."

I knew she more than liked me. She had told me often

enough.

"Yes, I like a drink, but I don't have a problem. I will prove it to you," I said as I departed.

It was time for me to settle down, so I made some plans.

Over the next few weeks I phoned her every day, sent flowers and didn't drink any alcohol at all. Why would anybody think I had a problem? For ten weeks I drank lime and soda and felt justified in asking Evelyn again and again to marry me.

I wanked an awful lot, because I'd also decided that I owed it to my intentions not to play around. Trouble was, my obsession with my genitals made me wonder whether I was a bit addicted to sex. I'd heard a long discussion on the radio about how to identify a sex addiction, and I think I complied with everything that it included.

Firstly: *Preoccupation with sex, and a great difficulty in stopping behavioural thoughts.* Well, definitely that was true. *Getting a feeling of a high followed by feelings of shame and sometimes depression.* Yes, I had to admit I did get a certain amount of low moods after sex. *Depending on sex to numb out negative emotions and difficult experiences or past traumas.* Guess that could be true too! *Betrayal and deceit, anger, shame, self-doubt, secrecy and avoidance.* I knew that to be true. I was secretive and avoided explanations. I guess I did really have a bit of a problem in that area, but I would prove that I could cope with it.

I resolved to be honest with her too, but I was concerned. I did believe that the truth may not always be desirable, that revealing how incredibly disloyal and untruthful I'd been would not lead to a resolution. So, despite knowing that she deserved the truth, I was unwilling to step back into the shadows of my past. But I really did want to change, and absolutely believed that I could control my sex addiction, if that's what it was, if I was more settled.

I could be a good husband I was sure.

CHAPTER 10
Marriage February 1993

EVELYN JOYNER/DAVISTEIN

Looking back to the day we married was painful. I was terrified. Sleep had been difficult. There was a little voice in my head asking questions I couldn't answer. The ceremony in the registry office, the church blessing and even the reception were a mixture of happiness and dread.

Although it was a lovely day, Leo seemed to me to be unchanged, both during and after the ceremony. Uncomplicatedly happy to be there, wearing his immaculate suit, no jewellery and a beautiful haircut. He looked so handsome. Watching him as we said the unfamiliar vows, I felt that although he stood there, he was essentially just standing in. He could have been in his favourite bar looking around with his drinking mates, smiling, having another beer and letting the world go by.

I wanted him to be changed, stood next to me, altered by this new era of our lives.

He was my husband, my soulmate and the lover whom I craved. I was disappointed.

I knew I looked sleeker and more glamorous than I could possibly have imagined in my long cream dress. My copper hair was glossy and pinned up with apricot roses to match my bouquet.

"Mum, you look like a princess," declared Lily happily as we stepped into the black limousine.

"So you do," said my serious Dan, who had been the one to show concern about this wedding. He was pretty astute for a ten-year-old. He had seen a few tears in the past year but I had tried to assure him that Leo was determined to make us happy.

"Good. I want you to be happy," he'd said seriously, but I

wasn't certain that he was convinced.

I loved Leo, but was I sure? Here I was on our wedding day, already disappointed.

Neither Sally nor Jude had been happy about my decision, but they had been finally convinced by Leo's sobriety and he'd assured them both of his good intentions. Swayed by his inordinate amount of charm, they too had believed him. Who wouldn't? He was so convincing.

The wedding reception was in Guisborough Hall with all our friends. Leo's mother Jeanette, aunts, uncles and cousins, Vic and Cathy, and Jeff and Nick from the cricket club were there with their wives and children.

My lovely mum Sonya took charge of Dan and Lily, who looked scrubbed and beautiful in their new outfits. The Joyners came too. It must have been difficult for them to see me married again. My wedding to their son Matt had been a grand affair and we had both been so young and hopeful. None of the family had been aware that when Matt was killed at work we had been on the verge of a friendly separation. We'd grown apart even before Lily was born, and Matt had already made arrangements to move out. I'd told no one except Sally who had helped me enormously, especially with Dan who was only four at the time and broken-hearted to lose his dad.

Looking around I realised how lucky I was to have such a supportive group of family and friends.

I watched Leo standing by the bar with a silly grin on his face. He wasn't drinking. I knew he was enjoying the day as a whole and that he was happy to be getting married, but…

"Are you happy?" I made myself ask Leo as we sat down to our meal.

He seemed startled by the question. "Of course, aren't you?"

"Oh, Yes… It's just that you…" I wanted to say, 'Haven't been moved by it,' but I said, "You haven't said very much."

"Haven't I?" he replied as he flicked my napkin across my lap. "Course I have."

I let my reservations go and enjoyed the rest of the day.

We'd started our married life with such good intentions. Within a few weeks I'd sold my house and we'd moved into Leo's in Great Ayton, a village which I'd always loved. We extended and upgraded the house. He allowed me to decide what it was to be, and to have it decorated to my taste throughout. It took nearly a year to complete. It was a good year. Leo and I enjoyed working together, decorating and moving furniture around to fit our new lifestyle, and it kept him at home in the evenings instead of at the pub or the cricket club bar.

Dan and Lily settled and were happy at school. Each had their own room, both of which looked out into the garden and across the meadows that circled Roseberry Topping. Living so close to the forest and hills afforded adventure for them, summer and winter.

My acceptance of marriage had come with a strict warning that Leo was never to be jealous of my love for my children, to which he agreed wholeheartedly.

I vowed that I would give Leo the stable, loving relationship that he'd obviously never had. He really loved us all and I was sure that he was contented at first. He rarely drank too much or behaved badly in front of Dan and Lily, but... there was a pattern developing and slowly things started to change. His mood would suddenly alter and he would disappear for the evening, come back late and sit around till the early hours watching television and drinking. I learned very quickly to leave him to it, go to bed and act as if nothing was amiss. The following day he would get up without any indication that anything was wrong, without the slightest hangover and go to work. He ignored my concern.

"What's wrong, Leo?" I asked on many such occasions.

"Nothing, no, nothing's wrong," he'd say, but I could see that he was closed, boxed up somehow, and a feeling of dread would sweep over me.

Our first Christmas together as a family came and went, too many presents, family fun and Leo passed out in the bedroom by 7 p.m. on Christmas Day.

On New Year's Eve, after threats of death, he saved his drinking until midnight and then disappeared off to the cricket club on his own, to reappear New Year's Day.

That was the first occasion that he didn't come home at night since we'd been married, and I hoped that he'd slept on someone's couch. When he arrived home in the morning he looked like hell, but laughed at me when I suggested he'd been with a woman.

"No, my darling," he said. "I've been in the cricket club all night. Fell asleep behind one of the benches. Old Jonesey found me when he came this morning to clean up. Good job we've got such an efficient caretaker or I could have been locked in there all holiday."

He laughed as he headed up the stairs. "Got to sleep."

He slept all day while Dan, Lily and I headed off out into the unexpected sunshine. By the time we came back home, Leo had showered and was busy preparing macaroni cheese for supper.

CHAPTER 11
A Good Life

EVELYN

By the summer of 1995 we had adopted a little mongrel from the R.S.P.C.A., and Dan named her Scruffy. Lily had always wanted a pet rabbit so we got two baby girls and called them Trisha and Cheryl after some characters on the television.

Life was good, but slowly Leo's moods became much more significant and, after we'd ceased to be so busy in the house, his evenings out and his drinking slowly increased again. I felt the cold thump in my heart when I saw it happening and begged him to stop. It would start out of the blue, because he'd had a difficult day, argued with his boss or I had bristled or raised my voice with an opinion that didn't agree with his. I don't know why, but a couple of drinks would never be enough. He couldn't stop, and he was often hurtful and bullying. Everything about me would irritate him, even though mostly his bad temper was nothing to do with me. I was aware of how quickly his moods changed and I blamed it on the alcohol. I became fearful. According to Leo there was always a reason and an excuse for it!

By then Dan was twelve years old, football mad and growing tall and dark like his father. Lily was nearly nine, darker-haired than me but with striking sea-glass blue eyes. She was a confident, athletic girl, bright as a button and passionate about the care of her pets. She was certain that she would eventually train to be a vet.

They both had such a busy social life that at least three evenings a week they were at karate, football, gymnastics, dancing or singing lessons, so mostly they saw little of Leo except at the weekends. He played cricket in the summer months at the weekend, and on a good day we would take a picnic down to the club to watch him play. We would return home, sun-flushed and full of crisps and cake, to the television and bed. Leo rarely returned until much later and usually quite drunk.

As the first few years passed, we were generally contented. What I recorded was mostly good, although I know some of it was awful, especially later on, but in those early days of our marriage I still believed in him. Every day that he was sober seemed right and potentially exciting and positive. All that is history now, stored away somewhere in the universe, the feelings, the disappointments folded somewhere in the black holes of time and space. Recorded forever, if not perfectly in my memory.

I'd never seen Leo display anger by raising his voice or slamming doors as I did. But I could feel it. It bubbled beneath the surface. It lurked in his eyes, in his tight jawline. It ate away at him like a growth, festered and grew, until I knew that someday, when he'd had enough to drink, it would burst open like a pus-filled boil.

I let myself be drawn into his needs, letting my own go unnoticed and unsatisfied. In truth I suffocated my feelings. I buried them in denial as I tiptoed around my husband's moods hoping that I could make him feel good, see his lovely smile and hold him close, so that he would feel how much I loved him.

I still often got the sensation that we'd already played this same scenario before, and that the Karmic residue was once again having an impact on this, our present life. How pompous that sounded; that I considered the fated power of our journey together was both special and tragic, and above mere worldly affairs.

It's not easy to pinpoint exactly when my feelings changed, and no moment of revelation, just a series of déjà vu incidents that felt familiar and unexplainable. I knew that he had started to lie to me again.

In my mind, once you'd made a commitment you had to stand by it, through thick and thin, in sickness and health, the good times and the bad. Wasn't that what it was all about? But Leo was still so unpredictable. Sometimes he was kind and loving, sober and helpful. Then he would say he'd be home for dinner and stay out most of the night, coming home drunk and collapse into bed. He'd tell me that he was going to a game or a match with a friend and then never move from the sofa. I used to think it was because he was used to being on his own, having the choice to do what he pleased, but I hated the way he just assumed everyone would fit in with him. I disliked it even more when we had made arrangements with other people and he didn't turn up.

One morning after the children had gone to school, I couldn't keep quiet any longer, so I challenged him.

"Before you go off to work, Leo, can you tell me where you were last night? I know you weren't at the cricket club because I telephoned them and asked if you were there."

"No, I wasn't there."

"You'd obviously been drinking."

"I had a few, that's true." His answers were guarded and vague, and left me feeling uncomfortable.

"Why are you being so deliberately evasive? You didn't come in until one. Where were you?"

Leo coughed and cleared his throat. That was one of the ways he gave himself time to think.

"Are you playing about, Leo? You've been behaving in such a secretive way again." As I questioned him, I was aware that my voice had risen, and resentment was colouring the conversation. I asked him several times what was going on.

Leo looked me straight in the eye. "You've got it all wrong again."

He turned and left, pulling the front door behind him, leaving me quite convinced that he was cheating again. But, as usual, he had not answered my questions. He was brilliant at leaving things up in the air, not answering, but using one of his stock replies, "It wasn't like that" – "It's not as it seems" – "Think you've got that wrong."

But most annoying of all when I challenged him was his total silence.

CHAPTER 12
Downhill Again 1997

LEO DAVISTEIN
When we married, I thought that my intentions had been highly honourable, but, as the years passed, I have to admit it didn't take long for me to wrap myself back into the feeling of self-doubt that haunted me. I'd wanted to be a good husband. I loved Evelyn, the best way I could. I wanted her to love me, but I convinced myself that she didn't really. Heaven knows why I had such a belief, because Evelyn was always caring and sincere, and showed her love willingly, but I let myself wander down the same pathway, believing I needed more.

How could she love me anyway? I didn't deserve to be loved. I had sex with other women. No, more than that, I had affairs with them. Full blown 'I love you, want to be with you forever' alcohol-induced affairs. None of which had much meaning to me really, as I was only satisfying my need for an ego boost and my insistent itch for sex.

Evelyn was singularly, simply, the most interesting, good-hearted woman I had ever known. Even though she had all manner of annoying habits and foibles. She was emotionally volatile, forgetful, hard to impress and impossible to beguile. She had no time for fools or laziness, she was impatient and demanding, and I loved being with her even though I still felt myself unworthy at times.

But, in truth, I had always been blowing through life; alcohol, affairs, lies, deceit and selfishness without a clue to the harm it was doing to our relationship. I was the worst sort of husband, an idiot and a weak-willed penis-follower.

More and more I drank myself into oblivion, whether from guilt or pleasure I'm not sure. I always blamed her for my moods and bad temper and rarely remembered what I said, but the devastating effect it had on her only made me feel guilty, so this added to my deep shame that sent me back to the bottle.

Waking in the spare bedroom, still in my grubby clothes and finding Evelyn with eyes puffy from the tears that she had shed, and with a gnawing knowledge that I had been vile to her, upset me intensely. Twice I'd even vomited in our bed, and she would silently strip it and clean up while I showered and hated myself. I could never find enough words to say how sorry I was, but that was all I could say, "Sorry, Evelyn."

It had been said too many times to be of any value to her, so once again I would walk away, holding my bitter regret deep inside like a growing boil of resentment. Eventually it had all been too much for her, because with the drinking had come more of the other women. Women who stroked me, made me feel better than I was, liked my casual, laid-back, easy-to-please attitude, and some who could drink me under the table. I spent a great deal of time with anyone who would accompany me into the hazy world of alcohol-induced revelry. I usually ended up back at the cricket club bar before returning home.

Evelyn would regard me with icy disdain, walk away and go to bed while I fixed myself a nightcap.

One morning she screamed her frustration at me. "So, what's the excuse this time? You rolled into the house at two a.m. I spent all afternoon cooking because we had visitors. Jude and Frank came to dinner. On *your* invitation, as I remember."

"Oh God, yes, I forgot," I replied, devastated.

Evelyn's eyes filled with tears. I hated to see her cry, and turned away unable to fathom what to say.

"You're pathetic. Nothing means anything to you at all," she spluttered. "Are you going to say something or are you going to just stand there buttering that toast like a retard?

Don't you feel anything? I suspect you were out with one of your floozies, Leo. It's not acceptable. Aren't I paying you enough attention? Tell me."

"It's not that at all."

"What then? Why do you try to make *me* feel guilty? I've done nothing and I am devastated, Mister God Almighty, selfish, guilt-ridden bastard that you are." She yelled at me and tears of anger flooded her eyes and poured down her flushed cheeks.

"Evelyn, don't, please. It isn't like that."

"It isn't like what?" she demanded.

I wrapped my arms around her shaking body and tried to reassure her. "I'm so sorry about last night. We'll ask them another night."

"No, we will not," she shrieked. "I am not going to be embarrassed by you again. Just get out of my sight."

"I'm so sorry, Evelyn."

Her face crumpled as she pushed me from her and walked away, sobbing uncontrollably.

CHAPTER 13
1997

EVELYN

Sally came over for a coffee after the children had gone to school and Leo had left for work. She saw immediately that I was suffering. My frustration and anger had become a throbbing headache. I felt emotionally battered and was not making a lot of sense, because I truly couldn't find any excuse for him.

When Sal asked me what was going on, I started to cry again, unable to hold back the continuing sadness that had become part of who I was. All the feelings that I'd kept so securely locked up were tearing through me in big shuddering sobs. The relief made me dizzy, and Sally held me steady as I heaved and choked out my grief.

"I hate to see you like this, Ev. What are you going to do?"

I blew my nose and swallowed hard. I wasn't going to let this rule my life, so I replied, "Hope he'll see sense. I'm going to try to convince him to get some help. I can't let him go on like this."

"Is it just the drinking or is he playing around again?" Sal asked with a concerned frown.

"Both. Yes. Don't know why. He won't tell me. It all starts with the drinking. I've watched him. He can't drink in moderation or stop when he knows he's had too much... he's always sorry," I added lamely.

"He can't really love anyone, you know, and in the end such people are always alone, no matter how much other people love them. I doubt whether he's really involved with someone else." Sally sighed as she said, "You still love him, don't you?"

"Yes, of course I do," I replied, although I couldn't

explain any of it.

"Doesn't he give a damn about how his actions hurt you, or is he some sort of sociopath or psychopath or whatever the terminology is nowadays for those who don't care about others' feelings?" Sal looked sceptical. "Trouble with you, Evelyn, is that you like a challenge. If anyone can get him on the straight and narrow it will be you."

"I can't, Sal. But I'm going to make him get some help. Do you think he would respond to some psychotherapy or anger management?" I asked.

"Anger management?"

"Yeh, I know he doesn't show great noisy displays of anger like I do, but he's what's called an imploder, rather than an exploder. His anger bubbles away silently as if he can't release it. I've been reading some theories on the subject. I have even managed to wade through Freud and Jung and I'm now on to Adler. They all have different theories about how damage in early life can create repeating messages in our heads."

"Like how?" Sally asked.

I hesitated. I knew she was listening intently as she had some theories of her own about men's behaviour and sex. We'd discussed them at some length when she'd told me she would never marry again. She believed men were totally incapable of relating to a woman's emotional needs, and so therefore it was best to have no expectations whatsoever. Sally considered herself immune to anything other than a good lay and a bit of fun.

"So, these messages?" she repeated.

"Well, like a tape that continues to give us wrong information that we learned when we were young as feelings, even before we could talk or had any way to intellectualise them. Stuff picked up on an emotional level only, and so never processed into rational thought. But the imprint is there."

Sally lifted her eyebrows in surprise. "Wow, when are you going into business, Ev? That makes so much sense, but how can we alter those 'tapes'?"

"Don't know, but I am determined to learn. All the courses I'm doing are giving me a little insight on where I am going with my studying. When I've finished my massage and reflexology I'm going to concentrate on mental health."

CHAPTER 14
Vicious Circles 1998

LEO

"You can never get too much, can you?"

"Okay. Repeat that," said Jeff, my mate at the cricket club. He looked shocked. He, being a boring forty-something, married for eighteen years, two kids, mortgage and no sense of humour type.

"A man can never get too much sex. We think about it all the time," I said with absolute conviction. "It's natural. So it can't be wrong, when the ol' man rises up, to find a suitable partner."

"Not when you've got a lovely wife at home," Jeff responded, clearly not condoning my illicit affairs. He'd been at our wedding, had met Evelyn on several occasions and thought that she was terrific. I thought she was terrific too. But so what?

"Get yourself home, Leo, you're bloody drunk," Jeff insisted.

"No, I'm not."

Although Evelyn went on and on about my drinking, I never really thought I was out of control, but I guess I was always a couple of pints ahead of everyone else. With a few drinks my horizons changed, altered my whole perception of things. Right or wrong things, mostly, but it never occurred to me that I needed to be different, or make any decisions that I had to reconcile myself with. Life had done what it had. I'd rarely been alone because I didn't have to be.

Sex was the name of the game. You work, you eat, you had sex, you sleep, and you move on. So, I was married! So what? After a few drinks I felt no guilt about it at all. Until the next morning anyway!

I had to admit it was disposable sex with disposable

women who meant nothing to me. A quick physical burst of pleasure and gratification, a pathetic ego boost at its best. The need to use my body in a sexual way gave me such intense satisfaction. As if I'd been deprived. Like being hungry and not knowing where the next food was coming from, so I gorged when I could. Like a good meal, soon forgotten.

My need for constant sex surprised even me sometimes. Although I did really enjoy it, surely it should've shown me how good Evelyn and I were together. It should've made me realise about love and relationships and how to make them work.

I knew I'd always felt that Evelyn was too good for me, too clever, too special. I tried to tell myself that it didn't matter, but I always felt less than her, smaller somehow, and then somebody came along who made me feel big, smart and special, clever and attractive. If I felt randy and someone was at hand, well, hey – why not? Not a problem. Or so I thought. What the hell!

But sadly it wasn't until many years later when my life fell apart that I seriously questioned my motives, my sad little ego trips, taking whatever was on offer, and understood about commitment and loyalty. It was a long time later that I learned not to hide behind my insecurities.

"Monogamy wasn't designed for men or, at least, it's not natural is it? All men will cheat sooner or later. Jus' natural behaviour. Anyway, I don't want to go home, everything I say leads to a row," I mumbled.

Jeff grunted. "That's hardly surprising, you knob-head. Stop messing her around and appreciate what a great woman you've got."

So, Jeff thought me a dope, and he was probably right.

I stared at my pint and shook my head. I had already had too many to go home. "Yeh, you're right, mate."

I'd had my fair share of totty over the years, but perhaps I should learn to be more discreet in the future. Old habits die hard, though!

"Right, I'm off," I told Jeff. "I know where I will be made welcome."

Jeff's look of disgust as I turned away did prick my conscience very slightly, but my penis was already responding to my thoughts of Mo.

Everyone knew Mo.

Go-MoJo-Go had a reputation for having a libido the size of Europe. She was married to Keith who worked offshore on one of the Shell oilrigs and only came home every twelve days or so. When he was away, Mo was always available and Keith had no idea.

What a perfect arrangement that was turning out to be!

CHAPTER 15
Facing the Problem 1998

EVELYN

When Leo finally did come home that night, he'd lost his keys and I had to get up to let him in. He burst through the door with a gush of cold air following him. He was shivering and breathing hard.

"Where the hell have you been, Leo?"

"Don't ask," he snarled as he leaned over me, grabbed the front of my dressing gown, and pushed me backwards as hard as he could. His features were contorted and he was drunk. I thought he might have been sick, as I could smell vomit somewhere on his dishevelled shirt. I knew he had been with another woman too.

I was horrified at the state of him. "Please don't wake the children, Leo," I asked as I released his hands and backed away from him.

He swayed to get his feet moving forward, and in an exaggerated whisper said, "Mustn't wake the children."

I was afraid that the angry boil was about to burst, so I went into the bathroom, locked the door and sat shivering. I knew that he would have another drink and collapse. I waited until I could hear no more movement. Stiff with tension, I tentatively opened the door and tiptoed along the corridor to look in the spare bedroom where he usually collapsed. As I expected he was snoring loudly, half undressed, his shirt and socks on the floor, his trousers draped around his hips. I was relieved and took myself to bed but was unable to sleep. I vowed that I would not allow this to happen again.

Without waking me, he'd left for work very early the next morning.

That evening I'd taken Lily to her dance class, and Dan was staying with a friend overnight.

I pulled myself together and decided that I wouldn't cry, but would put a rational argument to Leo to get some help.

Lily and I arrived home to a half-prepared dinner, and Leo was mowing the lawn. He came rushing in and pulled me into his arms as Lily rushed up the stairs to practise her pliés.

He moved me into the kitchen and said, "I'm so sorry, Evelyn. I'll make it up to you, I promise."

I wasn't going to be seduced back to him that easily. I pushed him away from me but he held onto my arms.

"Evelyn, please listen," he pleaded.

"Why should I? So, you're sorry and you're not denying that you've been playing around again?" I hissed. "Who is it this time? A local barmaid or someone else's wife? Don't think I don't know. This is a small place and people talk."

"It's not like that. I got a bit carried away, that's all, and I'm really sorry."

I was so angry. I pulled myself away from his grip and backed away from him. "Stop saying you're sorry. I don't want contrition. I want to understand. Love doesn't have to be perfect but it needs to be true. I want you to get some help."

"What for?"

"For your disgusting, aggressive behaviour and your drinking problem."

"I don't have a drinking problem."

I felt my insides shrink at his denial, "You *do* have a problem," I snapped. "I might as well talk to the bloody wallpaper. You don't love me enough to listen. It is getting out of control. Why can't you see that?"

My head was reeling. Anger was throbbing through my body, so acute was the feeling of betrayal. I was getting hysterical and there was a part of me that wanted to punch him. If anyone could incite violence in me where there was none before, it was Leo. I lifted a fist and banged it against his chest as I shouted, "I was a fool to marry you, I know, but you haven't given our marriage a chance. It might mean nothing to you but I bloody well care about it... and... I care about you. I've every right to disapprove of your affairs, the endless drinking, and the way you ignore me. I can't put up with it any longer. You're disgusting and you do have a problem," I shouted as I brought my other fist up and hit him as hard as I could.

He stood still and didn't argue or disagree or say a word. I was furious. In spite of my resolve I was crying with anger and frustration and I couldn't stop. "And I always make excuses for you and tell myself that you've had a difficult emotional past. But there is really no excuse, you just won't help yourself... you're just a sad, angry individual. What you inflict on me when you have been drinking is destroying me and my love for you. Are you going to explain yourself? What the fuck is going on with us? I want to know. It's time this was sorted once and for all."

I stood furiously with my nose dripping, waiting for a response, but before Leo could say a word, Lily came rushing down the stairs, her face flushed with worry. "What's happening? Are you fighting?"

I'd got so carried away in my anger that I had forgotten about Lily. I took a deep breath to calm myself.

"It's okay, Lily, just needed to get something off my chest. Back in a mo'." I quickly retreated to the garden, rubbing away my tears and sniffing loudly.

CHAPTER 16
Coward

LEO

I couldn't even remember coming home the previous night. I'd returned in a bad mood because Mo had kicked me out after I'd been sick in her kitchen. It was cold and wet but I remember very little.

Waking in our spare room at six a.m., I knew I'd behaved badly and, coward that I was, I fled. I went to McDonald's for breakfast before I headed off to work.

On my return to the empty house that evening, I'd set to and started preparing the supper. I was ashamed of myself for being such a fool.

When Evelyn and Lily came home I could see that she was angry and upset. She refused to speak to me until Lily disappeared upstairs. As usual all I could do was apologise. "I'm so sorry." I'd learned not to argue with Evelyn. What could I say, anyway? I knew she was right about me and far cleverer with words than I. She could analyse the situation, verbally address it, whereas I could not. Above all, Evelyn hated to be ignored, and so, with the skills of a master, she berated me.

When Lily had come rushing down the stairs, upset on hearing her mother's angry words, she stood and glowered at me as Evelyn headed for the garden.

I'd taken her hand and told her calmly, "It's all right, darling, I think Mum's a bit hormonal and I haven't been here to help her much lately."

With a disbelieving look, Lily pulled her hand from mine and rushed out after Evelyn. I followed, distressed that she should be alarmed, but Evelyn had mopped her face, turned and hugged Lily tightly.

Lily let out a shuddering sob. "Mum, what's going on?

577

You're upset."

"It's all right, baby. We're not really fighting, just a little disagreement, that's all. Everyone has disagreements sometimes." She gave me a warning look over Lily's shoulder. The last thing in the world Evelyn would allow was for her children to get upset.

Having calmly reassured her, Evelyn silently retreated to the kitchen to continue with the cooking. Lily went back to her room, so I went to finish cutting the lawn.

"I'm sorry, I shouldn't have spoken to you like that, or hit you, but this really can't go on," Evelyn told me quietly later that evening.

I accepted her apology, knowing I didn't deserve it, but I decided that she was right and I shouldn't inflict my poor behaviour on her any longer.

As the three of us sat down to dinner, our smart twelve-year-old Lily was concerned. "Is everything okay now?" she asked.

"Of course it is, Lil," I said, pushing my face into a smile, but I felt so guilty. "I shouldn't upset your lovely Mum. But we're sorted now."

Evelyn, too, reassured Lily with a smile. She had calmed down during dinner but had told me later, "You do need some help you know, Leo. This can't go on."

"I know," was all I could reply.

CHAPTER 17
Leo's Mother

EVELYN

Day by day the atmosphere in the house grew worse, and Leo had done nothing about getting help. It was a week later when things came to the boil again. Just as we sat down to eat, the phone started to ring, and Dan and Lily had come bounding downstairs ready for their supper.

Leo answered the telephone, looked at me and mouthed 'Mother'.

For Lily's sake I pasted a smile on my face. Dan was busy hunting for the tomato sauce.

"Who is it on the phone?" asked Lily, always wanting to know everything that was going on.

"It's Leo's mummy, Grandma Jeanette."

"Oh, her." Lily knew that I found Jeanette hard work, and Lily herself had proclaimed that she wasn't like most Grandmas.

Even though they lived in Doncaster now, Granny and Granddad Joyner still came every month, just for tea or to take the children to the cinema or the theatre, whereas we had only seen Jeanette here once since the wedding. Of course, Dan and Lily weren't Leo's children, so it was different, but we'd tried really hard to include her into our family. We'd invited her to stay, visited her in Manchester several times, taking presents and flowers, but her constant criticism of everyone she knew or had dealings with wore us all down. She took little notice of the children, and we usually left earlier than we intended and headed for Chester Zoo or the beach at Blackpool.

Whenever Jeanette phoned she only ever wanted to talk to Leo, so I knew that he would be ages.

We'd finished our meal before Leo got off the phone, and

Lily and Dan took themselves off to their rooms to do their homework. Leo put the telephone down carefully, so as not to show his frustration, but I could see the hard set of his mouth. His mother had obviously been working her power over him.

"What did she have to say, Leo?" I asked.

He sighed, "Oh, the usual. Why haven't I phoned? – I am obviously too busy to think about her needs? – She is lonely on her own – I am not being a very good son by being so far away – She needs help with the garden. Why the hell she doesn't pay for someone to help her, I don't know. She can afford it. I'd pay for a bloody gardener if she would get someone, but no, she would rather have a go at me."

"Have you still got issues with your mother? Is that it?" I asked him slowly, watching his stricken face.

"What do you mean, issues?"

"Well, you don't have the best relationship in the world, do you?"

"Perhaps not. Why would we? She doesn't care about me. Never did. She didn't want me, you know that. She likes to make me feel guilty as if –"

"Well, that's why you don't understand loving at all, isn't it, Leo?" I interrupted sarcastically. "We learn about love from our mothers. Jeanette loves no one but herself. She sits on the sidelines of life, smirking at the players. Her specialty is making people feel bad about anything she can. I'm probably the only one that she hasn't reduced to tears of frustration, and that is only due to the fact that I am perfectly confident about who I am. Why do you let her make you feel unloved and unlovable?"

I felt myself flush with anger as I watched his miserable face. I was convinced it was her lack of love for him that made him treat women the way he did. I knew that Leo had never felt any affection from his mother and I couldn't gauge it, as I'd had the love of both parents and had been treasured for my whole life. Having no father in his life meant everything he'd learned came from his mother. I felt protective towards him but resented the impact it had on our relationship.

"I know she didn't want you. Loads of babies are born unwanted. So what? It doesn't mean that no woman will want you, the real you, or that you have to pretend so that you *can* be loved. You bend over backwards to get her approval. You know you never will, but she has taught you to obey, be dutiful, but not how to love. You don't really love her at all. I have never once seen your mother touch you. Do you know that, Leo? That's not normal. She's as cold as a bucket of ice."

"Oh, come off it, Evelyn. What makes you such a fucking expert?"

I could see that he was getting angry now and I didn't care.

"Being married to you, that's what! I wanted your love so much, but you pretend, pretend and go on pretending. Because your mother didn't love you? Well, so what? It doesn't give you permission to behave badly towards me, does it? Or cheat on me, does it?" I insisted. "How do you think you make me feel with your false promises and declarations of love, and then you go elsewhere for sex when you've had a drink?" He stood facing me with a look of such absolute desolation, but I couldn't let go of my anger, "Say something." I waited. He said nothing. "It's the thing I most detest about you – your sad inability to respond or get angry or even look as if you understand what I'm saying." When I got nothing but a blank, stony stare, I raised my voice into an angry whisper and stormed off to the kitchen.

"You're such an arsehole. I can't stand it any longer."

CHAPTER 18
Pain and Loss 1998

LEO

We limped through the next few months, my moods getting worse and my inability to love her in the way she wanted more obvious. Becoming more and more frustrated as time passed, we were both clearly unhappy, but as much as I wanted to change, I continued to see Mo and occasionally others every time I'd had too much to drink. What possessed me, I couldn't tell, but I used the bottle like a comfort blanket and it became a vicious circle yet again.

Evelyn began to suffer from severe headaches, and I knew that it was because of the stress I was causing her. And I had started to dream again. Sad, violent dreams about pain and loss, guilt and remorse. Not quite the same dreams as when I was a child, but they concerned me. I would lie shaking and fearful to wait for the real and illusory worlds to fall back into place, but my relief on waking did not entirely dispel the fears that the dreams evoked.

When I was very young and I lived with my mother in our tiny flat, I slept in a room no bigger than a cupboard just off the living room. I had bad dreams, terrible nightmares. More often than not it would be the same one that would terrify me, so much so that I would wake up screaming.

A great curved knife would appear in my dream as I ran and played with a small horse that was my friend and playmate. We were in a desert full of prickly bushes. Even though I was hot and sweaty, we played and ran together, jumping and sliding in the soft, sandy hillocks. Suddenly the huge curved knife would appear, slashing and slicing, swooping up and around my body, trying to cut me to pieces. The sun was high in the sky as the knife flew above my head and swooped downward, but it pierced my horse instead of me. He cried and whinnied in pain. I was bereft. Then, falling into a great dark hole, blackness surrounded me as I fell deeper and deeper, my head spinning. All I could hear was my beloved horse crying. My terror as I woke from this terrible place left me sobbing and afraid.

My mother would shout from her armchair, "What's all the racket about? You're not crying, are you?" And if I continued to make a noise she would rise with a sigh and lock the cupboard door.

Of course I was crying! I had lost something precious.

CHAPTER 19
November 1998

EVELYN

One Saturday in the autumn, Dan and Lily were going out with Aunty Sally. She had promised to take them to Flamingo Land while I studied for my next exam.

After another evening's row, Leo had been quiet and unresponsive, and we had gone to bed without any resolution. I was still determined to encourage him to get some help. I'd heard of a very good therapist/counsellor, and the night before had left her card next to Leo on his bedside table.

Feeling totally miserable I dragged myself out of bed and organised the children for their outing. They had been looking forward to it for weeks, and when Sally arrived I managed to see them off with a smile.

Today had to be better, so I made the coffee and forced myself into a positive frame of mind.

"Good morning, darling," I said to Leo's sleeping bulk as I put the cup of coffee next to him on the bedside table. He'd opened one eye and glared at me for a few seconds, readjusted the duvet and slumped back into an untidy lump. He looked pasty and tired, and I wondered again at his ability to drink so much and never have a headache.

"Coffee, Leo," I said as brightly as I could manage, but he ignored me, so I left the cup and went and sat in our sunny kitchen, watching the birds and wondering how I'd allowed this to go on for so long. I should have chucked him out the first time I knew that he was playing around. It didn't make sense. I was usually so strong and he'd tested me to the limit. My world seemed to be dissolving around me.

Sipping my coffee, mulling over the arguments and rows that we'd been having, I started to cry again. Scruffy nuzzled her wet nose into my hand, instinctively knowing my torment. I bent and wrapped my arms around her soft, shaggy body. She had a warm, reassuring doggy smell that comes from a healthy life. Her tail spun at my attention and she gave me a slobbery kiss.

"Come on then, Scruff, we'll go for a stroll in the woods and walk off my terrible feelings."

I went upstairs to tell Leo that I was going out. The card I had left him was on the bedroom floor. He was seated on the edge of the bath, still in his pyjamas, sipping his coffee and saying nothing. Even his body language was blank. He looked up at the ceiling and didn't even register I was there.

"Leo, I'm going out with Scruffy." He didn't move or look at me. Totally ignored my presence. I waited.

"You bastard... speak to me," I tried to curb my impatience.

Leo turned and looked at me steadily, without a shred of emotion, and said, "What do you want me to say?"

I could feel an icy knot forming in my stomach, and his question made me want to run away and hide.

How could he say that? As if I could tell him the words I wanted to hear, and he could repeat them, and everything would be all right. I was wasting my breath again.

At that moment it was hard to see the man I loved. He looked sad and isolated, boxed in his deepening, dark moodiness, but I couldn't take it anymore. I'd lavished so much feeling into our situation, I felt exhausted.

"Fuck you," I shouted, and ran, slamming the door as I went and headed downstairs. Scruffy was still waiting patiently for her walk.

It really was time to make some serious decisions. We couldn't go on like this. My children were growing fast and they needed me to be happy and capable. My next exam was looming and I wanted to do some serious studying if I was going to qualify. Things had to change.

It was a cold November day so I wrapped myself well,

grabbed Scruffy's lead and headed for the door. I spent the next hour walking and climbing and making myself think seriously about our future, while Scruffy enjoyed the special smells in the woods and the pleasure of chasing rabbits. I felt calmer when I returned and decided to try to talk to Leo again. As it turned out, I didn't need to make any decisions. Leo had already made other plans.

The following day he broke the news. "I've been banned from driving for a year and I've been given a month's notice from Robert Preston & Son. I'm about to lose my job. I didn't tell you because I knew exactly what you would say. You've been warning me about drink driving ever since I met you. Well, you were right. I got stopped a month ago..."

"Oh, Leo," was all I could say, but he held up his hands.

"But the good news is, I've been offered a job in Milan for a year starting next January. It's a company of architects and builders that specialise in large car parks and public buildings with a project about to start. I can live in the city and won't need a car as Milan has brilliant transport systems, trains, buses, trams, the lot, so they won't expect me to drive at all."

He hesitated a moment before telling me, "I've already said yes. It will give us the space that we're obviously needing."

Leo had told me all this without looking at me. He didn't want to see my hurt, but I was no longer prepared to show it anyway. But then he added, "You could come with me."

"No, I think not. Why? You said it yourself, we need some space away from each other. Even if I wanted to, I couldn't just leave. What about Dan and Lily? I couldn't take them out of school, and I'm studying, as you well know. I need it to keep me sane."

I felt as if a weight was lifting off my shoulders. I'd be happy to see him go. I could get on with my life without the endless worry and disappointment. He was on the way to self-destruction and pulling me with him. Our relationship had deteriorated too far.

I knew, too, that he was getting sex elsewhere. I wondered how he'd feel if I found someone else, so next morning I thought I would test the waters.

"It's good that you are going away as I'm already involved with someone else. Well, not really involved yet," I lied, "just having an odd meal or a coffee and chat really, but I have kissed him, and he wants me to go to bed with him. He's very good-looking."

"Really, is that all?" Leo had said as he buttered his toast. I could see the slow burn of jealousy that was creeping up his spine, but he didn't alter what he was doing, and calmly asked, "Okay, tell me why."

"What the fuck do you mean? Why? Why do you think I'm telling you? To show you that I'm still attractive to other men, good-looking, sexy men who like me. I want to make you jealous, Leo. I know that must sound immature to you and it is. I know it is, but I want you to get angry, to be possessive and caring and to know how it feels to be mortified that the person you love could consider having sex with someone else. But look at you," I waved my arms at him. "You look as if you don't care at all." I had broken down into angry tears again. "You really don't care, do you?"

"I do care," he said, but still made no move.

"I don't want to go with you, anyway," I said bitterly. "I don't think I want to be with you anymore."

I know I sounded distant and cold. It broke my heart because I didn't really mean it, but I continued, "I'm not actually seeing anyone else. I only said it to get some sort of reaction from you and you let me down again. So, if you want to go, go. You can buy really cheap wine in Italy so you'll be able to drink yourself to death if you want. And the good thing is I won't be there to watch you doing it."

CHAPTER 20
On the Wagon 1998

LEO

That morning, the door banging behind her had brought me round. I'd watched her brittle, determined figure walk away with Scruffy and knew that we had to have a break from each other.

I was causing her distress and was sick at heart with it. I wanted to shout, 'Don't go, Evelyn.' But the words wouldn't come. I couldn't imagine being away from her, but knew that we were heading for disaster if things didn't alter. I hadn't told her that I was about to make some radical changes to our life. Would she be happy about it? I wasn't sure, but I knew she wasn't going to put up with me for much longer. I had a great deal to do. Firstly, I needed to concentrate on making a good impression on the company with whom I was about to start work. Aldo Rossini's Architecture was well known in Milan and, working there for them, I'd be earning a good deal more than in Darlington that was for sure! It was sheer chance that I had seen the advertisement in the Architects' Journal and found they were interviewing in Newcastle. I hadn't told Evelyn, but didn't quite expect the response I got when I told her.

It would take a few weeks to organise because it was nearly Christmas again. The job would start officially on the second of January, so I made a few other decisions. I didn't want to leave without putting things right.

Firstly, I would stop visiting Mo, and secondly, cut off the short relationship I'd been having with Nina, a delectable little secretary who had a convenient basement flat in Darlington. I'd got into the habit of popping in there after a couple of drinks, for an hour or so, before going home.

She was a pretty, dark-haired, raving nymphomaniac

who admitted that her day wasn't complete without a good fuck. I could certainly oblige there!

Other than her body she didn't have much going for her, as she was singularly lacking in any sort of taste. She dressed as if she had just fallen out of a charity sack, and her home was a flashy, oriental-inspired mistake. Her sole topic of conversation, when she wasn't partaking of my penis, was her passion for Indian food and Rod Stewart, neither of which held my attention for more than a minute or two.

She was devastated when I told her that I was going abroad to work, as she had decided that we really should get together on a more permanent basis. She'd happily forgotten that I had told her right at the beginning that I was married.

It was only when Evelyn told me that she was seeing someone else I had felt for a moment that I shouldn't go, but I didn't react as I was meant to, which brought about her denial. She loved me and she wouldn't cheat, I knew. It was me who cheated.

I stopped drinking alcohol and returned to the lime and sodas to show Evelyn that I didn't have a problem at all!

CHAPTER 21
Leo's Departure 1999

EVELYN

He left a week after Christmas, but surprisingly it had been one of the nicest Christmases and New Years we'd ever spent together. Leo hadn't had any alcohol, didn't disappear in the evenings and came straight home from work. He collected a Christmas tree, helped me decorate it, and we'd shopped together for presents.

On the surface we appeared to be a happy, well-adjusted couple, but I was twisted with jealousy and anger, and in his unusual state of sobriety I could see that Leo was feeling guilty and afraid. The atmosphere was forced and uncomfortable, but we managed to not let it affect Dan and Lily who were excited about Christmas.

Lily and I spent nearly a whole day making chocolates and sweets to give to Grandma Sonya and Granny and Granddad Joyner. We even made a pretty box up for Grandma Jeanette in Manchester.

On our visit to her the week before Christmas with gifts and good wishes, all she said was, "Yes, well, I for one will be glad when it's over."

Her only advice to Leo about going to Milan was, "Don't eat too much of that disgusting Italian food, Leo. You'll get fat like Pavarotti."

"I like Italian food, Mother," he had laughed, but I could see that he was disappointed that she hadn't asked when he would be back or suggest that she might miss him.

"I suppose it will be too expensive for you to telephone me and make sure I'm all right while you're away?" she asked sarcastically.

"I'll call every week as I always do." I knew he would too.

Granny and Granddad Joyner spent Christmas Eve with

us and left us a pile of presents including one for Leo. My mother Sonya arrived Christmas morning, and Leo and I put on our best happily married faces, and pretended great excitement at the suggestion that the children and I would whizz to Milan at every opportunity.

We carried on the pretence of perfect married bliss throughout the holiday. Neither Leo nor I ate much and rarely spoke to one another, using our visitors and the children as our allies and smiling a great deal, exclaiming at our gifts and generally play-acting at being excited about the future. I kept busy, but I think I was counting the hours as the cold knot of anxiety increased. I went to bed early, got up early, and walked a great deal with Scruffy in between preparing vegetables and cooking soups and stews from the leftover turkey and ham. I made cakes and pies, stuffed mushrooms and attempted a soufflé.

The moment I sat still and thought about the future I found myself in a ditch of self-pity. I wasn't usually like that at all, and could always lift myself out of any sort of low with my positive affirmations and gratitude for my life, my beautiful children, family and good friends.

Regardless of how busy I kept myself, I was aware that my feelings could flare into anger or tears at any time, as I still had a gaping wound and a painful icy lump burning inside me.

An outsider watching us might assume a perfect family. While we ate, Dan and Lily prattled on about their pets, their exams and the classes they would attend in the new year. I found myself grateful for their noisy chatter, covering up the silence that had descended on Leo and me.

Watching Leo fork his food into his mouth, the mouth that I had kissed with so much love and passion, I visualized him kissing his 'other' women and something inside of me snapped. With chilling clarity I knew this would have to end.

Up until the final day I hadn't shed a single tear at the thought of him going. I had a duty to carry on as normal, especially where Dan and Lily were concerned.

Leaving Leo at Teesside Airport was difficult. He looked so unhappy, but I knew that it was for the best. When the children and I arrived home, I was bereft and sobbed uncontrollably until Dan put his arms around me and said, "Don't worry, Mum, I'll look after you."

I suppose it was arrogant of me to think I knew what was going on for him; I was beginning to understand his lack of self-worth and deliberate use of alcohol to hide his vulnerability, but I wasn't prepared to let him cheat on me and put such a strain on my life.

Ridiculous, I knew, but I missed him so.

CHAPTER 22
Working in Milan January 1999

LEO

Although I was sad to leave, I knew that no amount of being sorry would make things better.

I'd decided that while I was away, I would do my best to get my problems in hand. Well, my penis at the very least, because I had every intention of remaining faithful.

Evelyn's bitter remark about drinking myself to death had also been a warning, and I was very careful for the first few weeks in Milan to limit myself with my alcohol intake. I immersed myself in my work and got on well in my new role. I had a good team, was well liked and started to feel some purpose, as the job was far more challenging and much more interesting than what I'd been doing in Darlington. It gave me the incentive to improve myself. So I filled my evenings getting to grips with the projects I was working on and I started to learn Italian.

After a month I moved into a little flat just outside Milan and struck out to find some good places to spend my spare time. The venues were endless. Pretty little taverns and cafes, rough-looking places that served fabulous wines and where the freshly prepared pizzas, pastas and vegetables were wonderful. I met an eclectic mix of people, many working in the city on contracts like myself.

I missed Evelyn and telephoned at every opportunity, told her what I was doing and how positive I felt about the future. I assured her that all would be well and we would make our marriage work, be even better, because the separation would give me a chance to get to grips with my problems. I did believe it, but as I settled into my new life I found endless reasons not to limit my alcohol, and the women in Milan were exceedingly glamorous and available.

No one kids as well as a kidder! However, nearly three

months passed and I was rejoicing at the 'new' me who had not been unfaithful. I *had* masturbated every time I took a shower, the erotic allure of women still at the forefront of my mind. I limited my alcohol intake, and on only two occasions got home without remembering how. I was proud of myself, in fact so proud that I wanted Evelyn to come and visit to see for herself how much progress I'd made.

I telephoned and asked her the following day. "Please, Evelyn, come and see me. Come for the Easter holiday. I promise I won't drink while you're here."

"Really? Could you do that?" she enquired.

"For you, yes, of course I could. I miss you so. I couldn't even look at another woman again. You're all I will ever need."

I believed it was true and I didn't have a problem with not drinking. I'd proved over Christmas that I was quite capable of abstaining. For Evelyn, I knew, it would mean so much if I could do without a drink whilst we were together.

"Bring the kids, the flat's not very big, but I can borrow camp beds for them. I'll take Dan to San Siro Stadium to see Milan play football. You and Lily would probably like Herb Ritts's photo exhibition in the Palazzo della Ragione. There are also lovely parks and places to go while I am working. I can probably get a few days off. Please come, Evelyn. I miss you all so much."

I knew that having them there would help me to stay on the straight and narrow.

CHAPTER 23
Easter 1999

EVELYN

I have to admit that I was concerned when I agreed to go to Milan. When he left I was so sure our life together was finished and was still so bitter and angry with him. I remembered what a relief it had been when he'd gone. My unhappiness at his infidelity and inability to explain had diluted into something else. I'd convinced myself that whatever I felt for him was not good for me and I didn't want it anymore. His absence had allowed me to focus on my own needs, to spend more time with Dan and Lily and to breathe back my own confidence as I had resolved to do. But it was really the children who decided for me. Dan had spoken to Leo on the telephone and the suggestion had been made.

Dan's eyes lit with excitement. "Will we get to see Paolo Maldini play? Right. Great, we will definitely come. I'll convince Mum."

Dan handed me the phone with an enormous grin on his face. I knew it had to be something to do with football, but was not sure exactly who Paolo Maldini was.

"Footballer in Milan," he mouthed as he whizzed up the stairs to tell Lily that we were going to Italy.

They were so excited about the prospect of flying to Milan and seeing Leo in his new environment that I couldn't let them down.

As we walked through the airport gates, there he stood, his suntan giving him a healthy, sun-kissed look, his welcoming smile completely overlaying my fears of seeing him again. He held out his arms to me and I stepped back into our marriage.

"I've missed you, so much." His expression showed me

that he had.

"Have you, my darling?" I whispered. I was happy to see him looking so healthy and pleased to see us.

"You two as well," he said as he hugged Dan and Lily who beamed and hugged him back, excited at the prospect of us all being together. I knew they'd missed him too. The holiday started well and as his arms encircled me and we kissed, the familiarity of him warmed me yet again. I felt the soft press of his lips, smelled his familiar scent. I loved the smell of his skin better than any perfume.

Later, our lovemaking was heightened by all the emotional rawness of the reconciliation. Holding him tightly I felt the intense excitement of our bodies. We needed to touch and indulge each other, renew the certainty of our love. No talking or confrontation, no reference to his previous behaviour could bring us close.

We only had five days there, but it renewed my feeling of absolute certainty of our bond and our need to be together. I loved him so sincerely. I found it extraordinary that I could think it so after the events of the previous year. Already it seemed to me they were misted into nothingness. But it *had* all been real, and a tiny voice warned me yet again, *It won't last. It can't last. It's too fragile to cling to.*

Perhaps if I stayed loyal and loving we could repair the damage and hold our marriage together. The world is full of damaged, unwanted people, and without those who were strong enough to help, by being capable and sane, no one would be safe.

I made a mental promise to myself that while Leo was putting so much effort into reform that I too would try to develop more understanding and empathy, instead of constantly being hurt. After all, it was his burden, not mine, but I would be there for him.

Dan and Lily loved being in Italy, and during the daytime we explored and enjoyed Milan and all it had to offer. Dan's visit to the San Siro Stadium with Leo was the highlight of his holiday and he couldn't stop talking about it. He'd managed to get Paolo Maldini's and George Weah's autographs and he was beyond ecstatic. Lily and I had visited the Milan Zoo, fed ostriches and monkeys, and arrived back at the flat exhausted and full of inspiration, her passion for animals renewed her ambition to be a vet.

The pizzas that Leo and Dan brought home were devoured, and we each laughed at the others' enthusiasm about our day out.

In the evening we strolled the parks and open spaces, found fabulous places to eat and even indulged in an Italian film, '*Il tenente dei carabinieri*', with subtitles, which we didn't really understand but Leo explained it all on our way home.

"Not much to it really," he concluded, "two funny cops trying to stop a robbery."

"Well, it was funny," said Lily, "but I liked the dog in it best."

"There wasn't a dog in it," retorted Dan.

"Yes, there was. He was called Pejay."

"Was there a dog in it?" Leo asked, teasing Lily and making her pull a face at him. "Was there, Evelyn?"

"No idea," I laughed as we held each other close, bathing in the warmth of not only the evening but of the fun that we'd had together. I thought it boded well for our future.

True to his word, throughout the time we were there Leo didn't drink, and behaved in such a way that I couldn't imagine that he would resort to his previous behaviour.

How wrong I was.

CHAPTER 24
Getting Fit

LEO

I was happy and satisfied with the way the holiday had turned out. I hadn't had a single drink of alcohol whilst we were together, and Dan and Lily had had a wonderful time. They were growing so fast and kept us amused and busy. Both were so smart and good-looking like their mother. I missed them all, so in the days that followed I immersed myself in work.

The weeks passed without me losing my way too much, and I started to look forward to my leave at the end of June. The job wouldn't be finished until December, but I'd already been offered another project for the following year. I'd decided to see how things went with Evelyn before telling her, or even asking her. It was important to know how she felt about me being away for so long.

Looking at myself in the mirror after they had left, I was far from pleased with what I saw. My mother was right. With all the fabulous pasta and pizza dishes available here I'd put on a great deal of weight. I decided that I should find a gym and get fit before my summer leave, so I joined a small local establishment called The Studio. The fact that I had cut down on my drinking inspired me to visit often, and within a couple of weeks I began to feel the difference.

I telephoned Evelyn as often as I could, and she was encouraging and enthusiastic about how well I was doing.

All through May and until the end of June I worked hard at my health and fitness and managed to drop about twelve pounds. I flew back to Teesside looking better than I had done for years. Evelyn was there to meet me and we greeted each other with absolute certainty that we had overcome our problems and all would be well. Even though little had changed in my feelings about myself, I now felt more in control. I knew I had to maintain my resolve or I would lose my family. I spent time doing jobs around the house and renewing my contacts at the cricket club, but kept my drinking to the minimum. This was harder for me than abstaining altogether because once I had a drink I could rarely stop. Did this mean that I had to stay on the straight and narrow and give up altogether?

That was unthinkable!

But being back home and in such a good place mentally and physically, we obtained a closeness that we hadn't had for a long time.

A new massage couch arrived and we turned our rather unused dining room into a therapy room. I helped Evelyn design a leaflet with the treatments she was going to offer and I was quietly proud of her achievements in such a short time. I found myself ferrying Dan and Lily to the after-school activities while Evelyn studied for her qualification.

I was a willing guinea pig, but the massage practice, although started seriously, usually ended up a lot of fun. Our passionate lovemaking brought us close again and we had an amazingly happy time.

CHAPTER 25
Feeling Good

EVELYN

On our return home from Milan I had started my massage course in York. I knew from the very first class that this was something that I was naturally good at. I'd never imagined that I could enjoy it so much. It was like being offered a gift. The gift of hands-on healing. I saw how people were transformed by professional massage, turning them from the grey stiffness of pain and tension-wracked bodies when they arrived to soft, smiling, relaxed fluidity after a good treatment.

The course would take over a year to complete but I practised on anyone who would lie down for me. I finished my anatomy and physiology, took my exam and passed it easily. I was happy and optimistic about the future.

Time passed quickly after our wonderful holiday in Milan and I missed Leo, even though at times I felt that I was perched on a mountainside in a high wind. I would catch my breath as I remembered something he'd said or done when he was drunk, how I felt knowing of his intimacies with other women, and having no understanding of why.

But as I climbed into the shower on a sunny May morning, I realised how good I felt about life. I was busy doing something I loved, had some really good friends, it was a beautiful day, but, best of all, Leo seemed to be more settled. Why that should make such a difference to how I felt, I couldn't understand, but it did. It's one of the unexplained mysteries of my life that this man should have such a profound effect on me. His mood, good or bad, had an immediate impact. He lived so far away and yet he could affect me so much.

I was worried that the Easter break had been too short a

time to renew and heal our marriage, but Leo assured me that he was still not drinking too much, had joined a gym, and was looking forward to his leave in June.

It's amazing how little we know about what provokes our responses. But what I'd come to realise was that I couldn't fight it. I knew that he was leading a life without me and I had absolutely no doubt about the strength of his feelings for me. Whether I could translate those feelings into my own interpretation of love I didn't know, but I read somewhere that, 'just because someone doesn't love you the way you expect to be loved, doesn't mean that they don't love you.'

I couldn't wait for him to come home. I'd been so uplifted by our visit at Easter. The assignment was obviously helping Leo, as he was achieving high applause for his designs and marketing plans. He'd already been told that there was a possibility of another year there. I wasn't sure how I felt about that, but the salary was not to be sniffed at and Leo seemed to be making good personal progress.

By the time he arrived back for his holiday he looked like a different person, toned, fit and healthy. My optimism soared.

Although the visit was good and I took time off to spend with Leo, I still felt that his drinking wasn't yet completely under control. Only once did it get out of hand. We'd gone to Scarborough for a weekend with my mother, and whilst there Leo drank far too much.

"What's it like when I can't have a drink on holiday?" he whined when I complained. I walked away as he belched loudly.

I didn't hear what he said next, but Dan had and was furious. He told me later that Leo had said to him, "It was that horrible fish pie that your grandmother made. It's given me heartburn."

Dan wouldn't allow anyone to be rude to his grandmother, so he'd steered her away from Leo, saying,

"Come on, Gran. Don't you take any notice of him. He's pickled. Everyone loves your fish pie."

I was disappointed in Leo, but eventually he fell asleep in the back garden and we left him to sober up. He did apologise, of course, and my lovely Mum was charming and conciliatory.

"Perhaps there was a little too much pepper in it, dear." She smiled at Leo's worried frown.

Other than that brief occasion, the leave went well and we were both sad and quiet when he went back to Milan in the middle of July. Unless we went for an October half-term visit, we wouldn't see him again until Christmas, when we would have to make a decision about our future. Being away and completely involved in the job obviously suited him, and I didn't want his new confidence in his body and his career to dissipate. The long-term future still seemed uncertain, but slowly over the last year he'd made such an effort that I was proud of him.

CHAPTER 26
Meeting Sheila

LEO

Returning from my June holiday I was pleased with life. We'd had a happy time together.

Back in Milan I had another big project to set under way, so, for the whole of July and August I spent a great deal of time in my tiny, air-conditioned office. My flat had no such luxury and the weather was unremittingly hot and humid, so I bought a large fan that enabled me to sleep at night.

The summer passed and I continued to go to the gym, and although my drinking had gradually increased again, I felt I was in control. I was beginning it find it a strain being on my own, and my initial resolve was slowly weakening.

The evening when I first met Sheila had been a stunningly hot day in late September. She didn't attract me at all at first, but as she lifted her eyes and smiled, I knew she would be available.

A colleague from Rossini's who had joined me for a drink had introduced us.

Sober, I wouldn't have looked at her twice, but two days later I met her again in The Neapolitan Bar. I was on my own and I'd just arrived at that cushioned glow of feeling where I could breathe again after a taxing day at work, and felt that life was turning out just fine. The result of a bottle of red and two martinis.

Sheila looked good; her rounded, busty body encased in a chocolate brown linen dress that just touched her fleshy knees, her soft blonde hair tied back, and a large smile of recognition as she swayed toward me. It set off a firecracker of excitement in my boxer shorts. She was brilliantly sexy and I dropped all pretence of indifference.

"Having a good day by the looks of it." She indicated the

seat beside me and I smiled my assent.

"I am. Join me. What would you like, pretty lady?"

"G and T please. Two, I think, if I'm going to catch up with you. Name's Sheila by the way, in case you've forgotten."

"Sheila, yes... how could I forget? A good-looking girl like you." And she did look good, surprisingly so, and I needed someone to talk to, didn't I? The familiar stirring in my loins gave me a favourable feeling. No harm in that.

"Are you meeting someone?" I asked.

"No, I come here every evening on my way home."

"Are you in Milan for long?"

"I have a year's assignment but I can extend it if I want to," she twinkled her reply. "I work for a broadcasting company and we're doing a documentary on the Mafia. I'm only in the office so don't see any action."

She laughed, and I noticed her lovely, even, white teeth. "Six months left on this assignment, possibly going to do another one afterwards about shark fishing or something. I love Italy and I'm enjoying Milan so far. How about you? Do you like working here?"

"It's getting better by the minute," I smiled.

"Good," she said, as she leaned forward and kissed me hard on the mouth.

I was taken aback, but, hell, I wasn't going to look this gift horse in the mouth. I kissed her back.

That is how easily it began. I don't remember having sex with her that first time. Did it count as infidelity if you couldn't remember doing it? I do recall the surprise and guilt waking up next to her the following morning, though. She was fast asleep and a wave of disgust overcame me. But it was only a fling, a bit of fun, a sport really and a form of release. In my mind it didn't encroach on my love for Evelyn. I have a knack for the game whilst I'm playing it. What harm could it do?

Over the next few weeks I allowed myself to revel in the sexual excitement she stirred in me. She was a lusty girl.

CHAPTER 27
November 1999

EVELYN

Leo had told me about the possibility of another assignment for Rossini's the following year. I wasn't sure whether it was a good idea to be apart for so long, but felt that time would tell. If he went, it would give me the chance to finish my courses, get my business started and give up the magazine articles that had become repetitive and dull. Three times in the past year I had to cover exhibitions of light industry and try to write something interesting about rubberised bolts, electric hair styling products and non-scratch pans.

It was time for me to concentrate on my practice. By October I was well into the massage course, working on my case studies with only four more to complete. Next I needed to finish my research projects, a comparison of holistic and modern methods of treating respiratory complaints, diabetes and irritable bowel syndrome.

Jude, Sally, Doreen and several other friends lined up willingly for me to practise my massage skills. I insisted that they gave me feedback. All agreed that to be touched in a loving, non-sexual way was nourishing and necessary. Even Dan concluded that it was 'rad', whatever that meant.

Sally had recently returned from India where she had had several massages. "Touch is too often neglected in our nanny society, with so many rules about non-contact," she told us. "In India everybody from little kids to old granddads practise massage. Apparently it is part of their learning and it's accepted as a natural human need. I had an Indian head massage in the street in Kerala, with dust and flowing traffic all around, but it still calmed me down. Everyone should do it. By the way, that was pretty darn good for an amateur," Sal said seriously to me after her treatment.

Almost everyone I practised on looked at my leaflet and booked a 'proper, paid-for' treatment even though I wasn't yet fully qualified.

Looking back, I knew from the start that I had a gift for helping people, but I needed to learn more so I enrolled for another course at the local college. It was called psycho-immunology, essentially about the mind/body links. Mostly it was psychology linked to physical symptoms and included investigating not only normal human behaviour but also mental and physical health.

'The Body follows the Mind' was the subject of the first class.

I was intrigued, and started to read self-help books and literature about positive thinking. The more I learned the more I wanted to study. The course was a long one and it would probably take me a couple of years to complete. So, in the meantime, I concentrated on my massage qualification. I was slowly increasing my knowledge of the use of natural products and essential oils to help healing and general health.

Our teacher at the college told us, "We could teach a monkey how to massage, but it takes a skilled practitioner to give a good treatment that will be beneficial on more than just a muscular level." I very soon learned that she was right, and not only practised my techniques but also my concentration and energy skills.

The psycho-immunology course taught me to listen carefully, be empathetic, non-judgmental, read between the lines and look for the underlying reasons that people got ill. Dis–ease took on a whole new meaning to me. Dis-against, ease-rest. I became obsessed with learning about human behaviour.

As feedback from my case studies was positive and rewarding, I grew more and more competent and confident. After a full day massaging clients, then ferrying Dan to football and Lily to gymnastics, I set to preparing some vegetables and chicken to make a quick stir-fry. My busy babes were always starving hungry when they got home. As I had finished my essay on the merits of complementary medicine versus modern, I was so pleased with my work that I wanted to tell Leo about it.

Having half an hour to spare before I picked up the children, and because I hadn't heard from Leo all week, I decided to telephone him. I knew he had another new project, on the outskirts of the city, so he was often really late home. Nevertheless, it was already nine o'clock there so I guessed he would be back. I wanted to tell him about my coursework and how I was learning about early conditioning and behaviour patterns. I was beginning to feel that perhaps he could benefit from reading some of my wonderful books. Shakti Gawain's 'Living in the Light', the amazing books by Louise L. Hay, and 'I'm OK – You're OK' by Thomas A. Harris M.D., who demonstrated ways of stripping old patterns of negative thinking that hampered good relationships.

I was enthused by the thought that instead of condemning Leo, I could perhaps help him.

The phone only rang once and Leo answered as if he'd been expecting a call.

"Oh, hi. It's you," he muttered, a note of disappointment in his voice. I could hear music and laughter in the background.

"Are you having a party?" I asked, as a knot tightened around my heart.

"No, no, but I'm a bit busy at t'e moment." He was obviously very drunk.

"Who is there with you?"

"A few mates from work and my special friend Sheila."

My earlier enthusiasm disappeared like smoke in the wind, and I was aware of my heart beating fast in my chest.

"Who the hell is Sheila?" I asked carefully. I could hear his visitors in the background, talking and laughing together.

"Jus' a few people around for a drink," he'd said again. "Sheila's a friend. I jus' told you."

"What's going on, Leo? Are you sleeping with her?" I knew instantly that he was. He laughed and it was for the benefit of whoever was listening

"Are you in-sin-uating something, Evelyn? Nuffing is going on," he slurred. "What are you in-sin-uating is going on? Why'd you get on the phone and spoil my day, eh? What's going on with you, eh? Passed your exams, have you? Good, well, I'm busy now." I heard him shift and knew he was about to cut me off.

"Don't you dare put the phone down on me," I said angrily, but the line went dead before I'd a chance to say more. My heart was pounding. I hated the familiar emotions that surfaced. I couldn't shake the mental image of him, laughing and pouring another drink and dismissing the interruption of my phone call totally from his mind, then carrying on with his evening without a care in the world.

Does he think I'm stupid? He's told me over and over that there was no other woman in the world for him, and yet here he was too busy having fun with Sheila to talk to me.

I wasn't the sort of woman to wrap myself in livid tangles of nasty imaginings, but with the cobweb of alibis and excuses about failed phone calls of the past, it was obvious that he was having another affair. He'd promised me that he wouldn't go down that road again, hadn't he?

I knew then that I must divorce him, but I'd seen many women emotionally knocked off their feet by divorce. I was still studying and too busy setting up my practice to be worrying about all that it entailed. Strangely it still didn't feel that it was the right time.

If we got divorced I knew I would sink into bitterness and depression, but for the moment we were far apart and I was feeling strong and capable.

Let him get on with it! I wasn't going to allow him back in the house ever again.

So much for trying to help him! He could go screw himself!

CHAPTER 28
December 1999

LEO

I was due my leave in December, as Rossini's would start their next project again in January. I'd decided that I would return as the job was exciting and my career self-esteem was high. I'd already made a decision to carry on working for Rossini's. Sheila, too, would be returning to Milan in January. I hadn't yet completely tired of her. That night of the party was a silly mistake, and if I hadn't drunk so much, Evelyn would never have known about Sheila.

Through my own stupidity Evelyn had refused to speak to me after informing me that I was not to return to Great Ayton under any circumstances. The day I was ready to return to Teesside, I called in a last-ditch attempt to convince her that all would be well.

"Go and stay with Jeanette," she'd shouted down the phone. "I will not have you here."

"Evelyn. Please, I don't want to go to my mother's. I want to come home for Christmas," I pleaded.

"Spend it with your 'special friend' Sheila then. You're not coming here. I've already told the kids that you've an emergency building project you have to deal with and can't come back. Go anywhere, but don't come here," she continued. "Keep out of my life. Do you understand, Leo? I will not be cheated on again."

CHAPTER 29
Christmas

EVELYN

This time there would be no turning back or forgiving, no more understanding. I wouldn't allow him to cajole, play the lonely neglected husband, or blackmail me emotionally as he had done previously. I remembered how it had been for us when he was home in June, and the lovely holiday we'd had at Easter. Although it was only a few months ago, our visit to Milan now seemed like a dream, a shadowy memory.

We'd made love, made promises about the future as we'd lain naked and happy together. Did it make sex more exciting for him knowing that he was leading a double life? Juggling with two women? The idea of his body linked to mine, his whispered vows of devotion and love, his sexy nuzzling made me feel sick to my stomach.

I had to find the strength to cope, but when he phoned I found it hard. He thought he could come back for Christmas and play happy families again. He kept phoning and pleading with me, but I'd made up my mind.

"Please, Evelyn," he begged, "I miss you. I need to come home. It'll only be a week, as I have to be back for the new job on the first of January."

"No," I shouted down the phone. I was furious that he could think he could come home and play happy families again.

His tone changed as he realized that I would not be persuaded. "It was you who chose not to come with me so that you could follow your own career. Do you know how I miss you all? How lonely I am? Do you expect me to sit by myself all the time?"

He knew he could make me feel guilty for not being with him, but I wasn't having it.

"So what?" I yelled.

"Who is it that is funding the mortgage and the bills? It's my home too, and you are the ones enjoying living and now working in it. Don't you think I'd rather be there with you?"

"Justifying your behaviour again, are you?" I retorted angrily.

"It must be so exhausting being such a bitch. No wonder we're living apart." He slammed the phone down.

I needed to focus on what was important. But what was that? I felt lost. Should I be with him for the sake of our marriage? No, I have my children, a life and a course to finish. My days are so much more peaceful without him, and my stress-induced headaches had all but disappeared. When I put the phone down, I sat with my hand across it, knowing that there was no point in beating myself up. How could I have been so naïve? He hadn't changed at all. He was a liar and a cheat and I'd heard all the excuses. All happy thoughts about Christmas were now blotted out, so I took myself to bed, making excuses to Dan and Lily of an impending cold and sore throat.

The following day was Christmas Eve and I was putting on a brave face, making a supreme effort not to be affected by Leo's absence. Packing all our gifts and my contribution to the Christmas food, we set off for Scarborough where we would spend the next week.

I didn't want Leo turning up on our doorstep in Great Ayton, even though he had promised to go to his mother's and not come anywhere near us. Nor did I want Dan or Lily to know that he was in England. They were concerned when I refused to post his presents and cards to Italy.

"We'll deliver them at half term… in person. It'll be fine," I told them. At that time I didn't know whether he would even still be in Milan.

Christmas Day was bright, cold and sunny, and as Mum watched the dinner, we marched down to the windy beach with our excited Scruffy, who was hung with pink ribbons and bells that Lily had bought her for Christmas.

"Aren't you going to telephone Leo, dear?" Mum asked when we arrived back, pink and shivering, scattering mitts, scarves and puffer coats around the tiny hall.

Looking through the window and avoiding her gaze, I said, "I think it might snow, you know. Just look at those clouds."

"Evelyn?"

"Mmm, no, can't, Mum, his phone's out of order. He'll call when he can, I'm sure."

And he did, just as we finished eating our Christmas dinner. My heart skipped a few beats as Mum answered the phone. She carried the handset into the dining room and handed it to Dan.

"He wants to speak to Dan and Lily first."

I busied myself clearing the table and stood quivering in the kitchen. I could hear the children, first Dan and then Lily, laughing, telling him about their presents and asking him questions.

My mother watched me and said quietly, "Is there a problem, dear?"

My carefully arranged Christmas face had paled and I was trembling. I'd managed so well up until that point. I nodded, but took the phone from Lily. She had it at arm's length as she shouted, "Happy Christmas, Leo." She sped off into the conservatory where Scruffy and Dan were playing.

I heard Leo's cheery reply to Lily as I put the phone to my ear.

"Yes, Happy Christmas. Are you okay, Leo?" I said.

The tone of his voice changed instantly. "Of course I'm not okay. You obviously haven't told your mother or the children that you have banned me from coming home."

"No." I walked into the now deserted dining room and shut the door.

"Evelyn, we need to talk."

"About what?"

"I want to talk to you about our future."

"We don't have a future. I'm going to file for divorce."

"Of course we have a future. You and me, we're meant to be together."

"Not anymore."

He didn't reply but I could hear his intake of breath. I couldn't help myself asking, "What about the lovely Sheila, then?"

"This has nothing to do with her. There's nobody else, never has been, never will be. It's our marriage that's important."

Mum had obviously heard the tension in my voice and stayed in the kitchen. I paced around quietly, holding the phone. I heard Mum closing the doors so that the children couldn't hear me.

"Go to hell, Leo," I hissed into the phone. "Presumably our future, as you put it, didn't feature so much when you were busy fucking your tart in Milan."

I could hear his breathing and knew he was distressed, but he said quietly, "That's not important, it's in the past now. It doesn't matter."

"It bloody well matters to me. It might be in your past, though I doubt even that, but it is my everyday waking nightmare. I'm filing for divorce. There is no going back, Leo." I slammed the phone back into its cradle in the hall and, shaking like a leaf, gulped down the remains of my coffee. How dare he make me feel like this?

He didn't call again. Christmas and New Year came and went. It took so much adjustment, so much relinquished hope, endless days and nights of aching loneliness. I missed him so much and grieved for him, but I hardened my heart at last and made myself believe it was for the best. I assumed that he had gone back to Milan to start the new project and back to his 'friend' Sheila. She was welcome to him. New millennium. New life!

CHAPTER 30
Spring 2000

LEO

After a stressful Christmas with my mother in Manchester, and with a heavy heart, I returned to Milan and moved in with Sheila. I'd continued to delude myself that I was fine, that it was all just fine. I had a good, rewarding job in a fabulous city, and Sheila. She was so different to Evelyn, not clever or witty, nor terribly bright, but a fun girl who was always up for a tumble. She had managed to get another secretarial post with a firm of solicitors in Milan so that she could stay with me instead of going to Corsica and writing about shark fishing.

Although she was demanding and possessive, Sheila had no problem with my drinking. She could pretty much keep up with me and would accompany me everywhere. Her whole social life focused around me. She had no other interests and few friends, so we spent a great deal of time together. I grew tired of her within a month of returning to Milan.

What did that say about me? I'd lost the most wonderful woman, my wife, because of her. But no, to be fair, it wasn't because of her. It was because of me. All my previous affairs had been acquisitions, brief, and satisfying in the short term only. When I saw someone I wanted, I never had to do anything really. Smile, compliment them, sit back and wait. Let them offer. Isn't that what I'd done with Sheila. Did she mean anything to me? I wasn't even sure. My need for constant sex was certainly satisfied, and I made the most of it. After a drink or two it was all that mattered, and, yes, for a short while I thought I was fine.

The truth was, I missed Evelyn and everything about her. Her bright, pretty smile, and her fabulous body that encased me with the sort of love I'd only ever dreamed about. Our meals together and the fun we'd had on outings with Dan and Lily. I was surprised how much I missed them too.

Sheila's bedroom antics and exuberant foreplay were inventive to say the least, but no longer satisfied me.

"I'm off to the gym," I told her one evening.

"I'll come too."

"No, Sheila. I want some time to myself. You have a G and T and I'll be back within an hour. It wouldn't harm you to get us some supper ready."

She pouted childishly and pushed her body toward me. "Can't I come with you?" Her plump little fingers began to massage my dick. "I don't know why you go to the gym anyway, you're fit and gorgeous already." Pulling away, even though my manhood was already half-erect, I said, "No, I'm going on my own."

Never having been known to turn down a fuck in my entire life, I was surprised at myself. I left her sulking. She was still sulking when I returned a couple of hours later, but after a bottle of wine and a warmed-up pizza we were in bed and she was groaning happily.

So life continued, and although I called Evelyn regularly, she refused to speak to me. She changed her phone number after a couple of months. I know it was because I had pestered her again, late at night, when I was very drunk.

CHAPTER 31
New Beginnings!

EVELYN

Nearly two months passed and I was gaining more and more confidence in my practice. My life without Leo was painfully sad at times, but I was being happily rewarded by my success in my newfound career. My aromatherapy course over, I enrolled in a reflexology course in Nottingham. I travelled every other weekend down to the university while Sally stayed with Dan and Lily. I loved every minute of it, met some fabulously inspiring people, and after completing five modules would take the exam in the autumn.

I learned about energy pathways; that each area of the foot related to a part of the body. I practised the technique of thumb walking across the feet, pressure, and how to make clients feel secure and safe with their treatments. Each day I studied; learned how to complete a full health record from genetic background to symptomatic problems.

I still continued to write an odd article here and there for magazines, as I was not sure that I could earn quite enough without it yet. Writing articles for magazines was a lonely profession, and I felt that being able to help people with relaxation, depression, pain and anxiety was so much more rewarding. I bored all my friends with my new knowledge, and knew that I would eventually make it my full-time career. My practice was expanding rapidly and I loved it.

I already had quite a few clients, and the best hours of my days were those spent with the complexities of muscles, tension and stress. People learned to trust my advice and I wanted to do more. Each client came with a set of life puzzles from their symptoms, what their doctors had advised, their relationships, what was happening to them as a result of failed marriages, unruly neighbours, out-of-control children and unsatisfying jobs. I knew that I would have to study a great deal more to be able to help everyone enough. Some people were more locked into their problems than others, some easily swayed into positive thinking and some so low in spirits that I felt compelled to advise that they go to someone more qualified than me. But I was slowly learning counselling skills as my practice increased, and every course that I had attended so far had put a great deal of emphasis on listening, being non-judgmental and treating every client as an individual. I realised more and more that it was not only my practical accomplishments that people found so helpful, but also my ability to give advice and the tools to help them improve their lives.

It was about this time that I became more aware of the power of my therapies and my own energies. When I was working and concentrating on my clients, I began to feel that I had some hidden hand helping me. I seemed to know instinctively how to treat and advise people. It felt as if I had another energy in the room with me, guiding me and sometimes whispering in my ear. The more I concentrated the more I became aware of it. It was a small female presence, and whilst I was massaging, she quietly surrounded me with her loving aura. I couldn't exactly see her but I could feel her presence. I could smell her too. She smelled like a garden full of flowers. She moved around me like a cloud of silk, and after my first feelings of hesitation I welcomed her into my life. She seemed to come when I was most perplexed or worried, and she was strangely familiar. I was never happier or more efficient as when she was around. I liked to think that she was my guardian angel. On one occasion, when I was mixing a prescription of essential oils for a lady suffering with a nasty skin disorder, I heard her voice in my ear, "Mix the geranium and chamomile into the calendula oil to relieve the inflammation." I had been about to mix something else, but instinctively knew that the right prescription should indeed include the chamomile and the calendula. I felt as if she knew so much, but as soon as I had thought it I heard her say, "So do you."

To my great surprise, at the end of February, on the day of our wedding anniversary, a large bouquet stuffed with roses and lilies arrived from Leo. It was beautiful, without a message, but what could he say at this point in time? We hadn't actually spoken to each other for two months.

I had received a letter from him the previous week telling me that he couldn't bear the fact that I wouldn't talk to him. That he was missing me and wanted us to reconnect! Did he really have such a short memory? Doesn't he remember that he was cheating on me? Does he think everything he does is excusable?

In my mind there was no way back.

When Sally arrived to pick me up for lunch, I was carefully arranging the flowers, thinking of all the times he'd done this. He knew that I loved flowers. My husband certainly knew how to get under my skin.

Sally raised an enquiring eyebrow.

"Today is our seventh wedding anniversary. He's telling me how much he loves only me." The note of irony in my voice was obvious.

Sally looked surprised. "Would you have it any other way?"

"Yes, I would. I would like to feel nothing. The opposite of love isn't hate, you know, it's indifference, and that's where I want to be. I don't want to feel so moved by a bunch of fucking flowers."

"True," she conceded, "but given the choice you want him back?"

"No, I don't."

She waved her hands to silence me. "You do, you know you do. Love is very insecure at the best of times, isn't it? That's why we get married, to pull in the insecurities. But sadly marriage doesn't protect anything. It gives us a false sense of security. Why can't you just divorce him? Or are you really going to let him back into your life again?"

"Only if he got some help and gave up alcohol altogether. It just seems to affect everything he does, thinks and feels. In particular his judgment and his ability to justify everything, even the bloody affairs. I can't have him back because he won't do it. Even though he says he can, it's only a ploy. Bloody man, I hate him."

I stopped and took a breath, and sniffed as a tear escaped and rolled down onto my collar.

"Strong emotion, hate," Sal declared.

"Yep, that's what I mean. I want to be indifferent but I can't be. Look at this." I couldn't help laughing as I showed Sal the letter he had sent the previous week.

"Couldn't he have waited a bit longer?" she smiled. "It's almost two months since he left; he hasn't exactly come running, has he? Doesn't he realise the pot is off the boil?"

"What about him wanting to reconnect with the strongest part of himself?" I said.

"I can only think that his tart has cut off his dick." She doubled over laughing at her own joke and I couldn't help joining her.

We both knew that we were joking about it because that's how we women dealt with that sort of pain. We talked to our friends. Real friends knew that even though we sometimes bored them to tears, they would listen, console and try to help however they could, just as I would do for them. 'The Sisterhood', as Jude calls it, works for those who are lucky enough to have good friends.

Sally knew exactly what I was suffering. Her alcoholic husband, whom she'd married at eighteen and divorced when she was twenty-one, had led her a merry dance and made her so unhappy that she had contemplated suicide. She'd vowed never to do it again. And she never had. She hugged me tight. "Okay, kiddo, let's go get some lunch. We'll not talk about him anymore."

CHAPTER 32
June 2000

LEO

It was in the middle of June that Rossini's general manager told us that our job would be finished by the end of August. We were to take two months' paid leave because we had done so well. Five of us were asked if we wanted to be included in the deal. They were already working on a contract in Barcelona. What a chance!

Evelyn had not acknowledged the letter or the flowers I'd sent for our anniversary in February, and, although I'd written regularly, I'd only received a card from her on my birthday in May.

Inside was a short letter, wishing me a happy birthday and informing me of the children's progress. She told me of her new business and how many clients she had, how satisfying she found it. Nothing contentious or complaining, but she didn't tell me she missed me or that she'd started divorce proceedings. So I knew that there was a possibility that she would allow me back, even if it were only for a short while.

My only thought was that I should return to Great Ayton and try to put things right. Sheila would not be pleased, but that relationship had run its course anyway, and I knew that she would stay in Milan.

I wrote a long letter to Evelyn explaining the situation and asking if I could stay with them for the two months. I told her how much I would like to see Dan and Lily and my mates at the cricket club. I promised that I wouldn't drink at all while I was there. I explained that there was a job for me in Barcelona in October so I wouldn't be there long. I felt that she might allow me to stay if she knew it was only for a short time.

She still hadn't done anything about a divorce, and in my head I once again resolved to make things right between us.

CHAPTER 33
July 2000

EVELYN

By the time I received Leo's letter I was in a better place. My headaches had stopped and I'd been able to concentrate on Dan's and Lily's never-ending demands, and my rapidly expanding practice. Dan was taking his A-levels and had decided that he wanted to study chemistry. Lily was still intent on becoming a vet and had become a volunteer at the R.S.P.C.A.

I'd just had a wonderful and inspiring two days in London at the Institute of Optimum Nutrition when Lily arrived home, carefully carrying a small box. "I've brought home some babies," she announced. "Their mummy has been run over. Please can we take care of them?" Three tiny kittens lay sleeping in the little carrier that she carried. They were so small they had only just an odd eye open.

Life was pretty hectic, and the thought of having to feed such tiny babies was a bit daunting. "Oh, I don't know, Lily," I said, but Lily was adamant.

"We can take turns. They need milk every hour or so but I can do a rota. Please, Mum? We can, can't we?"

Dan was intrigued. "I'll help," he offered, and Lily grinned happily at his support.

So, over the next few weeks we took turns to bottle feed them. Scruffy was a happy observer but occasionally got overly enthusiastic with cleaning them up and licked them until they looked like drowned rats. In between kitten duty, I reorganised my therapy room. While I had been in London, Sally and Lily had spent much of the weekend Chinese brush painting, something that Sally seemed to have a talent for. The results were hung on my therapy room wall, which was beginning to look very professional. They joined the growing number of diplomas I had worked so hard for.

I wanted to create a safe space for people coming for treatments, and the colourful little bird and orchid paintings looked perfect.

The kittens grew into entertaining little bundles of mischief. Lily wanted to keep them, but when they were weaned they returned to the R.S.P.C.A to find homes; we missed them terribly. I had no doubt that they wouldn't be the last needy animals to cross our threshold.

Having the babies to look after had taken all thought of Leo coming back out of my mind.

I'd read and re-read his letter, wondering how to respond. If he came it would bring everything back into focus. Was that a good or a bad thing? We really needed to finalise things properly and go ahead with the divorce. But was that the answer? I had convinced myself that it was only fair to allow him to come back. I couldn't expect him to go to Jeanette's for two months. This was still his home after all.

Later that day I was alone, idly wandering in the garden as I deadheaded a few roses, and all the past was swirling around in my head. My husband's secret flings, his strange moods, his inability to see the hurt he caused, the endless arguments and how much easier life had been with him away. Had I stopped loving him? It was a question I never asked myself. Although my life was satisfying and relatively content, I knew that there was a chunk of my heart missing. Memories stirred of Leo's sweet words, his soft touch and the magic of loving him: the cruellest and saddest moments were blurred by repetition of remembering and the pain was distant and dim.

One by one I pushed these thoughts aside. I was becoming quite good at focusing on other things: Scruffy's next injection, Lily's desire to get her own horse, Dan's exam results, and my next client who was due in half an hour.

It was several days before I emailed a reply to Leo's request. It took me over an hour to write, and I didn't say anything about how the thought of him coming home made me feel.

In the end I kept it simple.

Dear Leo, Of course you can come back here on your two months' break, but only on the understanding that you do not drink at all and that we talk about the divorce in a civilised way. We must do something soon so that we can both get on with our lives. I do not want Dan or Lily upset, so I will arrange for them to be away with my mother when you first get back in August. I will meet you at the airport if you let me know what time your flight arrives. Please let us settle this once and for all.

Love, Evelyn

It sounded so neat and flat. I felt a cold knot of pain as I hit the send button.

CHAPTER 34
Return August 2000

LEO

As I walked towards Evelyn my stomach was twisted in knots but I kept smiling. It was now over a year since we'd been together. I was so happy to see her. For a moment I imagined that arriving and kissing her would erase the past or make it inconsequential, that whatever happened from that moment on we would still have a marriage.

We were guarded in our conversation but we were meeting from different places. Life for us both had changed and moved on, and the rules were not the same anymore. I knew the notion of a fresh start was fleeting and unreal. I'd have to change. Not sure what to do though! Perhaps I would get some therapy, but for now I had to try to convince Evelyn that I'd do anything she wanted of me to prevent us parting forever.

Her expression remained clenched and unforgiving as I approached, and in the car on the way to Great Ayton she made it clear that she'd made up her mind. I decided to wait awhile before asking for another chance.

Evelyn had cooked a meal for me and prepared the spare room. There was no alcohol anywhere to be seen and I wanted to reassure her that I had no intention of breaking my promise.

"I've come home to ask for your forgiveness," I said later that evening, "I'm not entirely sure that you can ever forgive me. I don't understand why I'm like this, but I'm going to change, get some help as you suggested before."

She gazed at me as if surprised.

"Is it too late, Evelyn? Can you ever trust me again?"

"Yes. It is too late, Leo. I can't forgive you." She took a deep breath, and with a cold steely look, asked, "What happened to Milan? Sheila? New life?"

I shrugged. "I needed you."

"You mean you failed," she said somewhat sarcastically.

"Yeh," I sighed. "I failed. I can't fool you, can I? I'd like to say it was wonderful, but in the end I only cared about you."

Her face crumpled but I turned away. I didn't want to see her pain. Evelyn couldn't hide her feelings, and I knew she was holding back her tears as she said, "I think you should know I spoke to Sheila this morning. She called me just after you'd left for the airport. After you had finished with her, told her you were coming back to me. And you couldn't even tell her the truth, could you?"

"What do you mean?"

"You told her I was ill and needed you back. I put her right on that one, but she found it necessary to tell me all about your relationship. Your amazing sex life. How you were planning marriage −"

"No, that's not true. I never asked her to marry me. She's deluded."

"But you did convince her that she was the love of your life. Did you not?"

"*You're* the love of my life," I told her, and I meant it sincerely. "I'll do anything to have you back."

"Are you surprised to know that I don't believe you? It trips off your tongue so easily, Leo. It's almost funny." Evelyn spat the words at me. "She also said that you had told her I was having affairs all the time. That *I* was a scrubber. Yes, she called me a scrubber! She knew you were married and she had the cheek to call me names! What sort of tart does that make her? You told her that I'd begged you to come home because I couldn't live without you and that I would try to kill myself if you didn't. You told her you loved her and promised her your commitment, and then when it suited you just walked away. She was even prepared to go to Barcelona with you. Why would you do that to anyone?"

What could I say?

"Answer me!" she demanded.

"Are you just going to rant and rave and keep bringing up the past?" I eventually replied. I couldn't bear her anger.

She had started to cry. "It might be the past in your mind, but it is *my* daily nightmare. If you keep lying and avoiding the truth, you will pay for it somewhere along the line. Lies will always do the most harm to the person who tells them."

"I think you are the one worried by them."

"Yes, of course I am. I'm so hurt… but I'll get over it. You never will. I can never forgive you for cheating on me. How can I when you do it over and over again?"

"I've always loved you," I said. "I'm weak and stupid and lost my way."

"Lost your way!" she shrieked. "Explain that to me. I don't understand. You lost your way? What was it? Just one of those things – you had too much to drink and you just happened to find Sheila on the end of your penis? Did you fall over and there she was, attached to your oh-so-ready dick?"

Fire flashed in Evelyn's eyes and I recoiled at the venom in her voice.

I was furious that Sheila had telephoned her, so I retorted, "She's lying. I never told her that she was the love of my life. I might have told her some things… but that didn't mean marriage. She's being vindictive because I left her and told her I loved you."

"Are you surprised? Of course she's being vindictive. You're pretty shitty to them, your women, when you leave them, aren't you?"

"What do you mean?"

"You string them along so heartlessly."

I nodded, "I close doors. Yes… and I forget about them because I love you… Can I take you out to lunch? We could talk properly and I'll tell you what I've decided to do."

She hesitated and I thought she would concede, but she frowned, puzzled, and said carefully, "No, no way! We'll talk here and make some decisions about the divorce before the children come back. I don't want them to see us upset."

"No, of course, neither do I."

It hit me for the first time that she really meant to divorce me, and I felt wretched.

CHAPTER 35
Decisions Made

EVELYN

He sat silently, obviously saddened by my remarks, but I really didn't care. He'd reduced me to this snivelling, emotional wreck in less than a day.

"I couldn't even consider having you back," I told him when I had calmed down enough to articulate properly. "I need more from you, Leo. I need to be exclusive with your love and your body. There's no way. You hurt me with your –"

"No, I know that, Evelyn, and you know I'm sorry for… everything. I've never meant to hurt you. I'm so sorry."

"Sorry doesn't count anymore, Leo."

"It's over. I've told her it's finished and that it didn't mean anything."

"I'm sure you have, but that doesn't mean you can step back into my life."

As usual, his refusal to explain shattered me as nothing else had. But the conversation with Sheila made me more and more demanding that he explained why.

"Why? How could you? Don't walk away from me." I grabbed his arm as he turned, and he shook me roughly away from him. I watched his mood change, his face frozen in a hard grimace and his anger bubbling just below the surface.

"I don't know why. I would tell you if I could. I don't know why I do it…" Leo said as he marched away from me.

"Tell me, I need to know," I insisted.

His brow darkened and he went into the bedroom, covered himself with the quilt and shut his eyes. "Leave me alone now," he muttered.

I followed, stood in the doorway, my face contorted in

anger and running with tears, my nose dripping and my sobs audible while he turned to sleep, just as I stood there.

It was so easy being the victim.

"What are we doing?" I screamed at his inert body. "I hate you… I hate you for making me feel like this. I can't accept it anymore. I wanted so much to help you but you're beyond help because you won't admit that you have a problem, will you?"

He ignored me.

It's like a recurring dream. I'd let it happen yet again. I couldn't help it, when I was with him I wanted to touch him, draw him to me and keep him forever. But it caused me so much pain. I constantly questioned myself. Why couldn't I just walk away?

As the days passed, all his flaws seemed more significant; his black moods, the frustrating implacability during arguments, his untidiness and the constant search for possessions that had 'been moved' since he'd been away. They all seemed innocuous enough, but we still hadn't talked properly about divorce. Dan and Lily came back from Scarborough.

We'd all been invited to my cousin Sylvia's marriage to Roland in the middle of September and we had decided to go together.

Leo and I explained as calmly as we could to Dan and Lily that we were going to separate when he went off to Barcelona in October. We didn't mention divorce, and they both thought that nothing would change very much. After all, he had been away for over a year and they had become used to his absence.

"Okay," said Lily, but Dan glowered. He was old enough to work out what was going on and he could see how distraught I was, even though we were both being very civil to each other. The happily-married faces were maintained throughout the following days and especially for Sylvia's wedding. It was there that we'd met Pierre Renard, Sylvia's boss at the investment company where she worked.

At the beginning of October, I had to go to Nottingham to take my reflexology exam. I was tired and distracted and knew I could have done better. Nevertheless, I'd managed to pass with reasonable grades, but on my return to Great Ayton was unhappy and resentful.

Leo and I had still not reached any conclusion about getting divorced, and it was almost time for him to go to Barcelona.

"You're quiet tonight, Evelyn," he said a week before his departure. "Are you going to talk to me?"

I felt there were no more words left to say, so I nodded. "I'm just tired of it all but I still don't know the answer."

He looked at me questioningly. I'd said so many words through the years. Words that hadn't changed anything. I had an overwhelming sense that dealing with Leo had worn me down to a point where rational thought evaded me. We were both still struggling, me with my anger and bitterness and Leo with his guilt. We seemed to be locked into a lifetime of conflict, but I knew I had to be the stronger and make the decision.

"Are you willing to try again, Evelyn?" he asked as I stood to get us some tea.

I lifted my head and his misery was plain to see.

Afraid of what his face was exposing, he walked toward me, pulled me close and ran his hands over my buttocks, gently rubbing and caressing. I felt him hard and demanding, and wondered again at the rise and fall of his sex drive. He stroked my neck and I could feel his fingers linger on my birthmark. But I willed myself not to be drawn back and pushed away from our desire for each other.

It was still such a strong feeling, but I said, "No, definitely not. We don't seem to be able to get what we want from each other. I frustrate you and you hurt me with your drinking and your adultery, so that we have this circle of guilt and resentment that we can't climb over, no matter how hard we try. Leo, I know it's the right decision to separate. Your actions puzzle me and it's painful, but I'm tired of the conflict, and I can't trust you. There is no point anymore. The children would feel it all the time and that would only make me unhappy. Your stunning lack of understanding of what you've done, where you've taken us with your inability to take responsibility for your actions, is unforgivable. I just can't take the chance. Nor can you."

"I don't know what to say. I know you're right, but I can't imagine it, nor do I want to be without you," Leo said as he gazed at me. He sighed deeply. I'm not sure whether out of sadness or regret or just for effect, but he said slowly, "I can't change who I am, and I can't go on apologizing for it. Yet, I can't live without you in my life."

"You will in time," I replied, trying not to let my breath stop in my throat and choke me.

"My first thought every morning and every night before I sleep is about you. I wonder what you are doing, where you are. I know how strong you are, so I don't worry, but I need you."

"Even when you are with someone else?"

"Oh, yes, definitely."

"There is no need to lie to me, Leo. I can't live like this. It makes me feel worthless."

"You know I don't feel that."

"It's not about how you feel. Aren't you listening? It's how it makes *me* feel."

"I'm sorry."

"Don't. Please don't keep saying you're sorry. Sorry only works when a mistake is made, not when a trust is broken. I want you to find someone you don't have to say sorry to. Someone who makes you feel good about yourself, because I obviously don't."

I stopped; forced myself to sound more amenable. "Don't you see how toxic we've become? I'm not abandoning you, I'm freeing you."

"It's not what I want."

How could he feel like that and still behave the way he did?

"Look how many times you've said you're sorry and sworn never to hurt me again. You can't keep your promises to me. Leo, we have to do this. We have to separate completely."

"If that's what you want, Evelyn. I will go."

I was too exhausted to say more. There was nothing left to say anyway.

Leo left the following day. It should have felt like a relief, but I was inconsolable. We had not spoken of divorce!

Dan and Lily went with Granddad and Granny Joyner down to a cottage in Cornwall for a holiday, so I was alone and allowed myself to sink into a pit of self-pity. I cancelled all my clients and took myself to bed.

Each night I craved sleep, but, despite the gnawing grief and fatigue that overwhelmed me, it evaded me. The days passed, and each morning as the thin bleak light of dawn appeared, I knew it would soon be time to start another day without him. I'd been without him for a year, but now I was without the *hope* of him. Without whatever it was in my heart that knew we were meant to be together. Tears welled up in my eyes and slid slowly over my nose into my hair and onto the pillow as I tried to shut out my persistent thoughts. My despair caught in my throat, and huge, body-shaking sobs engulfed me. I was surprised by my shameless need for the animal contact of the man I loved but who had been unable to love me back.

CHAPTER 36
Needing Help

EVELYN

He cannot be gone. I rested my forehead on the bedhead and wept.

I only got out of bed to feed the animals. On the third day, Jude arrived offering food and advice. She ordered me to eat what she had made for me. I hardly tasted anything as I shovelled in mouthfuls of omelette, but I was much hungrier than I'd realised.

Jude sat, her chin in her hands, and stared at me.

"Think it's time you got up. Let's go to the park and get some fresh air, we'll invite some friends over for supper and have a cook-in. Finish that and I'll run you a bath and then we'll make plans."

Up she leapt and sped off, calling as she went, "I'll ring Sally and Doreen and perhaps our gay neighbours, Philip and Terry. They're a hoot. You need a good laugh. I'll bring Frank. We'll have a get-together." Therapy for Jude was brisk and to the point, always involved cooking, usually for others, with plenty of wine and company.

I immediately felt better. There was something pleasantly anaesthetizing about being looked after. Perhaps things would soon get back into perspective and I would stop crying. My friends had listened to me pouring my heart out for the past hour. The good company and the several glasses of red wine had relaxed me and I was feeling more positive.

"He seems to be looking for the self-esteem he doesn't have," said Jude sagely when everyone but she and Sal had left.

"It's true," I answered, "it comes from his mother's inability to appreciate him. She is such a cold person and always seems to disapprove of him. I'm sure she doesn't mean it, but it has given him a distorted response to the opposite sex. Definitely unresolved Oedipus complex." We all laughed at my tipsy philosophy. "He's a troubled man, you know, looking for a loving mother in all women, but of course he'll never recognise her when he finds her."

"Are you saying that you're the one that is unrecognised? Is that it?" Sally sniffed and continued. "Doesn't excuse him for fucking around."

"I know, but it's not just sex he's looking for, that just comes with the bargain. He's getting his ego as well as his dick stroked."

"Ha. What kind of woman does he attract then? Good mother types? I think not, he's just an old-fashioned prick getting himself a bucketload when you are out of sight, and blaming you too. Selfish through and through like all men." Turning back to the sink, Jude picked up a tea towel and muttered, "Get shot of him for good."

"I will, this time I am certain that I will, but I do understand him, you know. It's really nothing to do with his feelings for me."

Jude hadn't got time for all this analysis, so I stopped. It was simple in her eyes. They did you wrong. You got rid. Full stop. End of story! Sal pretty much agreed, and I felt like a snivelling child who had lost her lollipop.

Time to close a door!

It should've got easier, but I continued to simmer with anger and pain. One of the things I had learned about human behaviour was that sometimes help was needed to get things into perspective again. I definitely needed some help!

In my psycho-immunology course we had an excellent tutor, Patrick Lowther, who was also a counsellor of some regard. I decided I would make an appointment to see him as a private client. He already knew a little about me as we had covered various things in class including grief counselling and relationship battles and their association with the onset of disease. I knew I might need a bit of help to come to terms with my feelings of failure.

Patrick was a kind man and we had spoken about forgiveness in class, but I couldn't yet relate it to my situation. I was the one who had been wronged.

Why would I forgive him?

Why would I let him go on hurting me?

I was so angry. It was eating away at me so that there were days when I really couldn't work. I made an appointment to see Patrick, and he welcomed me into his office with a smile.

"Evelyn, my dear. You have need of my professional services? How can I help you?"

I explained to Patrick about my failed marriage, my feelings toward Leo and the ties that seemed to bind us. He listened, nodding and accepting, as I prattled on about how I'd decided it was for the best we part, and yet I still yearned for him, even though I couldn't let go of not only my desire for him, but also my anger. How the dilemma was not improving with time either. Saying it all out loud stirred me so emotionally that I began to cry. Tears came so easily when my feelings for Leo were exposed.

Patrick let me sob and then said quietly, "When we wrestle with rage and emotional pain, our bodies are filled with adrenalin which makes it difficult to find clarity. Instead of fixating on how and why Leo has hurt you, look within. Seek to understand yourself and your expectations. Look after yourself and recognise that you have needs that he didn't, or maybe couldn't fulfil."

"How can I do that without blaming myself?"

"You don't need to beat yourself or him up. Can you find any empathy for him? At this moment, it may seem as though he deliberately did you harm, but this is often not the case. His actions weren't necessarily intentional or vindictive, but rather an attempt to get his own unmet needs handled. Leo is also a vulnerable, flawed human being."

"Blaming me is an excuse for him to hold on to," I sobbed. "And he's getting his needs fulfilled elsewhere."

"I don't think we are talking about the same needs, Evelyn," Patrick said as he handed me another tissue.

"It all sounds so simple, but it's so hard. I wish I'd never met him at that dinner party. I only decided to go at the last minute." I'd finally stopped crying. "My life would have been so different."

"I don't believe that anything that happens is random," Patrick said. "The universe is bound by unseen threads moving us into situations that we need to untangle to see the entwined patterns unfold. Forgiving is the only answer. But it will take time. Very few people have the courage to work at it, but it's the only thing that can free us. Whilst we fail to forgive we're holding the hand of the offender that will pull us backward again into the tangled web of bitterness and bad behaviour."

"Perhaps I can never forgive or forget, but if I can live without anger or pain it'll suffice."

Patrick assured me that it was possible, but added, "It does involve you allowing yourself to be vulnerable, though. Forgiving someone means letting go of your anger and letting go of the 'moral high ground'. It can also be difficult, as it may involve having to consider how you, yourself, contributed to the problem. Although it's tempting to imagine ourselves as completely in the right when it comes to disagreements, there are usually other things that we need to take into consideration."

"Yes, I can see that, but my resentment is so deep set now. It won't go away."

Patrick held up his hand, and said with a smile, "There's a famous quote that goes: 'Holding onto resentment is like drinking poison and expecting the other person to die.'

Forgiveness isn't just about retaining harmony in your relationship; it's also about being kind to yourself. If you're not careful, anger can eat away at you and even affect your attitude towards relationships in the future, making you feel more defensive or untrusting."

"Yes, I believe that."

"Can you let him go? You know by staying with him you are involving yourself in his problems, you've become the rock that he hangs onto because he knows you love him. Your love is his prop. Do you understand what I am saying?"

"Why does he need other women then?"

"I can't answer that."

"I'm sure he attracts needy women too."

"That's for him to deal with, not you."

CHAPTER 37
Years Apart

LEO

It was not my choice when Evelyn and I separated, but neither was it hers exactly. We'd just come to a place in our lives that we couldn't sort out. There was no clear climatic moment that brought it to an end, just a realisation that we'd become toxic to each other.

Parting with Evelyn had been swift and difficult, but for me a step backward. I retreated further and further from really taking responsibility for anything, or allowing myself to give any real commitment to anybody. As the years passed I'd gone on having affairs, endless rather useless sex with women I cared little for. Pushing myself into a woman gave me so much satisfaction only while I was doing it. But I could argue myself into acceptance. It was my right, was it not? Why else would I have a penis that gave me so much pleasure?

The strong sexual urges that I had daily had started when I was very young, about eleven, I think. I had discovered myself in the early hours of the morning, my dick in spasm, pushing out hot, sticky juice. I had been dreaming the same dream again, and the knives in my dream had been aiming for my penis, and I'd been screaming and fighting, but was not sure who was there or who was attacking me. A faceless enemy and the fear were all I remembered on waking. My pyjamas were full of slimy liquid and my mother was furious.

"Keep your hands out of your pants," she shouted as she stripped my sodden pyjamas off me.

"I didn't do anything… I didn't touch –"

"It's disgusting. Go and wash yourself."

It was my hidden pleasure from then on, and I actively

encouraged the feelings. I took care to use a big washable hanky that I kept hidden from my mother.

My first act of intercourse was incredible. Fifteen-year-old Anna Blunt was known as the 'school bike' and was a willing teacher. I was only twelve and I very quickly became addicted. I'd never grown out of the need for the instant gratification it brought me. So when Evelyn and I went our separate ways, I was again able to indulge without any feeling of guilt or recriminations. But I was not happy, and nothing had ever seemed totally worthwhile since Evelyn and I had parted. I missed everything about her. Nothing I did seemed to make up for my loss.

Thank heavens that the job in Barcelona was so demanding. Although I liked the place less than Milan, it kept me working long hours and was satisfying. I missed the Italian food. Tapas seemed a poor substitute for the garlic-laden tagliatelle and the wonderful variety of cheeses and mushrooms that adorned almost every dish in Italy. I did like the Spanish wine and brandy, though.

I met and enjoyed for a short while several gorgeous senoritas, and a friendly interpreter called Julia who occupied my bed for a few months, but I soon tired of them all. I drank myself into oblivion every time I allowed myself to wallow in the loss of my lovely wife.

I didn't contact Evelyn, as I found it too distressing to talk to her, but I did occasionally send her an email. When she replied, she told me about Dan's exam results and Lily's newest foster care, but little about herself. We made arrangement for the household bills to go into her name and I was happy to continue to pay the mortgage.

As time passed, I knew that she had been right about me. I had to do something about myself before it was too late, because my one all-abiding thought was to get us back together and treat Evelyn as I should have done when we married.

I was hurt and lonely and I was tired of lying. I was tired of myself. That sounded pathetic when I said it out loud, but I was moving toward fifty, and although I'd gained some satisfaction and security in my career, I couldn't settle without Evelyn.

I still believed somewhere in my distorted brain that we would get back together when I finished in Barcelona, but, as time passed, I realised that it was unlikely.

CHAPTER 38
Pierre Renard

EVELYN

I took Patrick's advice and started meditating on the words and affirmation that he'd given me, but it was difficult. I still had days of such intense rage toward Leo.

Gradually, as time passed and with the therapy that I was receiving, I found myself letting go of the anger and pain, and allowed myself to accept that Leo was who he was, and no complaining on my part could alter that. Only by his own resolve could he change.

In the months that followed I was working hard, and felt more strongly the presence of my guardian angel. I needed her loving energy, so I would often ask for her help whilst I was meditating or working. It gave me such a strong positive feeling, difficult to describe but it felt so good and her advice washed through my thoughts, helping me become more confident. It was the strangest sensation, as if I had a friend and guide always at hand. I told no one about her, though, as I knew my earthly friends would find me more than fanciful!

Leo didn't contact me very often, and I was relieved. I decided to get out and learn to enjoy myself again. I resolved to 'have some fun', although was not really quite sure whether that would entail a passionate sexual encounter with the next eligible man I came across, or just a few drinks with the girls.

My forty-fifth birthday was on the horizon, and I found it increasingly difficult to go to places that I had enjoyed in the past. I guess at the time I was probably still too full of bitterness and regret to start any sort of relationship, so I concentrated on my growing practice. In truth, I really was far too busy to think about it anyway.

It was a year later that cousin Sylvia and her husband Roland invited us to dinner to celebrate their first anniversary and the fact that they were expecting a baby. My mum was coming from Scarborough, plus several close relatives and a couple of Sylvia's workmates, as she was planning to leave work early.

Pierre Renard was there, and I found myself enjoying his company. He had deliberately worked the table so that we could sit together. I'd seen him asking Roland if he could change places with Uncle Ted who was to sit beside me.

"Is Leo here?" Pierre enquired as we took our seats. I was aware that he knew full well that I was on my own, but I smiled and shook my head.

"No, we are separated now. I think everyone knows that."

"Good, I can ask you out then. Sylvia wasn't sure what the situation was when I asked if you were coming. Would you like to have dinner with me?"

I hesitated only for a moment. Sylvia had told me on several occasions about her good-looking, flirty boss, who was obviously worth a mint, drove a Jaguar, and had a house in the southwest of France and a manor house on the edge of the moors. Also that he changed his lady-friends as other men changed their shoes. I didn't mind. I had no interest in long-term arrangements anyway. He was a very pleasant-looking man with soft greying hair, a little paunchy but immaculately dressed and with an air of supreme masculine confidence. Maybe this was just what I needed. A light-hearted fling would do me the world of good.

"Oh... Yes, that would be great," I declared, delighted at the prospect of a proper date. I had dated a few times, mainly an odd lunch out or a trip to the cinema, but here was a good-looking man who wanted to take me to dinner. Bring it on!

I got into the habit of seeing Pierre on a regular basis, was taken to the theatre, concerts or dinner, and often to his fabulous manor house overlooking the Yorkshire hills.

I had told him little about my situation with Leo, and he only asked me once if we were getting divorced.

"Eventually, yes," I'd replied laughingly. "It's on my 'to-do' list."

"Good. Because I think you and I have a future together."

Ah well, I'm not so sure about that!

By the summer of 2002 both of my children were doing well. I had a busy practice, was involved in several complementary studies with the local hospital, and was also getting recommendations from our medical centre to help patients with pain, depression, and such things as fibromyalgia, arthritis and diabetes.

With the help of my guardian angel I'd also worked hard at letting go of all my bad feelings toward Leo.

I still dreamed of him. Sometimes they were sexy and disturbing, full of passion and emotion. In one I had sudden images of both of us happily running and laughing together. I saw us with a host of children, singing, working with horses and other farm animals in a soft green valley close to the sea. Amongst our family, a happy black face and a tall red-haired man who worked alongside us. From this dream I would wake up happy and convinced of a great love between us. In another dream I was holding him in my arms, as if to protect him, with feelings of such intense love and closeness. It made me believe that our paths would certainly cross again.

I told Patrick of my dreams and the feelings of happiness that they often left me with. I also told him about the extraordinary feeling of a bond that I believed I had with Leo. Patrick was one of the few people who didn't scoff at me, and said, "I wouldn't be at all surprised. I believe that reincarnation brings people with unresolved Karmic issues back together for another chance."

"Does this mean we've failed again in this life?"

"Not necessarily, but who knows. It could be your life's lesson or just another step in your soul's journey. It could be some great masterplan or totally irrelevant."

I was pleased that Patrick had said that, because time was passing and my feelings toward Leo had changed. I no longer harboured the bitter regret of the past and had begun to let go of any expectations of him.

Whenever Leo contacted me, he always told me that I was still the love of his life and that he regretted hurting me. And in my heart I knew it was true.

My therapy with Patrick helped me release and feel strong again. Whatever life had in store I was prepared to go with it. In fact, I considered myself lucky as I no longer mourned for Leo but had slowly accepted that he was treading his own pathway.

Dan was now at Chester University studying Biochemistry, while my beautiful Lily, so full of passion and love for animals, was struggling with her exams. She had given up the gymnastics and fostering to concentrate on her studies, but continued with her singing and dancing lessons.

They both got on well with Pierre, who was attentive and kind to them. Although I liked him too, I couldn't honestly say that he stirred any great feelings in me. He, on the other hand, was encouraging me to divorce Leo and settle down with him. I often stayed overnight with him in his house in Helmsley where the windows looked out over the spectacular North York Moors. I found the extravagant lifestyle pleasing, and, waking in such an ideal environment, I started to wonder seriously whether I could move on with Pierre.

But there was always something missing.

I lay quite still and waited for passion to rise in me as Pierre pulled me toward him and whispered, "I'm so in love with you, I don't think I've ever felt like this before."

I smiled at him and caressed his soft curly hair. He was so kind and loving, I wanted to breathe him in as if by doing so I would salve the pain that I still felt deep inside. Pierre's hands caressed my body, asking for a reaction. He kissed me at first, hard and demanding, but, getting no response, kissed me gently and kindly as if instinctively knowing what I needed. I sighed deeply and he paused, waiting expectantly, but I went on caressing his cheek and his hair almost as one would caress a puppy or a kitten, smoothing, touching, reassuring, but my thoughts were drifting and my mind wandering. I forced myself to press my body close. I wondered why I couldn't respond. Years ago, before Leo, I would've responded with equal pleasure, supping the passion, devouring the heat, enjoying every sensual and sexual moment. But I felt dulled, anaesthetised, stilled in my responses and so tired. I must be growing old, as sex with Pierre was forced and full of pretence.

Every word, every sigh and every gesture I'd experienced before with Leo, and all had turned out to be meaningless, of the moment only, without substance and barely touching reality. Pierre felt my reluctance, and being a gentle soul released me so that he could look into my eyes. His kindness made me want to cry.

"You can trust me, you know, Evelyn."

"I trusted Leo."

"Will you marry me and I'll prove it?"

"I'll have to get divorced first, but yes, I think I will marry you."

CHAPTER 39
Paris 2003

LEO

Meeting Evelyn in Paris was like a star falling from the sky. We'd been married and lived together on and off for nearly ten years, and now it was probably about three years since we'd parted. I knew instantly that I'd do anything to be back with her. She lit up my life. When she told me about Pierre Renard I felt the bottom drop out of my world, but I was still determined.

Seeing her tears stirred such a desire in me that I reached forward and took her hand. I was trembling.

"Come back to my hotel and let's really talk, please, Evelyn," I pleaded.

"Talk?"

"Whatever you want. I won't touch you if you don't want me to, but I need to tell you... I'm back in London next week. I was going to get in touch... I need to talk to you."

She hesitated but stood and nodded slowly. I could see that she was battling with her emotions just as I was, but I wasn't going to let this moment pass. I paid for our coffees and pulled her gently towards the door of the cafe.

We ran together through the driving rain and arrived in the foyer of the Hôtel d'Aubusson where we stood laughing as we shook off the worst of the rainwater. As we passed reception, I gave Margarita, the old receptionist, a sly wink and ordered a bottle of champagne. "My wife is visiting from England."

She pursed her lips, shrugged her shoulders as the French do to suggest it was all part of what went on in life and, with a nod, passed me the key.

I had been staying there since coming to Paris from Barcelona. It was a charming old townhouse hotel with beautiful gardens and quaint romantic rooms.

"Oh, it's lovely, Leo. We are staying at the Plaza Athenee, and it's overly posh and haughty. This is so much nicer."

"Where is Pierre now?" I asked casually as we rode the lift.

"Gone to see a client who has made a fortune and looking for investment deals."

"Will he be gone long?" I asked, hoping for much more time with Evelyn.

"All day."

"Good."

By that time we'd reached my room. I wanted so much to wrap my arms around her, but she backed away from me. I wanted her to feel at ease so I let her go. She took the single armchair, ignoring the couch and the huge bed, and solemnly gazed out of the window. It was still pouring with rain, but the soft gold and honey colouring of the room lent us exactly the right warm and comfortable atmosphere that I felt we needed.

I poured the champagne when it arrived and knelt beside the chair so that I could look into her eyes.

"I will do anything, Evelyn."

She smiled at me then. "I know your intentions are there, my darling. It's the capability that worries me."

"It's all been a mistake, Evelyn, I know that now," I said.

"A mistake made more than once is a bloody decision," she said sadly.

"Please let me back into your life."

Her face creased and she shook her head. "I'm not sure that I'm prepared to take the chance."

I put down my champagne glass. "Starting from this moment I will not drink at all. Never. I know that I'll find it hard, but I'm prepared to do anything you want."

"Will you have some counselling too?"

"Yes."

It was in that very moment that I knew that I could, and would, do whatever she wanted and not renege on my promise ever again.

CHAPTER 40
Paris 2003

EVELYN

He didn't have to speak to exert his will; all he had to do was look at me with those little boy eyes. Eyes that told me he was unhappy, and that the only thing that made his life bearable was being with me... But, wait... Haven't we been down this road too many times before?

I shivered violently. With fear? With joy?

I'd caught his reaction when I told him about Pierre and instinctively knew that I could not marry anyone else.

It was the measure of how persuasive he could be that I went back to his hotel with him and immediately he tried to fold his arms around me.

"Please don't touch me. I can't bear it," I'd said as I backed away to sit by the window.

I had known that we would have to meet sometime to sort out our finances and the divorce, and in my logical head that was what we should do. But... I was reacting to him again, and all my resolve was disappearing, just as it had in the past.

Sipping the champagne brought back happy memories of birthdays and celebrations, but also the echo of his drunken behaviour and the pain it had brought into our lives.

He had put his glass down and made the promise. Such a big promise!

The glass sat there, like a warning.

"Let me hug you, Evelyn," he asked. "I know you want it too."

Slowly, I stood and let him wrap his arms around me. Then he kissed me with all the tenderness I remembered. His hands were in my hair, tipping my head so that he could kiss my neck. His fingers searched for my birthmark, which he stroked reverently. He kissed me over and over, moaning softly. Oh, how badly I wanted it and needed it. My whole body yearned for him, as for no other man.

Deep within me I knew that I should hold back or he would absorb me again into the belief that he would stay, honour me and be true to me. He would make me believe that he was sincere when he'd proven over and over that he was not. Was he trying to punish me? Why would he?

I stepped away from him and wiped my hands impatiently across my wet face. I hadn't been aware that I was crying again. Leo stood, holding his breath hard in his chest as though holding a guarded pain. He lifted his hands toward me but I put my hands up to prevent him taking hold of me again.

"Please don't, Leo."

I felt pulled and pushed and emotionally drained. I took a deep breath and wondered where the hell this was leading. He took my hand and we sat together on the bed. Again I was moved by his closeness. His eyes were misted and pleading.

"Can we try again, Evelyn? I realise with every part of myself how wrong I've been and I want to make amends. We're meant to be together. I know that now. I want to come home, be with you and the kids, and talk and live with you all again, so that you will see I'm sincere. This time it'll be different. I need to reconnect to you and show you my true self, the self that loves only you, that wants to spend the rest of my life making you happy."

"Only if you get some help," was my immediate response. I couldn't yet just believe in him. He had to do something. "Listen, Leo, I needed some therapy after you left and it helped me so much. It made me realise so many things about my expectations of you. It could help you too. I know you've fought against it before, but it is only your fear that holds you back. That will go as you release and look at you own needs."

"Have you forgiven me then, Evelyn?" he asked.

I could feel my heart thudding in my chest as I answered. "I'm not sure. Forgiveness is an aspiration, not a fact, and it's to be worked through continually. I've come a long way toward it since we parted, but I have to admit I struggle with it. What I do know, Leo, is that I love you, and I want us to be together. Different rules, though."

"Yes, I know, I still have the card you gave me for the counsellor lady. As soon as I get back I'll make an appointment to get some help. I know I must change, and if you believe in me it will help me. I'll do it. I won't come back home until I've got my head sorted. Please believe me, Evelyn, I want to make this work. We've been apart far too long. I'll book into a hotel. I won't expect to just walk back into your life as I did before."

As he gently pulled me across the bed and we lay side by side, I could hardly believe I'd allowed this to happen. Was I convinced by his promises to get some therapy and address his drinking? I think I was.

We moved through the need of mutual forgiveness, and we absolved each other in our passion and love for each other. I was paying a high price for this ecstasy of the flesh. While we made love I insisted that he looked at me, I wanted him to be completely and absolutely with me. He was!

Later we lay for a long time in each other's arms, talking about being together, our future and our pasts. I watched his mouth and his hands, wanting them on my body, wanting so much to be kissed again and to feel him close. I think we even slept a little. I glanced up at him, at the closed eyes, the flesh of his lips and the outline of his body. He opened his eyes, and as he got up, he was smiling, pulling on his boxer shorts in the untidy way he had, leaving one buttock partly exposed. Oh, Leo, how I adore you, but something inside you holds you back, prevents you from leaping into the happiness of living and loving. Will you walk away from me as soon as someone else strokes your ego or your dick? Will you put me into the recesses of your mind and selfishly move on again? Or will you turn your life around and come back to me, whole and happy?

I watched him for a while, still luxuriating in our reconciliation. He hadn't touched a drop of the champagne.

This time, said a voice in my head.

As I lay wondering how I was going to explain to Pierre what had happened, I recalled Patrick's words when I'd told him of my passion for Leo and how he responded.

"Addiction to anything, be it drugs, behaviour, alcohol, sex, religion, nicotine... anything, is a disease of feelings. It covers up what's really going on, and dulls the bad bits, so that emotions can't be felt and dealt with."

I realised that I was addicted too. Both of us had a lot to deal with.

CHAPTER 41
Therapy at Last

LEO

I started therapy the week after arriving back in North Yorkshire. And I kept my promise to Evelyn that I wouldn't bother her until I'd conquered my drinking and my fears, so I booked into a hotel in Guisborough and made an appointment with the counsellor.

Her name was Angela Stroud and she was a warm, likeable, grey-haired woman with a wide mouth and a comfortable, full body.

'A. Stroud, Counsellor, Creator of New Realities and Endless Possibilities.' So declared the sign outside the red brick house that housed her office. I was already impressed.

Angela held out her hand to me. I put my hand in hers, and it was firm and large and reassuring. "Leo Davistein? Pleased to meet you. Would you like to sit or lie?" she asked as she led me into her office.

"Sit, I think." I didn't feel ready to lie on the big red couch.

She sat opposite and folded her hands comfortably across her ample stomach.

"What would you like to talk about?"

I swallowed hard but I wasn't panicking, so I tried to remember what I'd rehearsed to say.

"I want my wife back. We've been living apart for several years and I think we should be together."

"Why did you separate?"

I wanted to find the right and the most honest way of explaining. "My fault, I know, but it's not easy to explain."

"Close your eyes and relax and just let the words come."

"Okay," I said as I leaned back and tried to relax. I started slowly. "My wife thinks I have a drinking problem... Well, I do… not just a drinking problem… more what it leads to. I went away because of it and I've been working abroad. We've been apart a long time. I've just come back from Paris last week. I want to change, so that Evelyn and I can get our marriage back again."

I found myself babbling on, but Angela Stroud said calmly, "What do *you* think?"

"Me… what do I think? I know she's right. I've done things I shouldn't when I've been drinking."

"Things? Like what, Leo?"

"I cheated. I can't explain why, because I love my wife. I always felt guilty and then I would drink again," I said. "Cheating, alcohol, or the guilt, a vicious circle. I'm not sure which came first or which came last."

"Did you remember what you'd done?"

"I couldn't always remember. Sometimes I drank too much and said and did things I didn't mean, terrible things sometimes. When she told me what I've said or done, I didn't believe I could be like that… So I found it hard to take responsibility for something I couldn't remember saying or doing. I didn't feel… perhaps, it's just that I didn't feel bad enough. It's like it was nothing to do with me. And yet, I felt guilty because I knew I'd hurt her."

We talked endlessly about what it was like being an only child, having no father figure in my life and about the fact that my mother had to work to support us.

"My wife thinks my mother neglected me, but I don't know whether she did or not. She certainly didn't want me, I've always known that."

"Did she tell you she didn't want you?"

"Sort of, perhaps not told me exactly, but she made it perfectly clear that her life would have been better without me," I explained. "I've always felt as if I was invisible."

"And?"

"I know she's never loved me," I said, then added

reluctantly, "even now."

"Perhaps she just doesn't know how to show it. Do you know anything about her life before you came along?"

"She was an orphan brought up by her gran, who died just after I was born, so she had no other family."

"That must have been difficult for her?"

"Yes, it must. She told me once that her gran had loved her, left her money and a car, but I think my father took it all when he left. He left her skint and pregnant, so she blames me, I guess."

"So, she lost her gran and her husband at about the same time?"

"Yes, and I got the blame, didn't I?"

"Stop thinking like a victim. People stay stuck because they have a very rigid, narrow story that keeps them trapped. Rather than focusing on how your mother undermined you in the past, think about how, as an adult, you have the freedom to make decisions that might support who she is, and how her life affected her."

"Yeah, I can see that, but it doesn't help explain why I behave the way I do to Evelyn."

"Right, explain how you feel before and after cheating on your wife."

I felt myself fidgeting in my seat and I struggled to explain, but eventually I said, "I don't feel good about it. I tell lies to the women and to Evelyn. But telling someone what they want to hear isn't really lying, is it?"

"It's the worst sort because it doesn't reflect you, or who you are, or what you're really feeling. There is too much guilt."

Already in the first session we were talking about my feelings. I told Angela all of the things I'd been waiting to say. Everything just came spilling out of me. Angela listened, her dark eyes never leaving me for a moment. She didn't make any notes, just listened, her hands still, and her face expressionless.

Eventually, seeing that I couldn't say more, she nodded and asked, "Do you feel ready to take responsibility for what you've done?"

"Yes, exactly."

"Even though you don't understand why you do these things? Are you ready to forgive yourself?"

"Do I need to?"

Angela Stroud leaned toward me and made me look her in the eye. "Learning to forgive your own behaviour is vitally important, Leo. Hurting yourself, by refusing to forgive yourself, hurts others also. Why go on punishing yourself? The more you deny it, the less you have to give. The less you have to give, the less you can benefit those around you. Why be invisible? When you stop limiting what you receive, then you stop limiting what you can give. Everyone benefits, as you then allow much more good into your life, and have a lot more to share with those you love. You won't feel invisible anymore."

"I need to change, I know. I have always deliberately found women who I could easily keep at a distance, either very young or married, or just sexually demanding and wanting nothing else from me. Not Evelyn, of course. All of the others have become invisible to me."

"That is what you've learned is acceptable. A learned behaviour can be unlearned, Leo."

Our sessions certainly gave me plenty to think about, and Angela suggested I looked at the anger that I held so tightly in my chest. She said 'heart', but I was aware that the inner fury that I harboured and nourished affected my whole chest area not just my heart. It wasn't a pain exactly, but a feeling of being contained and restricted.

"It's anger, Leo," said Angela carefully. "You will have to address that, you know. Also, you will have to forgive your mother."

Within the next week I had signed into a three-day anger management course that she recommended in Brighton. I have to admit that I went feeling that there was little they could tell me, but I was wrong. The weekend blew away all my previous feelings about what was acceptable in a loving relationship.

John Briggs, our facilitator, had an applied psychology and criminology degree and taught at the University of Brighton. With him, the group – around twelve of us – explored the need to allow anger to express itself in a controlled way, not suppress it as I'd done for so many years. We role-played and talked, did exercises to explore behaviour and responses to emotional pressures and situations.

"Sometimes people are not aware they have an issue with anger or managing it. It often brings denial," John explained. "Getting to the bottom of your anger source is a hard journey, especially if you don't express it. Because it's one of the most powerful emotions we feel, it's often difficult to understand. Anger can stem from any number of events or reasons. It may be from childhood, violent or unhappy parents or experiences, rejection or lack of love. It can even be from grief or depression."

It all made so much sense. My therapy with Angela Stroud and the anger management course had exposed what I suppose I already knew but had never accepted. The angry moods that were suppressed were the reason that I drank to excess. It was so easy to blame the alcohol, but, as my real needs became exposed, I was aware that I had to look at the reasons straight in the eye if I was to be able to tackle them.

"Expose what is buried deep down and talk about it. It will happen slowly," explained John, "you will find your boundaries blurring and fading, your needs and expectations changing as you release them."

It was as if I hadn't been able to see clearly. Slowly I felt myself changing. I needed to be my own man, not directed by physical urges or erotic fantasy or distorted images of my life through an alcoholic glaze. I wanted to stop being ambushed by visions of my childhood, my mother's disinterest and coldness needed to matter less somehow if I was to do this. I knew I had to talk to my mother.

Slowly it did matter less, and the tight band around my heart started to release.

CHAPTER 42
Waiting

EVELYN

Returning from Paris with Pierre had been more than difficult. Amid my tangled emotions I'd tried hard to explain to him, both after my meeting with Leo and when we arrived back home. He'd been silent on our return journey and quite hostile. He declared that he wanted nothing more to do with me. I couldn't blame him. We'd gone to Paris for a romantic holiday and I'd treated him appallingly.

After seeing Leo, I knew that I couldn't marry Pierre, but explaining was almost impossible, as I was hurting someone who had only ever been loving and kind to me. The hardest part was losing him from my life.

Although I hadn't been in love with him, we'd been good friends, and the children found it hard to understand why I'd let him go so easily.

There were many tears after that day, for my disloyalty and my inability to explain why I was even thinking of allowing Leo back into my life. My friends were appalled and I couldn't blame them. Sally, in particular, constantly asked what I could possibly see in Leo when I had the gorgeous Pierre in tow. I couldn't explain.

Work again became my focus. My passion for what I did brought me back into reality and made me feel worthy again.

I knew that Leo was close by, living in a hotel. He telephoned me daily to tell me about his therapy and his progress. Despite my reservations I had a good feeling. I also knew that we would stay together. We had to build on our hopes for the future. If we kept looking back, we'd be destroyed forever.

Leo was doing well, and for the first time in his life

stopped talking about his loneliness and isolation as a child, and spoke of his mother with an attitude of acceptance and forgiveness, and slowly with love.

Since coming home from Paris I'd come to terms with what had happened, but needed to explain to Dan and Lily about meeting Leo and how it disturbed me.

"We've always known that you loved Leo the most," Lily told me with a grin.

Dan had nodded his agreement before warning, "Don't let him mess you around again, though, Mum."

I assured them the best way I could, because I did know that Leo's promises had more *intent* than they'd ever had before.

In the last year we'd managed to adopt another couple of rabbits and a one-eyed cat because Lily just couldn't resist them. I have to say the cat was a delight. His soft purring calmed my restless thoughts and tangled feelings.

Dan passed his driving test and I gave him my old Ford.

Leo's BMW, which had sat in our garage all the time he'd been abroad, was serviced, polished and became mine. He bought himself a new car and planned to go to Manchester to talk to Jeanette.

If he made any sort of peace with his mother, I would never know, because he'd become very emotional when I asked him if they'd talked about his childhood. All he told me was that she'd convinced him that she'd done her best. I was sure that she had!

In the meantime, with the therapy and no alcohol to blur what was going on in his life, Leo decided that he needed to make peace with others whom it had affected. He went to visit Dan in Chester and my mother in Scarborough. He talked to both of them about what he was hoping for and what he was doing to recompense for his previous behaviour. Dan phoned me and told me of the day he had spent with Leo and how impressed he was with his sincerity.

"Do you know, Mum, I often wondered how you put up with him. He was such a plonker when he'd had a drink. He's changed… a lot. He even told me about his affairs. Not that I really wanted to hear, but it was as if he was trying to get it off his chest. I wanted to punch him for treating you so badly, but I didn't," he laughed, and then asked me seriously, "are *you* okay with it?"

"Don't know, Dan. He has already given up drinking but… I want to forgive him, but we do have some bad history to deal with."

"Deep down he's a good bloke, you know, Ma'."

"I do know, but thanks for seeing it, Dan."

I was pleased. Leo had progressed so much, but I knew in my heart that he could never alter his past or completely let go of the fears that he had absorbed as a child. But the anger management course and the therapy had at least opened a small doorway of understanding about his inability to trust 'honest' loving. Whatever Leo understood about his early experiences of rejection and loneliness, I knew that I would have to change my expectations too. I still needed to learn to live with the waves of resentment about his infidelities. I was so lucky to have been involved in the coursework and Patrick's therapeutic counselling that had enabled me to stop being unhappy because of those negative feelings.

It took nearly three months for me to be convinced about accepting Leo back into our home.

Lily was in the garden feeding her rabbits when Leo first arrived.

"We've acquired a few more lodgers, I'm afraid." I laughed as we watched her on her knees, playing with the newest arrival, a little, flop-eared rabbit with a bad leg. "We've got a cat too," I told Leo. "Named Long John, because he only has one eye."

"I don't care if we've got a zoo full of animals, I'm just so happy to be here," Leo told me as we walked into our diminishing garden.

We already had at least four pens for the rabbits, a chicken-house and run, plus a little wooden-boxed house with special rooms for hedgehogs to hibernate. Lily was caring for one who was already tucked up for the winter.

She lifted her eyes with an air of enquiry. "So, you're back, Leo. Are you staying this time?" asked my dark-haired beauty of a daughter. At seventeen, she was a stunner, totally disinterested in boys and completely absorbed with caring for her animals. She was always dressed in the same faded jeans and DMs, and would soon be leaving home to travel south to a college where she would start her studies for animal nursing, the first step on her journey to being a veterinary surgeon.

She got quickly to her feet and hugged Leo as he replied, "I am indeed, if there's room for me now."

Lily tilted her head prettily to one side and grinned at me. "There is, isn't there, Mum? Will you give him another chance?"

"There are conditions."

Lily clearly thought that was a good idea. "Course there are, quite right too."

Not surprisingly, in the weeks that followed she kept an eye on both of us and could easily pick up whether I was discouraged or worried. It was going to take a while.

At first it *was* heart-breaking and intense, but slowly we began to laugh again, and the first time we had a row, and Leo lost his temper, was a triumph. He was stone-cold sober and angry with me for taking his favourite golf clothes and shoes to a charity shop. He stomped around and shouted and I was delighted. Previously he would have sulked and taken to the bottle.

A victory indeed!

CHAPTER 43
Home

LEO

The project in Paris had been successful and there was another job in the offing, but in the meantime I was enjoying being back in Great Ayton. I didn't want to think about leaving.

It was a lazy Saturday morning in November and I'd been home for a few weeks only. Lily was at the R.S.P.C.A. centre walking dogs or mucking out or whatever it was that she did there. Evelyn and I lay in bed comfortably wrapped around each other. Her head was tucked onto my shoulder; her right leg over my body and her free hand was caressing my face and neck. I was so happy. I hadn't had a drink for months and we had made love. Her gentle touch sent tingling warmth down my body and I felt myself beginning to harden again. As her finger stroked my chest and hairy nipples, I started to turn toward her but she stopped suddenly. She pressed my breast with the heel of her hand, and hesitated a moment before sitting up abruptly.

"Leo. There's a lump in your breast. Here, feel." I sat up and rubbed my hand across my chest.

"How long have you had this lump?" she asked.

"What lump?" She moved my hand to where the ominous bulge pushed my nipple out of shape. It was quite large.

"Feel it? There... that needs checking out." She was already getting out of bed to phone the doctor.

"I had a medical when I came home from Paris. Company insists on it every few years," I told her.

"Didn't they check your breasts?" she asked, pulling on her dressing gown.

"No, only my testicles, which is what they usually do.

Had blood tests and such..."

I had no inclination to alarm myself, but I could see by Evelyn's expression that this was not something to sweep aside.

"Leo, this is serious," she told me.

Almost at once I felt a hint of fear. "What does it mean?"

"Right. Step one, diagnosis. Step two, we sort it," she said, and headed straight for the telephone.

CHAPTER 44
Cancer

EVELYN

He grinned, his expression unchanged, and I knew that he had not realised the implication of such a lump. I'd learned enough in the past few years to recognise a tumour and know that it could be cancerous. A hot panic swept through me as I called the surgery to make an appointment.

Within days we saw the doctor, then Leo had the biopsy. We had to wait an alarming number of worrying days before we got a call from the surgeon who had the results of the biopsy.

It was serious!

Mr Guy, the surgeon, informed us solemnly, "Breast cancer in men is a rare occurrence and I personally have dealt with very few. Only about two hundred a year in the UK, and we are still unsure what causes it. Yours is a grade three tumour, and rather an aggressive one, I'm afraid, Leo. That's why you haven't noticed it before. It's grown rapidly and needs removing very soon."

Leo held my hand tightly. His palms were sweating and he was trying to be calm, but his voice wavered as he asked, "What will happen?"

"We'll have to do a full mastectomy and take tissue from the lymph nodes. If they appear to be infected, we will remove them as well," Mr Guy told us carefully. "Do you understand?"

"I had no idea men could even get it," Leo said.

"We've established that it's not genetic in your case, but you do have high levels of oestrogen in your body, and that is associated with liver damage. And *that* is usually definitely alcohol-related. Sad to say, because I like a drink of wine when I knock off here," he laughed. "But without a doubt, alcohol consumption is contributory, as are many other things, of course. I believe that cancer is an illness of the mind, body and spirit. Sadly, I can only deal with the body, and the program we set out for its treatment."

"My wife believes that too," Leo told him, "and is insistent that I cleanse my mind as well as my body. She has already changed my diet considerably. I'm also having therapy for anger issues and what my therapist calls pre-learned behaviour which I am trying to change."

Mr Guy beamed at us. "Good. That's excellent. We'll book an immediate surgery. We'll take away the tumour and the surrounding lymph nodes to check on its spread. After we look at the tissue, we can decide what will be the next step."

"I'll support him through this, whatever happens," I added as calmly as I could.

Leo was completely stunned and quite unable to believe that anything like this could happen to him. He'd pulled down the cuff of his sweater and was working his thumb against the wool. I reached for his hand again to steady it, and he said quietly, "Is it usually successful… with men?"

"Usually, yes," Mr Guy responded, "but we need to check the other breast as well, so that we can make sure it hasn't spread. A mammogram is the next step, and we'll see if we can get you in quickly. The next couple of weeks are busy, but after that … say, end of November, beginning of December?"

Mr Guy's tone was light and encouraging, and I felt I had to ask some questions as Leo had paled and his lips were clamped together. "Can we do anything positive to help the process?"

"Of course, a healthy body heals faster than an unhealthy one." Mr Guy already knew what I did for a living and was encouraging. He agreed that a strict regime of diet and exercise before surgery was a good idea, and informed us, "To heal well, the body needs as much help as you can give it. I, as a doctor, can only recommend the set protocol that we practise, surgery and either hormone or chemotherapy after we know the extent of the problem. We have no control over your lifestyle, but a healthy body heals the best, I can tell you. Also, I have to say in your case that giving up alcohol is the best thing you could do to help yourself."

"I already have, and intend never to drink again," Leo said quietly.

Leo's state of shock and his total lack of ability to have a rational, productive thought about what was happening allowed me to impose a strict regime. He willingly read all the information both from the hospital and from alternative and complementary practices. Together we scanned books and the Internet, studied various forms of detoxification, Ayurvedic and Chinese practices, castor oil packs and a dozen books on fitness and diet. I'd already set into action a plan to eliminate certain acidic foods from our diet. Apparently cancer loves an acidic diet!

The prognosis was not good, but over the past few years I'd learned that there were ways of improving survival of almost any disease, providing it had not spread too far.

"Firstly, we must clean your body ready for the surgery," I told him.

I'd already read Professor Jane Plant's books and knew that a pure, natural diet was essential to start cleansing the body, so we started to follow her guidelines. After all, she herself had recovered from several tumours. All alcohol, dairy products, meat and sugary snacks disappeared from our house.

It was the time to put all my skills into practice, so I spent hours concocting new recipes. I liked cooking and creating really delicious meals out of limited ingredients. It wasn't only gratifying but also strangely sensual. It was something I was good at, and it quieted my mind from the worry of the consequences of this awful disease and its treatment. I cherished the routines of chopping and preparing, the juicing and the experimenting. I knew that I was getting help from some unknown source because I often had random ideas that popped into my head. 'A little more garlic – Try it with grape juice – Cook it less – Make it stronger – Add some mint.'

I liked to think that I had a wise friend? A mother? A mentor? Someone whom I glimpsed in the side-line of my brain but that I couldn't quite see or remember. All I knew was that a loving hand was guiding me.

Leo was passively allowing me to take charge as if he knew that I'd go to the ends of the earth to help him recover healthily. I didn't tell him that I thought I was getting help from an ethereal being. He would only laugh at me.

I chopped and minced, peeled and prepared the best food possible, and it helped to keep my restless thoughts steady. Could this be the turning point that Leo needed? Would he survive? Would he understand the meaning of his disease and work toward dispelling forever that tight, enclosed heart of his?

I knew that the therapy he was doing with Angela was helping, and I hoped that he would go back for more, as and when he recovered from the surgery.

CHAPTER 45
Preparation

LEO

Evelyn found an old copy of the Times and a report by the science director about a cancer study in China. Given a combination of Vitamin E, beta-carotene and selenium, cancer deaths were reduced significantly. On investigation and with the advice of the vitamin company, with whom she had opened a practitioner's account, the said vitamins were ordered. I took everything she offered. We drank a dozen different juiced concoctions, including beetroot juice for my liver health. I learned to drink herbal teas, some of which tasted like last night's leftover greens, but Evelyn was insistent.

I found that there were days that I wanted alcohol to wipe out the misery of my expectations, but I wasn't going to let Evelyn or myself down. Gradually even the desire for a drink disappeared. I'd finally come to the conclusion that, although I couldn't see myself as an archetypal alcoholic, it'd had such a profound effect on my behaviour and my moods that it was definitely an addiction.

I was still convinced that any sort of cancer was a death sentence, but Evelyn would have none of it. She knew that I needed constant encouragement and told me about several surviving cancer clients who came to her regularly for massage or reflexology, both of which I was encouraged to have. I allowed myself to be indulged and enjoyed the attention that Evelyn was giving me.

Nevertheless, I was still sure that I was about to die!

I was also convinced that this was something I deserved. I could no longer hide! But, with help from Angela and John Briggs, I allowed myself to look wholeheartedly into my motives, emotions and insecurities, and I hadn't liked what

I'd found.

I understood what Angela meant when she insisted that I needed to forgive myself. At the time it seemed pointless and ridiculous, but now I was seeing myself from a totally different perspective.

Evelyn explained that she had come to believe that there was always a reason for everything that happened, and that this had come along as a test to set us on the right course for the rest of our lives.

"Perhaps this is the lesson that we need to learn in this lifetime," she told me seriously one evening when I'd been particularly low in spirits.

"Do you truly think that?" I asked. "I can't quite get it."

Evelyn moved close to me. She took my hand and squeezed it gently. "Leo, if we *were* meant to meet for a reason, and I think it *must* be, because we've been dragged back together for something, don't you think? We've been through such a lot of drama and misunderstanding, it must mean *something*."

That did make me smile, and I said, "You've always been convinced that we were together for a reason, I know."

She nodded. "I have. I've always been certain that I already knew you. That somehow we were predestined to meet. Perhaps what I'm saying is that our role together in this life must be to sort out some Karmic issues from previous lives. All the dreams I have about you appear to have been lived and imprinted on me from somewhere else. I've never really understood you, Leo. However much I've tried. I probably never will, because I haven't had the same experiences that you've had. I'm not excusing anything that's happened. We can't change them."

She laughed. "I know it all sounds a bit crazy to you, but just think, if you'd been born in a different time, to a different mother, how unlikely it would be that you would be experiencing what is happening now. It must all be for a reason, surely."

"I do understand that... Yes, I do. My dreams about my genitals... Do you think there could be a Karmic reason why I have been so obsessed with them?"

"Perhaps, but we will never know. What I'm trying to say is that we don't need to necessarily understand what we are or where we've come from. What we do need is to accept that we're all made up of different experiences, emotions and insecurities, and often it is impossible to know. But we've definitely been together before."

We spent the following hour or so discussing what could possibly have brought us to this point in our lives, and came to the conclusion that we only needed to love and be true to one another to be happy.

Even so, sometimes I couldn't always prevent myself from dropping into a pit of no-hope, but talking together helped me release my fears and worries. I'd never told her how scared I was, but she instinctively knew and was constant in her belief that all would be well.

On the day of my surgery I felt that I'd done all that I could. I was toned and fit, my skin was better than it had ever been, and if it hadn't been for the ominous lump in my chest, I would have thought myself well.

CHAPTER 46
Surgery

EVELYN

Lily would not go to school, Sally was by my side on the day of the operation, and Jude was constantly on the phone reassuring me. The waiting was terrible and, although I had managed to be positive, I still had some reservations.

I confided my fears to Sally.

"I'm so worried that he won't pull through this. We've made some incredible changes since he has been home and he deserves some happiness."

"I'm surprised that you're back with him," Sally said. "I know you love him. Not that I understand why or what you could possibly love about him. He hasn't exactly made you happy, has he?"

"No, but now I don't see it as his responsibility to make me happy. It's my choice, isn't it?"

"He denies the beautiful, loving person that you are. You deserve to be loved. Does he love you enough to make that sacrifice?"

"Oh, Sal, I am loved. It's my expectation of how that manifests that I've changed. Love comes in many forms, but Leo and I belong together. I have to be strong enough to love him unconditionally."

"Yeh, right." Sally was unconvinced.

Leo had his surgery. The waiting was terrible, but it had all gone well and he was home within a couple of days. The long, livid scar across his chest was still painful, but unlike a female mastectomy was not noticeable under his clothes.

"Doesn't mean it's gone, does it?" he asked as he sat uncomfortably in bed on his second day home.

"Leo, my darling, the results are good and this is a disease like any other. You are doing all the right things for yourself and your future health. You'll get through this."

"I might not."

"You will," I reassured him.

I knew that he wasn't convinced, but I was. We had to wait for the decisions to be made from the results of the extracted tissue to see whether any other treatment was recommended.

Although I had a panicky sense of needing answers more quickly than the scientific methods required, I was convinced that whatever was found, we could deal with it. In my heart I believed that there were ways to manage and possibly prevent the spread that did not entail harsh clinical measures. I knew instinctively what was good for Leo and what would help him recover. I felt surrounded with such good energies. Where it came from, I didn't know, but whatever it was gave me such a surety. It became my strength and my mentor. Everything I mixed or cooked came not only from what I'd learned, but also from some deep hidden knowledge that I was unaware I had.

And I no longer harboured any bad feeling toward him.

After a few days in bed, Leo was still encased in gloom. He was sitting in the most comfortable armchair, dishevelled and unshaven. His usual good-looking face was dull as putty, his eyes red from lack of sleep. His hoarse breathing frightened me, and he finally gave way to a spasm of choked sobs. I wrapped my arms around him. There was nothing I could say. I could see he was still in pain, but mainly it was the fear of death that shadowed his eyes.

He quickly drew a breath as Lily came bounding into the room. She was immediately concerned and offered to make him a cup of tea. "You look a bit rough. What you need is Long John."

"Tea will be fine," Leo replied morosely.

But Lily insisted that Long John sat on his lap, and instructed Leo to stroke him.

"It improves the immune system, Leo. Seriously, it's been tested. Stroking a cat or any animal will improve your immunoglobulin count, reduce your risk of a heart attack and change the biochemistry of your brain," she told him seriously.

Leo started to laugh. "You're sounding more like your mother every day."

"Good, drink your tea and stroke the cat." Lily pranced off to tend to our ever-increasing menagerie.

I was bursting with pride that my daughter was so concerned and special. Leo had immediately brightened and he kept Long John purring happily on his lap all morning whilst he snoozed.

CHAPTER 47
Recovering

LEO

I know I was not a good patient, but I did as I was told, ate what Evelyn cooked and drank the concoctions she made for me.

When we returned to the hospital to see Mr Guy, he was delighted to tell us, "There was no problem with the lymph and it appears that we have managed to remove all the offending tissue. We must now look at what we do next."

Evelyn was sceptical about the idea of any sort of artificial therapies or programmes, and when Mr Guy suggested that I had hormone therapy, she was adamant that statistically it didn't help at all. It was also fairly untried on male patients and could produce distressing symptoms, so I refused. Mr Guy shrugged and basically agreed that perhaps Evelyn was right, and what we were doing on a day-to-day basis was probably the best approach.

My whole life had been turned upside down, and as I started to recover I became aware of what a close call I'd had. What if Evelyn had not allowed me back into her life? I might never have found the lump or had the courage to tackle my drinking and behaviour problems. What if I had continued to harbour and contain those angry thoughts towards my mother? So much could have been different.

I had intended to discuss my anger with Jeanette when I saw her, but she hadn't allowed me to. I'd started to tell her how I'd always felt unwanted and unloved, but she'd stared at me blankly and turned away.

My heart had gone out to her when she mumbled, "I did what I could, you know."

"Of course, I know that, but I wondered whether you knew how I felt."

"No, I didn't know."

I had attempted to take her hand, but she had quickly moved away, saying, "I can't change that, can I? You're okay, aren't you?"

"Yes, I am now, Mother," I assured her.

I decided that it was no good expecting her to explain anything after all. She probably had her own regrets.

I recalled Angela's words. "We must not make judgment about others. Nobody can dictate the feelings, actions or the thoughts of another person when we don't know what motivates them."

It was my problem to deal with, and I was prepared to try as hard as I could without blaming her or anyone else.

CHAPTER 48
Happiness

EVELYN

Forgiveness is a dark and lonely place when you still feel the hurt. It took me a long time to let go of my passionate need for Leo to be what *I* wanted. Folding away my own needs into oblivion did not mean that I didn't care for them any longer, just that they were unimportant for me to be happy. The key is not to struggle with them. I forgive him, but it doesn't mean I accept his behaviour or trust him again. It means I forgive him for me, so that I can let go and move on with my life. While I have expectations of him I can never be happy. Whether it's resentment, sorrow or a need to please, I knew I could not cling to things that ultimately held me back. It was time to consider what no longer served me, and to let go, just like the leaves dropping from the trees as they do in the autumn, readying themselves for the transformation that spring will bring.

I no longer wake up sad. I feel I have reached a milestone in my understanding.

We need to be a family again. Dan and Lily are now grown and are walking their own pathways of hope, disappointment, joy and learning, but they still need our unity.

I watched him as he made the coffee, humming softly. He is no longer looking pained. He turns toward me and smiles. He looks so different, healthy, strong and happy.

"Why so serious?" he enquires.

"I was admiring how different you look."

"Do I?"

"You do. Better than you have ever done. I wish..."

"What?"

"That we could have done better, sooner. We know each

other so well now, but I guess the past is unchangeable. We can reinterpret it but not undo it. Shall we try?" I ask, as I wrap my arms around him.

"What are you saying?"

"I can't know what forced you into such behaviour. But I hope it has changed."

"Evelyn, I am a different person. The perceptions of my life, particularly of my sexual needs, have gone. I'm no longer holding anger in my heart or my chest. It has all gone, physically with the tumour and intentionally with my ability to see how I held it there. Everything has changed. How I stuffed my grievances about my mother into my heart and let them fester. How my feelings about women have been so wrong, selfish and unfeeling. But how can you ever forgive me?"

"I am not sure that I need to forgive you. I can't begin to understand why you have lied and betrayed me all these years, but neither can you understand what you call my pig-headed attitude, my jealousy, my need for you to be honest and strong and most of all to be there when I needed you."

"I'm beginning to."

"I know I'm bossy and take charge, but it's because you don't. All I know is that we destroyed what we had. But I can put it aside if you can. Shall we try?"

"Tell me what I need to do, Evelyn."

"Be true to your commitment, to our marriage, your love for me, and put aside your insecurities about sex and love."

"I think I already have."

"Let us just love each other in the best way we can? We are all a mixture of right and wrong. I'm working on letting go of what's gone and look forward to what comes next. Oh, Leo, let's be grateful for what we have. Don't judge but stand up for what is good and honest with love and hope."

We hold each other and know that we are finally safe. We are aligned. Love renewed is not love redeemed exactly, but it is I that needs to chase those doubts away. It is not easy. It will take time. Leo will always be puzzled by how little he understood or in fact even now understands, but I know he is changed. Finding happiness is more elusive. I have made the commitment and renew it every moment of every day. But, happiness? How is it measured? It comes in moments only. Those are the times to treasure, and my expectations no longer interfere with it.

There is, after all, nothing to forgive.

THE END

AUTHORS NOTES & BIBLIOGRAPHY

This book is a work of fiction and the main characters exist only in my imagination. In each book I have aimed to create a world that is convincing and authentic, but each is the world of the two characters and theirs alone. I do not pretend to be a historian but have tried to keep the events that affect the stories as accurate as possible. Historical research and abstract ideas alone will not bring a novel to life, so it is the characters that must be real. It was important for me to see the characters as on-going rather than leaving the void that often happens when the body ceases. The variation of human existence and experience could occur in many lives; the lessons unlearned, the feelings unexplored, potential never released taken into the next incarnation.

Part 1- Guilt - Leon and Eva
The story of the bloody crusade against the Cathars certainly happened, but I have taken liberties with the evidence and place names on occasion. The description of Aleth les Bains, although true with regard to the healing waters and spa facilities has been exaggerated to include the underground tunnels and caves of which I can find little evidence.
Simon de Montforte was the soldier who led the Crusaders to victory. He was hungry for land and wealth and had the fighting skills that the Pope needed to lead his army. The atrocities committed are well documented as are the trials of the Cathars, but little is known of the ordinary soldiers who fought in the Crusade. I hope Leon's journey has interested you as it has me.

The Cathars by Sean Martin

The Perfect Heresy by Stephen O'Shea
Cathar Country by Michèl Aué
Guide to Carcassonne
The Cathar Religion by Didier Poux

Part 2- Revenge - Leopoldo and Evangelina
The places and dates of the events are certainly accurate, but the existence of the convent is unlikely. Certainly, the procedure that Inquisitors would use to announce their arrival in a town in advance so that everyone was 'invited' to attend and confess their errors, is based on fact. When the Inquisitors arrived 'volunteers' were interviewed. If they confessed to relatively minor misdeeds, were prepared to swear fidelity to the Catholic Church, and were willing to provide useful information about others, even to the extent of pointing a finger at friends and family then they were given a small penance, considered to have genuine zeal and commitment and the matter was closed.
Torture became a favourite method of extracting confessions for offences both real and fabricated. Inquisitors and their assistants were permitted to absolve one another for applying torture. Instruments of torture, like crusaders' weapons, were routinely blessed with holy water.
I have taken a few liberties with the evidence of the poisons being readily available in the area at the time.

The Spanish Inquisition (a history) by Joseph Pérez
Torquemada and the Spanish Inquisition by Rafael Sabatini.
The Poison Diaries by The Duchess of Northumberland
The Complete Guide to Aromatherapy by Salvatore Battaglia

The Encyclopedia of Herbs and Herbalism edited by Malcolm Stuart

Part 3 – Remorse - Leoska and Evina
I have given artistic treatment to reliable evidence of the life of Jan (King John III of Poland) and Marysieńka Sobieski. In the National Library of Poland there still exists many of the letters that they wrote to each other during the campaigns against the Tatars and the Ottomans.

Arojka Institution is an invention, but it is well documented that the health care for the wealthy in mental hospitals was relatively good.

Leoska's play with anorexia stems from his mistrust of his mother and fear of poison; a residue from his previous incarnation as Leoploldo

Primus interpares: The First Among Equals – the story of King Jan III.

Marysieńka, Marie de la Grange D'Arquien by K Waliszewski – translated by Lady Mary Loyd.

Jan Sobieski: The King who saved Europe by Miltiades Varvounis.

Part 4 – Understanding - Eveanya and Leonard
I wanted this part to show that the love and understanding Leonard and Eveanya had for each could outshine the cruelty of being sex slaves to the same master.

Musqat is the perfect place to set this story, as the history of the slave trade there is immense. It was in 1822 that a formal agreement by the British with the Sultan succeeded in legally abolishing the slave trade even though it continued as an integral part of the long and established customs of the peoples of Arabia, India and China. Another treaty in 1845 allowed the British Royal navy to watch and capture any dhows or ships involved in the trade. Even so it wasn't until

1867 that the British were authorized to try subjects accused of taking part in the trade.

I spent six wonderful years living in the Musqat area in the 80's, enjoyed the magnificent shoreline, the amazing wadis and the generosity of the people there. It is easy to see the impact that slavery had on this country, as the population is diverse and multi-coloured even with the occasional redhead!

The British influence is still well preserved.

A short history of Slavery by James Walvin.
Britain in the Persian Gulf by J B Kelly.
Arab Slave Trade Wikipedia.
The Quran.
Enchanting Oman by Shirley Kay.

Part 5 - Forgiveness – Leo and Evelyn
Is it possible that unresolved lessons, denied or avoided, emotional experiences, thoughts and beliefs could affect what we choose to learn in our next reincarnation so that previous experiences in past lifetimes, control some of our thoughts, actions and beliefs in our present incarnation?

Perhaps the avalanche of pain and drama that engulfs the relationship of Evelyn and Leo from the moment of their meeting is a result of just that. They fall in love, but everything seems to be out of the ordinary as they are unable to form the commitment necessary for a happy relationship.

Leo's sexual and alcohol addiction could be a result of the Karmic issues of Leonard's life as a eunuch and Evelyn's need to be loved perhaps a result of unsatisfactory relationships with men in previous incarnations.

We will never know but all is eventually healed, not by understanding, but by forgiveness.

You Can Heal your Life by Louise L. Hay.
Living in the Light by Shakti Gawain.
Overcoming Sexual Addiction by Thaddeus Bichard.
Your Life in Your Hands by Professor Jane Plant.